CHRONIC CITY

Jonathan Lethem is the author of eight novels, including *The Fortress of Solitude* (2003) and *Motherless Brooklyn* (1999), which was named Novel of the Year by *Esquire* and won The National Book Critics Circle Award and the *Salon* Book Award, as well as the Macallan Crime Writers Association Gold Dagger. He has also written two story collections, a novella and a collection of essays, has edited *The Vintage Book of Amnesia*, guest-edited *The Year's Best Music Writing 2002*, and was the founding fiction editor of *Fence* magazine. His writings have appeared in *The New Yorker*, *Rolling Stone*, *McSweeney's* and many other periodicals. He lives in Brooklyn, New York.

JONATHAN LETHEM

Chronic City

faber and faber

First published in 2010
by Faber and Faber Ltd
Bloomsbury House
74–77 Great Russell Street
London WC1B 3DA

Typeset by RefineCatch Limited, Bungay, Suffolk
Printed in England by CPI Bookmarque, Croydon
All rights reserved
© Jonathan Lethem, 2010

A CIP record for this book
is available from the British Library

ISBN 978-0-571-23567-4

10 9 8 7 6 5 4 3 2

For Amy and Everett

CHRONIC CITY

I first met Perkus Tooth in an office. Not an office where he worked, though I was confused about this at the time. (Which is itself hardly an uncommon situation, for me.)

This was in the headquarters of the Criterion Collection, on Fifty-second Street and Third Avenue, on a weekday afternoon at the end of summer. I'd gone there to record a series of voice-overs for one of Criterion's high-end DVD reissues, a "lost" 1950s film noir called *The City Is a Maze*. My role was to play the voice of that film's director, the late émigré auteur Von Tropen Zollner. I would read a series of statements culled from Zollner's interviews and articles, as part of a supplemental documentary being prepared by the curatorial geniuses at Criterion, a couple of whom I'd met at a dinner party. In drawing me into the project they'd supplied me with a batch of research materials, which I'd browsed unsystematically, as well as a working version of their reconstruction of the film, in order for me to glean what the excitement was about. It was the first I'd heard of Zollner, so this was hardly a labor of passion. But the enthusiasm of buffs is infectious, and I liked the movie. I no longer considered myself a working actor. This was the only sort of stuff I did anymore, riding the exhaust of my former and vanishing celebrity, the smoky half-life of a child star. An eccentric favor, really. And I was curious to see the inside of Criterion's operation. This was the first week of September—the city's back-to-school mood always inspired me to find something to do with my idle hands. In those days, with Janice far away, I lived too much on the surface of things, parties, gossip, assignations in which I was the go-between or vicarious friend. Workplaces fascinated me, the zones where Manhattan's veneer gave way to the practical world.

I recorded Zollner's words in a sound chamber in the technical wing of Criterion's crowded, ramshackle offices. In the room outside the chamber, where the soundman sat giving me cues through a headset, a restorer also sat peering at a screen and guiding a cursor with a mouse, diligently erasing celluloid scratches and blots, frame by digital frame, from the bare bodies of hippies cavorting in a mud puddle. I was told he was restoring *I Am Curious (Yellow)*. Afterward I was retrieved by the producer who'd enlisted me, Susan Eldred. It had been Susan and her colleague I'd met at the dinner party—unguarded, embracing people with a passion for a world of cinematic minutiae, for whom I'd felt an instantaneous affection. Susan led me to her office, a cavern with one paltry window and shelves stacked with VHS tapes, more lost films petitioning for Criterion's rescue. Susan shared her office, it appeared. Not with the colleague from the party, but another person. He sat beneath the straining shelves, notebook in hand, gaze distant. It seemed too small an office to share. The glamour of Criterion's brand wasn't matched by these scenes of thrift and improvisation

I'd gathered in my behind-the-scenes glimpse, but why should it have been? No sooner did Susan introduce me to Perkus Tooth and give me an invoice to sign than she was called away for some consultation elsewhere.

He was, that first time, lapsed into what I would soon learn to call one of his "ellipsistic" moods. Perkus Tooth himself later supplied that descriptive word: ellipsistic, derived from *ellipsis*. A species of blank interval, a nod or fugue in which he was neither depressed nor undepressed, not struggling to finish a thought nor to begin one. Merely between. Pause button pushed. I certainly stared. With Tooth's turtle posture and the utter slackness of his being, his receding hairline and antique manner of dress—trim-tapered suit, ferociously wrinkled silk with the shine worn off, moldering tennis shoes—I could have taken him for elderly. When he stirred, his hand brushing the open notebook page as if taking dictation with an invisible pen, and I read his pale, adolescent features, I guessed he was in his fifties—still a decade wrong, though Perkus Tooth had been out of the sunlight for a while. He was in his early forties, barely older than me. I'd mistaken him for old because I'd taken him for important. He now looked up and I saw one undisciplined hazel eye wander, under its calf lid, toward his nose. That eye wanted to cross, to discredit Perkus Tooth's whole sober aura with a comic jape. His other eye ignored the gambit, trained on me.

"You're the actor."

"Yes," I said.

"So, I'm doing the liner notes. For *The City Is a Maze*, I mean."

3

"Oh, good."

"I do a lot of them. *Prelude to a Certain Midnight* . . . *Recalcitrant Women* . . . *The Unholy City* . . . *Echolalia* . . ."

"All film noir?"

"Oh, gosh, no. You've never seen Herzog's *Echolalia*?"

"No."

"Well, I wrote the liner notes, but it isn't exactly released yet. I'm still trying to convince Eldred—"

Perkus Tooth, I'd learn, called everyone by their last name. As though famous, or arrested. His mind's landscape was epic, dotted with towering figures like Easter Island heads. At that moment Eldred—Susan—returned to the office.

"So," he said to her, "have you got that tape of *Echolalia* around here somewhere?" He cast his eyes, the good left and the meandering right, at her shelves, the cacophony of titles scribbled on labels there. "I want him to see it."

Susan raised her eyebrows and he shrank. "I don't know where it is," she said.

"Never mind."

"Have you been harassing my guest, Perkus?"

"What do you mean?"

Susan Eldred turned to me and collected the signed release, then we made our farewell. Then, as I got to the elevator, Perkus Tooth hurried through the sliding door to join me, crushing his antique felt hat onto his crown as he did. The elevator, like so many others behind midtown edifices, was tiny and rattletrap, little more than a

4

glorified dumbwaiter—there was no margin for pretending we hadn't just been in that office together. Bad eye migrating slightly, Perkus Tooth gave me a lunar look, neither unfriendly nor apologetic. Despite the vintage costume, he wasn't some dapper retro-fetishist. His shirt collar was grubby and crumpled. The green-gray sneakers like mummified sponges glimpsed within a janitor's bucket.

"So," he said again. This "so" of Perkus's—his habit of introducing any subject as if in resumption of earlier talk—wasn't in any sense coercive. Rather, it was as if Perkus had startled himself from a daydream, heard an egging voice in his head and mistaken it for yours. "So, I'll lend you my own copy of *Echolalia*, even though I never lend anything. Because I think you ought to see it."

"Sure."

"It's a sort of essay film. Herzog shot it on the set of Morrison Groom's *Nowhere Near*. Groom's movie was never finished, you know. *Echolalia* documents Herzog's attempts to interview Marlon Brando on Groom's set. Brando doesn't want to give the interview, and whenever Herzog corners him Brando just parrots whatever Herzog's said . . . you know, echolalia . . ."

"Yes," I said, flummoxed, as I would so often later find myself, by Tooth's torrential specifics.

"But it's also the only way you can see any of *Nowhere Near*. Morrison Groom destroyed the footage, so the scenes reproduced in *Echolalia* are, ironically, all that remains of the film—"

Why "ironically"? I doubted my hopes of inserting the question. "It sounds incredible," I said.

"Of course you know Morrison Groom's suicide was probably faked."

My nod was a lie. The doors opened, and we stumbled together out to the pavement, tangling at every threshold: "You first—" "Oops—" "After you—" "Sorry." We faced each other, mid-Wednesday Manhattan throngs islanding us in their stream. Perkus grew formally clipped, perhaps belatedly eager to show he wasn't harassing me.

"So, I'm off."

"Very good to see you." I'd quit using the word *meet* long ago, replacing it with this foggy equivocation, chastened after the thousandth time someone explained to me that we'd actually met before.

"So—" He ground to a halt, expectant.

"Yes?"

"If you want to come by for the tape . . ."

I might have been failing some test, I wasn't sure. Perkus Tooth dealt in occult knowledge, and measured with secret calipers. I'd never know when I'd crossed an invisible frontier, visible to Perkus in the air between us.

"Do you want to give me a card?"

He scowled. "Eldred knows where to find me." His pride intervened, and he was gone.

For a phone call so life-altering as mine to Susan Eldred, I ought to have had some fine reason. Yet here I was, dialing Criterion's receptionist later that afternoon, asking first for Perkus Tooth and then, when she claimed no familiarity with that name, for Susan Eldred, spurred by nothing better than a cocktail of two parts whim and one part guilt. Manhattan's volunteer, that's me, I may

6

as well admit it. Was I curious about *Echolalia*, or Morrison Groom's faked suicide, or Perkus Tooth's intensities and lulls, or the slippage in his right eye's gaze? All of it and none of it, that's the only answer. Perhaps I already adored Perkus Tooth, and already sensed that it was his friendship I required to usher me into the strange next phase of my being. To unmoor me from the curious eddy into which I'd drifted. How very soon after our first encounter I'd come to adore and need Perkus makes it awfully hard to know to what extent such feelings were inexplicably under way in Susan Eldred's office or that elevator.

"Your office mate," I said. "They didn't recognize his name at the front desk. Maybe I heard it wrong—"

"Perkus?" Susan laughed. "He doesn't work here."

"He said he wrote your liner notes."

"He's written a couple, sure. But he doesn't *work* here. He just comes up and occupies space sometimes. I'm sort of Perkus's babysitter. I don't even always notice him anymore—you saw how he can be. I hope he wasn't bothering you."

"No . . . no. I was hoping to get in touch with him, actually."

Susan Eldred gave me Perkus Tooth's number, then paused. "I guess you must have recognized his name . . ."

"No."

"Well, in fact he's really quite an amazing critic. When I was at NYU all my friends and I used to idolize him. When I first got the chance to hire him to do a liner note I was quite in awe. It was shocking how young he

7

was, it seemed like I'd grown up seeing his posters and stuff."

"Posters?"

"He used to do this thing where he'd write these rants on posters and put them up all around Manhattan, these sort of brilliant critiques of things, current events, media rumors, public art. They *were* a kind of public art, I guess. Everyone thought it was very mysterious and important. Then he got hired by *Rolling Stone*. They gave him this big column, he was sort of, I don't know, Hunter Thompson meets Pauline Kael, for about five minutes. If that makes any sense."

"Sure."

"Anyway, the point is, he sort of used up a lot of people's patience with certain kinds of . . . paranoid stuff. I didn't really get it until I started working with him. I mean, I *like* Perkus a lot. I just don't want you to feel I wasted your time, or got you enmeshed in any . . . schemes."

People could be absurdly protective, as if a retired actor's hours were so precious. This was, I assume, secondhand affect, a leakage from Janice's otherworldly agendas. I was famously in love with a woman who had no time to spare, not even a breath, for she dwelled in a place beyond time or the reach of anyone's Rolodex, her every breath measured out of tanks of recycled air. If an astronaut made room for me on her schedule, my own prerogatives must be crucial as an astronaut's. The opposite was true.

"Thank you," I said. "I'll be sure not to get enmeshed."

8

Perkus Tooth was my neighbor, it turned out. His apartment was on East Eighty-fourth Street, six blocks from mine, in one of those anonymous warrens tucked behind innocuous storefronts, buildings without lobbies, let alone doormen. The shop downstairs, Brandy's Piano Bar, was a corny-looking nightspot I could have passed a thousand times without once noticing. BRANDY'S CUSTOMERS, PLEASE RESPECT OUR NEIGHBORS! pleaded a small sign at the doorway, suggesting a whole tale of complaint calls to the police about noise and fumes. To live in Manhattan is to be persistently amazed at the worlds squirreled inside one another, the chaotic intricacy with which realms interleave, like those lines of television cable and fresh water and steam heat and outgoing sewage and telephone wire and whatever else which cohabit in the same intestinal holes that pavement-demolishing workmen periodically wrench open to the daylight and to our passing, disturbed glances. We only pretend to live on something as orderly as a grid. Waiting for Perkus Tooth's door buzzer to sound and finding my way inside, I felt my interior map expand to allow for the reality of this place, the corridor floor's lumpy checkerboard mosaic, the cloying citrus of the superintendent's disinfectant oil, the bank of dented brass mailboxes, and the keening of a dog from behind an upstairs door, alerted to the buzzer and my scuffling bootheels. I have trouble believing anything exists until I know it bodily.

Perkus Tooth lived in 1R, a half-level up, the building's rear. He widened his door just enough for me to slip inside, directly to what revealed itself to be his kitchen. Perkus, though barefoot, wore another antique-looking

9

suit, green corduroy this time, the only formal thing my entry revealed. The place was a bohemian grotto, the kitchen a kitchen only in the sense of having a sink and stove built in, and a sticker-laden refrigerator wedged into an alcove beside the bathroom door. Books filled the open cabinet spaces above the sink. The countertop was occupied with a CD player and hundreds of disks, in and out of jewel cases, many hand labeled with a permanent marker. A hot-water pipe whined. Beyond, the other rooms of the apartment were dim at midday, the windows draped. They likely only looked onto ventilation shafts or a paved alley, anyway.

Then there were the broadsides Susan Eldred had described. Unframed, thumbtacked to every wall bare of bookshelves, in the kitchen and in the darkened rooms, were Perkus Tooth's famous posters, their paper yellowing, the lettering veering between a stylish cartoonist's or graffitist's handmade font and the obsessive scrawl of an outsider artist, or a schizophrenic patient's pages reproduced in his doctor's monograph. I recognized them. Remembered them. They'd been ubiquitous downtown a decade before, on construction-site boards, over subway advertisements, element in the graphic cacophony of the city one gleans helplessly at the edges of vision.

Perkus retreated to give me clearance to shut the door. Stranded in the room's center in his suit and bare feet, palms defensively wide as if expecting something unsavory to be tossed his way, Perkus reminded me of an Edvard Munch painting I'd once seen, a self-portrait showing the painter wide-eyed and whiskered, shrunken within his clothes. Which is to say, again, that Perkus Tooth seemed older than his age. (I'd never once see Perkus out of some part of a suit, even if it was only the pants, topped with a filthy white T-shirt. He never wore jeans.)

"I'll get you the videotape," he said, as if I'd challenged him.

"Great."

"Let me find it. You can sit down—" He pulled out a chair at his small, linoleum-topped table like one you'd see in a diner. The chair matched the table—a dinette set, a collector's item. Perkus Tooth was nothing if not a collector. "Here." He took a perfect finished joint from where it waited in the lip of an ashtray, clamped it in his mouth and ignited the tip, then handed it to me unquestioningly. It takes one, I suppose, to know one. I drew on it while he went into the other room. When he returned—with a VHS cassette and his sneakers and a balled-up pair of white socks—he accepted the joint from me and smoked an inch of it himself, intently.

"Do you want to get something to eat? I haven't been out all day." He laced his high-tops.

"Sure," I said.

Out, for Perkus Tooth, I'd now begun to learn, wasn't usually far. He liked to feed at a glossy hamburger palace around the corner on Second Avenue, called Jackson Hole, a den of gleaming chrome and newer, faker versions of the linoleum table in his kitchen, lodged in chubby red-vinyl booths. At four in the afternoon we were pretty well alone there, the jukebox blaring hits to cover our bemused, befogged talk. It had been a while since I'd smoked pot; everything was dawning strange, signals received through an atmosphere eddied with hesitations, the whole universe drifting untethered like Perkus Tooth's vagrant eyeball. The waitress seemed to know Perkus, but he didn't greet her, or touch his menu. He asked for a cheeseburger deluxe and a Coca-Cola. Helpless, I dittoed his order. Perkus seemed to dwell in this place as he had at Criterion's offices, indifferently, obliquely, as if he'd been born there yet still hadn't taken notice of the place.

In the middle of our meal Perkus halted some rant about Werner Herzog or Marlon Brando or Morrison Groom to announce what he'd made of me so far. "So, you've gotten by to this point by being cute, haven't you, Chase?" His spidery fingers, elbow-propped on the linoleum, kept the oozing, gory Jackson Hole burger aloft to mask his expression, and cantilevered far enough from his lap to protect those dapper threads. One eye fixed me while the other crawled, now seeming a scalpel in operation on my own face. "You haven't changed, you're like a dreamy child, that's the secret of your appeal. But they love you. They watch you like you're still on television."

"Who?"

"The rich people. The Manhattanites—you know who I mean."

"Yes," I said.

"You're supposed to be the saddest man in Manhattan," he said. "Because of the astronaut who can't come home."

So, no surprise, Perkus was another one who knew me as Janice Trumbull's fiancé. My heart's distress was daily newspaper fodder. Yes, I loved Janice Trumbull, the American trapped in orbit with the Russians, the astronaut who couldn't come home. This, beyond my childhood TV stardom, was what anyone knew about me, though some, like Susan Eldred, were too polite to mention it.

"That's what everyone adores about you."

"I guess so."

"But I know your secret."

I was startled. Did I have a secret? If I did, it was one of the things I'd misplaced in the last few years. I couldn't remember how I'd gotten from there to here, made the decisions that led from my child stardom to harmlessly dissipated Manhattan celebrity, nor how it was that I deserved the brave astronaut's love. I had trouble *clearly recalling* Janice, that was part of my sorrow. The day she launched for the space station I must have undertaken to quit thinking of Janice, even while promising to keep a vigil for her here on earth. I never dared tell anyone this fact. So if I had a secret, it was that I had conspired to forget my secret.

Perkus eyed me slyly. Perhaps it was his policy to make this announcement to any new acquaintance, to see what they'd blurt out. "Keep your eyes and ears open," he told me now. "You're in a position to learn things."

What things? Before I could ask, we were off again. Perkus's spiel encompassed Monte Hellman, Semina Culture, Greil Marcus's *Lipstick Traces*, the Mafia's blackmailing of J. Edgar Hoover over erotic secrets (resulting in the bogus amplification of Cold War fear and therefore the whole of our contemporary landscape), Vladimir Mayakovsky and the futurists, Chet Baker, Nothingism, the ruination Giuliani's administration had brought to the sacred squalor of Times Square, the genius of *The Gnuppet Show*, Frederick Exley, Jacques Rivette's impossible-to-see twelve-hour movie *Out 1*, corruption of the arts by commerce generally, Slavoj Zizek on Hitchcock, Franz Marplot on G. K. Chesterton, Norman Mailer on Muhammad Ali, Norman Mailer on graffiti and the space program, Brando as dissident icon, Brando as sexual saint, Brando as Napoleon in exile. Names I knew and didn't. Others I'd heard once and never troubled to wonder about. Mailer, again and again, and Brando even more often—Perkus Tooth's primary idols seemed to be this robust and treacherous pair, which only made Perkus seem frailer and more harmless by contrast, without ballast in his pencil-legged suit. Maybe he ate Jackson Hole burgers in an attempt to burgeon himself, seeking girth in hopes of attracting the attention of Norman and Marlon, his chosen peers.

He had the waitress refill his gallon-sized Coke, too, then, as our afternoon turned to evening, washed it all down with black coffee. In our talk marijuana confusion now gave way to caffeinated jags, like a cloud bank penetrated by buzzing Fokker airplanes. Did I read *The New Yorker*? This question had a dangerous urgency. It wasn't any one writer or article he was worried about, but the *font*. The meaning embedded, at a preconscious level, by the look of the magazine; the seal, as he described it, that the typography and layout put on dialectical thought. According to Perkus, to read *The New Yorker* was to find that you always already agreed, not with *The New Yorker* but, much more dismayingly, with *yourself*. I tried hard to understand. Apparently here was the paranoia Susan Eldred had warned me of: *The New Yorker*'s font was controlling, perhaps assailing, Perkus Tooth's mind. To defend himself he frequently retyped their articles and printed them out in simple Courier, an attempt to dissolve the magazine's oppressive context. Once I'd enter his apartment to find him on his carpet with a pair of scissors, furiously slicing up and rearranging an issue of the magazine, trying to shatter its spell on his brain. "So, how," he once asked me, apropos of nothing, "does a *New Yorker* writer become a *New Yorker writer*?" The falsely casual "so" masking a pure anxiety. It wasn't a question with an answer.

But I'm confused in this account, surely. Can we have discussed so much the very first time? *The New Yorker*, at least. Giuliani's auctioning of Forty-second Street to Disney. Mailer on NASA as a bureaucracy stifling dreams. J. Edgar Hoover in the Mafia's thrall, hyping Reds, instilling self-patrolling fear in the American Mind. In the midst of these variations the theme was always ingeniously and excitingly retrieved. In short, some human freedom had been leveraged from view at the level of consciousness itself. Liberty had been narrowed, winnowed, *amnesiacked*. Perkus Tooth used this word without explaining—by it he meant something like the Mafia itself would do, a whack, a rubout. Everything that mattered most was a victim in this perceptual murder plot. Further: always to blame was everyone; when rounding up the suspects, begin with yourself. Complicity, including his own, was Perkus Tooth's only doubtless conviction. The worst thing was to be sure you knew what you knew, the mistake *The New Yorker*'s font induced. The horizon of everyday life was a mass daydream—below it lay everything that mattered. By now we'd paid for our burgers and returned to his apartment. At his dinette table we sat and he strained some pot for seeds, then rolled another joint. The dope came out of a little plastic box marked with a laser-printed label reading CHRONIC in rainbow colors, a kind of brand name. We smoked the new joint relentlessly to a nub and went on talking, Perkus now free to gesticulate as he hadn't at Jackson Hole. Yet he never grew florid, never, in all his ferment, hyperventilated or like some epileptic bit his tongue. The feverish words were delivered with a merciless cool. Like the cut of his suit, wrinkled though it might be. And the obsessively neat lettering on the VHS tape and on his CDs. Perkus Tooth might have one crazy eye, but it served almost as a warning not to underestimate his scruples, how attentively he stayed on the good side of his listener's skepticism, making those minute adjustments that were sanity's signature: the interpersonal realpolitik of persuasion. The eye was mad and the rest of him was almost steely.

Perkus rifled through his CDs to find a record he wished to play me, a record I didn't know—Peter Blegvad's "Something Else (Is Working Harder)." The song was an angry and incoherent blues, it sounded to me, gnarled with disgruntlement at those who "get away with murder." Then, as if riled by the music, he turned and said, almost savagely, "So, I'm not a *rock critic*, you know."

"Okay." This was a point I found easy enough to grant.

"People will say I am, because I wrote for *Rolling Stone*—but I hardly ever write about music." In fact, the broadsides hung in his rooms seemed to be full of references to pop songs, but I hesitated to point out the contradiction.

He seemed to read my mind. "Even when I do, I don't use that *language*."

"Oh."

"Those people, the rock critics, I mean—do you want to know what they really are?"

"Oh, sure—what are they?"

"Super-high-functioning autistics. Oh, I don't mean they're diagnosed or anything. But I diagnose them that way. They've got Asperger's syndrome. I mean, in the same sense that, say, David Byrne or Al Gore has it. They're brilliant, but they're *social misfits*."

"Uh, how do you know?" As far as I knew I'd never met anyone with Asperger's syndrome, or for that matter, a rock critic. (Although I had once seen David Byrne at a party.) Yet I had heard enough already to find it odd hearing Perkus Tooth denouncing misfits.

"It's the way they talk." He leaned in close to me, and demonstrated his point as he spoke. "*They aspirate their vowels nearer to the front of their mouths*."

"Wow."

"And when you see them talking in groups they do it even more. It's self-reinforcing. Rock critics gather for purposes of mutual consolation, though they'd never call it that. They believe they're *experts*." Perkus, whether he knew it or not, continued to aspirate his vowels at the front of his mouth as he made his case. "They can't see the forest for the trees."

"Thelf-reinforthing exthperts," I said, trying it on for size. "Can't thee the foretht for the threes." I am by deepest instinct a mimic. Anyway, a VHS tape labeled ECHOLALIA lay on the table between us.

"That's right," said Perkus seriously. "Some of them even whistle when they speak."

"Whisthle?"

"*Exactly*."

"Thank god we're not rock critics."

"You can say that again." He tongued the gum on another joint he'd been assembling, then inspected it for smoke-worthiness, running it under his funny eye as if scanning a bar code. Satisfied, he ignited it. "So, I'm self-medicating," he explained. "I smoke grass because of the headaches."

"Migraine headaches?"

"*Cluster* headaches. It's a variant of migraine. One side of the head." With two fingers he tapped his skull—of course it was his right side, the headaches gravitating toward the deviant eye. "They're called cluster headaches because they come in runs, every day for a week or two at exactly the same time. Like a clock, like a rooster crowing."

"That's crazy."

"I know. Also, there's this visual effect . . . a blind spot on one side . . ." Again, his right hand waved. "Like a blot in the center of my visual field."

A riddle: What do you get when you cross a blind spot with a wandering eye? But we'd never once mentioned his eye, so I hung fire. "The pot helps?" I asked instead.

"The thing about a migraine-type experience is that it's like being only half alive. You find yourself walking through this tomb world, everything gets far away and kind of dull and dead. Smoking pulls me back into the world, it restores my appetites for food and sex and conversation."

Well, I had evidence of food and conversation— Perkus Tooth's appetites in sex were to remain mysterious to me for the time being. This was still the first of the innumerable afternoons and evenings I surrendered to Perkus's kitchen table, to his smoldering ashtray and pot of scorched coffee, to his ancient CD boom box which audibly whined as it spun in the silent gap between tracks, to our booth around the corner at Jackson Hole when a fierce craving for burgers and cola came over us as it often did. Soon enough those days all blurred happily together, for in the disconsolate year of Janice's broken orbit Perkus Tooth was probably my best friend. I suppose Perkus was the curiosity, I the curiosity-seeker, but he surely added me to his collection as much as the reverse.

I did watch *Echolalia*. The way Brando tormented his would-be interviewer was funny, but the profundity of the whole thing was lost on me. I suppose I was unfamiliar with the required context. When I returned it I said so, and Perkus frowned.

"Have you seen *The Nascent*?"

"Nope."

"Have you seen *Anything That Hides*?"

"Not that one either."

"Have you seen *any* of Morrison Groom's films, Chase?"

"Not knowingly."

"How do you survive," he said, not unkindly. "How do you even get along in the world, not understanding what goes on around you?"

"That's what I have you for. You're my brain."

"Ah, with your looks and my brain, we could go far," he joked in a Bogart voice.

"Exactly."

Something lit up inside him, then, and he climbed on his chair in his bare feet and performed a small monkey-like dance, singing impromptu, "If I'm your brain you're in a whole lot of trouble . . . you picked the wrong brain!" Perkus had a kind of beauty in his tiny, wiry body and his almost feral, ax-blade skull, with its gracefully tapered widow's peak and delicate features. "Your brain's on drugs, your brain's on fire . . ."

Despite this lunatic warning, Perkus took charge of what he considered my education, loading me up with tapes and DVDs, sitting me down for essential viewings. Perkus's apartment was a place for consuming archival wonders, whether at his kitchen table or in the sagging chairs before his flat-screen television: bootlegged unreleased recordings by those in Tooth's musical pantheon, like Chet Baker, Nina Simone, or Neil Young, and grainy tapes of scarce film noir taped off late-night television broadcasts. Among these treasures was a videotape of a ninety-minute episode of the detective show *Columbo*, from 1981, directed by Paul Mazursky, and starring John Cassavetes as a wife-murdering orchestra conductor, the foil to Peter Falk's famously rumpled detective. It also featured, in roles as Cassavetes's two spoiled teens, Molly Ringwald and myself. The TV movie was something Mazursky had tossed off around the time of the making of *Tempest*, the latter a theatrical release featuring Cassavetes and Ringwald, though not, alas, me. That pretty well summed up my luck as an actor, the ceiling I'd always bumped against—television, but never the big screen.

Cassavetes was among Perkus's holy heroes, so he'd captured this broadcast, recorded it off some twilight-hour rerun. The tape was intact with vintage commercials from the middle eighties, O. J. Simpson still sprinting through airports and so forth. I hadn't seen the *Columbo* episode since it was broadcast, and it gave me a feeling of seasick familiarity. Not that Mazursky, Falk, Cassavetes, and Ringwald had been family to me—I'd barely known them—yet still it felt like watching a home movie. It led to the curious sense that in some fashion I'd already been dwelling here in Perkus's apartment, for twenty-odd years before I'd met him. His knowledge of culture, and the weirdly synesthetic connections he traced inside it, made it seem as though this moment of our viewing the tape together was fated. Indeed, as if at twelve years old I'd acted in this forgettable and forgotten television show alongside John Cassavetes as a form of private communion with my future friend Perkus Tooth.

Perkus paid scant attention to the sulky children tugging at Cassavetes's sleeves—his interest was in the scenes between the great director and Peter Falk, as he scoured the TV movie for any whiff of genius that recalled their great work together in Cassavetes's own films, or in Elaine May's *Mikey and Nicky*. He intoned reverently at details I could never have bothered to observe, either then, as a child actor on the set, or as a viewer now. He also catalogued speculative connections among the galaxy of cultural things that interested him.

For instance: "This sorry little TV movie is one of Myrna Loy's last-ever appearances. You know, Myrna Loy, *The Thin Man*? She was in loads of silent movies in the twenties, too." My silence permitted him to assume I followed these depth soundings. "Also in *Lonelyhearts*, in 1958, with Montgomery Clift and Robert Ryan."

"Ah."

"Based on the Nathanael West novel."

"Ah."

"Of course it isn't really any good."

"Mmm." I gazed at the old lady in the scene with Falk, waiting to feel what Perkus felt.

"Montgomery Clift is buried in the Quaker cemetery in Prospect Park, in Brooklyn. Very few people realize he's there, or that there even *is* a cemetery in Prospect Park. When I was a teenager a friend and I snuck in there at night, scaled the fence, and looked around, but we couldn't find his grave, just a whole bunch of voodoo chicken heads and other burnt offerings."

"Wow."

Only half listening to Perkus, I went on staring at my childhood self, a ghost disguised as a twelve-year-old, haunting the corridors of the mansion owned by Cassavetes's character, the villainous conductor. It seemed Perkus's collection was a place one might turn a corner and unexpectedly find oneself, a conspiracy that was also a mirror.

Perkus went on expounding: "Peter Falk was in *The Gnuppet Movie*, too, right around this time."

"Really."

"Yeah. So was Marlon Brando."

Zing! Another dot connected in the Perkusphere!

■

I was at first disconcerted, perhaps jealous, when I learned other beings could breach the sanctum on Eighty-fourth Street. First was Perkus's dealer, he who provided the tiny Lucite boxes of Chronic. His name was Foster Watt. Watt, young and suspicious, hair brushed forward into spikes, wearing a red vinyl jacket and black jeans, carried a beeper, and only returned calls to established customers—to join his roster you'd have to meet in person, or he'd shun your number. Perkus assured him I was "cool," explained that I only happened to be visiting, wasn't a candidate to join Watt's rolls. There, businesslike Watt's interest in me died. Chronic was just one of his wares: Watt showed off a whole menu of marijuana brand names, each fertile sprig behind its Lucite

23

pane labeled SILVER HAZE, FUNKY MONKEY, BLUEBERRY KUSH, MACK DADDY, or, eerily I thought, ICE. There might have been a dozen more. Perkus shopped among the brands with random eagerness, refreshing his supply of Chronic but adding several others. (These I'd go on to smoke with Perkus, and I could never tell the least difference: every one of Watt's brands got me devastatingly high.) Deal done, Watt scrammed.

More important, though he never actually entered the apartment, was Biller. I learned of his existence by a rattling at Perkus's window, the window onto the airshaft at the building's rear. I heard the intruding sound first— I'd just come up, and Perkus was beginning to expound, to spread his wings—and ignored it. Then Perkus, without explaining, shifted his attention, became silent. He didn't go to the window immediately, instead scooping together items from his linoleum table, items I now saw had been arrayed, made ready. A bagel, fixed with cream cheese and smoked salmon, in wax paper—an overlooked breakfast, I'd thought, wrongly. An antique Raymond Chandler paperback with a gorgeous cover, like those Perkus shelved in little glassine pockets, *Farewell, My Lovely*. A joint Perkus had rolled and set aside, and which he now ziplocked into a tiny baggie. And a wad of dollars, fives and ones, bunched as if withdrawn from a pocket and tossed aside. All went into a white paper sack, recycled, perhaps, from the original bagel purchase. Then Perkus opened his window and waved at someone standing below. The threshold's height, from the bare cement courtyard, meant Biller must have tapped the window with a tossed pebble, or reached for it with a stick or wire coat hanger. Straining up, he was just able to accept the white sack as Perkus lowered it. Leaning from my seat to see, I first saw his fingers, brown and dusty-dry, groping for the gifts. Then I stood and saw the whole of him.

This was early October, six or seven in the evening, barely dusk, barely chill. Yet Biller was forested in jackets and coats. Some seemed turned inside out. Before I registered his dark face I saw a golem of cloth, all rumpled plaid linings and stained down-filled tubular sections. His large, crabbed hands thrust the white sack Perkus had given him under a layer, into a canvas shoulder bag, silk-screened BARNES & NOBLE, that swung beneath the outermost coat. Now I resolved Biller's face in the gloom. Though his cheeks and neck were aggravated with ingrown beard hairs, impossible to shave, and his Afro looked both patchy and greasy, knitting into proto-dreadlocks, within that frame handsome eyes showed a gentle reluctance. I felt I'd betrayed them both, rubbernecking Perkus's charity. I sat again and waited.

"Who's that?" The man's voice was soft and sane.

"Don't worry," said Perkus. "He's a friend."

"I've seen him. I thought he might be from the building."

"He's not from the building. You might recognize him from somewhere else."

I fiddled with a small plate of Italian cookies Perkus had laid out, while they discussed me and I listened. Coffee percolated, an irregular gurgle—Perkus had just put it on before the window tap.

"I didn't mean to surprise you with a visitor," continued Perkus. "I thought you'd be here earlier."

"It was the tiger," said Biller. "They practically had to close down Second Avenue. I couldn't get across."

This was the first I'd heard of the gargantuan escaped tiger that was ravaging sections of the East Side. Or if I'd heard, I'd forgotten. Either way, I didn't have any reason not to credit it as some fancy of Biller's. A tiger could be a homeless man's emblem, I thought, of the terrors that pursued him. No wonder he needed all those coats.

Perkus responded neutrally. "It doesn't matter. Can you get back?"

"I'm going downtown." For someone glomming bagels at a back window, Biller sounded peculiarly intent. Second Avenue, downtown—how broad was his orbit?

"Okay. See you tomorrow."

"I thought he'd be gone before you came," Perkus told me after he lowered his window and told me the apparition's name. "He prefers not to be seen. He used to wait for me in front, then some assholes from my building called the police three times in a row. So I showed him how to come around the back, where Brandy's puts out their garbage."

"Where does he live?"

Perkus shrugged. "I don't know that he particularly lives *anywhere*, Chase. He sometimes sleeps under a pool on Orchard Street, he says it's a block run by Mafia, so no one would ever suspect or bother him. I believe he often simply sleeps on the subway trains when he goes down there."

26

"But why . . . does he go . . . down there? Or come . . . up here?"

"I never asked." Perkus poured two cups of coffee. He rolled another joint out of the loose dope scattered on the linoleum, to replace what he'd added to Biller's care package. The brand was Silver Haze. Sharing it with Biller seemed at once a kind of communion, lowered from above to those supplicant hands, and a gesture of egalitarian comradeship: I self-medicate, why shouldn't you? And the Chandler novel with the vintage cover art—did Perkus have two copies of that, or was he gradually feeding his precious collection out onto the street to Biller? For Perkus, books were sandwiches, apparently, to be devoured.

Perkus was alert to my fascination. "I'll introduce you," he said. "He's just shy at first."

Marijuana might have been a constant, but coffee was Perkus Tooth's muse. With his discombobulated eye Perkus seemed to be watching his precious cup while he watched you. It might not be a defect so much as a security system, an evolutionary defense against having his java heisted. Once, left alone briefly in his place, among his scattered papers I found a shred of lyric, the only writing I ever saw from Perkus that wasn't some type of critical exegesis. An incomplete, second-guessed ode, it read: "Oh caffeine!/you contemporary ~~fiend~~ screen/~~into your face I've seen/into my face~~/through my face—" And yes, the sheet of paper was multiply imprinted with rings by his coffee mug.

I pictured the fugue that resulted in this writing being interrupted by a seizure of migraine, the pen dropping from Perkus's hand as he succumbed to one of his cluster headaches. It was impossible not to picture it this way because of the day I walked in on him in the grip of a fresh one. He'd called to invite my dropping by, then fell victim. The door was unlocked and he beckoned me inside from where he lay on his couch, in his suit pants and a yellowed T-shirt, with a cool cloth draped over his eyes. He told me to sit down, and not to worry, but his voice was withered, drawn down inside his skinny chest. I was persuaded at once that he spoke to me from within that half-life, that land of the dead he'd so precisely evoked with his first descriptions of cluster headache.

"It's a bad one," he said. "The first day is always the worst. I can't look at the light."

"You never know when it's coming?"

"There's a kind of warning aura an hour or two before," he croaked out. "The world begins shrinking . . ."

I moved for his bathroom, and he said, "Don't go in there. I puked."

What I did I will admit is unlike me: I went in and cleaned up Perkus's vomit. Further, seeking out a sponge in his kitchen sink I ran into a mess there, a cereal bowl half filled with floating Cheerios, cups with coffee evaporating to filmy stain rings. While Perkus lay on the couch breathing heavily through a washcloth, I quietly tinkered at his kitchen, putting things in a decent order, not wanting him to slip into derangement and unhealth on what it had suddenly occurred to me was *my watch*—he appeared so disabled I could imagine him not budging from that couch for days. Not counting

28

Biller, who'd stayed outside the window, I'd never seen another soul in Perkus's apartment except for his pot dealer. The dinette table was scattered with marijuana, half of it pushed through a metal strainer, the rest still bunchy with seeds. I swept it all back into a plastic box labeled FUNKY MONKEY and scooped the joints Perkus had completed into the Altoids tin he kept for that purpose. Then, growing compulsive (I do keep my own apartment neat, though I'd never before felt any anxiety at Perkus's chaos), I started reorganizing his scattered CDs, matching the disks to their dislocated jewel cases. This kind of puttering may be how I set myself at ease, another type of self-medication. It was certainly the case that blundering in on Perkus's headache had made me self-conscious and pensive, but I felt I couldn't go. I made no attempt to conceal my actions, and Perkus offered no comment, apart from the slightest moan. But after I'd been clattering at his compact discs for a while he said, "Find Sandy Bull."

"What?"

"Sandy Bull . . . he's a guitarist . . . the songs are very long . . . I can tolerate them in this state . . . it gives me something to listen to besides this throbbing . . ."

I found the disk and put it in his player. The music seemed to me insufferably droning, psychedelic in a minor key, suitable more for a harem than a sickroom. But then I really know nothing about music or headaches.

"You can go . . ." said Perkus. "I'll be fine . . ."

"Do you need food?"

"No . . . when it's like this I can't eat . . ."

29

Well, Perkus couldn't eat one of Jackson Hole's fist-size burgers, I'd grant that. I wondered if a plate of some vegetable or a bowl of soup might be called for, but I wasn't going to mother him. So I did go, first lowering the lights, but leaving the creepy music loud, as Perkus wished. I found myself strangely bereft, discharged into the vacant hours. I'd come to rely on my Perkus afternoons, and how they turned into evenings. The light outside was all wrong. I realized I couldn't recall a time I'd not come back through his lobby, brain pleasantly hazy, into a throng of Brandy's Piano Bar patrons ignoring the sign and smoking and babbling outside on the pavement, while piano tinkling and erratic choruses of sing-along drifted from within the bar to the street. Now all was quiet, the stools upturned on Brandy's tables. And all I could think of was Perkus, stilled on the couch, his lids swollen beneath the washcloth.

The next time I saw Perkus I made the mistake of asking if his tendency to veer into ellipsis was in any way connected to the cluster migraines. He'd been bragging the week before about his capacity for shifting into that satori-like state; how, when he ventured there, he glimpsed bonus dimensions, worlds inside the world. Most of his proudest writing, he'd explained, was born of some glimpse of *ellipsistic knowledge*.

"There's no connection," he said now, where we sat in our Jackson Hole booth, his distaff eye bulging. "Cluster's a death state, where all possibilities shut down . . . I'm not myself there . . . I'm not anyone. Ellipsis is *mine*, Chase."

"I only wondered if they might somehow be two sides of the same coin . . ." Or two ways of peering out of the same skull, I thought but didn't say.

"I can't even begin to explain. It's totally different."

"I'm sorry," I said spontaneously, wanting to calm him.

"Sorry for what?" He'd spat out a gobbet of burger in his fury at refuting me.

"I didn't mean anything."

"Ellipsis is like a window opening, Chase. Or like— art. It stops time."

"Yes, you've said." The clot of chewed beef sat beside his napkin, unnoticed except by me.

"Cluster, on the other hand—they're enemies."

"Yes." He'd persuaded me. It hadn't taken much. I wanted to persuade *him*, now, to see an Eastern healer I knew, a master of Chinese medicine who, operating out of offices in Chelsea, and with a waiting list of six months or more, ministered to Manhattan's wealthy and famous, charming and acupuncturing away their ornate stresses and decadent ills. I promised myself I'd try, later, when Perkus's anger cooled. I wanted so badly for him to have his ellipsis, have it wholly and unreservedly, wanted him to have it without cluster—however terribly much I suspected that one might be the price of the other. I wanted this selfishly, for, it dawned on me then, Perkus Tooth—his talk, his apartment, the space that had opened beginning when I'd run into him at Criterion, then called him on the telephone—*was my ellipsis*. It might not be inborn in me, but I'd discovered it nonetheless in him. Where Perkus took me, in his ranting, in his enthusiasms, in his abrupt, improbable asides, was the world inside the world. I didn't want him smothered in the tomb-world of migraine. Perkus was the opposite of my distant astronaut fiancée—my caring for him could matter, on a daily basis.

2

Perkus Tooth was right. I may as well acknowledge I function as an ornament to dinner parties. There's something pleasant about me. I skate on frictionless ball bearings of charm, convey a middling charisma that threatens no one. As a retired actor I evoke the arts, yet feature no unsettling aura of disgruntlement, striving, or need. Anyone can grasp in a single word —*residuals*— where my money comes from and that I have enough of it. People with money don't want to wonder, in their private evenings, whether their artist friends have enough (or worse, be certain they don't have). It was during one of these evenings at their most typical, swirling with faces I'd forget the morning after, that I came to be introduced to Richard Abneg.

Maud and Thatcher Woodrow's duplex apartment took the disconcerting form of a small town house that had sidled against a representative Park Avenue monolith of an apartment building and been absorbed and concealed there. Entering through the lobby after having passed the doorman's muster, a visitor veered left, shunning the burnished, inlaid-rosewood elevators leading to the ten-million-dollar apartments, up a small interior stoop, six marble steps narrowing to an ornate doorway, to be greeted inside by another, finer, more scrupulous and savvy doorman, the Woodrows' alone, who spoke the name of any guest before it was given, even at a first visit. This house-within-a-building functioned to enunciate to dwellers in those apartments, elevator-sloggers who imagined they'd come to one of life's high stations, *your indoors is our outdoors, that's the exponential degree between us.* Distinction from merely heedless wealth was tough to obtain on Park, but the Woodrows had purchased some. If it took a surrealist flourish to do so, fair enough. Inside, there was nothing to say the Woodrow dwelling wasn't some stupendous and historical town house, now widened to modern style, walls layered with black-framed photography and paintings as crisp as photographs, behind dustless glass, and with a curving interior stairwell as much a proscenium for entrances as that in *The Magnificent Ambersons*. Yet their home was invisible to the street. It had nothing to enunciate to the street.

A certain script pertained. I wouldn't speak of my astro-fiancée, off trapped behind her thin steel-and-tile skin against the unfathomable keening void, during cocktails. No, I should reserve the material. There would come a point in the dinner, after some fun had been had, candles burned two-thirds down, glasses just refilled, when someone to my right or left would inquire and as if by previous agreement other talk would fall off, so the whole table could listen as one to my sad tale. Janice Trumbull's drama, to which I was attached, wasn't going to go unmentioned, and it was hardly secret—they'd after all been following her fate in the papers. So with earnest concern in their hearts, the guests would lean in unashamed to hear what I knew, the "real story," maybe. And to moo sympathy, like the approval an audience shows a poetry reading.

Cocktails were for smaller talk. Eight or nine of us mingled in that plush drawing room, counting Maud and Thatcher, our hosts, while their staff wove amid us, harvesting drink orders and sowing canapés. Naomi Kandel, the lesbian galleryist, tipped her glass in salute when I came in, and I drifted in her direction. Stout and handsome in her evening dress, eyes drowsy with congenital irony, Naomi bore the promise of deadpan commiseration here. Though we'd all chosen to accept this invitation, we had to make ourselves feel better about the decision by imagining ourselves enslaved. Naomi stood with another woman, a curvaceous, fortyish socialite in a sparkling ginger-threaded dress. Together they stood regarding a framed drawing, perhaps a new art acquisition of the Woodrows', a crisp architectural-style rendering of a dark pit that plunged between two Manhattan office towers, viewed from above. Tiny figures were also represented, gazing into the pit's depths from the sidewalk.

"Do you know Sharon?" asked Naomi.

"I haven't had the pleasure."

"Sharon Spencer, Chase Insteadman."

"I'm a fan of your work," said Sharon Spencer. She weighed my handshake for an extra instant. I wondered which work she meant. Was she a fan of *Martyr & Pesty*? Few bragged of this. And Sharon, attractive as she was, seemed a bit old for that sitcom's hey-day. She was being polite, I decided, or coy. I joined in gazing at the drawing.

"Laird Noteless," said Naomi, naming the artist. "It's a study for *Expunged Building*."

"Are you his dealer?" I asked Naomi.

She shrugged no. "There's nothing to deal. Noteless doesn't usually let go of his sketches. He likes to hoard or destroy the evidence, leave only the major works behind. I think Maud and Thatcher are helping him get *Expunged Building* past city council."

"It's not *built* yet?" said Sharon Spencer, surprised.

"Not yet."

She shook her head. "Preposterous, the hurdles they set up."

"Where's your husband, anyway?" said Naomi dryly, not concealing her boredom, and maybe wishing to squash any flirtation.

"Reggie's coming late," sighed Sharon Spencer. "He's stuck at work. It's all dreadful down there now."

Reggie, I understood, was one of those who shifted the money around, trying to make it get bigger. They all deserved our pity, clearly enough. The money men, effortful and exhausted, slumping through the gray fog. Compared to their wives they were peons.

Maud Woodrow found me next, and broke me away from Naomi and Sharon Spencer to meet Harriet Welk, an editor at Knopf. Maud and Harriet had met when a photographer needed permission to reproduce some of Maud's collection for a coffee-table book on nineteenth-century folk jewelry. Harriet, though she might have been the youngest player on this intimidating stage, was commanding and keen, and easy to want to charm. It was Harriet who'd brought Richard Abneg along. He was still across the room, getting button-holed by Thatcher Woodrow. No male arriving in the Woodrows' circle was ever spared preemptive mark-ing with Thatcher's scent. When spirited off to another duty, Harriet retailed a few facts about Richard, who she called her "secular date."

"You mean 'platonic,' I think."

"Platonic, secular, old friends. Anything between us is unimaginable." She pointed Abneg out, a short, stolid fellow who appeared, in this company, like a cartoon Communist in his wide-legged charcoal suit, untucked flannel shirt, and a black beard encroaching on his sul-len cheeks and fierce eyes. He stood nose to nose with Thatcher, gripping a martini's neck like the handle of an ax he'd use to hack his way free if Thatcher didn't quit bragging.

"Clear enough," I said. "You're a pair of solo opera-tors here. Lone wolves."

She explained that they were high-school friends, went all the way back to the corridors and water foun-tains and sexual embarrassments of Horace Mann. "You know when you've known somebody so long, you're familiar with all their self-reinventions?"

"At least he's bothered with self-reinventions."

Richard Abneg had begun as a radical, an anarchist. His formative event the Tompkins Square Park riots, when the police quelled the rebel spirit of the Lower East Side. (I faintly recalled these facts, another version of the city's Original Sin.) Abneg had spearheaded a squatters' seizure of a famed building on Ninth and C, a cherished last stand, a toe stuck in the slamming door of progress. Out of this had come a career in tenant advocacy, bulldog negotiations on behalf of those sidelined in gentrification's parade. Now, ultimate irony, Abneg worked for Mayor Arnheim, managing the undoing of rent stabilization. He'd become a major villain to some who recalled his earlier days, Harriet Welk informed me. Yet Abneg clung to his sense of duty, always alluding to how much worse it might all be without his interventions, a jaw-clenched claim on a higher realism. His intimates, like Harriet, could see what it had cost him, going to that crossroads, making that devil's bargain. They kindly left the ironies unconfronted. What Richard Abneg had carried forward, always, anyhow, was a certain sense of his own crucial place in the island's life. He'd never copped out. And the beard, that too was uncompromised, continuous. He grew it when he was fifteen and reading Charles Bukowski and Howard Zinn and Emmett Grogan. I soaked up Harriet's description and braced myself. What she hadn't warned me was that I'd like him.

Richard Abneg scotted over to us now. Stuck out a horny hand for me to shake, but while I held it, addressed Harriet Welk.

"You see her?"

"Who?"

"Don't look, don't look. The ostrich-woman."

He meant Georgina Hawkmanaji. I'd seen her come in. For her hair pinned in a high, plumed construction, her long pale neck and narrow shoulders, her lush

38

bottom, *ostrich-woman* was a fair summary. Worth twenty million or so of inherited Armenian plunder, educated in Zurich and Oxford, but sure, ostrich in stature and perhaps soul as well. She stood a foot taller than Abneg.

"Sorry," he said abruptly. He introduced himself, and freed my claustrophobic fingers. "Don't get any ideas, I'm going home with her."

"I'll give you an advantage," I said. "She lives in this building, the penthouse."

"Well I'm getting clear go-signals."

"Go-signals from the ostrich-woman."

"Yeah, exactly."

"Never ignore those," I told him.

"I never would."

When it was time for dinner Richard Abneg and I were seated on either side of Georgina Hawkmanaji, as it happened. His strategy, which given its unhesitating launch must have been instinctive, was to more or less shun Georgina completely and at the same time physically occupy her lap, in an ostensible campaign to impress himself on *me*. Repartee with Georgina could, in my experience, be a tad Sisyphean—she wasn't dumb, on the contrary, astute on nearly any subject, but her formality and deliberateness were a type of damp weather. So I admired the stunt. Abneg used Georgina for triangulation. She didn't have to keep up, only periodically ratify something particularly emphatic in his talk. That, and tolerate his spittle landing on the breast of her high-necked silk dress, tiny glints accumulating like a new constellation in the night sky.

Richard Abneg liked to dynamite his own ego, with tales of deals struck in offices where you counted your fingers after handshakes and found a few missing, where believing you'd won meant you'd misread the stakes. Between the jokes I heard him rationalizing a life's arc of excruciating compromise. He painted himself as a specialist in sheltering sand-castle idealisms against the undertow of the city's force of change, a force not so much cynical as tidally indifferent. Coughing up the lion's share of what you'd sworn to protect, in days of privatizing plunder, might be to keep from losing it all.

Abneg's voice was insinuating and sarcastic, a bully's, though he bullied only himself. At some point Thatcher Woodrow's internal testosterone meter tipped, and he leaned over to our end of the table. "Do you actually *know* Mayor Arnheim?"

Abneg had just hoisted a whole duck's drumstick out of his risotto, leaving a fat white spear of asparagus to ooze back into its sucking footprint. He seemed to revel in being framed in atavistic tableau, ripping at the glistening flesh with his teeth an extra moment while Thatcher waited for a reply.

"I work for him," said Abneg, swallowing. "I didn't say I know him. Sure, we've met a few dozen times, half of those in public where you'd hardly say it counted as a meeting. Look, Arnheim has fifty guys like me, farmed out covering his ass in one particular or another, sweating bullets on a daily basis. I don't flatter myself that he wants to be seen with me."

"We used to play in an all-night poker game, before he ascended to the throne," said Thatcher. "He and

I and Ted Koppel and Ahmet Ertegun, and George Soros, when he was in town. Killers all. I'm not sure it fits the people's image of their mayor, but he was the biggest killer among us. I'm no lightweight, but I was fighting for my life at that table."

If I knew Thatcher he'd look for an opening to tell us the cost of a buy-in at that game, too, before he was done. The minimum bets, the big and little blinds, and so on. But Richard Abneg stemmed this curtly and deftly.

"I work mostly with an aide to the mayor you probably didn't play poker with," he said. "Her name is Claire Carter. A killer too, of a different type. When we go to lunch she always insists on separate checks."

I laughed, liking how Abneg checked Thatcher's one-upmanship with one-downmanship. Georgina laughed too. Maybe Abneg would land his ostrich-woman after all.

At the appointed time the Woodrows' table turned its search-light on my woe. I played my part in what was a kind of kabuki enactment. There wasn't any real news—like the whole city, they'd devoured Janice's famous epistles from outer space. They only wanted to savor their lucky intimacy with the glamorous would-be astronaut's-husband. Janice was up there and I was down here. It was a rebus of heartbreak, misfortune a dog could parse. The Woodrows and their guests wanted a confession of something, but my only confession I wouldn't offer: my emotions were bogus as long as they were being performed in a setting like this one. I might love Janice, yes, but what I showed these people was a simulacrum, a portrayal of myself.

41

Harriet Welk asked the usual question. "They publish her letters to you, but do you write back?"

"I used to," I mumbled in my shame. "But Mission Control needed the communication time for ... other stuff. At some point they told me not to bother."

I was rescued from painting the last brushstrokes of my picture by the haggard entrance of Reggie Spencer, Sharon's husband, the funds manager who'd been delayed downtown. I thought I could see shreds of the gray fog still clinging to his creased pinstripe three-piece, to his scuffed chestnut wingtips. Certainly the gray fog was still reflected in Reggie Spencer's eyes as he rolled them upward and faked a smile and slid into the seat that had been kept open between Naomi Kandel and Harriet Welk. There was something tragical about the men who worked downtown, never more than when they were expected on return to manfully reassert their role entertaining ladies at parties, or cheerfully take over on weekends from nannies in Central Park, in order to remind their children of who their fathers were or had once been.

"Sorry, folks," said Reggie Spencer. "You don't want to know about it." Judging from his wife's expression, truer words couldn't be spoken. Staff were just clearing our ruins, pouring coffee from silver. "The F ground to a halt and just sat whining at Rockefeller Center. Eventually I got out and took a cab, I don't know if it was a mistake or not. Traffic was a nightmare. The cabbie was saying something about that escaped tiger getting loose again on Lexington Avenue."

"One hears continually of this . . . *tiger*," said Georgina Hawkmanaji. "It is supposedly of a tremendous size." She spoke as if this represented some personal provocation, from which adequate skepticism could offer insulation. I sympathized. I'd heard of the tiger perhaps three or four times now myself, yet found it difficult to bring into focus as a real and ongoing problem, something capable of bollixing traffic on Lexington. My fault. It was too long since I'd read a newspaper.

"See, they should let a few of us who know what we're doing track that baby down," said Thatcher Woodrow. "I ought to give Arnheim a call and suggest it. Can't imagine what's taking so long with one little old tiger." He raised his arms and squinted one eye like a five-year-old to mime bagging a moving target with a blunderbuss or elephant gun, alluding, I suppose, to facts we were supposed to have absorbed during some earlier dinner, about Thatcher's record of accomplishments up against big game. I thought I remembered something Hemingwayesque in his background, and maybe, god knew, a room full of pelts and heads lurked in the duplex somewhere, quarantined by Maud in favor of Diane Arbus and Gregory Crewdson prints and studies for sculptures by Laird Noteless.

"It isn't that kind of tiger," said Richard Abneg. His tone was dismissive. These two, Thatcher and Abneg, were going to be at it all night long, I saw. They'd find materials over which to dispute through the dessert, and through the round of Cuban cigars Thatcher always loved to personally distribute, and the seemingly spontaneous offerings of brandy and Armagnac Thatcher would haul out after the cigars, to distend the evening into a contented, blithering haze, meanwhile instructing the staff to do the final clearing in the morning, to Maud's disgust. (This was Thatcher's real enmity, anyway. Maud's conversational prerogatives ruled while conversation was possible, so Thatcher worked steadily to numb our tongues with stimulants, until we were reduced to the humming and grunting and Morse-code glances he preferred.)

"What's that supposed to mean?" asked not Thatcher but Naomi Kandel.

"Just that it isn't that kind of tiger, where you can, you know, kill it with a well-placed shot between the eyes or something."

"I have heard it is quite ... sizable," murmured Georgina, allying herself with Abneg.

"Yeah, it's big. A big *problem* is what it is. You have no idea." Was Richard Abneg implying that as a mayor's aide he was privy to facts about the tiger not printed in the *Times*? His heavy glances seemed to say *Yes I am*. He adjusted the collar of his shirt, grimacing sweatily, as if adding *and I've got claw marks on my back, they itch like hell*. Thatcher Woodrow seemed to take this as a signal to depart, without explanation, for a visit to the bathroom, or possibly to his humidor, to poison Abneg's cigar in advance.

■

Of course, there was no poison in Thatcher's cigars. Or, only a kind of poison we craved. An hour later, with all of us sprung from the vise of Maud's table, sprawled

44

on her white couches, snifters hovering at the level of our heads, hostilities were forgotten. Or drowned. Thatcher, in his absurd maroon dinner jacket with its college emblem, was our champion, keeping those snifters full of colored fluids with magical properties. He always had another exotic bottle that cried to be sampled, always with a name I instantly forgot, thinking instead: *Funky Monkey, Blueberry Kush, Chronic*.

Now we all loved one another to death. Which is to say, until the end of the evening. There was no other place to be, it was unimaginable not to float on our backs in this ocean of luxury, an archipelago of personalities lobbing witticisms across one another's beaches. Only I'd lately become irresolute in my dissolution. Gazing up at blue from my island, I'd begun to wonder how near that sky was. Whether it was some ceiling, perhaps a tissue I could rend with my fingertips if I only reached up to try.

Georgina Hawkmanaji and Richard Abneg sat side by side in the center of the largest and whitest of the couches, a kind of centerpiece around which we'd deferentially arrayed: Maud and Sharon Spencer and I bunched at one end of a facing couch, with Reggie Spencer asleep, face propped, curled knuckles indenting his sallow cheek, at the other; Thatcher coming and going from his terrific caramel-leather throne of a chaise longue, and Harriet Welk in another, smaller chaise, with Naomi Kandel camped out on the carpet at her feet—I spotted Naomi reaching casually to caress Harriet's sheer-stockinged calf for emphasis at some point she was making, but this gesture was going absolutely nowhere, only being blithely tolerated by Harriet. (To be honest I was being similarly molested by Sharon Spencer, and it mattered as little.)

It was Georgina's and Abneg's coming together that formed the main action here, a show we all consented to see slowed to a crawl by Georgina's elegant jitters and Abneg's distractibility. The show's progress was slowed, too, even if sponsored, by the flow of Thatcher's brandies. Our delight in the exhibition wasn't unkind. It was simply a real pleasure to witness Georgina uncorked by Richard Abneg's coarse, crazy appetite for her. In glimpses, between harangues on one subject or another, when he didn't seem to notice Georgina at all, Abneg appeared not to believe his fortune. You'd have thought their sweet collision was Maud's engineering—I envisioned her taking credit, with relish—only it became clear Maud couldn't have known whom her new friend Harriet Welk would bring along to dinner.

Abneg, somehow, had gotten onto the subject of a visit he'd made, some time ago, to Stonehenge. "You park in this little area, it's across the road, and then you buy a ticket, just to be allowed to cross the street. There's this underground tunnel, you mill through like sheep. And there's nothing to do except trudge like that, all the way around the thing. They've got you in a kind of track, restrained from Stonehenge itself. You can't go near the rocks. And that's it. You trudge around single file in a circle, the thing looks a little smaller and less mysterious than you'd hoped, and you go back through the tunnel and maybe stop at the gift shop or the restroom, then back to your car."

"Unimpressive," grunted Thatcher.

"Well, sure," said Abneg. "Totally unimpressive. I wanted to be like one of those apes in whatchamacallit, *2001*, by whatsisname, Kubrick, you know, kneeling in fear before those slabs, getting brain-zapped."

"I never saw *2001*," said Harriet. "It's about *apes*?"

"Ape-*men*," said Thatcher helpfully.

"They should change the name of that movie," said Sharon Spencer beside me. "Since the real *2001* turned out so different."

"Listen," said Abneg, with exasperation that we hadn't caught his real drift. "I'm trying to tell you about the Stonehenge restroom. I had to piss, so I went in there, it was a completely modern men's room, with all these floor-length ceramic urinals. They didn't have the wit to arrange them in a circle, but the resemblance was obvious. And whereas everyone was jabbering when they walked around Stonehenge, all the moms bargaining with the whining children, in here the men were all silent, avoiding one another's eyes. Each of us standing at a urinal or waiting our turn, and this profound truth comes over you, a feeling much bigger than anything available outside and across the road, which is that everyone in that restroom just did the exact same thing you did."

"Which is what?" said Naomi Kandel.

"*Looked at Stonehenge*," said Abneg. "And now you were taking a piss, and then you were going to get back in your car."

I tried to understand, and almost did, and then found myself wondering if Abneg was emphasizing the word

47

piss so strongly in order to force Georgina to visualize the existence of his penis. It was forcing me to visualize it, anyway.

"That . . . is . . . not . . . deep," said Naomi Kandel conclusively.

Thatcher, Abneg's biggest fan, seemed to get it. "Got a place like that in Australia," he said. "Ayres Rock, only you're supposed to call it something else. Biggest rock in the world, takes a coupla hours to walk around it. Same thing, though. You go around in a track. Center of the country, nothing around for a thousand miles, no other reason you'd ever stop there. Rock has its own damn airport."

Abneg was thrilled, though it seemed to me his point, if he had one, had been hijacked for Thatcher's imperial scorn. "Fantastic! So, basically, that airport's just the world's foremost example of a *Stonehenge restroom.*"

Thatcher toasted this, a little uneasily, with a hoist of his snifter.

"In a thousand years," continued Richard Abneg, "they'll probably lead walking tours around the perimeter of the ruined airport."

"Huh," said Thatcher, less and less sure.

"It would be a terribly *disappointing* walking tour," said Georgina Hawkmanaji, with a sly smile to make us know she was playing along. Abneg, who'd snaked a densely haired forearm around Georgina's tiny waist at some point, drew her nearer to him now, proud to be understood. His grip accordioned a coo from Georgina.

"Very few people know this," I heard myself saying, "but Stanley Kubrick once tried to make a film with the

Gnuppets, if you can believe it." I'd been silently drunk for so long my voice startled me, but for that same reason some participation seemed demanded of me, to prove I'd been listening. Idiotically, I'd fished up this secondhand anecdote too late, after the Kubrick interlude had passed, and everyone looked at me a little daftly.

"Urgghh, I *hate* Gnuppets!" said Sharon Spencer. She formed her hands into tortured upright figures, snarling at them so we couldn't fail to taste her avid revulsion.

"Sure," I said, then tossed a life preserver after my drowning remark. "But just picture it ... a *Kubrick* film ... with *Gnuppets* ... it might be kind of *incredible* ..."

"You sound like someone I know," said Richard Abneg. "I've got this one friend who's always trying to make you imagine films that don't exist." He squinted as if seeing me for the first time. I might have returned a similar look. "Actually, he was talking about the Kubrick Gnuppet movie just the other day."

Busted. It was Perkus Tooth I was parroting in the first place. Of course Abneg knew him. As the tumblers slid into place, I understood that the tone of Abneg's Stonehenge story had unconsciously reminded me of Perkus, and made me wish to smuggle him into the conversation, to impress, or perhaps test, Richard Abneg.

Then Abneg shocked me. Looking me in the eye, he lifted thumb and forefinger to his lips as if smooching the damp stub of a joint. It was hardly that marijuana was taboo here. The shock was in how the gesture so carelessly pierced the bubble of harmony that had formed, against the odds, among us. In his contempt for our bonhomie, he also showed me how it was still in some way sacred to me. How I was in the business of protecting, and flattering, the Woodrows' vanities. It felt as if Abneg had undone his fly and pissed on the Woodrows' carpet.

His message to me, if it wasn't too much to read into the single gesture, seemed to be *See you later, at Perkus's. Away from these fucking rich people*. Or maybe I'd invented that last, out of my wish that Abneg could detect my own degree of defiance, of bad faith in this company. Anyway, our instant of collusion was finished. As if at some established cue, Abneg swept in and finished what it looked like he'd never even get back to: spiriting Georgina Hawkmanaji up from that couch and out of the duplex, presumably upstairs, to her penthouse apartment, to prove definitively to her the existence of his penis, or to have her prove it to him. We all sat pretending not to be fascinated at how neatly he sheltered Georgina from her own shyness at being extracted from our nodding assembly. I'll admit she was revealed (too late) (and unimportantly) as erotic to me, as she'd never been until seeing Abneg's hairy fingers brushing the nape of her neck, and guiding her, like a virtuoso repositioning a cello, by the hip. So I learned how Richard Abneg, like Perkus Tooth, was someone who could uncover what hid in plain sight.

I only had to arrive fifteen minutes early at East Eighty-fourth Street one day to discover Oona Laszlo existed. Perkus buzzed me up and I entered to find them standing there, in front of their chairs at his kitchen table, shuffling as if apprehended at a crime. Almost one in the afternoon, but I'd broken up a breakfast scene, coffee, cheese Danish sliced into fingers on a grease-marked white sack, a thin joint modestly half smoked and perching in a cleanish ashtray. A pair of Lucite boxes labeled WHITE RHINO, one of Watt's brands. *The New York Times*, which Perkus never read. I assumed it belonged to his guest. A book Perkus had been reading last I visited, a gigantic novel entitled *Obstinate Dust*. Also, non sequitur, *A Field Guide to North American Birds of Prey*, a sturdy blue trade paperback, inverted on propped-open pages. I did my best to conceal my surprise at this woman's presence. The foot traffic was a little thicker in Perkus's apartment than I'd previously understood. It might be that he booked us one after the next, his secret life bustled with visitors, his lonely lobby a revolving door.

Needless to say my first thought was that Oona Laszlo was Perkus's lover. I was wrong. Yet this error, the tender cameo it conjured in my mind's eye, is still, weirdly, a place I can retreat to in memory and think *It might have been better. It might have been nice.* I can still see them there, framed in my mistaken assumption, and feel thrilled and relieved for Perkus, who, in dwelling in that imaginary frame, remains as I first knew him.

The two fit, inviting the mistake. If not lovers, they might be brother and sister. Oona shared Perkus's marionette-ish aspect, large head connected to a tiny frame and seeming to sweep her nervous limbs behind its weight. She wore black (another hint, I thought, that they'd spent the night together—she seemed dressed for the previous evening), making her like a marker scribble, a silhouette in spastic motion in that cramped kitchen. They were expensive clothes, too—I noted that automatically. Expensive for Perkus's kitchen at least. Black hair, too, in bangs and a neat bob. Had Perkus spilled a pot of coffee on his tiles and the coffee sprung to life as a woman an instant before I opened the door, it would have explained her perfectly. Oona's mouth alone confessed female ripeness, seeming to stand for secret curves unrevealed by her silhouette. Her canines caught on her lower lip just as our eyes met, drawing it into an expression faintly lascivious and wry. Or perhaps those tooth tips tended to catch there. This might be her default look, teeth too much for lips to contain. Above this expression Oona's eyes flitted, measuring distance to the exit. Yet if Oona was Perkus's female synonym, she was younger and, I had to admit, alluring. If they were siblings, she'd gotten the looks. If they were lovers, I found myself thinking, he'd gotten lucky.

Perkus didn't seem flustered, exactly. Aggravated was more like it. His independent eye tried to follow Oona as he turned to me.

"Chase, Oona. Oona, Chase." He discharged the formality, then practically threw down his hands in disgust at his own obedience.

"Hello."

Oona stared at me with her crooked smile. I wasn't totally unfamiliar with the starstruck gaze, but Manhattanites usually did a better job of concealing it, especially those dressed in black.

"Sorry," she said. Instead of offering a hand, she crossed her arms, fitting plumlike breasts over her forearms. "I've always sort of wanted to meet you. But then again, sort of wanted not to, *at all*."

"Okay," I said, as generous as I could manage under the circumstances. People might dialogue in their own heads with famous or semi-famous strangers. I preferred to think it a fundamental minimum standard that they keep it to themselves. Nothing in Oona Laszlo's manner suggested any self-reproach. She examined me like a portrait painter seeking a better grasp of the play of light over my facial planes.

"You're from somewhere really weird, aren't you?" said Oona Laszlo. Before I could answer she supplied it herself: "Indiana."

"Yes." If I didn't think of it I often forgot. My home was far away, if it was my home.

Perkus had plunked back into his chair. He relit the joint, and scrabbled in a pile of loose CDs, then shoved one into the boom box. "So," he said. Slumping beneath the bridge of his own templed hands, he drew on the joint centered in his lips so that it crackled, then pinched it from his mouth and waved it free. "I got sent a dub of Gillo Pontecorvo's *Burn*, it's eighteen minutes longer than the release cut, some kind of early assembly, maybe we should watch it—" Perkus spoke as if to one of us alone, only I was unsure which. Was he resuming a conversation with Oona or beginning one with me? All talk was a resumption. I couldn't remember who Pontecorvo was, though I knew I was supposed to.

Perkus pounced, as ever, on my hesitation. "Pontecorvo. He did *The Battle of Algiers*. You know, *Burn*, with Brando."

"Oh, sure."

"Yeah, this is pretty much how I pictured it," said Oona Laszlo. She gathered up a sweater, also black, from the back of her chair. "You guys are pretty sweet, and I'm going to go now."

"Sweet how?" I asked. "What's so sweet about us?"

"Just, you know, watching old Brando movies together in the afternoon, then deconstructing the universe for dessert. It's like you're helping Perkus with his homework."

"See you later," said Perkus. He was, I understood, very eager to have Oona leave, to avoid having us here together. Which made me eager for the opposite. Oona Laszlo's little jibe at Perkus made me understand that they weren't lovers, at least not anymore. She and I shared a protective impulse toward him. Also, an unrelated insight, I'd begun to find Oona beguiling, despite her pointed gawking. It was a little boyish

54

around here, now that she'd pointed it out. She could be the cure.

"Why don't you stay and watch with us?" I said.

"I would, but I just saw that movie, and Perkus hates it when I shout out the dialogue just before the actors say it."

"Oh?"

"That was a joke. Forgive me. There's something about running into you here that's making me babble."

"You don't have to be so self-conscious."

"No, actually, I do. I'm one of those subtext-on-the-outside people, which is why I should really go."

She then surprised me by gathering up one of the Lucite boxes of White Rhino and shoveling it into her purse. And then was gone. Perkus barely glanced after her.

"She took your pot."

"It was hers," he said, not glancing at the table either. "I scored it for her, as a favor. She doesn't like to deal with Watt." He invented tasks for himself, sweeping imaginary crumbs into his cupped palm, fiddling with the volume, jumping up to rinse a glass, seeking, with his whole being, to exorcise the obvious subject. I didn't allow him.

"An old girlfriend?"

Perkus shook his head. "Just a friend."

"She's a funny one. How'd you meet her?"

"Oona's great, when you're in the mood. She used to be a kind of intern of mine, I guess that's what you'd call it. She answered an ad I placed at the New School, she used to help me pasting up broadsides . . ." His voice trailed, even as his desublimated eyeball zipped to walls of the living room, rolling wildly to indicate the framed and unframed manifestos of his youth.

"Oona was your glue-girl!" I said.

"Something like that. My apprentice."

"Every mad scientist needs an apprentice."

"Fuck you."

"She didn't want to change the world, I suppose? Or what did she call it—deconstruct the universe."

"There was this editor from Viking Penguin, uh, Paul somebody. He proposed to do a compilation of the broadsides, and took us out for drinks. I didn't care to do the book, but Oona ended up with a job in publishing. She was looking for a writing career, and I guess she felt it was her way in."

"Why didn't you do the book?"

"We differed on . . . context."

"He saw you as a rock critic?"

Perkus nodded.

"So she's in publishing?"

"Oona?" he asked, as if we'd dropped the subject hours earlier. He stood and put his back to me, fussing at his coffeepot. "Nope, she's a freelancer. A self-admitted hack."

"I'm interested in hacks, Perkus, being one myself. What does she write?"

"Nothing under her own name. She ghostwrites. Autobiographies of people who can't write their own. She brought one around once—here." He'd poured us fresh coffees. Now he clapped these, with a pair of spoons, on the table before me, then moved into the living room, to burrow into a stack of unsorted books at the foot of a shelf.

The hardcover Perkus delivered into my hands was unexpectedly garish and grim: *Across Foul Lines*, by Rose Arbogast, the memoir of a seven-foot-tall WNBA center who as a high-school star had been abducted and serially tortured by a teenage gang, then rescued by a federal agent she'd married a decade later. "This is shit," I blurted.

"Read the inscription."

"What?"

"On the title page."

Someone, Oona Laszlo, had printed in a stenographically precise hand *To Perkus Tooth, who taught me to lay up, not lie down, warmly, R.O./O.L.* "She's become a specialist in traumatized athletes, frostbitten Everest climbers who have to wear plastic noses, etcetera, a narrow field she dominates. She fully knows it's shit. How she gets through her days is another question."

"The same way you do," I suggested. "White Rhino." I nodded at the remaining container.

Perkus ignored me. I learned nothing further about Oona Laszlo that day, nor did Perkus and I get around to viewing the early-assembly dub of Pontecorvo's *Burn*, though the videotape sat talismanically before us through the afternoon and into the evening. For lately, with the addition of Richard Abneg, my Perkus afternoons had distended into Perkus-and-Richard nights. I'd begun to let other priorities shrivel in favor of these bouts of epic squalor. It was easy to drop out of my drifting existence. The Eighty-fourth Street apartment was

57

a container bigger on the inside than the outside, and days there might seem to hold thirty or forty hours, yet more and more I reeled home in dawn light, along a Second Avenue mostly vacated, the downtown stream of empty wishful taxicabs all veering to toot their horns at me until I waved them off, pavement deliveries of Italian loaves and kaiser rolls and bundles of tabloids under way—the clocks outside hadn't stopped, after all. Richard Abneg was the one among us with an office, a morning agenda shackled to those unstopped clocks, yet he drove us maniacally through the night, toward daybreak, as much as Perkus (or his coffeepot, or dope supply) or myself, more perhaps.

Was the afternoon when Oona first appeared the third or fourth Richard and Perkus and I spent together? Or the hundredth? I can't say. In the swamp of memory I can only confidently fix that occasion to Richard Abneg's eagles, and that only because of *A Field Guide to North American Birds of Prey* which lay propped open on the table from which Oona retrieved her stash before vanishing. I was always foolish to slight any clue at Perkus's kitchen table, for what seemed to happen to occupy space there was always destined to colonize my brain soon enough. (I suppose I could say the same about Oona. Soon. Soona.)

■

Richard Abneg came in enraged about eagles. He liked to come in enraged about something. Hadn't I read the front page of the Metro section? The answer was no. Richard found this incredible. My neglect of the headlines was practically as egregious as the birds themselves. Richard nearly slammed down his bottle of wine, Rioja in a paper sack. He always arrived with one in tow. Not a gift, since Perkus wouldn't touch red wine, a trigger, he claimed, for his cluster migraines. Richard and I would drink it later, in the smaller hours. For now it sat.

Perkus tossed the relevant section into my lap and resumed rolling a joint to welcome and soothe Richard, to whatever extent he could be soothed. Richard jabbed his finger at a newsprint photograph, so my attention wouldn't wander. A pair of enormous birds perched on the massive lintel of a prewar building's entranceway, each with a beak-borne branch. Between them stood the object of their efforts, a conical structure of twigs and leaves. HOMECOMING OF MATING PAIR REWARDS 78TH STREET FAITHFUL. "Okay," I said.

"Not okay," said Richard, poking harder at the newspaper on my knee. "That's my fucking window."

"You live there?" I asked, trying to catch up.

"My headboard's against that wall. Right above the scratching, whining, gobbling fiends themselves. They don't sound like you'd think eagles should sound, Chase. They sound like vampires. Vampires at a buffet of dying rodents."

A joke occurred to me. "Well, you know what they say. Go to bed with the Hawkman, wake up with the eagles." It was now three weeks past our fateful introduction at the Woodrows' Park Avenue duplex, and Richard Abneg had surprised me, and perhaps himself,

59

by persisting in an affair with Georgina Hawkmanaji, Turk heiress. He called her, in his irascible way, Georgie Hawkman. Or the Hawkman, or the Hawk. The complicity between us, my having seen him infringe on Georgina's rectitude the first time, formed the backdrop to our new friendship, a ready-made history we could allude to. If Richard seemed to bristle when I mentioned her, this was only ritual. He loved being reminded I knew of his conquest. Perkus was the one whom mentions of the Hawkman truly provoked. Perkus was a possessive friend, true enough. But he also cringed at evidence of my migrations, or Richard's, through a milieu he viewed as corrupt.

Richard only glowered. "It's not funny. I've been spending nights at the Hawkman's just to sleep. She thinks I can't get enough of her."

"If it's your window, can't you have the nest removed?"

"You really live in a cloud, don't you?"

Perkus had done tonguing the new joint's glue, and he handed the result to Richard. "So, about six weeks ago Richard opened his window and pushed the whole mess into the street. The eagles went into mourning, started wheeling around crying, and all the TV news stations picked it up. The eagles flew off to Central Park, I guess. It seemed like it was going to blow over, but then the other apartments got together and held a press conference saying they loved the eagles, that the lone pusher didn't speak for the building's wishes. Richard got hung out to dry. That's what they called him, *the lone pusher*."

"The president of the co-op board didn't give my name, mercifully. But I've had to creep in and out of the building for weeks. The *Post* published a telephoto picture of me in my Fruit of the Looms. Now the feathered monsters are beginning again with the nest, and everybody's so thrilled. I'm totally stuck. There's this bored old television star on the eighth floor, she's made the eagles her whole raison d'être."

"What television star?" I had an odd feeling I knew.

"You know, what's her goddamn name?" Richard slurped air around the joint's tip, waved his hand.

"Sandra Saunders Eppling," supplied Perkus. "She was married to Senator Eppling for a while. She was the one who spoke at the press conference."

"Sandra Saunders played my mom on *Martyr & Pesty*," I said. I felt, as I often do at those rare times I actually choose to speak of my child stardom, as if I was boring my listeners with information too familiar to mention, and yet also evoking a distant pocket realm no living human could imagine. In either case, the result felt as though I were being humored. Possibly I did live on a cloud.

"She was in an Elvis movie," said Perkus, frowning at me for not citing the more salient fact. I'd noticed— this may have been when I first noticed it—how Perkus didn't browbeat Richard Abneg for his cultural illiteracy. He had me for that.

"Right, that's the one," said Richard, uninterested in anything but his nest. He seized the newspaper section from me now. "These days she's a kind of fundamentalist vegetarian eagle-advocate. It's horrendous luck for me she doesn't have a real career to keep her busy. My whole building's brimming with mediocrities and has-beens."

"The whole *island's* brimming with them," said Perkus agreeably.

"Yes, but your bedroom isn't full of the smell of moldering underbrush and the death screams of squirrels and pigeons and sewer rats," said Richard. "Look at this." He handed the fuming joint to me and raised the newspaper for us to consider, folded to the photograph of the eagles and their startlingly large construction. "It's obscene. It's practically . . . pubic."

"Yes," said Perkus. "Your building is definitely wearing a merkin."

"That's a *polite* word for it." Richard stroked his beard, perhaps unconsciously making an association.

"I don't think merkin is the polite word for something," I said. "It's more specific than that—"

"Read it to me," interrupted Richard. Perkus had taken up the book, the *Field Guide*. I now saw it lay flapped open to the entry on eagles, Perkus having already delved into study on Richard's behalf. "I've got to find some way to eradicate them that can't be traced back to me . . ."

"I guess if you got a dog it would bark at them." This was my pallid contribution, while Perkus studied the pages, tilting the book to favor his orderly eye.

"No, it can't be inside my apartment, it has to be something that will crawl up the front of the building. Besides, I hate dogs." We were deep into crime melodrama, a caper, Richard and Perkus collaborating on the perfect interspecies murder. "I'm going to need an alibi, too. I can't be anywhere in the vicinity when those eagles go. That building is ready to come after me with torches and pitchforks."

"So, here's the thing." Perkus held up a finger proclaiming *Eureka*! He was forever ferreting out the key, always distilling essences. "*Majestic in his privilege,*" he narrated from the *Field Guide*, "*the bald eagle knows no natural enemy apart from Man.*"

"What a freight of shit," said Richard.

"Why?"

"There's something totally insane about saying a frigging psychotic serial killer has no natural enemy! What they *mean* is the eagle's enemies don't stand a chance. All those mice and squirrels and pigeons, believe me, they'd *gladly* define themselves as enemies in that instant before the talons tore through their hearts."

"In nature I think a thing doesn't qualify as your enemy if it can't fight back," I said. "It's just a victim."

"Maybe we could corral a whole bunch of mice and squirrels and pigeons together," suggested Perkus. "If they somehow were all run up the side of the building at once, when the eagles were sleeping . . ." He flipped eagerly through the *Guide*'s back pages, perhaps scanning the index for some precedent.

"No." Richard leaned forward, grabbing for the joint I still held. He took it and drew in a puff and shook his shaggy head. "No, it won't do." His grave tone suggested real deliberation. "Prey is prey, I'm sorry to have to disenchant you two dreamers. You total Communists. If you'd heard them whimper and die, the way I have, you'd understand. A *million* mice couldn't do it."

"Didn't mice kill the dinosaurs?" asked Perkus.

Richard shook his head. "The dinosaurs were stupid, they were on their last legs. Anyhow, the mice had help, they needed comets and glaciers, all kinds of stuff. I'm pretty certain the mice just jumped in at the end and administered the coup de grâce, then took all the credit."

"We need a predator," said Perkus.

"Exactly."

"We should go up there, the three of us," said Perkus. "Not now, but later, when it's dark, when they're sleeping." We were always, Perkus Tooth and Richard Abneg and I, on the verge of some tremendous expedition, like Vikings spreading nautical charts across a knife-scarred table, laying plans for plunder. Oh, how Manhattan yearned for our expert intervention! We never budged from that kitchen, however, unless if it was to tumble out coughing into the fresh chill air, and around the corner, to pile into a booth at Jackson Hole for cheeseburgers and Cokes.

"The thing about animals," Perkus said, "I remember this clearly, is that when you bring in, you know, *kangaroos* to chase away *monkeys*, then you have a kangaroo problem. Then you bring in *zebras* to chase off the kangaroos, and you're overrun with zebras, and so on."

"You learned that in a Dr. Seuss book, didn't you?" said Richard.

"What about the tiger?" I said. "What if somehow the tiger could be brought into play?"

Perkus gave Richard a look of horrified helplessness, seeming to say at once, *Don't blame me, I didn't suggest it*, and *Well, why not?*

Richard tittered. "The tiger?"

"Sure."

"Sure, that's just what my apartment needs, Chase. That tiger destroyed one of the city's primary water mains last week. I mean, totally shattered layers of concrete and brick that had held since the nineteenth century, it's going to take *months* to repair it."

"Okay," I said. "Well, maybe the tiger could be . . . blamed somehow."

Richard snorted smoke through his nostrils. "Blamed when I *off the eagles*, you mean?"

"Sure."

"Brilliant." At this Richard Abneg dissolved in giggles, sweeping Perkus Tooth along with him. And soon enough myself, too. "Blame the tiger!"

Let this stand for a typical night in our company there. I don't remember them all in such detail.

∎

I met Oona next at a funeral, the funeral of a man I didn't know, a purportedly great man. I had to cross the park to be there—the services were held at the Society for Ethical Culture, on Central Park West—and when I saw how populous the congregation was, I felt foolish for troubling. Emil Junrow was a famous science-fiction writer of the 1940s, a lowly career he took upmarket by being also an accredited (if undistinguished) scientist, and a famous humanist who'd uttered fine early doubts

65

about the Cold War, a sort of Einstein without any theory. He'd then gone on to become a relentless prose-lytizer for the peaceful exploration of space, appearing many times before Congress and in public forums, a dwarfish wizened presence in bolo ties and flyaway hair (I learned all this in tributes presented during the long memorial presentation, including video clips that made me realize I'd seen Junrow on television without registering his name).

It was in this last role that Emil Junrow had once or twice been photographed in the company of Janice Trumbull, lady space-explorer. My receiving an invitation wasn't anything personal, however, a fact that was made plain the instant I entered. Some publicist, knowing the cavernous size of the society's hall, had emptied his Rolodex into the invitation list. In range of my glance I spotted Salman Rushdie, Charlie Rose, and Lou Reed. There were surely many others I didn't recognize. Despite being a low-grade semi-celebrity myself, I'm rotten at picking out any but the cartoon-obvious among us. I felt like an idiot, dressed to the nines, alone and invisible in the dim back rows as the stately figures spoke one after the other on the distant stage. I'd attended out of an absurd pity, imagining an old man who'd been exaggerating his connection to Janice, and therefore to me, not remotely guessing that Emil Junrow's passing was an authentic cultural moment, and that with the gravity and glamour of those who'd come to pay respects no one would trouble to register my presence. I only stayed out of a mild curiosity, and discretion. No one should duck out of a funeral.

Oona found me just as the three-hour marathon of tributes concluded and the crowd broke into a buzzing mass, before I could sprint to the exit. Perhaps she'd spotted me earlier. She seemed, anyway, to be alone here.

"What did you think?" she said.

"It was all very impressive."

"For me, there was only one good line in the whole show," said Oona, oblivious to the risk of being overheard.

"What was that?"

"From when Emil Junrow was born, when he was handed to his mother in the hospital and she said, 'He looks like he can remember happier days.' "

The words had been offered up by one of the few family members giving testimony amid the parade of luminaries, a cantankerous elderly cousin, a woman as shriveled and fierce as Junrow. Hearing the quip, it was hard not to picture the newborn already possessing Junrow's white muttonchops and furrowed brow, his hectoring eyes.

"Sometimes one good line is enough," I said.

"Oh, absolutely, I wasn't complaining. Junrow's mom, she goes straight into the annals with that remark."

As we drifted out into the lobby a waiter appeared, balancing a tray of wineglasses, half of them filled with white, half with red. Oona and I each grabbed a white.

"Did you know Junrow?" I said. A stupid choice, since I wouldn't have wished to be asked the same in return. I was groping. My tongue felt cardboardy in my mouth. Yet other parts of me were unaccountably alive, all at once, despite the soporific effects of three hours in that whiskey-colored auditorium, and the sober and seemly procession of tributes.

"I wrote his last two books," she said, fixing me with that same steady, warmly sardonic gaze I'd faced at Perkus's.

"Ah. You know a lot about science, then?"

"Barely anything. I wrote his funny, personable books. *Junrow's Rules for Amateurs* and *I Can't Quite Believe You Said That, Dr. Junrow*."

"So you must have spent a lot of time together. I'm surprised you weren't invited up onstage to pay homage."

"My existence is meant to be a secret," she said, again with no concern for secrecy. "I didn't get where I am today speaking at funerals."

"Did you like him?"

"Picture one of those old *New Yorker* cartoons with the old man chasing the secretary in circles around the desk. Luckily he was easy to outrun."

"I read *Across Foul Lines* the other night—I mean, part of it."

"I'm guessing you mean Perkus Tooth's copy."

"It was pretty good, actually."

"Oh God, I can totally picture it, you and Perkus getting stoned and reading pages aloud and roaring with laughter, until the words quit making any literal sense. Am I right?"

This was closer than I wanted to admit.

"Did you guys do voices, trying it out as Donald Duck and Greta Garbo and so on? It's perfectly okay, sometimes I do that myself when I'm writing them."

"I'd like to hear that," I said, not wanting to put up a fight.

"Maybe you do a great Marlon Brando, Chase? I know Perkus would like that one."

Was Oona Laszlo mocking Perkus now? Our secret sharing of the apartment on East Eighty-fourth Street felt almost disagreeably intimate, here in this crowd. I went for a gulp of wine and found my glass was empty. "Do you want to go somewhere and get a drink?" I said impulsively. I had no idea how to navigate the West Side, but we were near Lincoln Center—there had to be something.

"There's plenty here, for free. I think they might even bring out some sushi or cocktail frankfurters if we play our cards right."

Oona Laszlo's teasing dared me onward. She was a sprite of sarcasm, even her pensive torso, her small breasts concealed in black silhouette, seeming to jape. I'd been immune for three hours to the shameful survivor's lust that I'd known to sometimes wash over me at funerals, the giddy, guilty apprehension of one's own continuing lucky freedom to feast and fuck and defecate, to waste hours flipping cable channels watching fragments of movies or half solving crosswords in ballpoint and then tossing them aside, to do pretty well anything but sit and honor the memory of another whose lucky freedom had run out. But now, three hours' worth of such lust seemed to flood me all at once, in retrospect. Oona and I were surely not the two youngest people in that crowded hall of five or six hundred, many of whom were just now filing through the doors into the lobby, being handed their first glass of white or red. But it felt to me at that moment as though we were teenagers who'd dressed up and snuck in.

"I'd be willing to pay for my own drinks or even cocktail frankfurters in exchange for a little privacy," I told her.

"You don't want to be seen with me?"

"I'd like to be seen with you," I said, "elsewhere."

"I don't believe you. I think you're afraid somebody's going to try to ask you for your autograph or to pose for a picture with your arm around Salman Rushdie, and then I'll slip away. Which I absolutely would. I'd be out of here like a shot."

"I—"

"We could go to the movies," she said, surprising me. "Or just find a doorway somewhere and make out awkwardly, then later not call each other, or call but not find anything to say."

"Let's go," I said, applying my palm to the small of her back, to guide her from the reception. Disconcertingly, her dress was cut out in a circle there, so my cool fingers slipped inside and made her jump. Then she smiled again, canines caught on her lip.

"Where?"

"Anywhere."

I only meant to insist that we go out of hearing range of the mourners and celebrants, though it had the effect of seeming to endorse her dizzy talk as a kind of plan. And as well to suggest I took the matter of my celebrity seriously in that crowd, as she'd joked. In truth, I doubted anyone cared. But *I* cared. It was my pitiful flame to nurture, that I should behave upstandingly as Janice Trumbull's signifier in public places, at funerals at least. I was arm candy on Janice's phantom arm, not much else. And the difference between this setting and Perkus's apartment, or even Maud and Thatcher Woodrow's, was real to me.

We stopped to get our coats from the checkroom, then stepped outdoors, into a street vacant in a gutter-choking rainstorm, the black sky seemingly half liquid, snail-crawling taxicabs hugging the gleaming avenue's crest for safety. I manage never to be prepared for the weather. Nobody else had left the hall, and as the heavy doors slammed behind us, all warmth and light seemed definitively on their backside, the reception an oasis we'd foolishly forsaken. Oona Laszlo was unsurprised. She produced a short black umbrella from her trench-coat pocket, and we struggled to shelter ourselves beneath it together long enough to put Emil Junrow and Ethical Culture behind us. Swirling wind made comedy of our attempt, and soon enough we found a doorway, just as Oona had scripted for us. I suppose she knew the weather forecast. Brass nameplates identified our hiding place as the entrance to a cabal of dentists. Across Central Park West trees lashed like an island's in a typhoon.

The shoulders of my suit were drenched, the shirt beneath pasted to my back, and my slacks to my calves as well. Oona had fared a bit better, centered beneath the shred of umbrella. Yet she was wet and cold enough to be shivering. I felt it as she nestled into me. The lintel above us played the role of a tiny Niagara, the sheet of droplets a white-noise curtain drawn against the city and the whole of the storm.

"This has to be a secret."

"I'm terrific at secrets. It's a professional requirement."

"I don't have a whole lot in the way of a public role. I'm only known for one thing: my fidelity to Janice."

"Oh wow, yeah, you scream *fidelity*."

"Look, it's all I've got."

"That's true. You're a very one-dimensional character."

Her gaze zipped shyly from the coursing street to my damp collar and tie, anywhere but to meet mine. Her tiny hand, sharp and mouselike, slid between my jacket and shirt at my ribs. It seemed I was waiting to understand. The West Side was a mysterious distance from the East, the howling park between us and home. There was no one there to protect us from each other. There never was. I thought, irrelevantly, of the tiger. This is too true of me: my thoughts migrate, precisely when I ought to be attending. I stare into one face and begin to recall tendrils of another conversation. Richard Abneg had mentioned that the tiger kept to the East Side. Maybe we were safer here, in that case. But now came a dozen questions I wished I'd been bright enough to ask. Where did the tiger go in the rain? Why wouldn't it want to take up in the park?

This night it might be fair to think such thoughts were the place I fled in a storm of guilt. I might not remember Janice very well, but wasn't I supposed to love her? Here, beneath this sill, I toyed with wrecking the greatest long-distance relationship in the history of the cosmos. Or at least the long-distantest.

"I didn't think I would like you," whispered Oona Laszlo, offering a glimpse of devastating tenderness toward us both. The tiny cracks in this woman's hard-boiled façade were as entrancing to me as the fine tracing of shattered glaze on a Renaissance portrait, vulnerable everywhere, though the face that glared from beneath dared you to waste any sympathy upon it.

My own words were more than usually missing. I let my hands play at Oona's hair and clothes, her perimeter, didn't plunge inside.

"Should we go to your place?" I asked.

"You'll never be invited to my place, Chase. Please don't suggest it again."

"Okay." I felt a little rapturous and awed, but completely tawdry, too. Oona seemed to demand it, the ticket price of entry. I was meant to ignore the shattered glaze.

"Have I insulted you yet?" she asked.

"I'm hard to insult, for the same reason you're good at secrets."

"Too delicate by half, Chase. Fucking kiss me."

4

The only role I ever played to anyone's complete satisfaction was Warren, on *Martyr & Pesty*. As the idealistic and dreamy boy intern to Gordon Pesty, the fulminating lawyer extraordinaire, I seemed, to myself and others, to embody . . . something. The show itself was avowedly "dumb" and we all (writers and actors, network, critics, audience) flogged ourselves those days for our complicity in its runaway success, but I, the exception, was unaccountably "soulful." Or, not I, but Warren Zoom, born on the wrong side of the tracks, single child of glamorous widowed mom, persistently seeking fatherly mentoring from the irate and disarmed Pesty. This Warren Zoom struck the viewer (or at least a critical mass of teenage girls, and a number of their mothers) as possessing some quantity of life outside the cold frame of the screen, beyond the rigid limits of what shadow plays could be mounted within that half-hour frame in the usual attempt to placate, amuse, and sell what needed selling. Short novels, geared to the teenage girls, were hurriedly commissioned by Ballantine Books (written, I suppose, by the eighties equivalent of Oona Laszlo), decorated with my face, and offered on drugstore and supermarket racks—new stuff to sell, exploding out of the old, the great dream. At one point, I remember, I had the cover of *TV Guide* and *People* in the same week. Everyone wanted to know or be Warren Zoom! And I was he! This all evaporated rather (extremely) quickly.

Now Warren Zoom and I have suffered a permanent rupture. We go our separate ways, he trapped in his rounds, ever youthful, pushed deeper and deeper into cable television's circles of hell (where I accidentally glimpse him from time to time, and hurriedly surf away). Me, aging, but not too badly, playing these other roles in my life here in Manhattan, for which Warren floats the checks, an elegant arrangement of mutual support and indifference. Or no, that's not true. I do nothing nowadays to support Warren Zoom. I'd say he owes me everything, but I'm not sure he'd agree.

I no longer act, that is unless you'd call my every waking moment a kind of performance. Apart from errands of good taste, like recording the Criterion voice-overs for Susan Eldred, I'm untempted. To be honest, few lately have sought to tempt me. A year ago I took a strange meeting with a couple of producers, young men with the bullish slickness of newly recruited spies or secret agents. They even dressed oddly, in twin black suits that cried for tailoring. Over an expensive meal the two propositioned me with the glib confidence available, it seemed to me, to those who not only had never known failure but were also spending someone else's money. They sketched, vaguely, "the role of a lifetime." I no longer remember the details of the pitch, or even the milieu—in truth, I wasn't listening carefully. I tried to tell them I no longer auditioned, didn't even bother to keep a relationship with an agent. My childhood fame had made me impossible to cast, and relieved me of the burden of ambition. I'd been returned to civilian life, I joked. They, in turn, proposed that it was my residual career, and my existence as a Manhattan gadabout, that made me so very perfect for the role in question. Defeated, I told them I'd be willing to look at a script. They promised it would arrive soon.

That was the last I heard from them. The encounter puzzled me.

I live in capital's capital, but I root against the Dow. I feel an instinctive lizard-thrill on those days when it collapses. I know I'm meant to feel we're all in something together, especially after the gray fog stretched out to cover the lower reaches of the island. I ought to feel sympathy for the moneymen, ashen and dim in aspect, forgetful, sleepy, never quite themselves anymore, like Reggie Spencer. Yet if I'm honest with myself, I'd like to see them stripped even of their fog-gray suits, reduced to suspenders and barrels, put out of their misery at last. Sometimes this Dow-enmity of mine seems like the worst secret I could disclose. I don't.

Though I do dwell among the money people, that's incidental to what I like about the Upper East Side, and to the matter of why I rarely go anywhere else. The secret of this place is its quarantine from the boom-and-bust of Manhattan's trends and fashions. Maybe someday, if the rumors are true, they'll build a Second Avenue subway line and all of this will change. For now, what's here is entrenched and immutable. The shopping-cart ladies and the fur ladies and the black-cocktail-dress girls, the preying, tie-loosened twenty-three-year-old junior partners, the reverse-slumming off-duty policemen, none has to glance at the others and wonder whether this place rightly belongs to them or anyone. The resonances and layers here are mysterious without being unduly impressed with themselves. (A few of the shopping-cart ladies will still roll up their sleeves and show you a bluish line of concentration-camp numerals, if you want to get your self-pity casually smashed.) Money has been here so long it's a little decrepit. If one of money's laws is that it can never buy taste, here is where it went after it failed, and here's what it bought instead. Much hides behind what's assumed about the East Side, even if what's assumed is true. There are things beyond what's assumed and true. East Eighty-fourth Street, the entrance beside Brandy's Piano Bar, and those who live there. Not only Perkus Tooth, though he's a fine example.

Biller, too. The homeless man lives here, at least sometimes, if it isn't more correct to say he lives in another world entirely.

I'm more and more a day sleeper. This trend, inaugurated before my friendship with Perkus Tooth, was certainly aggravated by it. The angle of light in my apartment makes it awfully easy: there's a sort of afternoon "dawn" as the sun at last breaks past the edge of the Dorffl Tower. (My building's board fought hard to prevent or modify the Dorffl, and lost. I never go to those meetings.) Like a restaurant worker I abide with the life of Manhattan as it slakes itself on sundown pleasures, as it dines and smokes and boozes, then I tuck it in for the night and go on. What's served with cocktails — a handful of wasabi cashews, a nice black-market unpasteurized *fromage* oozing off its board—is frequently my lunch if not breakfast. On this denatured island if I crave "breakfast" Gracie Mews Diner will gladly serve me two poached with bacon, and home fries with shiny bits of onion and green pepper, at four in the morning, before bed. That's when I crave it, if I do.

I'm outstanding only in my essential politeness. Exhausting, this compulsion to oblige any detected social need. I don't mean only to myself; it's frequently obvious that my charm exhausts and bewilders others, even as they depend upon it to mortar crevices in the social façade—to fill vacant seats, give air to suffocating silences, fudge unease. (I'm like fudge. Or maybe I'm like chewing gum.) But if beneath charm lies exhaustion, beneath exhaustion lies a certain rage. I detect a wrongness everywhere. Within and Without, to quote a lyric. It would be misleading to say I'm screaming inside, for if I was, I'd soon enough find a way to scream aloud. Rather, the politeness infests a layer between me and myself, the name of the wrongness going not only unexpressed but unknown. Intuited only. Forbidden perhaps. Perkus would have called me *inchoate*. He wouldn't have meant it kindly.

In that margin of sky granted to my apartment by the Dorffl Tower is visible another tower, a church spire three or four blocks away, something built in the nineteenth century. I don't know the name of the church, despite how easy it would be to discover. I'd only have to ask a neighbor. Or walk over. I know nothing about architecture, but I think the style may be Gothic. To confirm this, I'd simply need to pluck White and Willensky's

78

Architectural Guide to Manhattan from the place where I noticed it, in the bottom row on Perkus Tooth's living-room shelf. I never did.

The point about the church spire is that I take a moment every day on waking to glance at it to see whether the birds are there. It is a flock of . . . something—gulls? swallows?—with feathers white on top, darker underneath, that wheels and races in unrepeatable patterns around and underneath the spire, for sessions lasting usually fifteen minutes, sometimes as much as half an hour. I try to count the birds and settle, uneasily, at eleven, twelve, or thirteen. They dive, figure-eight, the flock's density bunching and stretching as it turns. They shoot left of the spire, tilting, seeming about to abandon the landmark, then abruptly turn, white tops flipping to gray undersides as if at a cursor's clicking, and recover their orbit. Sometimes, rarely, a sole bird turns the wrong way, parts from the group, and has to wheel in a phantom operation until it is swept up again in the flock. It is terribly easy to blink or look away and miss their unceremonious finishing, for whatever reason it is that they finish. They merely tilt and are gone from the spire, and from my slice of sky.

My ignorance of natural history keeps me from gaining traction on puzzles attaching to the birds themselves (Why that number? Why not eight, or fifteen? Do they live together all day and night, or gather only for these missions? What do they do on days when they don't visit the tower? Have Richard Abneg's eagles ever fed on this flock?), so I drift to truly unanswerable questions. Did the church attract birds when it was first built? Did the builders know it would? Did they intend it? The relation between those birds and that tower feels both deep and impossible. The longer one stares, the more the persistence of the vaguely medieval spire in the sky over Second Avenue seems to evidence a mystery in itself. If I could plumb it I'd perhaps begin to know why I live in this place and what it consists of. Instead I get about as near as those birds. Yet they're carefree, and I'm not.

On some days, while I'm watching the flock loop at the spire, a passing airplane putters at high layers past the top of my window frame, leaving a faint contrail. (This happened to be the case on that first morning after Emil Junrow's funeral, when Oona Laszlo crept from my bed and left me sleeping there.) A planeload of people on their way to somewhere from somewhere else, having as little to do with birds or tower as birds or tower have to do with each other. I am the only witness to their conjunction. The privilege of my witnessing is limited to that fact: there's nothing more I grasp. I suppose if, somewhere in the stratosphere beyond, Janice Trumbull's irretrievable space station could be seen in its orbit, it would have again as little awareness of or relation to airplane, birds, and tower as airplane, birds, and tower have to one another. Or, if relation exists, I don't fathom it.

◼

November 4
Dearest Chase,
I am trying to "feel" November, yours and mine. I'll make an imaginary diorama, like something from grade

80

school, an attempt to win a secret science fair of the heart: Janice and Chase's November. A mind's-eye miniature I can peer into. (I won't mention this project to the Captain, or the Russians, anyone. We all know too much about one another's little projects up here.) Is it cold yet? Is Manhattan beautiful? Have they put up the Christmas tree, or is it too soon? (I know you loathe Rockefeller Center.) Do you ever go to the Chinese garden at the Met, with the tiny gurgling waterfall, where we once went and laid our heads together on a stone and fell asleep? (I don't know whether I want to know if you go there without me or not, so don't answer that question.) Do I sound idiotic? Forgive me, I'm going a little bonkers up here at last. Since the antifreeze leak— explosion, really—things have not been right. I should organize my thoughts. It always helps put my feelings back in order, to write them to you. I'm sure Mission Control will have tried to keep any panic to a minimum, that's in their training, and even more, it's in their nature. (Hello, Ted! And how are you, Arun? Are you sipping Ceylon as you read this?) Even among us six, we've quit discussing the incident—there's always the new day's tasks to think of. But in truth we nearly lost both the Den and the Greenhouse. And without the Greenhouse, no food. And no air. No us. *Northern Lights* just an elaborate mausoleum, or perhaps a floating lab for an experiment in zero-gravity mummification.

Mstislav, the most dedicated gardener among us now that Sledge rarely emerges from the Attic, has been tinkering with the carbon-dioxide balance, a dangerous but crucial sport. At six or seven hundred parts per million, the air in here is dreadful but sustains life. Regular jiggering of organic functions are needed to keep the ratio from ballooning to something deadly. To make a long story short, after an alarmingly high reading, Mstislav discovered a mound of rotting mangrove fronds under a seemingly healthy hillock of wheatgrass—a camouflaged nightmare of poison-leaching compost. Endgame for us here could be that simple, that foolish. Everyone, even the Captain and Sledge, was required to take up pitchforks in an emergency campaign to clear the fermenting stew into garbage stockings, which then had to be banished from our air space, pronto. Now, for months Keldysh has been stuffing waste into one of the emergency modules, a reasonably nifty solution, with the notion that we'd eventually test our ability to launch the module and dump its contents at the edge of the Chinese scatter field. Perhaps our garbage, drifting slowly into Earth's gravity, could even take out some of the Chinese mines that keep us trapped here. A fantasy, perhaps. We'd have to eliminate hundreds for Mission Control even to begin to discuss reaching us with a shuttle. But we dream, why not? If Keldysh's scheme fell short, the worst would be to see a garbage-stuffed module destroyed on passage through the scatter field. We've got two other modules.

Well, this surplus of mulch-bulging stockings forced our hand, before Keldysh had any chance to chart a launch plan. Zamyatin was enraged at Keldysh for attempting the early launch, but we'd all encouraged him, Zamyatin included. And in truth, we were all exhausted from twelve hours of what Mstislav laughingly called "serf toil," one of the rare jokes among the Russians that even

Sledge and I could get. Also the last laugh we'd have for a while. Keldysh crashed the module. It rebounded off solar panel V, snapped off an antenna, and then clanged disastrously against the Den's exterior tile. Glued to the video feed like teenagers watching a horror film, we saw the module tumble unbraked through, yes, the Chinese mines. Then flare and vanish. (Honestly, I do think by then Keldysh had his head in his hands, and could have reversed course if he hadn't been so despondent at the earlier impacts. Mission Control will delete this parenthetical before releasing this letter. Howdy again, fellas.) Farewell to excess compost, to unrecyclable plastic waste, to irredeemably shameful diapers, and to the module itself. The flume of mute fire another warning, if we needed it, to recalibrate orbital decay daily. Like flossing. (I joke to keep your attention during the dry technical passages, my darling distractible Chase.) I don't think anyone thought to inspect the Den's interior for damage until we smelled the antifreeze, a skunk's reek speeding through *Northern Lights*' tiny atmosphere.

It was Mstislav who had the foresight to remotely seal the Den, then insist we don oxygen masks and investigate. Forget for now any damage to the interior—we were predisposed to concern ourselves with the rocket ship's hull, every spaceman's concern! By the time we reached the Den we'd lost Sledge somewhere, but the remaining five of us went in wearing masks and discovered the wrecked antifreeze line spewing turquoise blobs, which floated and shattered to paint every surface of the Den's interior. Mstislav and Zamyatin clamped the line. Then, fresh off our serf toil in the Greenhouse, we space janitors now set to scrubbing and sponging and wringing the blue goo into containers, a task much like the pursuit of Dr. Seuss's Oobleck. (I still want to have children with you, Chase.) At the finish our uniforms were coated. Mstislav, champion of this episode, reasonably pointed out that any droplet of the pollutant we exported from the Den was destined for circulation and, ultimately, our mucous membranes. Our bloodstreams. So we stripped and trashed the clothes. Picture us, five floating nudists in oxygen masks, ragged with fatigue and degrees of shock, squeezing last beads of antifreeze from our hair. (Don't be jealous. They've seen me naked before. Anyway, on our present diet I'm shrunken to a ten-year-old's gaunt outlines, not exactly turning heads. My periods have stopped, too. And yes, again, I still want to have children with you, Chase.) At last, and ignoring various bruises and scrapes that first-aid protocols would have had us tend immediately, we all slunk away to our various hidey-holes, each to strap ourselves to a wall for some desperately needed sleep. Starved as we were, I don't think anyone emerged for ten hours or more.

I won't tell you what Sledge was up to in the interval while we scrubbed the Den. I'm too tired.

Even omitting that, I can't imagine, having written it out now, that Mission Control will release too much of this report. Still, when our media-digest packet turns up (there's always so much demand for our scrawny bandwidth, so many technical transmissions in line ahead of anything personal, that the packet is usually delayed a week or two), I'm startled at how many columns they devote to us. How fascinating can we really be? They'll forget us soon. We've practically forgotten ourselves. That's why I rely on you, Chase, to believe in me. As I drift, you anchor me in reality. On Earth. In Manhattan, where you sit reading this, perhaps in that fake-French coffee shop (is it really called *Savoir Faire*?) with the amazing almond croissants you pretend to allow yourself only once or twice a month but in truth devour at least twice a week. That's where I picture you, Chase. With powdered sugar on your fingers as you open Mission Control's overnight envelope. The sugar on your lips and fingers and possibly on your nose, too—that sweet dust is me, your astronaut, your lostronaut, your Janice.

5

Perkus Tooth read *The New York Times* as he rode the F train downtown. He'd lifted the copy from a neighbor's doorstep—up at this ungodly hour, he felt entitled to it. He hadn't purchased a copy since the day Richard Abneg had called to insist he read about the eagles, and before that, not for many months. Perkus refused to pay for the *Times*, wasn't interested in giving subsidy to hegemony. The paper was nearly useless to him anymore. He used to light on items that spoke to him, elements in the larger puzzle. These he'd clip and try to shift out of context, pinning them above his kitchen table, onto the layered backdrop of his own broadsides, to see what age would do to their meaning as they yellowed, as they marinated in pot fumes. Lately this never happened. The front page seemed recursive, every story about either a species of animal collapsing into extinction or the dispersal of the Matisse collection of some socialite who'd died intestate. Yesterday a minke whale, its motives perhaps deranged by ocean fungus, had wandered up the East River nearly to Hell Gate: FROLICKING VISITOR DELIGHTS HEARTS, AND THEN DIES. Another animal story that had made the front page concerned the latest depredations of the escaped tiger, who'd razed a twenty-four-hour Korean market on 103rd Street.

Then there was the requisite update from space, another installment in the travails of Janice Trumbull and her Russian cohort, the crew doomed to orbit. The piece on the space station took up a third of the front page, and where it continued on the interior the *Times* had run substantial excerpts of Janice Trumbull's latest letter to Chase Insteadman. A soap opera. Perkus's attitude toward his new friend Chase's situation was an area of suspended judgment, only flooded with Perkus's usual conspiratorial searchlights. That the situation reeked of fakery was only natural—what wasn't? Oona Laszlo, too, had dropped a few hints, though she often teased Perkus's grave suspicions, and was at bottom untrustworthy. In making Chase's acquaintance, Perkus had alluded heavily that he not only knew but understood and forgave—for who hasn't found themselves enlisted in this city's reigning fictions from time to time? Yet Chase seemed entirely sincere and heartbroken, as much hanging on the updates from space as any other punter. Perkus felt sorry for him. But then the whole *New York Times* seemed phony to Perkus, even or perhaps especially when it featured his friends. He checked the Metro section, but there was no update on Abneg's eagles. The Arts section was of course useless. Perkus recognized none of the names. It struck him as largely consisting of rewritten press releases. Yet this paper as a whole felt more insubstantial even than usual—where were all those pieces nobody ever read, but everybody relied upon to be there? He glanced at the front, the top-right corner: WAR FREE EDITION. Ah yes, he'd heard about this. You could opt out now. He left the paper on his seat when he exited the train at Twenty-third Street.

Aboveground, he walked north on Sixth. This was the farthest afield Perkus had traveled in many months, perhaps in over a year. However absurd, he couldn't recall the time previous, or what exactly last had drawn him out of the bounds of what had become his quarantine: east of Lexington, north of Grand Central Station. Even midtown east, where he'd occasionally drop into the *Rolling Stone* or Criterion offices, was disorienting to Perkus; the part of Manhattan he encountered here, with its lingering echoes of an older, ethnic-mercantile realm, and the proprietary and jocular gay enclave that overlaid those garment-district ghosts, the complacently muscular pairs holding hands as they strolled—all this was like another city to him. Perkus joked uneasily to himself that he ought to have a guidebook, he felt so foreign here.

A pair of Chinese-dissident protesters occupied a part of the sidewalk on Sixth; they squatted in cages and wore T-shirts decorated with fake blood, commemorating some crackdown against their politicized variety of meditation or worship. One of these caged persons met Perkus's eye before he could avoid it, and pointed, first at herself, then at him, seeming to say, *You and Me Are the Same*. Another of their group stood beside the cages, urging pamphlets on passersby, all of whom veered expertly aside, alert within their cocoon of earbuds or cell conversation, raising preemptive hands like Indians in a Western. All except Perkus: he ended up clutching a scuffed and incoherent pamphlet. Glancing at it, he saw a primitive drawing, repeating the image of the sidewalk tableau, a figure in a cage barely big enough for a dog. He crumpled the pamphlet into a trash can and tried to walk as steadily as the human stream of which he was part.

In truth, Perkus felt ill. That was the reason for the jaunt and why he was so vulnerable to dislocation, yet it made him wish to reverse course before he'd taken some irrevocable step. He'd shaved and showered, for the first time in many days, understanding it was likely someone would be examining his undressed body. Then, defensively prideful, he'd donned his best suit, a deep-maroon pinstripe three-piece that would have risked seeming clownish had the vents and pockets not been so impeccably detailed, the fit to his wiry body so trim and modish. The suit wasn't tailored for Perkus. He'd gotten lucky, found it at the Housing Works Thrift Shop on Seventy-seventh. He made a daylight dandy in the maroon suit, and now, like a lush who'd woken drunk, weaved slightly on the pavement, he couldn't help it. The sun was bright and the day was bitterly cold. Better to get indoors and face whatever it was he'd gotten himself into. He found the building on Twenty-fifth Street and pushed a button at the intercom, gave his name, was buzzed into the lobby. These were the offices of Strabo Blandiana, the celebrated master of Eastern medicine, who catered almost exclusively to stars— Chase Insteadman had been in his care since that time, ten years past, when he'd qualified as something of a star himself. Chase had induced Strabo to make an exception

89

to his long waiting list for Perkus, then pleaded with Perkus to keep the appointment. Incredibly, Perkus had agreed. Now, at the threshold, he fought every impulse to flee.

Neither Strabo's candle-scenty reception area nor the gentle, fair-haired, dippily smiling young man who welcomed Perkus to a seat there inspired any hope that Perkus's prejudices against Eastern medicine might be disappointed. But the vibe, so to speak, was mellow, palliative in itself, and Perkus really didn't want to be out on the street again too soon. Couldn't hurt to fill out the clipboard's two pages of questions on health history and "Present Areas of Complaint" — Perkus laughed to himself that he had plenty of those. He specified "cluster headache, a subvariant of migraine," not wanting to be mistaken for having fantasized his symptom, and preemptively disdaining any curative gesture that veered too much into fantasy itself. Then defiantly listed caffeine and THC under "Medicines." Perkus had brewed himself a pot of coffee (Peet's Colombian roast) and smoked a joint (Watt's Ice) this morning before walking to the subway, and could feel both medicines still buzzing pleasantly in his bloodstream. He sat alone in the waiting room, apart from the blond kid, who each time Perkus looked up from the clipboard grinned welcome as if for the first time. No sign of other patients, no clue to what was expected of Perkus or what he should expect. Perkus reminded himself he wasn't into astrological symbols or archetypes of any kind. He had a fucking headache. Actually, it was gone, though this had been one of the cruelest, lasting a week and a half, with barely any oases of relief. In its wake he was enfeebled, that was all, and needed an infusion or two of what he liked to call, only half jokingly, "replacement lipids" — a Jackson Hole vanilla malted and an extra slice of Swiss on his burger deluxe.

When Strabo opened a door Perkus was disarmed utterly. The Romanian was so much younger than Perkus had imagined, and devastating in his calm. Strabo's personal style was minimalist, hair cropped in a close Caesar, the sleeves of his black turtleneck, some superfine knit, pushed to mid-forearm, revealing on his left a tremendous gold Rolex. No ascetic renunciation of worldly treasure here. Strabo's gaze penetrated quickly, satisfied itself, and moved on, declining to make a show of hypnotic spookiness. Despite himself, Perkus felt disappointed. Did he rate just a glance? Strabo hadn't even hesitated over Perkus's morbid eye.

Strabo Blandiana's examination room was neither encouragingly medical nor New Agey enough to justify Perkus's balking. Just a couple of Danish Modern chairs, in which the two now sat as equals, a brushed-steel cabinet on wheels, and beyond it a long, flat daybed covered with a neatly folded sheet. One silver-framed photograph, of an enigmatic orange-glowing ceramic vase against a blank white backdrop. From the moment Strabo opened his mouth no question of negotiation remained. He spoke decisively, each word acute. The tone suggested they'd agreed beforehand never to waste an instant of the other's time. Perkus's clipboard results were in evidence nowhere, and the word *headache* was never spoken.

Strabo explained quickly that Perkus was—surprise!—
"out of balance." He could see that Perkus worked
with his mind, and that he did so with the urgency of
one who knew that if he faltered in his chosen task no
one could possibly carry on in his stead. This sense
of special purpose motivated Perkus to accomplish
extraordinary things but also made him lonely, and
defiantly angry. Strabo surprised Perkus by finding
nothing shameful in this: Perkus evidently made use of
productive fear and rage. Each insight Strabo offered
as if describing the workings of a car, some fine-tuned
Porsche or Jaguar, to its interested owner. There was
no air of metaphysics. Strabo went on to explain that
Perkus's constitution was strong. If it wasn't he wouldn't
have made it even this far, nor accomplished what he
had. The suggestion being that this Porsche's owner had
brought his car limping into the garage just barely in
time. Strabo's intuition of Perkus's special accomplishments and challenges allowed Perkus to feel them himself as though for the first time. What burdens he carried!
That Perkus couldn't go on as he had been was simply
manifest and true.

Strabo Blandiana paused now, as if catching himself
too much showing off what one glance had collected
from the subject before him. He might be about to turn
to the question of treatment, whatever that consisted of.
Perkus was at this point only dazzled. Then Strabo again
turned that gaze of total discernment in Perkus's direction. "You understand," Strabo said, as if incidentally,
"that beneath your anger is really mourning. But you
feel you can't afford to mourn."

"Mourn who?" said Perkus, feeling a breath disappear, so he had to gulp to replace it. The description seemed to tip him headfirst into self-understanding, as if from a high diving board. But he hadn't hit the water yet.

Strabo shook his head, refusing the obvious. "Before your parents were taken from you, the loss you felt was already real." Yes, Perkus's parents had both died, but how did Strabo know this? Or was this one of those specious bold guesses with which a charlatan secured your confidence? Perkus's suspicions were aroused, but they were overrun by his hunger to understand what Strabo was on about. *What loss?*

"You mourn a loss suffered by the world. Something in living memory, but not adequately remembered. You see it as your sole responsibility to commemorate this loss."

With this astonishing pronouncement, Strabo shifted efficiently and permanently to the practical effort of the Porsche's maintenance. Was Perkus aware that he breathed only into his upper chest, never into his stomach? This distinction anyone would be likely to have noted a hundred times, but Strabo, with a guiding touch, made Perkus feel the difference. Perkus then tried to reopen the conversation, but Strabo, with a shrug, conveyed the sense that their talk had been conclusive. He deferred to Perkus's expertise. "You know what you need to do to continue your work, I can't teach you anything about that. Let's just get you balanced, and then we'll discuss strategies for leaving aside the useless pain. When you were younger you could carry more, but it isn't efficient or necessary now. Please undress and lie under the sheet, I'll return momentarily."

To reject anything now was out of the question. Perkus made himself ready, folding his suit neatly on a chair back. Strabo returned and got to business. Acupuncture needles didn't look as Perkus had imagined them, but then he'd never bothered to imagine anything other than a sewing needle. Thin as threads, each with a tiny flag at their end, they entered his body at various points, neck and wrists and shoulders, painlessly. Only a hint of tightness, a feeling he shouldn't move suddenly, confirmed Strabo had used them at all. Then Strabo lowered the lights and switched on some music, long atmospheric tones that might have been vaguely Eastern. "To someone like you this CD may sound a bit corny," he said, surprising Perkus. "But it's specially formulated, there are tones underneath the music that are engaging directly with your limbic system. It works even if you don't like the music particularly. It's inoffensive, but I personally wish it didn't sound so much like Muzak."

"Okay," said Perkus, just beginning to see that he was expected to reside with the needles a while.

"I'll be back for you in half an hour. Practice breathing."

"What if I fall asleep?"

"It's fine to sleep. You can't do anything wrong." With that, Strabo was gone. Perkus lay still, feeling himself pinned like a knife-thrower's assistant, listening as an odious pan flute commenced soloing over the synthesized tones, promising a long dreadful journey through cliché. Here Perkus was, supreme skeptic and secularist,

94

caught naked and punctured, his whole tense armor of self perilously near to dissolved. How had it come to this? How could I have been allowed to persuade him? Puttylike Chase Insteadman, so eagerly enlisted in absurd causes—*Chase* had talked *Perkus* into this?

■

Well, he'd frightened me. For a week Perkus hadn't answered his phone, nor his apartment buzzer when I resorted to dropping by unannounced. Then, my own phone had rung, at six thirty AM, an hour at which, even had I been driving deep through evenings in Perkus's company, I'd reliably have been dozing. I fumbled the receiver up to my ear, expecting I don't know what, but always guiltily terrified of dire updates from the space station, some further revolution in Janice's fate.

His voice was dim, smoke-tight, wreathed in hours. No question of his having slept anytime recently.

"So, I need your help with something."

"Yes?" I croaked.

"I have to talk to Brando. Can you get his number?"

"Brando?" I pinched the bridge of my nose, miming groggy disbelief for an invisible audience. "You mean *Marlon* Brando?" I thought Brando was recently dead, but this was exactly the sort of thing I get mixed up about. Maybe Paul Newman had died, or Farley Granger.

"Yes, Chase, Marlon Brando. Can you call, I don't know, someone at your talent agency?" However depleted, however absurd the hour, Perkus seemed in a rage of impatience.

"Doesn't he live on some island?"

"So you're saying you can't?"

"I—I don't know. I guess I can try."

"*Only Brando can save us.*" He croaked out the line as if he'd been saving it for the crucial moment, a bomb-shell revelation.

"Perkus, what's going on? What time is it? Are you okay?"

Silence.

"I tried to call, five or six times."

"I had cluster," he said after a moment, the grandiosity leaked from his voice. "I turned the ringer off."

"I rang your doorbell."

"I know. It sounded like an atom bomb, whistling toward the Nagasaki of my brain." Perkus tittered at his own joke, his voice seeming to fall away from the receiver. Having failed the Brando test, I was losing him.

"Have you been in all week? When did you last eat something?"

"I don't know . . ."

"Can I come over?" I asked, astounding myself. He didn't answer. "I'll stop at H&H and grab some bagels and stuff." Now I bargained, pathetically.

"Go to East Side Bagel, they've got better whitefish spread."

"Okay."

"And Chase?"

"Yes?"

"Get some extra for Biller. I haven't had anything for him for a couple of days."

It might have taken me an hour to rally myself, get bagels, and arrive to ring Perkus's bell. This was a day or two before Halloween, the morning fiercely cold, a first taste of winter. I worried for a long chilly moment on his doorstep that Perkus had changed his mind, but no, without troubling with the intercom he buzzed me through. His door was unlocked when I tried the handle, and a sour smell escaped to the corridor. Inside, Perkus's tightly managed chaos had tipped into squalor, his sink's basin like a geological site, heaped with unrinsed cups and a rain of grounds emptied out of his gold filter, ashtrays too, their contents muddily mixed with the coffee, his living-room floor a mad tatter of clippings, books with spines pressed open by whatever lay to hand—more coffee cups, a stapler, a brown banana, a pot of rubber cement—and with their pages mutilated, paragraphs excised and stickily transferred to gigantic cardboard backings, collaged into wild conjunctions, like vast scholarly punk-rock liner notes. I'd never seen Perkus destroy a book. Rather they were holy objects, whose safety he compulsively patrolled when he placed them in your hands, forehead veins bulging in panic if you turned one down on its open face, though he reserved the right to do this himself. But no more. Now his precious collection was only fodder on some quest. Perkus sat on the floor amid this disaster, his hair dripping wet, his chin and throat peppered with a week's beard, his expression smashed and dark. He wore a green shark-skin three-piece suit's pants and vest, nothing else—I suppose he'd made a last-minute effort to neaten up for me and could locate no clean shirts. His chest was, somehow, scrawnier than I'd allowed myself to imagine. The television screen was frozen on a stop-motion frame of Marlon Brando, smiling ominously as he scratched a large blue felt-and-fur tree-sloth Gnuppet behind its ears. I turned from him to the kitchen, pushed aside heaps of ancient magazines, *Rolling Stone*, *Playboy*, and *Esquire*, to clear a spot on his table for the bag of bagels and spreads, then went back in and confronted him.

"Perkus, tell me what's going on."

"I'm trying to reconstruct an epiphany."

"An epiphany? I thought you had a *headache*."

"I don't know if the cluster's passed, but I had a great ellipsis a few days ago, between episodes, really revelatory. I couldn't do anything about it then, I was so fucked up. I could barely walk for two days at the peak, Chase! The blot on my vision was like an elephant in my apartment this time, crowding to the edges of the room, I felt like I could stroke its pebbly hide." He spoke in a feverish rasp, all the while concentrating on piloting scissors to free a few sentences from their surrounding page. "Then the epiphany came, I could see everything, the whole landscape at once, like it was lit by the moon. This enormous undescribed thing in every detail, I have to get hold of it while I can, I don't know how long I'll be allowed this time."

"Get hold of the epiphany, you mean?" The Venn diagram of *ellipsis*, *epiphany*, and *episode of cluster* was already too much for my mind's eye. I feared what I would never again dare suggest: that it was All One Thing. The pebbly hide of the elephant and the moonlit landscape, the first so close it was oppressive and useless, the other so distant he'd never reach it even if he grew wings, One and the Same.

"Yes."

"So that's what all this is?" I indicated the project arrayed on the floor. "An ... epiphany ... from last week?" I craned my neck to read the filleted sentences draped in Perkus's hand—*The Beatles family goes back to Jack Kerouac and Neal Cassady. They want to get to American freedom; they don't understand that American freedom is itself horribly complicated and conflicted ...* Another slip continued, *There's also a kind of Less Than Zero thing about being the Beatles; they're not quite the Beats. There's a kind of Bret Easton Ellis about the whole Beatle phenomenon, and that has to do with the tragedy of John Lennon. Being a kind of Beetle, being a kind of insect in a way ...* And then a third excerpt, in a different font: *But in truth, moderns live in a world-order in which the primitive "physics" or "chemistry" of things ("reality," the measurable and controllable thingliness of things strictly taken) is overwhelmingly eclipsed, reduced nearly to negligibility by the power-relations or actualities that have strategized and shaped the thing-complexes among which moderns live ...*

"Not last week," said Perkus, patiently straightening me out. "Last week, I told you, I was in a death glaze, mostly. I'm reconstructing an epiphany from five years ago, at least. Probably ten."

I wanted many things, but for starters I wanted us to quit saying the word *epiphany*. "What do you want on your bagel?"

"Let's make coffee."

When I'd performed what triage I could on his kitchen and we sat with coffee in fresh cups and pumpernickel halves frosted with whitefish, Perkus said, "So, what about Brando?"

What about sleep? I wanted to reply. "I honestly think it'll be difficult to get hold of him."

"Sure, but we have to try." Between starved attacks on his bagel, gobbets of pureed fish and mayonnaise dripping from between his fingers, Perkus named Brando as the living avatar of the unexpressed, a human enunciation of the remaining hopes for our murdered era. His lordly vulnerability, his beauty overwritten with bulk, his superbly calibrated refusal to oblige, all made Marlon Brando the name of that principle which nemeses as varied as Mayor Jules Arnheim, the War on Drugs, Jack Nicholson's museum-defacing scene as the Joker in Tim Burton's *Batman*, and the Rock and Roll Hall of Fame had conspired to unname.

"You know Brando's single most crucial moment?" Perkus quizzed me.

"Uh, not *On the Waterfront*?"

"Not even close. Too compromised by McCarthyism."

I hated this game. "*Apocalypse Now*?"

"Well, that's an important one, with the whole *Heart of Darkness* subtext, but what I have in mind is when he sent Sacheen Littlefeather to accept the Oscar in his place. I mean, it's the most amazing conflation of the American Imaginary, just think about it! In one gesture Brando ties our rape of the Indians to this figure of our immigrant nightmare, this Sicilian peasant doing the American dream, capitalism I mean, more ruthlessly than the founding fathers could have ever dreaded.

We're as defenseless against what Don Corleone exposes, the murderous underside of Manifest Destiny, as the Indians were against smallpox blankets. And in the vanishing space between the two, what? America itself, whatever that is. Brando, essentially, *declining to appear*. Because the party's over." Here Perkus hesitated for breath, like a jazz soloist tipping his horn to one side. His unruly eye tested the bounds of its socket. He also snuck in another bite of whitefish and pumpernickel—at least I was getting some calories into him. "By refusing to show up Brando took on the most magnificent aspect, it's as if Toto sweeps the curtain aside and the great and powerful Oz has absconded, leaving you to contemplate the fact that *behind the illusion there's nothing*. The Oz of American history, for all its monstrousness, is all we've got. Brando could have done anything at that moment. Come home to us, instead of remaining in exile. He should have run for mayor of New York."

"Like Mailer?" I might not pass many tests, but I recalled a recent Tooth History of New York.

"Sure, but Mailer had it all fouled up, he still bought the romance of Marilyn Monroe, all that Andy Warhol crap. Brando was pure because he'd been out there, had Marilyn, knew it didn't matter. He was our captain. Maybe it's not too late."

"Not too late—?" To lure Brando here to run for mayor? I hesitated to complete the thought aloud, fearing I'd lead Perkus to this conclusion if he hadn't reached it already. I wasn't sure which was more worrisome, Perkus's careening logic or that I'd mostly been able to follow it.

"No, Brando's keeping faith. That's what I realized, Chase. He's still out there, sending up flares, if anyone's paying attention."

"What flares?"

"His most recent film, that spy movie, *Footholds*— you know how it was supposedly ruined by his battles with the director, Florian Ib, the guy who made *The Gnuppet Movie*? There's this one anecdote from the set, seems like typical Hollywood gossip, but I couldn't get it out of my head."

"Yes?"

"So, there's a scene they're shooting, Ib's setup calls for a wide shot, but Brando demands a close-up. They argue over it, but neither backs down, and then Brando goes back to his trailer, and when he comes out for the shot, *he's wearing only the top half of his costume*. Right there, with the whole crew watching, Brando's nude from the waist down. He's basically daring Florian Ib to shoot the wide shot."

"I'm somehow guessing Marlon got his close-up."

He tried to contain his impatience with me. "Sure, but if that was the whole point it wouldn't be more than showbiz vanity. The thing is, by that time Brando's figured out *Footholds* won't be much of a vehicle for what he needs to say, so he sends out this message."

"What message?"

"It took me a while to decipher it, but think, Chase— what's the Platonic form of a Gnuppet?" My baffled look told Perkus not to wait for my guess this time. "Your quintessential Gnuppet stands behind a *wall*, right? You only ever see them from the waist up. Remove the wall, or the edge of the frame, and you'd see the hands of the operators, making them move. I've been studying Brando's scene in *The Gnuppet Movie*, there's a reason he's pointing us back to that work—the key is the relation between the actors and the Gnuppets. We're players in a Gnuppet realm, reading from the same script. *We're All Gnuppets*. Brando was saying: abolish this boundary, tear down the wall or the curtain, and let's have a look at the Gnuppeteers."

"Or at his genitals."

"Haven't you wondered why the average consumer is uncomfortable with letterboxed movies? It isn't because most people are programmed to be Philistines, though they are. Cable channels go on offering scan-and-pan versions to keep people from having to consider that frame's edge, which reminds them of all they're not seeing. That glimpse is intolerable. When your gaze slips beyond the edge of a book or magazine, you notice the ostensible texture of everyday reality, the table beneath the magazine, say, or the knee of your pants. When your eye slips past the limit of the letterboxed screen, you're faced with what's framed and projected in that margin—it ought to be *something*, but instead it's *nothing*, a terrifying murk, a zone of nullity. But the real reason it's so terrifying is because it begs the question of whether they're *the same thing*. Maybe the tabletop or the knee of your pants bears no more relation to the contents of the magazine than the images on the screen do to the void above and below."

I rinsed a glass and handed Perkus some cold tap water, wanting to see something going in besides coffee.

"I think I ought to put up a broadside," he said.

"It's been a long time." I spoke cautiously, not wanting to jar him, and anyway uncertain of my facts.

"Yes."

We both glanced in at the paperscape of his living-room floor, the unreconstructed epiphany. Was it a broadside in progress? That groping collage seemed a kind of wan parody of the maniacal hand-scrawled rants of his heyday. It dawned on me that by lighting on a champion whose triumph was in *declining to appear*, Perkus might elaborately forgive his own years of inactivity, his hide-and-seek muse. That Brando had frittered away much of his prime gave them something in common. (Me, too, if I bothered to think in those terms.) Even better, absence could form a statement, especially if punctuated with a well-timed and phantasmal return, the broadside equivalent of Sacheen Littlefeather. Manhattan might have forgotten Perkus and his broadsides, but never mind. He'd send up a flare.

"Would you help me put it up?" he asked.

"Like Oona Laszlo?" I joked. "You want me for your glue-girl?"

"Seriously."

This figure before me—with bare-knuckly shoulders, cheek sinews tensed beneath beard bristles, fingernails mooned with newsprint dirt, unmoored eye careening—I'd sooner chaperone to Bellevue's intake door myself than allow onto the street to be swept up by Mayor Arnheim's quality-of-life squad. "On one condition," I said.

"What's that?"

"You'll let me make an appointment for you with my Chinese practitioner."

I didn't kid myself that Perkus felt obligated. Rather, he'd agreed out of a kind of pity for me that I pitied him, and out of embarrassment at my worry. Plus I saw I'd made him curious, with my wild claims for Strabo Blandiana's visionary and remedial powers. What if Perkus could be freed of the cluster headaches? How much more ellipsis would that leave time for? Any gambit might be worth that chance. Some rare medical gift might come shrouded in the mystical wrapping paper.

■

So here he was, pocked with needles, a Saint Sebastian of aromatherapy and pan-flute solos, when he could have been home studying Brando's Gnuppet moment frame by frame, like it was the Zapruder film. Well, it was relaxing, at least. Obediently breathing all the way to the pit of his stomach, he expected to feel sleepy. Instead experienced the opposite effect, grew strangely excited inside his total stillness, whether creditable to needles, the somatic tones dwelling underneath the fake-Asian music, residual traces of coffee and pot, or Strabo's uncanny pronouncements. *The loss you felt was already real. Something in living memory, but not adequately remembered. You know what you need to do to continue your work.* These phrases continued to sink through Perkus. He couldn't feel Strabo's needles at all, but if he closed his eyes his body seemed to float toward the ceiling, a disconcerting sensation he avoided by opening his eyes instead. There at the center of vision was the framed photograph he'd passingly noted before, of the orange ceramic vase glowing, as if lit from within, against the minimal white backdrop. The line of the table on which the vase sat was barely detectable, so near was the tone of the tabletop to the wall behind it. The vase was lit to throw no shadow against either wall or table. It had a translucence, perhaps *opalescence* would be the word, like something hewn from marble the color of a Creamsicle. Under the circumstances, the vase seemed to have its own message for Perkus: *Have you neglected Beauty?* Even as he believed he contemplated the photograph with idle curiosity, killing time as he would with a copy of *Sports Illustrated* in a dentist's waiting room, Perkus felt the tears begin to seep across his cheeks, toward his ears, the salt stinging tiny fresh cuts that edged his sideburns, cuts he'd incurred shaving with shaky hands.

Now Perkus felt himself float without closing his eyes. Not toward the ceiling, but up and, however impossible, *into* the orange vase in the photograph. He dwelled there, was held there, for a long and outrageously pure instant. The vase sheltered Perkus like a kindly cove. And when it couldn't continue to shelter him the failure wasn't a rejection, a spitting out, but a sigh. Perkus understood that he and the vase couldn't abide with each other any longer than that instant, not here in these absurd surroundings, not stuck full of acupuncture needles and separated by the boundaries of a framed photograph. This had been a mere taste. But what a taste. The orange vase spoke to Perkus, simply, of not the possibility but the fact of another world. The world Perkus or anyone would wish to discover, the fine real place where the shadowy, tattered cloak of delusion dissolved. The place Perkus had tried his whole life to prove existed. Only lately he'd lost the thread. Fuck ten-year-old epiphanies made of scraps of yellowing articles from the *London Review of Books* and *Comics Journal*! Perkus had nodded off the night before, seated on the floor, and woken to find his scissors nearly glued to his thumb and forefinger. But even to taste what the orange vase promised was to feel weariness lift away entirely. Just to know it was out there, like a beacon calling.

Strabo Blandiana returned and removed the needles, a process which Perkus now barely noticed, then allowed Perkus a moment to collect himself and dress. The exit interview was brief, Perkus as eager to wrap up as Strabo, who obviously needed the room for his next patient—Chazz Palminteri, or Lewis Lapham, or whomever. (It was this that always surprised and amused me, too, how Strabo whisked you through, as much as any Western doctor.) Perkus didn't want to stare at the vase too intently, fearing he'd give himself away. He did manage a quick inspection of the photograph's margin, to make certain there was no signature or other mark he'd need to memorize for his later quest. Unsurprisingly, there wasn't anything.

"How do you feel?" asked Strabo.

"Great," said Perkus truthfully.

"You respond well. We'll eventually want to talk about caffeine and other substances, but there's no hurry. For now I'd like you to think about your breathing, and this may seem strange to you, but I'd like you to eat more meat."

"I can do that."

"And while in the outer office I couldn't help noticing you came here wearing nothing but your dress jacket. You should have a coat in this weather."

"You're right, of course."

"If you'd like a copy of the CD I played, you can rebalance yourself at home this way. One purchases it from a Web site, it's quite simple."

Perkus consented, and Strabo scribbled the Web address on a slip. Then, before stepping out to take a receipt from Strabo's receptionist (I'd insisted on paying for the visit in advance), he asked about the photograph of the vase. It was silly to lose the chance.

"Ah," said Strabo. "The chaldron, yes, it's quite beautiful. A gift from another patient. At first I hesitated to place it so prominently, but as it happens several patients have mentioned that they find it quite consoling. I've forgotten the name of the photographer, alas."

"I'm sorry, what did you call it?"

"I understand that type of ceramic is called a chaldron."

"Thank you."

■

That evening, Perkus home from the fateful appointment, he called me and I hurried over. Appearing both radiant and exhausted from the adrenaline Strabo's treatments typically unblocked, Perkus effused as much as I could have hoped, but his exact subject bewildered me.

Crumbled marijuana buds from a container labeled ICE were strewn across the tabletop I'd sponged clean for him a few days before, and he waved a half-consumed, temporarily extinguished joint in his fingers as he explained that he'd already looked up "chaldron" on the Internet, and found two for sale on eBay, advertised with photographs much like that he'd seen on Strabo's wall. They weren't cheap, but he'd entered bids. He'd get one into his apartment as soon as possible, and then I'd see what he'd seen—that, in so many words, he'd detected proof of another, better world. "Like reverse archaeology, Chase, but just as thrilling as contemplating the lost remains of the past. A chaldron is treasure from the *future*, if we deserve a future that benign." Meanwhile, did I want to see an image of one? Even in cold pixels, he promised, they conveyed a certain force.

I slowed him as well as I could, as his tale tumbled out, frantic, careless, ridiculous, the whole visit a pretext for his encounter with the chaldron. Had I seen it myself? Yes, I recalled the framed print, vaguely. No, it hadn't had such an effect on me. Or rather, I hadn't credited any effects to the photograph. Was Perkus certain he wasn't transposing the results of Strabo's treatments—the twin penetration of his needles and his insights into Perkus— onto the artwork? Perkus corrected me: it wasn't an artwork, it was an *artifact*. Evidence. A manifestation. Furthermore, he wasn't so impressed with Strabo as all that. The acupuncture hadn't been unpleasant, but it also hadn't been anything at all beyond a self-evident placebo. Perkus found the propagation of ancient ritual into an upscale urban setting innocuous and charming, in its way. The needles imparted a gravitas to Strabo that his customers, who otherwise paid handsomely to lie on a table and be reminded to breathe, must find reassuring.

As for Strabo's so-called insight, Perkus was sorry I was so credulous. For it had only taken him a second thought to be certain Strabo employed techniques perfected by British mediums during the great Victorian craze for psychic phenomena of all types: safely evocative and flattering generalizations with which anyone would agree, combined with precise secret research into the subject's background in order to provide a clinching detail or two. I ought to do a little reading on the historical techniques, I'd find it fascinating. "Strabo's brilliant, I'll give you that, Chase. Unmistakably, he'd been reading my work carefully in those two days between your call and my appointment. He must have a hot-shit researcher tucked away somewhere. What's incredible is that he distilled my basic themes so quickly. He was feeding me back to me, neatly mixed up with his own brand of stuff." Perkus widened his eyes, his expression that of exaggerated admiration for what he regarded as a top-notch stunt. Where could I begin? To attack the first premise, that Strabo Blandiana—who'd added the appointment as a favor, and who was in my experience often sweetly oblivious that clients like Marisa Tomei or Wynton Marsalis were renowned themselves rather than merely friends of others he'd helped—could ever have had the interest or means to discover Perkus's marginal writings, might seem an assault on Perkus's frail sense of his own relevance. I said nothing. Perkus relit the joint and after drawing on it himself handed it to me. "Enough of this," he said. "Let's go win an auction!"

Well, we lost a couple. If anything epitomized Perkus's curious disadvantages, his failure to find traction in the effective world, it was the state of his computing. Perkus was the type to be Web-delving on some sleekly effective Mac, I'd have thought. Instead his lumpy Dell looked ten years old, Cro-Magnon in computer years. He connected by his phone line, which he transferred by hand from his living-room Slimline, and which bumped him offline if anyone rang, but also, it seemed, intermittently and at random. Watching that Dell painstakingly assemble a page view, images smoothed pixel by pixel, was agony. Perkus was enchanted—he'd just discovered eBay, by way of the chaldron hunt. The format and rules fascinated him, and as we watched the hour tick toward the resolution of the two chaldron auctions—one half an hour later than the other—he gleefully refreshed the pages again and again in turn, to see if anyone had trumped his bids. No one had. As things stood he'd be collecting two chaldrons, one for three hundred and fifty dollars, the other for one hundred and eighty-five. I suggested Perkus bow out of the first, but he waved me off.

Then, thirty seconds left, Perkus refreshed the page again. After excruciating delay, a verdict was coolly levied: another bidder had raised on Perkus with fifteen seconds to go. Unanswered, this rival had taken the chaldron. Better luck next time! Indignant, muttering, Perkus hastened back to the other auction. He lurked intently over the screen, as if the scouring of his hot breath might be telling in the effort. Again he looked to be in command with less than a minute to go, until a speedier bidder stole the chaldron away at the last instant. Game over.

I saw Perkus crumble then, drained of spirit, sagging into himself, an imploded building in slow motion. Despite all care he'd taken to shave and wash and dress for the morning's appointment, he looked heartbreakingly worse, his vessel stranded even higher on the shoals than before I'd sent him downtown. In my experience Strabo's needles uncorked vast energies in the weeks following a treatment, but on the day of their entry into one's body they took a severe toll. Even so, I had to persuade Perkus not to resume his hunt. If there had been two chaldrons the first time he'd looked there'd be more tomorrow. He'd mentioned Strabo's advice to him to eat meat, so what about a burger? I joshingly mentioned replacement lipids, appealing to his self-medicator's vanity. Perkus smiled wanly. He made motions of consent to the expedition downstairs, but couldn't seem to get out of his chair. I detached the phone line from the computer and replaced it in the telephone, enforcing my little prohibition. Someone might want to call. I might want to call. Perkus didn't have the gumption to argue. He moved through the French doors to his little bedroom, slid his jacket onto a hanger, then curled onto his bedspread like a dog. The temperature outside was dropping, in Perkus's kitchen I'd felt a chill draft on my neck from gaps in the window to Biller's inner courtyard, but the building's clanking, whistling radiators were at work and the bedroom was practically a sauna. Perkus's lids sagged to veil the good eye and the irascible one, which still lolled in the direction of the living room, seeking the Dell's screen, which had reverted to a screen saver featuring comical raccoons huddled in the upper branches of a towering redwood. Then his lids at last tucked over his aggravated orbs, to meet the parchment-yellow skin beneath. For what it was worth, my four-day campaign was victorious: I'd put Perkus to bed. As he drifted off, he honorably swore he'd wait until morning to chase chaldrons.

Oh yes, and one other thing: he still relied on me to locate Brando.

6

Oona Laszlo was bizarrely productive. She seemingly did nothing, when out of my sight, but dash off books. The week previous we'd strolled together though the Barnes & Noble on Lexington and, serene and dead-pan, she'd pointed out three she'd written just among the new releases. (Then again, she could have told me she'd written anything in the shop. Her name wasn't on the books.) Now she'd taken a new assignment, covert as ever: an autobiography of Laird Noteless, who'd received the commission for the *Memorial to Daylight* popular sentiment had demanded in reply to the gray fog downtown.

Noteless, legendary for his unbudging exile stance, his stark antihumanist vision, his clashes with borough presidents and local preservationist groups in attempting to mount his abysmal spectacles, was experiencing the kind of late-blooming legitimacy this town some-times accorded to avant-gardists who stuck around long enough. It might be the case that in this era of gray fog we'd caught up to Noteless's stark antihumanist vision, even found some flinty comfort there. Or perhaps it was simply that Noteless's Ivy League undergraduate friends were finally, four decades later, running the world, as they were always meant to. (Legitimacy settles on us in various ways.) Anyhow, Noteless was too occupied with the big controversial commission to pen his own memoir, so his publisher had found reliable, versatile Oona. Now she'd persuaded me to travel this morning to 191st Street, to have a look at *Urban Fjord*. Unembarrassed to inform me or the publisher that she paid contemporary art little attention, Oona wanted to gaze on a few of Noteless's works, to get a feel. She was at least that thorough, though she promised me she'd be concocting the book without much consultation with Noteless or his assistants, and that she preferred it so. She also bragged or confessed that she wrote with the television on, mostly *Top Chef* or *Next Year's Model*. This was the third morning we'd woken together. I'd still never crossed the threshold of her apartment building.

Despite all global rumors, the city was suffering a ferocious November. In a kind of wardrobe shock, nobody could locate their January gear, and on the street all hobbled like crooked insects, stunned by the knifing winds. Oona and I made it as far as Eighty-sixth and Third before ducking into the nearest shop, a Papaya Czar on the corner there.

"Why don't we take a cab?" I said.

"The subway goes right to it," said Oona. "Let's just warm up for a minute. We haven't had breakfast anyway."

"Fabulous suggestion," I said. "Let's go somewhere for breakfast." I gestured at the hot dogs browning on the grill, the dented tureens of sickly tropical beverage, covered with garish signage, that lined the walls, hoping my point was self-evident. I had good visions of a bowl of latte, something crumbly in my fingers, hot dough and caffeine. Then a U-turn route to my bed, which we'd vacated too soon for my taste, driven here by Oona's workaholic jitters. My own priorities would have kept us indoors, fugitive and warm, out of public view.

I wanted Oona in the morning. I could still conjure her slippery smoothness in my arms (and divergent cuppable breasts in my palms, where they left ghost trails of a peach's weight), but Oona had kept dunning lights and pulling curtains, and dressing and undressing stealthily, while I was at the sink or refrigerator, or asleep. When I asked, Oona informed me she was too skinny to look at. She might even be invisible, she joked. After I looked clear through her I'd see there was no one there at all. Well, I suspended judgment. Meanwhile, I campaigned to get her nude in a bed flooded with daylight. I really felt no call to visit any *Fjord* in this weather.

"This is a good breakfast right here."

"You're kidding." Oona had a thing for dodging my suggestions of bars or restaurants, I'd noticed. She'd claimed she lived on roast chestnuts and knishes from sidewalk carts, and takeout Chinese. Really, I think I'd seen only white wine, good Scotch, and Häagen-Dazs cross her lips.

"Papaya's fantastic for the lower intestine," said Oona. "I think it reverses cancer, too." She ordered herself a cup of orange stuff from an imperturbable Hispanic man in a white smock and mustache. Lodged beneath the glowing coils of ceiling-mounted heater, he might have been on some faraway beach, vending to bathers. Outside the shop window, a cyclonic wind had roiled a discarded

Times into a kind of whirligig, one which pedestrians had to dodge, with their hands protecting their faces.

"Have some. It really is an aid to digestion, it says so on this sign."

"Yes, that's why they sell it with hot dogs."

"Poor Chase. Is capitalism too paradoxical for you?"

"I'll take a black coffee," I told the counterman. Then I pointed at the hot dogs. "And two, with mustard."

"You're the astronaut's man," said the counterman suddenly, breaking what I thought had been a fourth wall between us.

"Yes," I admitted.

"Don't give up," he said, his tone conveying stoical solidarity. "She needs you, man."

"Thank you." I shook his hand awkwardly before accepting the hot dogs and coffee.

Oona and I stepped out to brave the wind again. It was then that, without trying, I spotted him, second from the corner in a long line of sidewalk peddlers, each behind their various tables full of socks and gloves, digital watches and batteries, pre-owned magazines and bootleg DVDs, a stilled caravan sloping down Eighty-sixth Street, the way we'd come. Biller. Oona and I had likely passed him once already, obliviously bantering, our elbows not linked but jostling together, on our way into the Papaya Czar. Biller's little card table was loaded edge to edge with trade paperbacks; literary titles, unusual ones, it seemed to me, even as it dawned that they must be Perkus Tooth's books. Stopped there, my dumb cardboard tray of coffee and dogs between us, I felt a strange guilt that Biller should catch me and

Oona together. Perkus was in the dark about us, so far as I knew. (Confronted with a vagrant, my mind also fled to vagrant guilts: that wind-whipped *Times* surely must contain the latest update on *Northern Lights'* damaged tiles, and the space walk the trapped astronauts had scheduled to tend them.) Whether Oona recognized Biller or not I couldn't guess.

"Here." I shoved one of the two mustardy dogs, in its crenellated paper sleeve, at Biller. He received the steaming gift in fingers bared by a woolen glove with cutoff tips, and only nodded. His eyes were as gentle as I recalled. So much so I couldn't discern whether they were also puzzled. He seemed to be forgiving me for the hot dog, even as he lifted it for a first bite.

"I'm Perkus's friend," I said. "Chase."

"Okay," said Biller.

"Those are some of his books you're selling, I see."

"He gave them to me."

"I wasn't accusing you of anything."

"I read them first."

"I'm sure."

This was small talk, but even as I made it, one title caught my eye, raised above the others by the book's thickness. *Obstinate Dust*, by Ralph Warden Meeker, the tome Perkus had had on his kitchen table or at his bedside the last few times I'd visited. Now, as though an involuntary detective action had been triggered in me by Biller's defensiveness, I also noticed the bookmark, a smoothed Ricola cough-drop wrapper, hanging like a tongue just a quarter or fifth of the way through the volume's heft. Perkus's bookmark, I knew it. Perkus sucked the Ricola drops to coat his fume-seared gullet, another of his self-medications—like papaya beverages to smooth the passage of frankfurters, it occurred to me now.

Oona tugged at my arm and scowled. I handed her the hot coffee, as though she'd requested it. Then continued with Biller, a little helpless to quit what had become an interrogation. I put my finger on *Obstinate Dust*. The book must have been a thousand pages long.

"You finish that one? Perkus didn't."

If I'd caught Biller in a lie, he wasn't chagrined. His attitude was still sympathetic, as though I'd come to him somehow penitently, to right a small wrong. Or perhaps the air of sympathy was directed at the absent Perkus.

"Mr. Tooth gives me books he can't finish," he said. "He's not reading a lot these days, I don't think."

"*Chase*," said Oona, butting her forehead against my shoulder, then closing to me for warmth. The sidewalk entrepreneurs to the right and left of us each jogged in place, fists deep in pockets. They eyed the transaction between myself and Biller, plainly envious to think the bookseller, of all people, had a customer in the impossible weather.

"Okay, I'll take that one." I had the wild thought I'd read it, and surprise Perkus. Maybe I could recapture his interest from chaldrons. I hadn't seen Perkus for three days, but we'd spoken on the phone. He'd reported that the going price of chaldrons was skyrocketing, not that he'd had a chance to pay it—he'd bid in seven auctions and lost them all. Before I could remind him of the joke about the restaurant-goer who complained that the food was bad and the portions small, he'd hustled me off the phone so he could resume scouring eBay for sellers. There were obsessions I could adore in Perkus, others which in their thinness broke my heart. I didn't want him to give up his books.

Biller quoted a price. "Ten dollars."

"Are you kidding?"

"Half price."

I handed Biller a twenty. He told me I was his first buyer of the day, and that he had no change. I waved it off, and shoehorned the brick of pages into my coat pocket. As if aping me, Biller crammed the last third of the hot dog into his mouth, then raised his half-gloved hand in salute, bare fingertips gripping the air, while Oona and I slanted off toward the subway entrance.

Oona's plan, which she claimed was impeccable, involved shooting downtown in order to go uptown. We took the Lexington line to Forty-second Street, then boarded the shuttle, in order to get on the 1 train up into Harlem and beyond, to the parklands alongside the Harlem River, where Noteless had constructed his *Fjord*. I couldn't imagine why we'd needed to cross to the West Side if our destination had been in the east all along, and after our second train began pleading with Oona to be reasonable and exit the system, but she ignored me, continued dragging me through passages like a ferret with a captured hare in its jaws. The New York subway is a vast disordered mind, obsessing in ruts carved by trauma a century earlier. This is why I always take taxicabs. Nevertheless, we eventually boarded the uptown

Broadway local, which poked its way unsteadily into unknown parts of Manhattan.

"*closing in dream the somnolent city—*"

"Wait, wait, that's the first sentence?"

I began again. "*closing in dream the somnolent city—*"

"No, stop, that's enough."

I'd unwedged *Obstinate Dust* from my coat's pocket and begun narrating its opening to Oona once we'd found seats on the local. Now she grabbed the book from me. Our subway car held a scattering of faces, none, after 125th Street, white as our own, and none interested for more than a glance-worth in Oona's and my own agitation. I am always nervous, I'll admit, in Manhattan's triple digits. (In my defense, I'm nervous in the single digits, too.) Fidgeting with the big paperback, we were out of place and to be ignored, painted over with everyday disdain. The train was clammily warm and malodorous. Riders sat with coats loosened, nodding in rhythm to earbuds or just the robot's applause of wheels locating seams in ancient track.

"No, no, no," chanted Oona, flitting through a few pages. "Not lowercase italics, they can't be serious, it's like *poetry*! Next thing you know the characters' names will be X, Y, and Z. I can't even *find* any character names."

"Maybe that's just a kind of overture," I suggested. "It can't really stay like that all the way through." I felt a kind of wilting despair, as though my plan to read the book was a real one, on which any hopes for Perkus's stability was contingent.

"Impossible. I don't want to know about it. I didn't get where I am today reading thousand-page prose poems. Please, sorry, but no."

This was one of Oona's recurring jokes: *I didn't get where I am today*. She never said, of course, where it was she claimed she'd gotten—the ghost, the invisible girl. I suppose that was the joke. That she'd gotten who knows where, but still had some standards. What I noticed now was how near she held the book to her face. I'd never before seen her reading.

"Do you need glasses?"

Oona replied idly, as if musing to herself. "Sometimes I wear glasses, but never in front of you. My god, it's *all* like this." She thrust the book in my lap, and I resumed the survey she'd abandoned. True enough, the look of the pages was consistent. . . . *he struggled to interest them in the concretization of listenality* . . . Why italicize an entire book? Was the whole of *Obstinate Dust* meant to be taken as a kind of parenthetical fugue, or as an aside to something else? And if so, what? Ralph Warden Meeker's other novels? Literature per se? The reader's mundane existence?

Doubt swallowed my fantasy. Even if I somehow managed to get through *Obstinate Dust*, and then to resuscitate Perkus's interest in it, was reading Meeker's opus in any way preferable to surfing eBay for chaldrons? Nonetheless, I felt I'd incurred a responsibility, was somehow doomed to the book. Biller had tricked me into taking a hot potato off his hands, just as Susan Eldred had booby-trapped her office by introducing me to Perkus in the first place.

"Is 'listenality' a word?" I asked Oona.

"So do you have, like, this whole network of spies on street corners giving you regular updates on Perkus Tooth's mental health?"

"I realize this sounds weird, but Biller lives in the air space behind Perkus's kitchen . . . part of the time, at least . . ." I attempted to explain the whole unlikely fact that Perkus had a dependent in this world. Meanwhile our train rattled out of the 145th Street station. The unfamiliar tunnels grew stained and decrepit, the tile more and more resembling Roman or Greek mosaic, those fragments entombed at the Met in dim vacant rooms one hurries through en route to the latest exhibition of Bacons or Arbuses.

Oona didn't mask her impatience. "I've seen him lowering leftovers out his window. But what's your role? Did you agree to keep buying back the junk Perkus gives Biller? A little triangular economy of pity?"

"I thought I'd return the book," I said, feeling pathetic. "I thought Perkus might have given it to him . . . by mistake."

"Tried to put Humpty together again," she possibly muttered, her voice engulfed in the train's clangor.

"Sorry?"

"Nothing."

"Why would pity be *triangular*?" I heard myself ask. "Perkus shouldn't pity me. Or Biller."

"Nobody pities you, Chase."

"Why are you angry all of a sudden?"

"I'm not angry. It's just I thought you and I were sneaking around behind *her* back." Oona jabbed a finger upward. Though we sped through an underground tunnel in a dingy earth rocket, anyone would understand she meant Janice Trumbull, the sky's noble captive. It was in the nature of orbit that Janice's presence blanketed the planet, overhead of any given location. She was like a blind god, one helpless at our lies, deceived effortlessly.

"We are," I told Oona, though I really barely did more than mouth the words, feeling dangerous stating it aloud. My guilt was as large as the sky, and I couldn't escape it underground.

"Really? Because it mostly feels to me like we're cheating on Perkus. Whenever you mention him, which is constantly, I feel like you're talking about your wife and kids and dog, waiting in a suburban home where you'll inevitably return."

"I'm *concerned* about Perkus," I blurted.

"Why aren't you concerned about your girlfriend? She's stranded in orbit with four horny cosmonauts, plus one American horticulturalist who's begun barking like a dog and won't come out of the storage attic. The plants are dying, the air's full of carbon dioxide, and now she's got these unspecified medical symptoms—"

My betrayal of Janice was compounded by Oona's details. "What medical symptoms?"

"You really should read the letters more carefully."

What had I missed? My shame took its place in a vast backdrop of shames—oxygen-starved astronauts, war-exiled orphans, dwindling and displaced species— against which I puttered through daily life, attending parties and combating hangovers, recording voice-overs and granting interviews to obscure fan sites, drinking coffee and smoking joints with Perkus, and making contact with real feeling unpredictably and at random, at funeral receptions, under rain-sheeted doorways.

Yet through shame and guilt I felt a sudden joy. Oona was jealous. To be jealous was to be in love. Oona would deny this on the spot, but the two were continuous territories on any emotional map I'd ever known. The realization unleashed delight in me, but Oona didn't seem delighted. She was gnarled in herself, peevish. Maybe she was sorry she'd mentioned Janice. I wanted to embrace and protect her, but she'd angled from me on the seat. How odd, really, that Oona felt pitted against Perkus. With their small bodies and large heads, their persnickety outfits and smoke-tinged tenors, I'd first taken them for siblings or lovers. Even now, in their vibrant wit and impatience, and for their revitalizing effect on my own life, I associated the two, no matter that each spoke dismissively of the other. I'd certainly fallen into this skulking romance partly because it sprang from the magical site of the Eighty-fourth Street kitchen. But it was obvious that poor Oona had displaced her jealousy: to directly compete with the stranded astronaut was too abysmal, so she projected the feelings onto Perkus instead. Yet under the circumstances, it didn't seem strategic to say so.

I had barely a chance to dwell on the dismaying cityscape as the train soared aboveground, the slate-brown monolithic prewar tenements, the rusted Coca-Cola-sponsored bodega signs, the glass-strewn lots full of twisted ailanthus shrubs, before we'd abandoned the elevated views and descended to that unfriendly map ourselves. I felt a little overwhelmed, being one who flinches from any wider world but prefers to feel at home in Manhattan, to glimpse the island's own provinces and badlands, its margins. The bitter wind had died, and the pavements were full of drifting souls, men in porkpie hats leaning on parked cars or arrayed in beach chairs, packets of schoolchildren not in school. Oona knew just where she was headed, putting the commercial avenues behind us, and then the tenements, too, as we crossed Fort George Avenue, into the parklands at the island's edge. I had to pee, but wasn't too tempted by the prospect of any restroom I'd find if we backtracked. Anyway, Oona was impossible to slow. Consulting some inner compass, she drew us to the cyclone-fenced perimeter of a wild steep slope, the ground tangled with underbrush, nothing like the tended river's edge I knew. A cleared ball field, its home plate caged to manage fouls, was partly visible below us, but I saw no evidence of a trail that would get us to it.

"We're almost there."

"Almost where?"

"We just have to find the entrance. Come on, Chase. Your shoes will be fine."

"I wasn't worrying about my shoes."

"Then stop looking at them."

That was when they appeared, on the trail through the brush the way we'd come: two black kids, boys rather than teenagers, not threatening in any way, though one carried a stick, picking along as if with a shepherd's crook. One wore a puffy fake-down coat, gold scuffed with black, and the other a New York Jets warm-up jacket over a hooded sweatshirt. They fell in with us easily, local guides to the forsaken zone, masking their curiosity with shrugging familiarity.

"Hey."

"Hey to you," said Oona.

"You lookin' for the Ford?"

"Fjord—yes."

"Fee-ord," repeated Puffy Coat, lightly mocking. "You goin' the wrong way."

"So take us the right way."

They steered us back uphill. The beaten trail at the base of the fence forced us into single-file, Oona ahead of me, the boys bracketing us protectively. It was Puffy Coat who led, foraging ahead with his broomstick crook. The one at my back, New York Jets, tapped my elbow.

"Where you from?"

It seemed odd to say Upper East Side. For one thing, his part of things was so much farther *upper*. "Downtown," I told him.

"You and her married?"

"No."

"You Zoom, right?"

"Sorry?"

"From that show, *Mister Pesty*."

There may be no way to say this sensitively: from my vantage, I've come to believe black people watch a lot of reruns. Or at least they tend to know me for my first fame, rather than my second, that social half-life at Janice Trumbull's side or in cocktail photographs in *New York* magazine.

"That's me."

"You look old."

"I am old. That was a long time ago." It occurred to me that he was probably near the age I was when cast for *Martyr & Pesty*'s first season.

"Why you never punch that dude in the face?"

"It's not me, it's a character. If it were me I would have punched him."

"Naaah." My interlocutor seemed to think I lied.

"Well, Zoom needed to keep his job, you know."

This answer satisfied him better, and he fell silent behind me for the time being. Oona was quiet, too, behind our leader, and we made a kind of reverent company as we picked our way up and down the scrubby rises led by these sprites, these ushers, who'd emerged from the wasteland. The ball field was in view for a moment, then it wasn't. Puffy Coat halted at a section of the cyclone fence where it was split and curled away from the ground as if by a raiding animal. He set his stick on the ground, then gripped the fence and widened the breach, nodding to indicate that we should duck through, his breath frosting in the air before him.

"This can't be what Noteless had in mind as an approach to his great work," I said.

Oona had wriggled past the barrier, and now beckoned me to follow. "I don't think he necessarily intends to make it easy to see. I've heard some people rent helicopters and fly over."

"What if we just took his word for it?"

A dust-trampled path led downhill from the damaged fence, into deeper brush. Bladder swelling, hands chapping in cold, I was just ready to despair totally when Noteless's *Fjord* erupted into view at our feet. The chasm seemed to have been hewn out of the earth by unnatural force, the ground's lip curling suddenly downward, bringing with it shrubs and small trees now turned horizontal to sprout from the *Fjord*'s walls. The artificial crevasse yawned at least fifty yards across, perhaps a hundred. On the vertiginous cliffs dangled dozens of pairs of sneakers tied together at the laces, lodged on all sides in the branches and scrub. Then I made out other stuff, on the ridge at our feet, junk which unlike the sneakers had perhaps been intended to finish a journey into the earth's craw but had fallen short: children's toys, kitchenware, electronics, knotted plastic bags of unspecified treasure. I made out a tricycle and a large nude doll, a smashed stereo turntable, a power drill. I wondered whether the refuse was Noteless's flourish, or the local community's spontaneous outpouring. In any event, the cascade of garbage was the only thing "urban" about his *Fjord*, since the city was entirely out of view. We could have been a hundred miles into forest, for all the skyline of treetops informed us. I wondered, too, whether I knew exactly what a fjord was, after all. Or maybe it was Noteless who didn't know what a fjord was. Shouldn't it be full of water? Perhaps it was, at the bottom.

We stepped nearer, the four of us. Beneath the lip of trees and grass and the crap that had lodged there, the earth gave way to an underbelly of roots and stones, and below that, darker stuff, veins of sunless soil, and shadow tapering to total blackness. It was as though a titanic ax had descended from heaven to sink its blade in the parklands, then be lifted away. Oona and I stepped as though hypnotized nearer to the lip—there was no definite limit to approach, only whichever foothold on that curled ridge of landscape you'd last judge safe to take. Trampled grass showed others were braver than ourselves. The boys hung back. Having marshaled us here, they seemed to want to let us steep in the site's insane grandeur undisturbed a while. The wind had died entirely by now, and the long tilt of clouds overhead seemed ready to close over us like the lid of a box. I took an involuntary step backward, and heard something glassy crackle underfoot. But I didn't take my eyes off the dark center before me. The longer I stared into the *Fjord*, the more likely it seemed that I'd pitch headfirst into that light-destroying well, so the sky could slam shut and entomb my tiny form inside.

"Okay, it's kind of incredible. Let's go home now."

"Wait, I want to take it in," Oona said. "It's a total vision of death."

"One hundred percent agreed. I'm cold and I have to pee."

"So go pee."

I stepped backward again, unwilling to trust the *Fjord* at my back. Again I felt a gritty crackling under my shoes. I turned one heel up, as if to check for dog shit, and found dusty shards of thin glass embedded in my sole's leather. Crack vials. That detail, I figured, was beyond even Noteless's vision. He'd had collaborators at this site.

130

"Can you believe they'd put the man who built this in charge of the *Memorial to Daylight*?" said Oona. "I wonder if those people have ever even *seen* this thing."

"Well, he'll obviously have to . . . compromise . . . on the memorial . . ." I'd found a discarded Starbucks cup and was using it to scour the glass from my shoe.

"Did you know he originally proposed *Urban Fjord* for Columbus Circle? Needless to say, they refused him."

"Pretty petulant of him to have put it here instead."

"You're projecting, Chase. Whatever you think of Noteless, there isn't a less petulant man alive."

"I've never heard you speak so reverently about one of your assignments. You're trying to make me jealous."

The boys stepped up beside us—like museum guards, it occurred to me now.

"What you gonna give?" asked Puffy Coat. Leaning on his broomstick crook, framed in wilderness, he could have made some mock Pre-Raphaelite tableau. But I needed to get a grip on myself. Not everything was in quote marks, or wearing some mystical halo of interpretation. I suffered Perkus's disease by proxy. I should focus on the real. Two badly parented boys had led us to see the freakish hole in the ground on this chilly bluff at the edge of their ghetto. They were playing hooky. Their older brothers would have mugged us.

"What do you mean?" said Oona.

"Everybody put in something," said Puffy Coat. "What you got?"

"An offering, you mean."

Puffy Coat only shrugged. That word was near enough to what he had in mind.

Oona looked at me, and pointed at the coat pocket where *Obstinate Dust* bulged. "He brought something," she told the boys.

"I want to return this to Perkus," I protested.

"Perkus gave the book away, Chase," said Oona. "Besides, what else have we got? I'm not tossing in my Treo."

"Do it, Cheese," said New York Jets.

I had to tell myself it wasn't Perkus Tooth I'd be symbolically interring in that pit, but Ralph Warden Meeker. From the sample I'd taken on the 1 train, he and Noteless deserved each other. *Obstinate Dust*, meet Obstinate Hole. Anyway, it would be a relief to walk the return path without the asymmetrical sink-weight in my pocket. I gave the book a spirited heave, wrenching my shoulder in the process. The tubby paperback fluttered softly as it dwindled to a birdlike speck, proving the real breadth of Noteless's monstrosity. Then it was gone.

"Ow." I cradled my shoulder, amazed at what a single effort could inflict. I hadn't been to the gym in months. At least I'd gotten the book past the crud-strewn whale's lip, into depths where its impact returned no sound.

The ceremony freed us from the *Fjord*'s spell. The boys turned and piloted us back through the tear in the fence, and up the last rise, until Fort George Avenue was evident ahead of us, and beyond it, hints of the wider city, even the reassuring far-off Chrysler and Empire spire-tops. There our guides soberly shook each of our hands, and turned back. Their graceful final silence would forever enshrine them for me as mythological chaperones. I peed behind a tree, then Oona and I found our way back into the streets. Oona was on the silent side herself.

■

Something was wrong at the 191st Street station. Reflective tape barricaded one stairwell entrance, and an orange-vested MTA worker, wearing a black woolen hat with earlaps and puffing out great gusts of breath steam, stood at the center of a teeming mob of disappointed passengers. Pushing into this congregation of the confused, we made our way near enough to overhear the worker, who in the most blasé tone possible announced that the subway was out of commission going downtown, and directed us to a nearby bus stop for a shuttle to 125th Street, where we could reboard the train. He parried all questions with a shrug, and rewound his spiel for the next party.

A bit stunned, Oona and I trudged with the others in the direction of the bus stop, two blocks down Nagle Avenue, on Broadway. The chaos there was more appalling than at the stairwell. One shuttle bus was loaded and just embarking, full with seated and standing passengers to such a point that I could hear its carriage sigh unhappily, promising breakdown in a mile or so. Another hundred passengers waited, in a streaming, hive-like circulation around a pole on which was taped a hasty, Magic Markered sign promising shuttle service at fifteen-minute intervals. A scene to crush your heart.

"What happened?" Oona addressed this as a kind of local petition to the five or six aggrieved passengers milling nearest. As in a street incident involving wreckage or fire trucks a volunteer explainer emerged, a middle-aged Hasid with curved shoulders draped in a long, soiled scarf, and bearing twin shopping bags like a milkmaid's yoke. He seemed drawn to Oona as another dressed in black.

"Somebody said the tiger again," he told her.

"They still haven't caught it?"

He made a sour face under his beard, as though tasting the civic ineptitude. "If it stays so far uptown, what do they care? Five, six times I've been forced to get off and switch to the bus."

"Really?"

He nodded, widening his eyes: really. "They claim it's tearing up the track. But then an hour later the train goes right through. A convenient excuse, that's all. So let it devour a small-businessman's livelihood now and again. People like distraction. They live on it, gobble it up."

I had to interrupt. "You're saying they . . . encourage the tiger?"

He shrugged. "Tolerate maybe. Encourage maybe. It's not mine to say. What they don't do is *catch*."

"Thank you," said Oona. She nudged us away before I could ask more.

"I don't completely get that man's theory," I said. "If there's really a tiger, then why would he call it an excuse?"

"Well, the MTA could be opportunistically lying about the tiger's whereabouts, I think that was what he meant."

"Where do you suppose he's getting his information?"

"Same as me, Chase. He's just repeating what he's heard."

"Please don't be so short with me. I think I dislocated my shoulder."

"Don't whine."

"Now I'm completely sure you brought me out today as some kind of esoteric punishment," I said. "I only don't understand what I did wrong."

Oona gave me a knifelike look. "You're a little confused, Chase. I brought you with me for protection. I was scared to come up here alone."

How quickly we'd become invisible to each other. I saw Oona Laszlo now, as if in a visionary flash, almost as if she were a blazing chaldron set before me. Pale, not so much dressed in black as feathered in it like a wounded bird, tinier in the white canvas tennis shoes she'd selected for the hike to Noteless's *Fjord* than I'd ever seen her before, blinking her mascaraed eyes at me with a self-loathing which, if I let myself truly take notice, never subsided. A sort of elegant fragment or postulate of a person, but not whole, not entirely viable, certainly not credible waiting to board a shuttle among all these stolid brown-faced citizens whose depressive rage hovered smoggily overhead, a communal rain cloud formed of a loathing so much readier, so much less curdled in irony. Of course Oona again made me think of Perkus, and of course again I wouldn't say so. I roused then what was best in me, what made me worthy of her or Perkus or anyone else who'd ever called to me for protection, and stuck out my expert arm and hailed an empty taxicab pointed downtown. It was hardly a miracle—this was Broadway, after all, never mind the high triple digits—but it felt like a miracle, one I'd summoned personally, in the manner of a quarterback's Hail Mary pass.

We plopped exhausted and relieved into the cab's backseat. The heater got my nose running and I snuffled happily. Even before Oona gave the driver her address we sped off, putting the grotesque scene of the bus stop behind us. We wouldn't be missed—more shamblers redirected from the subway were arriving there, in waves.

"Well, you got your cab ride after all."

"You want to make me feel guilty, but I can tell you're as happy as I am."

It was true, Oona was exhilarated, we both were, at the escape. If some standard of austerity, indicated by Noteless's unforgiving aesthetic, had seemed to require a pilgrimage to his artwork by public transportation, then it was as if with the taxicab I'd wooed Oona back from that grim brink.

I couldn't keep from gloating. "It's amazing how passive people get in the face of an authority figure like that bully in the orange vest. He told them to go and wait for the shuttle, and they were all doing it, like sheep."

"No doubt about it, Chase, those people would totally all hail cabs if they only had your iconoclastic courage."

"I'm just saying we were locked into some kind of collective trance."

"And then you recalled that you had a hundred dollars in your wallet, *et voilà*."

Oona's assault was fond, a sting with no venom. In one gesture I'd reclaimed her affection, and been forgiven my obsession with Perkus, too. I suppose I'd bargained for that forgiveness by surrendering *Dust* to *Fjord*. Our surrogates had canceled each other. In the delicious seedy security of the taxicab I felt I'd passed tests, survived fjords, ghettos, tigers. Even my shoulder felt better. My lust flooded back, too, the pang I'd felt earlier, of unfinished bed-business between us. Now I crowded Oona, in a pleasant way, and put my nose in her hair. The city seemed to be parting for us, the lights green in easy sequence, our cab already rounding Central Park's northeastern shoulder.

"What are you doing later? And by later, I mean pretty much anytime starting immediately."

She squirmed, also in a pleasant way, but farther from me. "I have to work. I want to get some impressions of *Urban Fjord* on paper while they're fresh."

"You sound like you're working on a serious book for a change." My jealousy wasn't too real, but I didn't mind striking the note.

"Oh, I didn't get where I am today *working on serious books*. If I ever write a serious book you'll be the first to know, Chase, I promise."

"So why not risk an impression that's . . . less than fresh?"

She used both hands to push me away. "I have to work, really."

"Okay, okay."

"Honestly, I have a lot on my plate."

"I'm glad you're being honest."

"Fuck off."

We'd pulled up to her building, at Ninety-fourth and Lex. The place had taken on a certain aura for my being excluded from it, and I turned my back to the entrance-way and faced the street instead, not wanting to stare like a tourist at the pyramids.

"Don't sulk," said Oona. "Maybe I'll call you later on. What are you doing?"

"Nothing."

"Nothing?"

"Well, I heard there was this fabulous crater on Thirty-fourth Street, I thought I'd wander over and have a look."

"Nice."

"I mean, I'd sing under your window, but I don't know which one is yours."

"I might not even have a window."

"I might not have much of a singing voice."

"Okay, well then, that sounds like a plan."

"Perfect."

■

In truth, I wasn't completely shattered at the prospect of our parting ways for now. I had an assignment, one I'd awarded myself at some point in the morning's episode, though I couldn't say exactly when. It would be a secret from Oona for now. I was going to visit Perkus again, but not alone. As Oona had dragged me to the rim of Noteless's bleak pit, I'd drag some sane witness into the present void of Perkus's obsessions, his unhealthy onanistic chaldron-hunt. This was overdue. Call it an intervention. So while I went on playing the role I'd been cast in, that of the fluffy vacant boyfriend, he who'd be doing nothing, only pining, while Janice or Oona carried on her important work, just beneath I was full of intent. (This might be seen as the mediocre actor's basic minimum threshold: to play two moods simultaneously, one on the top surface, the other below, and invest adequately in both.)

With whom to people this intervention, though? Well, my first impulse had been Oona herself. Her vibrant skepticism could be just the tonic Perkus required. I liked to find occasions for us to be around one another, these days. Yet that notion disqualified itself. The triangle between the three of us was a little fierce at the moment, even if Perkus had no knowledge of it. Oona might speak too scornfully, and so drive Perkus deeper into defiance. Anyway, I was already under suspicion with her now, of trying to reassemble Humpty Dumpty. I'd also considered inviting Susan Eldred, who after all had introduced us. Susan was the sanest person I was sure Perkus knew. Yet I had no reason to believe Perkus had ever welcomed Susan into his Eighty-fourth Street sanctum. I wouldn't want him to feel invaded or overrun. My sole option was that which had been inevitable all along: Richard Abneg.

I hadn't seen Richard in more than a week, but two days before I'd been summoned to lunch at Daniel with Maud Woodrow and Sharon Spencer, almost a sort of intervention of its own. Maud had refused to name the occasion on the telephone, but made my attendance mandatory. The two women wanted me to give expert testimony on Richard Abneg, though this agenda wasn't unveiled before I'd been plied with several rounds of the gratis appetizers Daniel made its specialty. It was a little early in the day for me, and I had to remind myself to quit draining half my wineglass for appearance's sake, since the staff hovered, ready to top it off after I'd had even a sip. Too late. I was a little sick from the rich food before we'd eaten a single item we'd actually ordered, and dizzy before the interrogation began.

"He's practically living at Georgina's," said Maud. "We keep seeing him crawling through the lobby at weird hours. He leers at people, Chase. He made friends with the night doorman, they were seen drinking together at four AM."

I understood the situation instantly: Richard's invasion of Georgina Hawkmanaji wasn't in Maud and Thatcher Woodrow's plans. To those Lords of the Building, he'd been amusing enough, turning up at their party as an outcropping of Mayor Arnheim's power, which seemed feeble contrasted with the deeper sway of the Woodrows' ancient dough. But Richard had overstepped his bounds by going after Georgina, though even that was diverting enough at first, and could have been a perfect scandal-in-a-martini-glass, if it had caused merely a little harmless wreckage as they'd wagered after the party. Georgina slightly broken by a taste of sex, Richard totally humbled by a taste of wealth: either or both of those outcomes would have been suitable. Instead

Richard, by succeeding with Georgina, threatened to make her not so conveniently absurd, less a container for their patronage and pity. Or anyway, that was what was at stake at this lunch. The women had no actual evidence of what had gone on, except that he was suddenly *in the building*. They only knew what Georgina had told them and, more important, what they'd invented by themselves. In truth, by threatening to be a Visigoth Richard had gratified their unacknowledged yearning for chaos, for the torching of their complacency.

"I first met Richard at your dinner," I pointed out. "It's not like we've got some huge history."

"But you're in that secret after-hours club with him," said Sharon Spencer. "He must confide in you, you must know what he's up to."

I raised my eyebrows. By what game of Telephone had my connection to Richard Abneg become an "after-hours club"? Georgina's arcane English might be partly to blame.

"By all reports Abneg's apparently a bit of an *animal*," said Sharon, her nostrils flaring while her mouth cinched in disdain. "If you can imagine Georgina Hawkmanaji waking up *handcuffed*."

"My problem is I can imagine almost anyone waking up handcuffed," I said irresponsibly.

"To her *toilet*."

"Perhaps Georgina's bed doesn't have an easily accessible frame?"

"He's taking advantage of her, Chase, anyone can see that," said Maud. "He's setting up some kind of beachhead in her apartment. What I can't imagine is why."

I didn't understand her implication. I really ought to push aside my wineglass. "There's a problem at his building," I said, stalling. "A problem . . . with . . . eagles."

"We've heard about the eagles, Chase," said Sharon. "That's a pretty lame justification, if you ask me."

"Thatcher was saying he thinks the eagles might have come specifically for Richard," said Maud. "He says they may follow him here now. Somebody told Thatcher they follow him *everywhere*, that when he leaves his building they fly overhead."

"That's impossible," I said. "We've been out together and I've never seen any eagles following him. They're nesting, Maud. They just happened to pick his window ledge."

"You and I both know these things don't 'just happen.' "

"I Googled him," said Sharon. "He has a history in this particular regard."

"What particular regard? Eagles?"

"Abneg began as a *squatter*," said Sharon. "He has a track record of colonizing apartments that don't belong to him. That's how he got his *start*."

"That's not the same at all."

"I admit it's not the same, I'm just saying there's a certain tendency in both."

"She's got a point," said Maud.

"No, she doesn't." I was eating something now that had looked like an oyster but when eaten tasted like foie gras, an item I distantly recalled picking from the menu. For some reason the courses seemed to be clumping around me at the table, while the women went on sipping at balloon-sized glasses of white wine and thimblefuls of chilled soup.

"You're protecting him."

"From what?"

"We don't *know*," said Maud, with great exasperation. She'd come to me with a problem, and I was refusing to help. "That's what's killing us, Chase. Georgina is so nuts, she just talks about him like he's her *boyfriend* now, she won't take a look at what's going on." The secret garden of sexual satisfaction was the only truly unimaginable thing. That two people might locate such joy on Maud and Sharon's watch would be worse for them, by far, than if Richard had been some indiscriminate seducer, bent on pillaging through their beds in turn. The problem might not be that Richard Abneg was an ogre but that he wasn't ogre enough.

"Now we've told you everything we've got," said Sharon Spencer, squinting fiercely. "You owe us the same in return."

I doubted I could reciprocate such a stew of nonsense, even if I'd wanted to. "I don't know Georgina, really," I said. "Maybe they're good together."

"Forget Georgina for a minute," said Maud, totally irritated by my answer. "Tell us about Perkus Tooth."

"Georgina told us he's the leader of your little club," said Sharon.

"Has she met him?"

"No, I don't think so. Thatcher's been asking why you've never brought him around. We're *all* wondering,

Chase. Do you and Richard think we wouldn't like him? Or wouldn't he like us?"

I tried to fit Perkus for Maud and Thatcher's compilation album, *Great Shrunken Heads of Manhattan*. It wasn't easy. Maybe ten years before, when Perkus had been just arriving at his brief moment of currency, with his bylines in *Artforum* and *Interview*. Even then it would have been an ill-fated encounter. Now, I couldn't even picture them in the same room.

Sometimes I wonder if I'm alone in knowing such opposite, such irreconcilable people: Maud at her regular table at Daniel, vibrantly awake to an invisible yet omnipotent web of social power, and Perkus, in his Eighty-fourth Street burrow, testing his daily reality on a grid of cultural marginalia, simultaneous views of mutually impossible worlds. Or do I flatter myself? Probably everyone feels this way. My distinction (if there is one) lies in the helpless and immersive extent of my empathy. I'm truly a vacuum filled by the folks I'm with, and vapidly neutral in their absence. Something in me defaults to an easeful plasticity, a modularity. I'd claim it as the curse of my profession, except I've forsaken that profession for so long now it defines me only in the eyes of others, not in my own.

And still I flatter myself: my empathy here was sharply circumscribed. I wasn't finding *the vacuum of me* too well fed by Maud Woodrow and Sharon Spencer. Actually, the domain of these hedonist inquisitors seemed, at this moment, the most undernourished I knew. For all the butter-poached and truffle-oiled fare, I felt drunk and annoyed and ready to behave a little badly.

"Do you know what a *chaldron* is?" I asked Maud and Sharon. I'd asked flippantly, but then felt keen to hear the answer.

"A what?"

"A chaldron. It's a certain kind of . . . very rare and desirable . . . ceramic."

"Er, no," said Maud. "Why?"

"That's Perkus's current interest," I said. "He collects chaldrons."

"Well, that's . . . terribly interesting."

"Yes."

"It isn't what I was expecting."

"No."

"But what's Perkus himself like?" said Maud.

"He's, I don't know, fairly *ellipsistic*," I said.

"Oh, really?" she bluffed.

"I imagine that's how he'd strike you, yes."

"I'd love to meet him."

"Let me see what I can do." There wasn't a chance I'd do anything to bring this about. I'd sooner ask my agent (who wasn't exactly pining for a call from me) to see if he could put me in touch with Marlon Brando's people.

At that moment I felt Sharon Spencer's stockinged toes flex against the inner curve of my thigh, then slither beyond, toward my crotch. I didn't move either to discourage or encourage this maneuver, took it rather as a neutral element in an environment already suffocatingly sensual. Given a pillow at my setting I could have begun napping at the table, with the warmth of Sharon's instep now cradling my penis. Her foot's adventure might not mean so much more, to either of us, than the redundant hors d'oeuvres that had slipped down our throats without our even pausing to hear their descriptions. Likely it represented less the divulging of some occult agenda for our lunch date than a local tactical response to what she'd found to be a dull stretch in the table talk.

Anyway, this lunch encounter had made me certain in my present plans. For it was evident Richard Abneg hadn't forgotten about Perkus Tooth, despite Richard's recent absence from the scene at Eighty-fourth Street, and no matter his involvements with eagles or Georgina Hawkmanaji's toilet. Like me, Abneg bore the matter of Tooth around with him wherever he went, and talked about him, too. He might not be up-to-date with chaldrons and other catastrophes, but he could be brought up-to-date. He'd rise to the occasion of my planned intervention. I'd only need to find and rally him.

7

I find I want to get this description right, or at least a little righter. With the possible exception of my own face in the bathroom mirror, the church spire outside my window is the sole thing I look at deliberately, consciously, every single day. Yet I glance in its direction as if in doubt, as though the spire's memory is only a rumor between me and myself, and one of the two of us doesn't completely trust the other. When my eyes do confirm the church's actuality (*buildings do persist, Manhattan does exist, things are relentlessly what they seem even if they serve as hosts, as homes, for other phenomena*), the sight acts on my mind like an eraser rubbing away the words that might describe it, into crumbs easily swept from the page. If I'm elsewhere, I have an easy name for the thing: a church spire, a few blocks away, and, sporadically, a flock of wheeling birds. When I look, however, language dies.

Against a white sky the stones of the church are gray-brown. They're smutched, like scraped toast. Against blue, the stones reveal an earthiness. Sienna? Umber? In sunset, the church nearly looks blue. Darker stones are bricked at right angles, lines of mortar visible between them, while lighter stones form the tight-jointed and apparently seamless triangular spires which cluster, one atop the other, each crowned with a small stone cross, nesting toward the single highest cross at the peak. The long A-frame roof is dusky black, not shingled but smooth, and lined with a ridged ornamental top and gutter, both a shade of copper-gone-green like that of the Statue of Liberty. Windows framed in lighter stone take the shape of a snub, rounded cross. (A Celtic cross, possibly? Or do I just mean it reminds me of a shamrock?) Other windows, in the smaller spires, are formed in clusters of three upright lengths, with arched tops. I've never seen anyone in any of those windows. I doubt they open. You'd think they ought to be colored glass, and perhaps they are, but they appear black.

Terms swarm up to tempt me in the course of this description: *Greek Orthodox, Romanesque, flying buttress,* etc. These guessing words I find junked in my brain in deranged juxtaposition, like files randomly stuffed into cabinets by a dispirited secretary with no notion of what, if anything, might ever be usefully retrieved. Often all language seems this way: a monstrous compendium of embedded histories I'm helpless to understand. I employ it the way a dog drives a car, without grasping how the car came to exist or what makes a combustion engine possible. That is, of course, if dogs drove cars. They don't. Yet I go around forming sentences.

One day recently I glanced out in the spire's direction and was shocked to see a bird passing, just at that moment, quite near the glass of my window. Not one of my birds (or perhaps I should say "the church's birds"), but a migrating duck, its Concorde-like shape unmistakable even if I hadn't seen a hundred drab paintings of winging ducks on the walls of cheap restaurants. The duck flapped in one direction only, intently passing through, so quick it was apparitional. Then, followed by others, twenty or perhaps thirty ducks, none so close to my window as the first, yet all flapping doggedly through the margin between my building and the Dorffl Tower. The ducks seemed a kind of eruption, a happening, yet they were too fixedly themselves, too plainly on a natural mission, to be a harbinger of anything but ducks. I yearned for the group to waver, to turn and linger, to sweep through my sky space a second time at least, but in a moment they were gone, another ordinary mystery, one discrete plane of existence momentarily intersecting with another, under my obtuse witness.

Today the tower's flock, the usual birds, flew in a kind of scatter pattern, their paths intricately chaotic, the bunch parting and interweaving like boiling pasta under a pot's lifted lid. It appeared someone had given the birds new instructions, had whispered that there was something to avoid, or someone to fool. I once heard Perkus Tooth say that he'd woken that morning having dreamed an enigmatic sentence: "Paranoia is a flower in the brain." Perkus offered this, then smirked and bugged his eyes—the ordinary eye, and the other. I played at amazement (I was amazed, anyway, at the fact that Perkus *dreamed sentences* to begin with). Yet I hadn't understood what the words meant to him until now, when I knew for a crucial instant that the birds had been directed to deceive me. That was when I saw the brain's flower. Perkus had, I think, been trying to prepare me for how beautiful it was.

8

It struck Richard Abneg that the appropriation of certain buildings—great museums and libraries, music halls, public atriums—for the throwing of benefit galas, those gatherings of social and monetary forces, dressed in their human costumes of ball gown and black tie, to dine at circular tables of ten or twelve, had the effect of seeming to reveal the provenance and rightful ownership of such spaces. Ten trillion schoolchildren might have tramped through these corridors, peered into spooky vitrines and dioramas to contemplate exotic tableaux frozen within: Serengeti lions, emperor penguins, a polar seal writhing in an orca's jaws. Richard had been one of those children himself, ogling this museum where bland informational placards barely veiled the revelation of morbid oddities, of Barnum voyeurism. But the mystery of a building as grand as this one was as deep as anything locked in the tormented gazes of the taxidermied dead.

To whom does New York City belong? Not to schoolchildren. Not to the citizen shuffling cowed and amazed across marble floors in the Frick or Cooper-Hewitt, or paging bug-like through some tome under the green lampshades of the Forty-second Street reading rooms. Money communes after hours in these places, after the turnstiles have been stilled. Money shows itself only when it cares to. Mostly it lurks instead in the high prosceniums and fitted-rosewood ceilings, the broad granite staircases, the fitted-veneer mosaic archways, and as well in the fitted tuxedos and fur coats slumbering in walk-in closets, the strings of pearls and antique diamond cuff links biding time in their felt-lined drawers. Then comes one morning in the mail the engraved invitation, the stamped reply card, with boxes to check, indicating numbers of seats at two thousand a pop, or the whole table at ten grand.

Richard Abneg loathed the fucking galas. He persistently rented his tuxedos, from Eisenstadt & Sons on Fifty-fourth, a musty theatrical institution, with framed autographed glossies of celebrity customers dating back to Ray Milland. By now for the accumulated sum paid to Eisenstadt he surely could have bought ten tuxes on the installment plan. Yet there was a certain liberty in renting. One of the city's truths he'd let slip through his fingers, right about the time he scrabbled together a down payment on the Seventy-eighth Street three-bedroom, now beset with eagles. Liberty in renting, greater liberty in squatting. He'd prefer to regard himself as squatting in the tuxedo, if squatting expensively.

Georgina Hawkmanaji had sprung for these seats at the Manhattan Reification Society's annual fund-raiser, in the room any kid in the city would know as the one with the blue whale strung overhead. This evening being at least in part a tentative experiment in appearing in public together. Indeed, the society's guest list proved an intersection of their worlds, though by definition a gala was more the Hawkman's vibe than Richard's. His tux itched at the crotch. Better update his measurements in Eisenstadt & Sons' primitive card-file system. Or maybe Georgina had given him crabs—hah! At Hunter College he'd battled them for a shameful semester, his hairy body their dream refuge. Shaved his pubes and the fiends packed off to his navel and the tuft above his ass, a little allegory of urban renewal and displacement. Well, he'd pay that price happily, that was the humble truth. He hadn't fucked like this since his Hunter days, either, since Marta Tristman, with whom in a sweaty, fly-infested Barnard dorm one famous July he'd once managed intercourse five times in a twenty-four-hour period. The whole month had been a marathon, he and Marta aching and giggling in their pot haze and falling asleep for ten hours on her perfectly filthy futon.

Not since then for Richard Abneg, nothing like that, not if he was honest. The insatiable Hawkman debased herself elegantly to him night after night, in positions and attitudes the involuntary recollection of which he found overriding his senses throughout the days between. For instance, now, here, at the gala. At two that same morning he'd had Georgina swinging in a rope chair she'd had installed at his whimsical suggestion, hung from a bolted hook on her ceiling, her legs spilling over the sides of the mesh seat in which her splendid bottom lay helpless to his savage ministrations. The situation was wildly odd and erotic, Georgina's hands bound behind her as she rotated in the squeaking device, head turned courteously to one side, ever and absolutely the aristocrat no matter how fiercely he worked to defile her. He'd heard her murmuring as she climaxed, "The best, the best, the best . . ."

The best!

Remembering it, Richard's crotch throbbed, grew hotter, the itching more intense. He reached down once to work the tux's fabric loose around his testicles, then tried to refocus on the dais, the society's oxygenless sequence of self-congratulatory speeches, the elaborate buildup to this year's winner of the Dorffl-Huxley Medal, whatever. Only worse thing would be to be ensnared in their table's mummified conversation, wives with hair precariously piled, exposing necks burdened with bling, husbands all in identical tuxes, with nostrils nicely groomed, gray sideburns and temples expertly carved. Richard Abneg's hair lapped his ears—that might qualify as his last stand. *If I'm ever trimmed so precisely around the curve of my ear let me die in my sleep. Let the eagles pluck out my eyes.*

With his fork Richard nudged the remains of the two-thousand-dollar pork medallion and scalloped potatoes facing him like a cameo on his navy-blue plate, sickened at what the price tag could have bought instead. He didn't so much have in mind hundreds of cleft-palate surgeries to brighten the prospects of African orphans, no. Richard had begged off such mathematics long ago. Worlds couldn't be seen to balance as on a seesaw; their relation was tangential, irreducible, oblique. Dollars resided intrinsically here in Manhattan. Their transfer elsewhere was only a mystical wish, as unlikely as the wish to see the gala's overdressed constituency suddenly swap existences with the long-dead dolphins and ocelots and forest gorillas trapped within the museum's glass cases.

Two days before, the steward at Arc d'X had accompanied their young, coltish waitress back to Richard and Georgina's table, to explain in the place of the frightened, voiceless girl that the credit card company had not only refused Richard's card for payment, it had commanded her to immediately scissor the thing into pieces, a command she'd followed. Doing so was contrary to the restaurant's policy, but certainly Mr. Abneg could understand how in the girl's deference to authority she'd obeyed the voice on the telephone. The quartered plastic card had been returned to him with this apology, in a Ziploc bag. Georgina had laid down her own card to pay for the meal, and treated the episode as an endearing joke, tipping the waitress unusually well for her trouble. But Richard was still without a replacement from the company that had canceled the card, his last. Georgina's four-thousand-dollar subsidy of this glum evening could have repaired his credit rating. Richard's embarrassment at thinking this, the one thing he'd never say, only amplified his rage at Georgina's sacred obliviousness.

At that moment she touched his arm. Their neighbors at either side stared at him with polite, puzzled expressions.

"Darling," she said.

"Yeah?"

"I think it is your cell phone."

Well, duh. Logically nobody else here would have a snippet of Richard Hell and the Voidoids' "Blank Generation" seeping from their tuxedo pocket. Richard knew the ringtone typified his strategy, a strategy also tipped by his beard and the hair overlapping his ears, to festoon himself with harmless signifiers of his past selves. The problem was that through endless repetition the song had become inaudible to him, providing only a mild affront in certain mixed companies, like this one. He should have set it to vibrate, but was grateful he hadn't. Fuck it, he was *important*, the mayor's fixer, not merely here as the Hawkman's hirsute man-candy. Let their tablemates feel the urgency of his business, an urgency they'd never know in their own coddled existences, that was unless the sky truly fell on all of them. Still, Richard imagined, the Manhattan Reification Society and its constituency here would manage to shore up their bubble of bemusement, of obliviousness. Not-knowing being the supreme luxury. As for Richard, he bore the heavy duty of partly-knowing. So he flipped open the phone and stepped away from the table, raising up a faux-apologetic hand and scowling his seriousness to Georgina as he left.

He glanced, but didn't recognize the number. "Abneg," he said.

"Richard? It's Chase Insteadman."

The actor. The dupe. Richard was chagrined at how fond he'd let himself become. It felt unwise. "What's up?"

"It's about Perkus." The actor then launched into an anxious jumbled monologue worthy of Perkus himself, something to do with Chinese medicine and the purchase of rare vases on the Internet, all in the cause, so far as Richard could tell, of saying that Perkus had suffered a bout of the usual headaches and madness, only much worse than usual. The actor was working to enlist Richard in something.

Richard retreated farther from the nearest table, under the overhang of the room's mezzanine, into a dark corner behind a caterer's table, near a long display full of penguins bunched on floes of ice.

"You think he's going off the rails, huh?"

"That's putting it lightly. I don't think he's been within sight of the rails in quite a while. I don't know if he's taking care of himself, Richard."

"Well, I've known Perkus a lot longer than you. He's always going off the rails, that's his signature. He'll be fine."

"I'd personally appreciate it if you'd come by and see if you think this is the same sort of thing."

"You sound like a man with a plan."

"Is there a chance you'd meet me at Perkus's tonight?"

Richard found himself almost interested, the actor's panic was so tangible—tangible, that was, beneath his archaically dapper reserve. (Who did he think he was, William fucking Holden? He'd starred in a *sitcom*, for crissakes.)

To care for Perkus Tooth, as Richard would have to confess he did, was to worry. But Perkus was also a perpetual motion machine, on an uncorrectable course, and quite ferociously selfish, too. He'd built for himself a protective armature of text and recordings, an exoskeleton that, however maladaptive in a wider sense, got Perkus through his days as well as anything, say, the denizens of the Reification Society's gala had come up with. Perkus had his little orbit: burgers, coffee and pot, free DVDs, acolytes like the actor. There wasn't much Perkus needed in the way of help. That was, unless he lost his rent-stabilized apartment, or the planners of the Second Avenue subway issued an eminent domain seizure of Jackson Hole, and tore the restaurant down. At that, Richard might feel some need to intervene.

But the actor's panic meant the actor identified with something in Perkus's plight, whether he'd admitted it to himself or not. That *was* interesting. More so, at least, than the evening at hand.

"Sure, I'll be there, just as soon as I can get away from this other thing," Richard said. He liked leaving stuff vague, putting it all on a par, *items on the agenda of Abneg.*

"Great."

Great, but the call was too short. Richard didn't want to be returned yet to the gala table. Retreating farther into the shadows by the penguin display, nodding and winking to a member of the catering staff who eyed him suspiciously, Richard pulled up his e-mail on the phone and began scrolling for something that felt like important business. Nothing much. At least forty new Reply Alls on the tiger Listserv—now there was one ad hoc committee he should never have agreed to join! He twitched Delete until his thumb got tired, then quit. Then glanced up, conscious of some other figure beside him in the penguin gloom. The caterer? No. A woman, another shirking gala attendee punching buttons on a BlackBerry. None other than Claire Carter.

Fuck me. Richard felt a vertiginous return of the disquiet he'd had to shrug off earlier, his scorn at an affair full of those who liked to imagine they ran the city just because they took their tuxes from their own mothballs instead of Eisenstadt's. Now Richard's undertow of apprehension tugged the other way: What was *she* doing here? Was the Reification Society in some way important? Worth the time of the mayor's *real* fixer?

"Hello, Richard."

"Claire."

"I wouldn't have assumed this was your sort of cause."

He shrugged. "I'm slumming. What about you?"

"I'm presenting the Dorffl-Huxley Medal." Lit from beneath by the tiny screen of her phone, Claire Carter's gaze appeared more than usually unearthly and impassive. She'd always struck him as ageless, but there was no mistaking that she was younger than he was, a member of the generation of automatons, her blond cowl of hair as immaculate and slick as a helmet. He'd never even bothered to wonder if he found her attractive before this moment. His erotic voyage into Georgina Hawkmanaji had sexualized his whole world, that could be the only explanation.

"How cool for you," he said. "Since you rarely get to do that kind of stuff." He meant it sarcastically. Claire Carter likely cut a ribbon or handed over a medal twice daily.

She ignored him, focusing on her own scroll of e-mails. Presumably she'd been blind-cc'ed on all the tiger stuff he'd just been looking at.

"I'm, ah, just going to get back to my table," he said, needing to be acknowledged.

"Excuse me, Richard," said Claire Carter, as if it were she who'd been rude. She was infuriatingly immune to his attempted slights. "I'm about to go on. Perhaps I'll see you at the after party."

"I doubt it."

As he slipped into his spot at the table Georgina touched his wrist and smiled, conveying an imperial pride and curiosity that he should have been called away. The Hawkman obviously got her rocks off on Richard's air of civic stewardship. He decided to push it. "I've gotta go," he whispered.

"Oh, no, what's the matter?"

Richard had been relying on implication to carry him, but found he couldn't lie baldly now that it was required. Georgina seemed too ready to be afraid for him. "It's a friend, actually. Probably nothing."

"What friend?"

"Perkus Tooth."

"He's sick?"

"Maybe."

"I'll join you."

He shook his head.

"Is there some secret about Perkus Tooth I'm not permitted to know?" Her voice had begun to rise.

"It's not that."

"Then I'd like to meet your friend."

"Listen, I'll go and see what's up, and meet you at your place by the time this thing is over." He slid his hand up her thigh, teasingly high into her softness, near

159

the frontier of her wild private hairs. "You can meet him anytime, I'm not hiding him, for fuck's sake."

"If you leave here without me, Richard, please return to your own apartment, not mine."

Richard Abneg felt a humid lurch in his gut, as carnal scenarios he'd been nurturing at some barely conscious level flatlined. Too, he hadn't confronted whatever waited for him at his own bedroom window in many days, and was hardly eager to try for a night's sleep beside that nest of horrors now.

"Fine, fuck it, come along."

The Hawkman had the refinement not to gloat. Her knit brow demonstrated only concern for his friend's needs. "Should we leave now?"

"After the award," he said.

Claire Carter apologized on behalf of Mayor Arnheim, who wished he could be with them, a version of a remark Richard had heard her convey half a hundred times, she the human emblem of Mayor Arnheim's non-presence. Then, platitudes as inaudible to Richard Abneg as his own ringtone. When she turned to an account of the honoree's accomplishments, Richard felt himself relax: the project was familiar. Richard even had his own hand in it. The winner was Abigail Friendreth, heir to the Friendreth Securities haul. The childless widow had converted a condemned pre-war apartment building for the cause of abandoned dogs, espousing a domesticated beast's need to inhabit human surroundings, even if there were no human to live with it, or to love it; dogs should live in homes, not cages. Hence the Friendreth Canine Apartments, maintained by a staff paid out of some bottomless trust.

Richard's part? He'd had to fend off advocates for the homeless, who'd claimed Friendreth's dogs lived better than some of Manhattan's humans. The truth that it was the widow's money to spend wasn't sufficient to blunt negative hype, so Richard had played his usual conciliatory role, diverting some Friendreth tax write-offs to a few key charities while preserving the Canine Apartments' charming halo. Another truth, that Manhattan had more advocates than it had homeless, wasn't politic to say. Richard had barely spotted one in months, apart from the oddball working Perkus Tooth's back window. Speaking of which, Hawkman or no, it was time to blow this popcorn stand.

Such was Richard Abneg's state of mind in the hour before he glimpsed his first chaldron.

9

I was surprised, to say the least, when a moment after buzzing Richard Abneg into Perkus's building I opened the door to find Georgina Hawkmanaji there, a vision in heels and floor-length fur, head topped with a towering sable hat, cupping her lips and nose with her black dinner gloves, puffing steamily into her fingers. Richard stood a little behind, easily a head shorter than his companion, stamping to defrost his feet, the collar of his inadequate coat turned up around his ears—this was the same frigid day, remember, as my jaunt uptown with Oona—and when I met his eyes they bugged. He mimed a comic groan to say he couldn't help arriving with company. I wasn't sure I objected. The ostrich-woman presented a certain awesome spectacle to see wading into Perkus's squalor, a scent of treasure and foreign shores that seemed to warp the rooms around her and might be a tonic for Perkus to contemplate. If old books and songs and cheeseburgers couldn't turn his head from this obsession, maybe she would. At the very least she bulked our numbers, gave my intervention ballast.

I'd been the one to buzz them up from the street because Perkus was already glued to his computer's screen, tracking a couple of auctions culminating later that night. I'd arrived less than half an hour before and hadn't yet been able to budge him. For the new visitors, though, he sprang up and rushed into the kitchen and began fussing at his version of hospitality. Richard had already chucked their mountain of coats and gloves and scarves onto Perkus's sofa, making a soft sculpture of black and fur, and uncovering Georgina's black-clad, pear-bottomed curves as well as his own ill-fitting tuxedo, gut straining like a sausage in its casing of cummerbund. Perkus didn't blink, as if their costumes were natural, fitting the unnamed occasion. (After all, he wore a suit himself.) He only introduced himself to Georgina, then clicked a new CD into the player, some kind of guitar drone again, and began rolling a joint at his kitchen table, gesturing for us all to sit with him. The brand of dope was always Ice now, the only product Perkus wanted to smoke since his revelation. I'd opened his freezer for cubes to chill a Dr Pepper a few days earlier and found a backup supply instead, the dealer Watt's Lucite boxes all labeled with the same name. When I'd joked to Perkus about finding Ice in his freezer he didn't seem to get it, as though verbal puns were among things left behind in the brave new state of ellipsis in which he now permanently resided.

"Chase says you're getting into trouble," said Richard Abneg.

Only his mutinous eyeball revealed annoyance with Richard's question, or with me for the obvious betrayal. The rest of Perkus couldn't be bothered. "Never been better. I'm glad you're here, Richard. I've been eager to get you in on this." He was so certain of what he was about to unveil, it was a bit unsettling to consider

I'd pitted myself against it. As it happened, nothing in Perkus's mien evoked the desperation I'd promised Richard Abneg would strike him as worthy of his concern. Possibly intuiting my agenda when I'd asked to visit, Perkus was showered and shaved, had a fresh shirt on under his navy pinstripe three-piece, and socks covering his knobby toes, black socks that if they weren't clean didn't reveal their footprints in filth, the THC dust-bunnies swirling under the little side table where he kept his computer. Hair still damp so it lay combed back to emphasize his widow's peak, Perkus resembled a tiny agitated banker, no worse. He'd certainly bounced back from the cluster headache. Even seemed to be thriving in his new pursuits. I could tell Georgina Hawkmanaji was already charmed, and it threw me to memory of Susan Eldred's office, how he'd swept me off my feet.

He sparked the first joint and passed it to Richard, then went on rolling two more, fingertips busy like a mad scientist at a console. "You'll want to be freshly stoned," he announced to no one in particular, to all of us. Richard didn't hesitate, leaning back in his tux, now untucked and unbuttoned and unzipped in several places, bow tie dangling like a tongue, and drew in a lungful, seemingly certain he could conduct a diagnosis of Perkus in a state of intoxicated complicity. Then made as if to pass the joint to me, skipping Georgina Hawkmanaji, who sat erect and curious, pleasantly impassive, between us. Georgina reached out to intercept it, her glance at him only sweet, unreprimanding. She crossed her eyes and pursed her lips kissingly outward, rather than clamping them together, painting the rolling paper with burgundy lipstick before curtly coughing out her portion and waving the joint in my direction. I had to cradle her hand to steady it, then pluck the joint from her trembling fingers with my other hand. If the Hawkman hadn't smoked, I suppose I might have abstained, too, the gesture of a gentleman. But I'd called this curious company together, and I wasn't willing to be left behind wherever they were headed. I nearly finished the joint. Perkus used what remained to ignite the next, which we also devoured.

"Hurry!" said Perkus, now sweeping aside the smoking materials and dashing from the kitchen. Enspelled, we crowded around his small computer screen, Richard pulling up a chair and patting his lap to invite Georgina to settle there. I stood and craned over Perkus's shoulder. I wondered at Richard Abneg's uncommon passivity, but then I'd hardly equipped him to grasp what was wrong here. He'd have to gather an impression before leaping in with the caustic force I'd been bargaining for.

Perkus rattled his mouse, trying to wake up the dial-up connection. "I think there's about twenty minutes to go," he said. "Chase, would you turn up the music? Thanks."

"What is that crap?" said Richard distractedly. A veteran of Perkus's enthusiasms, he'd obviously begun readying himself for some esoteric disclosure on the computer screen. The music was, I hoped, the first clue that we'd migrated out of the usual range.

"It's Sandy Bull," said Perkus, not turning from the screen. He'd called up eBay, and now tapped Refresh, so the page blinked and began redrawing itself. "So, Chase's acupuncturist was onto something, actually, there *is* some kind of tonality that resonates with the limbic system, and Sandy Bull's guitar has got it in spades. You'll see, it opens you right up to the chaldron. Chase explained to you about chaldrons, didn't he?"

"Oh, sure," said Richard, unflappably mocking. "All about chaldrons and acupuncture and limbic tonality in spades. You know me, Perkus, that's some of my favorite stuff."

"Be polite," said Georgina softly.

"It doesn't matter," said Perkus breathlessly. "You'll see. You have to be listening to the Sandy Bull and high on Ice when you see the chaldron, at least for maximum effect."

"I'm in your hands."

Well, we were certainly high. The four of us seemed to throb there where we'd gathered in Perkus's dim lair, Georgina gracefully flung across Richard's lap, long legs and elbows askew, hands gathered beneath her chin, Richard grunting slightly as he shifted her weight around trying to get vantage past her shoulder, the building's radiators cackling and whining as they beat back the chill seeping through window seams, the four of us like the chambers of a collective beating heart, pulsing with expectancy despite Richard's congenital cynicism or my heretical doubt. Perkus, the fugitive ecstatic, had infected us with zeal again, the critic's illness. Who knew, there might be something limbic in the music as well, only I wasn't sure I knew what the word meant. Just at the instant this occurred to me Perkus got the finished image of a chaldron, all the pixels now smoothed around the edges, centered on-screen.

There were words bordering that screen, I suppose — text with a seller's description, the latest bids on the item in question, also eBay emblems and advertisements, sidebars and rulers, and a margin of Perkus's computer-desktop bordering those. None of it pertained, no more than the dun-colored plastic casing of Perkus's monitor, or the dusty volumes on the shelves behind the table where the computer perched. The glowing peach-colored chaldron smashed all available frames or contexts, gently burning itself through our retinas to hover in our collective mind's eye, a beholding that transcended optics. Ordinary proportions and ratios were upturned, the chaldron an opera pouring from a flea's mouth, an altarpiece bigger than the museum that contained it. The only comparison in any of our hearts being, of course, *love*.

Georgina Hawkmanaji leaned a little into the glow. Perkus scooted aside to invite her nearer, a gesture of munificence now that we saw what it was worth to have his privileged seat. How could we have come so late to this knowledge? Sandy Bull's guitar, which a moment before had been a nagging schoolyard taunt, some universal *nyah-nyah* whine, now catalyzed and enlivened our desire for the chaldron, become less music than a kind of genial electricity, a subliminal correlative to our longing.

It was Georgina who placed the first words into this higher silence, her voice the first out of our joint trance. I think Perkus and Richard would have agreed she properly spoke for us all, her femininity and reserve the only appropriate thing, her trace of accent, formerly laughable, now a nod to the powerful essence of *elsewhere* radiating from the artifact. Our voices would have been too gruff and shattering to offer up.

"It is beautiful," she almost whispered.

What were we going to do, contradict her? There was nothing to add. We were silent.

"A door," Georgina added, even more completely under her breath.

I misunderstood and, not wishing her to be embarrassed, said gently, "I adore it, too."

She shook her head, never taking her eyes off the screen. "I feel it is a kind of *door*, this chaldron. One goes *through* it, to another place. I think I shall never completely return."

I myself wasn't positive I'd glimpsed the other place the chaldron evoked, yet Georgina Hawkmanaji's term stuck. I couldn't doubt the chaldron as a *door*, even if I hung somewhat at that door's threshold. But any such minor reservation found no voice, for if I was certain of anything it was that though the chaldron must have somehow been *made*—whether by the hands of some individual human genius, a Mozart of the potter's wheel, or by a machine or assembly line, was therefore some sacred accident of commerce—its effect was to make constructed things, theories and arguments, cities and hairstyles, attitudes, sentences, all seem tawdry, impoverished, lame. *Door* was good enough. I didn't need to form a better idea, a better name. The chaldron had pardoned me of that burden. It possessed *thingliness*, yet was wholly outside the complex of *thing-relations* (these peculiar terms appeared spontaneously in my thoughts, I couldn't have said how).

"I . . . want to . . . *fuck* it," said Richard.

"Richard!" said Georgina.

He pretzeled his arms around her waist, fingertips tickling high at her ribs, beneath her neat breasts, and ground upward against her from his seat. "I mean it makes me want to make love to you, my sweet!" Georgina squirmed happily even as she reddened with shame, her eyes wide. The atmosphere was helplessly giddy, we all streamed in the chaldron's light, like hippies in some LSD mud puddle. "I mean it makes me want to dance with you, my darling Hawkman . . ." Richard lifted them both from the chair, still pinning her around her waist. They shimmied together to one side of us, swaying to Sandy Bull's droning chords like the last couple on a prom floor, Richard clinging to Georgina, growling endearments with his beard crushed into her long, bared neck. The room flooded with their animal presence, and when Perkus turned from the chaldron I anticipated his disapproval at this outbreak of the corporeal in his dusty mental kingdom. Instead he grinned at them, another blessing that seemed to emanate from the chaldron. I grinned, too. Seeing them dance, I thought of myself and Perkus cavorting, months earlier, and Perkus's mad declaration that I was his body and he was my brain. Now, immersion in the chaldron's light refreshed this notion of a gestalt identity alive among us. The chaldron's door might open to a place where selves dissolved and merged. Anything was possible.

Perkus ushered us ever so delicately back onto earthly ground. This was an *eBay* page, after all. "So, I put in a reserve bid of eighteen hundred dollars. As you can see, that was surpassed ten minutes ago. It's already up to twenty-six, and there's still more than fifteen minutes left."

"Two thousand . . . six hundred . . . dollars?" I blithered.

"Yeah, they've gotten a lot more expensive," said Perkus, not without satisfaction. Why shouldn't the value of such a thing slide upward—why not a hundred thousand, or a million?

Richard quit dancing. "What are you talking about?" he said. "You don't have the winning bid?" He and Georgina crowded back into their one seat, as if the music had stopped in a game of musical chairs.

"Nope," said Perkus.

"Can you afford to stay in?" I asked.

"Oh, I don't know," said Perkus with a sweet sadness. "I couldn't afford the eighteen hundred, but it doesn't matter. I won't win."

"We'll see about that," said Richard Abneg furiously. Spittle from his lips arced onto the computer screen. "Make a bid, Perkus. I'll pay you back when you nail it."

"Sure, sure," said Perkus. His own fever was expended, now that he'd guided us into the chaldron's embrace. He was the mellow proprietor of tantalizing glimpses, we the sideshow customers, looking for a slot for our nickels, frantic to widen the peepshow's aperture. "There's no hurry, the action's all in the last minute or so, you'll see."

"*Bid, bid,*" grunted Richard, almost jostling Georgina off his lap.

"Sure, pick a number, how much do you want to see them pay?" said Perkus. "There's a certain pleasure in driving the bids up."

"I want us to *win*," said Richard.

"Of course you do," said Perkus delicately. "I used to feel the same way." We'd all leaned in, seeking reconnection with what now seemed such a dire commodity, feeling breathless at what could be taken away from us, a thing we hadn't even known to want a few minutes before. Chaldrons circulated in a zero-sum system, and those not winners were certainly losers. How could we have been so naïve? It was as if for a sweet instant we'd forgotten death existed, and Perkus had had to break the news.

"What do you mean, 'used to'?"

"I've come to see that it's enough to put on the music, smoke some Ice, and, you know, bid on them. Just that feeling is enough. It gets me through, knowing that it's out there. Increasingly, I think that's what they're *for*. It's like an indirect thing, who knows if it would even work if you had it right in front of you."

"Screw that," said Richard. "I want one in my *house*."

"You don't have a house anymore," I pointed out.

"Perhaps Richard means *my* house," said Georgina, teasingly.

"Okay, let's give it a shot," said Perkus equably, his fingers on the keys. Now he was our arbiter of the reasonable. "How much do we want to go in for? I'm warning you, coming in this early we're probably just forcing the price up for the eventual winner—even if it's somehow us. But you'll chip in if we nail it, right?" He appeared to find our eagerness somehow funny. His temper recalled, of all things, Strabo Blandiana's bedside manner with his needles.

"Go in hard, stick it to them, make them think twice," said Richard. "Five grand. We'll pay."

"Go ahead, Perkus," I heard myself say. "Do it, please." Meanwhile the chaldron just went on shining its strange light on our absurd lusts, egging us on and shaming us all at once.

"It's a good investment," said Richard, in his crude way reading my mind exactly. "That thing's obviously worth ten times that much. If it's trading like this on eBay, for fuck's sake, imagine what it would bring if it were handled *right*. It should be for sale at Sotheby's."

Georgina Hawkmanaji gripped Richard's arm. "You wouldn't dare speak of reselling it."

"No, no, I'm just saying we should blow these small-time operators out of the fucking soup. Bid already, Perkus."

"I am." He entered the five thousand as a reserve bid, to be allocated in hundred-dollar jumps, so when he checked the bid list his on-screen name—Brando12— now appeared at the top, bearing the current leading offer of thirty-one hundred. Someone else lurking as we were must have already offered a reserve to the tune of three thousand. We all four breathed at a different rate, breathed at all for the first time really, since learning the ghostly ceramic was destined for some other hands than ours.

Only Richard wasn't satisfied. "*Why doesn't it say five grand?*"

"We don't want to pay more than we have to," I said, thinking it needed explaining.

"To hell with that. I want them to feel who they're up against!" As if to confirm that our rivals were simultaneously more pathetic and more expert than ourselves, the bidders we'd topped were named Chaldronlover6 and Crazy4Chaldrons. That they seemed to have no other life confirmed that we deserved the chaldron more, yet this was no consolation, for not to have a chaldron was to have no life at all.

"Spoken like a representative of the Arnheim administration," said Perkus. "Maybe you should have the other bidders all arrested. Then you can seize the chaldron as evidence."

"No," said Richard, with a husky note of urgency, even terror, in his voice, as if Perkus's taunts outlined some real prospect, one within Richard's scope. "This isn't for . . . them. This is for *us*."

"Yes, for us," said Georgina, almost singing the words. Her tone, balm to Richard's fury, was at the same time beseeching, a prayer or invocation over the battle we'd entered.

"We'll keep the chaldron at my place," I said, thinking ahead. "Seeing as how I live sort of at the midpoint of our various apartments. We can build some kind of special display case—"

"Perhaps this marvelous pottery ought to spend time in each of our homes," said Georgina.

"I don't think it's appropriate to treat it like a child in a divorce," said Perkus.

"We need *four*," said Richard.

"We don't even have *one* yet," said Perkus.

We spoke wildly, one eye on the clock ticking down on-screen, feeling invisible enemies crawling nearer to our prize with each silent digital heartbeat. Maybe the music and Ice were wearing off, maybe we weren't entirely worthy, maybe we weren't remotely worthy, anyway somehow the chaldron seemed to recede before us, no less potent but more distant, as if preparing us for goodbyes. The chaldron wasn't to blame, we'd hardly hold it against that pale magnanimous container, but it seemed to wish to ease us toward an inevitable farewell, toward heartbreak. We were going to have to try to pretend we were content to be just friends. Perkus refreshed the page. The current bid was at five thousand and fifty. Perkus checked the history—the bidder was Crazy4Chaldrons. The auction closed in four minutes.

"Who are these fucking fucks?" said Richard.

"Tax-paying citizens like yourself," said Perkus impartially.

"You don't know for a fact that I pay taxes," said Richard. "Raise on them, hurry up."

"Five thousand, one hundred?" I suggested.

"Fifty-dollar increments is Tinkertoy stuff," said Richard. "That's how I know we're going to kick the ass of these clowns. Make it fifty-five hundred."

"Neither of these two is going to win it," Perkus predicted, even as he entered the new bid. "One of the really big players will be coming in any second now."

Perkus entered the bid, and we stared as his computer reconstructed the page with agonizing slowness. By the time it resolved an image our offer was irrelevant, had already been surpassed. The present sum was six thousand. Then, six thousand and fifty, Crazy4Chaldrons pitting against Chaldronlover6, ourselves an afterthought, fans in the upper deck bellowing inaudibly at the on-field action.

"*Nooooo!*" wailed Richard.

"Excuse me," said Georgina Hawkmanaji. "I fear I am going to be ill." She lurched out of Richard's lap. "Where . . . I'm sorry . . ."

"Off the kitchen," said Perkus, bearing down on his keyboard.

Georgina teetered on her heels. Richard didn't glance away from the screen. I took the Hawkman by the elbow and steered her through the kitchen, aimed her at Perkus's small bathroom. She raised her hand in hasty thanks, then shut the door behind her before finding the pull string for the bare bulb overhead. It was too late to point it out. I returned to Richard and Perkus and the calamitous auction. They'd bid seven grand, now waited for the screen to confirm it. With less than two minutes to the auction's close, the top number came in at seven thousand and fifty.

"More, more!"

Perkus tried, heartlessly, I could see. The number swelled to eight, then nine thousand, our own bids never even reaching the top of the list, perhaps not even driving the others. We never held on the item's main page long enough for Perkus's rotten dial-up connection to complete the chaldron's image, so it now remained elusive, jittery, wreathed in chunky pixels as if fatigued by our strident love. In the bathroom behind us Georgina could be heard decorously puking, the intervals between heaves filled by labored snuffling breath and a kittenish, unself-pitying whimper, as if in time to what now sounded like a psychedelic banjo number from Sandy Bull.

"Keep it on-screen!" yelled Richard. "Quit checking their names! Who cares!"

"You'll want to see this," Perkus promised.

"Richard," I said. "Do you want to . . . go to Georgina? Do you want me to do something?"

He waved me off. "She'll be okay. She barfs easily, it's no big deal."

What Perkus revealed to us was the list of bidders, Crazy4Chaldrons and Chaldronlover6, not to mention Brando12's feeble contributions, now buried beneath two other rivals whose names were veiled beneath the words "private listing—bidders' identities protected." From this vantage we watched as this masked pair ran away with the bidding, topping one another by hundred, then two-hundred, then at last five-hundred-dollar increments, each time Perkus tapped Refresh. Our pretenses were shattered. We'd never been in the game, never been near to in it. The Hawkman's heaving tailed away, and we heard the toilet flush twice. The digital clock ticked out the fateful irreversible instant. The chaldron had sold for fourteen thousand dollars.

"They can't hide like that, it's un-American," said Richard despondently, his heart not in his own bitter joke.

"So, the way I see it, Crazy and Lover are fools like us, they've never been any nearer than bidding, never held a chaldron in their hands, never even been in the same room with one . . ." Perkus began this monologue absently, to no one of us in particular. Richard and I had fallen back, distraught and disenchanted, from the screen, while Georgina staggered back into our midst, breathing heavily, moistening her lips with her tongue, and Sandy Bull put down his banjo and picked up his guitar again. Losing the auction felt like soul-death, or at least a soul-shriveling, like the endorphin debt incurred by an all-night binge on Ecstasy, a trauma for which all among us but Perkus had been grievously unready. "They never win, so far as I can tell. Who knows, they may have my attitude, that the rapture is contained merely in bidding. One of those anonymous heavyweights always blows them out of—what did you call it, Abneg?—the *soup*, at the last second. Collectors with money to burn, they're surely stacking up warehouses full of the things, like at the end of *Citizen Kane*. And their computers are probably a lot faster than mine, it's a terrific advantage. I've heard it's possible to set up subroutines that fire off a bid at the last second, mechanically ensuring that no one else can top it."

I understood that Perkus was applying a balm, filling the doomy silence, offering us at once a whole menu of the rationalizations he'd concocted for staunching failure at these auctions. Perkus really was the expert here. Even his arcane eye seemed now to glance at wisdom that lay outside the boundaries of these rooms. I wondered how many chaldrons he'd communed with and lost.

"We should break into their fucking palaces and steal their treasure," snarled Richard Abneg. He seemed to have reverted to a squatter's paranoia, some feudalist rage predating accommodation to his role at the mayor's hand.

"The prices really have shot up," I said, stupidly showing off my slender familiarity in front of Richard and Georgina.

"It's exponential," agreed Perkus. "Who knows how many people are only just learning about these things?"

I gulped back revelation of my guilty fear: that we'd been bidding against Maud and Thatcher Woodrow, or Sharon Spencer, or others of their acquaintances with bottomless funds, all the result of my daft teasing insolence in mentioning Perkus and his chaldrons, during that lunch at Daniel. Countering that uncomfortable suspicion was the sense that the vision the chaldrons had opened to our eyes, however hopeless to define generally, was in part a glimpse of a world in which the Woodrows and Spencers, their empire of inherited privilege, of provenances and exclusions, was exposed as ersatz, fever-stricken, unsustainable. The object seemed to explode in our hearts with a wholeness that disproved Manhattan's ancient powers, though those towered everywhere around us. A chaldron was fundamentally a thing beyond, or beside, money. Yet we'd done nothing but hurl cash at it, as if pitchforking hay into a furnace. Everything disproved everything else. The Hawkman might have been the one to vomit up the contradictions, but she'd done it for all of us. I felt ill.

I wasn't alone. We all wavered in the apartment as if aboard a seasick vessel. Perkus drew out four clean glasses and filled them with tap water, which we sipped thankfully. He switched the music, stuck in a Rolling Stones CD, *Some Girls*. Mick Jagger's cartoon raunch was another balm, beguiling us into a version of our worldly selves we could live with, the song "Miss You" calling up synesthetic recollection of discotheques, harmless sniffs of cocaine, skinny asses in gold lamé, stuff to make us grateful the chaldron hadn't translated us out of our discrete and horny bodies just yet. Perhaps a teasing glimpse of that possibility was enough, perhaps Perkus was right that we wished to be window-shoppers, not buyers, not yet, of the purifying apparition. Richard clutched Georgina to him and they danced again, with charming formality, as if suddenly aware they'd come bursting into this scene in a tuxedo and party dress. Then, keeping with the black-and-white motif, Perkus tore open a package of Mallomars, unveiling rows of nestling breast-like cookies, and we fell on them like grateful scavengers, even Georgina (though I did now spot a small pink crumb of vomit on her pale cheek), collapsing their marshmallowy tops to gunk in our back molars, causing our heads to swim with sugar.

We returned from the kitchen to the meager comforts of Perkus's living room, but his computer screen had defaulted to its saver, the branch-stranded raccoons, and none of us were troubled that one twitch of his cursor, or two, could feasibly unshade the light of a chaldron again. We were resplendent enough in the memory of the last one. And now, restored from the ordeal of losing the auction by pop songs and chocolate cookies, could afford to realize we were substantially *in the black* for the whole of the experience. We knew so much more than we had an hour before, never mind that it was nearly impossible to agree upon, or even to say clearly, what it was we knew.

"Perhaps you will understand when I say I felt undressed." Georgina gulped in embarrassment having blurted this, and for an instant I feared she'd flee the room again. Instead, divertingly, she whirled from Richard, putting her long arms in the air. It seemed in another moment she might whirl her dress off over her head.

Wishing in my genteel way to give sanction and cover to Georgina's observation, I found myself testifying, speaking in tongues. "For something so warm . . . it casts a sort of . . . brusque . . . watery . . . shadow . . . over so much else . . . that I took for granted . . ."

"Despite sounding like a retarded Wallace Stevens I actually get you," said Richard. "That thing's the ultimate bullshit detector—"

"Sure, and what it detects is that *your city's a sucker*, Abneg." Perkus spoke with startling insistence, but his tone wasn't needling. "Your city's a fake, *a bad dream*." This was somehow the case, the chaldron interrogated Manhattan, made it seem an enactment. An object, the chaldron testified to zones, realms, elsewheres. Likely we'd lost the auction because one couldn't be imported here, to this debauched and insupportable city. The winners had been rescuing the chaldron, ferrying it back to the better place.

"You think I'm going to get defensive, you guessed wrong," said Richard, watching the Hawkman sway to the Stones' "Just My Imagination." "I wouldn't defend anything right now, except, you know, *your right to say it*, and that with my life, Comrade Tooth."

"What . . . are we going to . . . do?" I said, gullible enough for anything. Was a chaldron a beacon of revolution, was that what Richard signaled in calling Perkus *Comrade*? One if by land, two if by sea?

"Make coffee," said Perkus.

"We're going to get our hands on one of those goddamn things, that's what we're going to do," said Richard.

Georgina Hawkmanaji had wound down, and curled her long body like a greyhound's on the heaped-up coats and furs on Perkus's sofa. She tucked her knees up between her arms, bracelets clicking together, her head slipping to one side as she began to snooze, revealing the curve of her neck, the pulse there. Richard and I were nicely energized, though, even before Perkus put mugs of fresh coffee in our hands. The evening, though filled with wild purpose, was slanting toward the shape of our old all-nighters, those corrosive binges that were only weeks behind us yet seemed a forsaken oasis, one island in time now revealed as a stop on our way to another. Perkus industriously rolled joints of Ice and changed the music again, Van Morrison's *Veedon Fleece*, something

Georgina could nap to and a transitional bridge (we didn't need to ask to be certain of this) back to the limbic strummings of Sandy Bull.

Richard hovered over Georgina, leering like a villain. "Look," he said, as he ran his hand over the astonishing contour that began at her long ribs and narrow waist, to the jut of her wide hip, his hand less than an inch from the fabric of her dress. Georgina slept on, languid breath rippling her upper lip. "Such an amazing shape. How can anyone ever sit in a meeting, or make a plan, or add up a column of fucking numbers, when there's a shape like that somewhere out there, a shape like that with your name on it, coming to get you? Where did it *come* from?" Richard didn't have to say what we were all thinking, that the curve of the Hawkman's bottom made us think of the chaldron, that we'd hopelessly muddled the lust for one with lust for the other. If we indeed were a kind of gestalt entity, Perkus the perennially overwrought brain, myself the trite glamorous face, then I suppose Richard Abneg was our raging erection.

"So, the next auction closes at midnight," Perkus informed us casually. "What I'd suggest is we hold off for another twenty minutes or so, the impact is usually best when it's nearer the finish line. Now that you see what we're after we don't have to fidget around, we can just reside with it, dwell in that place—"

"Are you saying we shouldn't bid?" asked Richard, with an edge of alarm.

"No, no, we'll bid. You get closest to the feeling in that instant when your name tops the list. But, you know, afterward we don't have to get so . . . frantic." Perkus was a master of the order, walking initiates through their graduation ceremony in advance.

"I wasn't *frantic*," said Richard, lapsing in his vow of undefensiveness.

■

Perkus had taken care of us, in every way so far cradled us through the bewildering night. How did I reward him? I began to cover the whole event in denial and, filled with the special arrogance of denial, tried to turn the tables, to take care of Perkus as I'd vowed to do. My tough-love intervention: I clung to that scrap of agenda in my confusion. I wanted Richard Abneg to understand why I'd enlisted him, and that even if a new religion or Marxist plot had been founded on Eighty-fourth Street tonight, Perkus was still crazy and helpless and needed our help, needed a reality check. I reminded myself that only that morning I'd discovered Biller on the Eighty-sixth Street pavement, selling Perkus's books.

"So should we talk about Brando?" I said.

"What?" said Perkus.

"Tell Richard about Marlon Brando, how you, you know, realized he was destined to save New York City from itself."

"What the fuck are you talking about?" said Richard.

Was it my imagination, or did the vigilante eyeball in Perkus's head rotate laser beams of hatred at me for this betrayal? I somewhat hated myself, but pushed on. "Perkus told me Brando was the key, but I didn't quite understand it at the time. Brando and Gnuppets."

183

"What does that have to do with anything else?" said Richard, suspicious of us both.

"Maybe Brando owns a chaldron," I said lamely.

"You have no idea what you're talking about," said Perkus. He leaned back in his seat, legs crossed ankle-over-knee, bare fringe of leg hairs exposed beneath his pants hem, held up a joint of Ice and his lighter, ready to bring them together but not doing it yet, and despite leaping into a verbal assault, kept his physical comportment cool, apart from that eye. "You're just staggeringly useless, Chase, to understand what's right in front of you. You're even *part* of this culture, albeit a foolish part, and yet you can't see it, or won't. The breadth of awareness that's embodied in a figure like Marlon Brando, the aspects of American possibility that he's tasted on all our behalves, well, that wouldn't probably interest you. The fact that for you he's maybe only some kind of laughingstock, that says it *all*, doesn't it, about what flourishes in this world of commodities and cartoons. And about what's exiled, made into a safe caricature, or just outright expunged and forgotten. Brando's a figure of freedom, just as much as that chaldron we just saw, yes, sure, and fuck you totally, Chase."

"He's not a laughingstock to me," I said, unable to keep a little hurt from my voice. Brando and I were members of the same guild, after all. "He's our greatest living actor, everybody knows that."

"He's not an actor," said Perkus with stubborn ease.

"He's not *living*," commented Richard, but we paid him no attention, not yet. We spoke in full voice, giving no consideration to Georgina Hawkmanaji's nap.

She slumbered on in our midst, tucked pet-like atop that mound of coats, sublimely oblivious.

"I agree with all of what you say." There was a stubborn part of me, too. "I just hoped you'd explain to Richard about how Brando was coming out of exile soon, to overturn all this plastic stuff. You said he might run for mayor. You wanted me to get in touch with him for you."

"My mistake," said Perkus stiffly. "I'll contact him another way."

"Listen, guys, not that Marlon Brando wouldn't make a fucking excellent mayor," said Richard, chortling in his beard. "But nobody's contacting him anytime soon, because he's kaput." Richard reached out, took the joint and the lighter from Perkus's hands, and ignited it. "Big fat old corpse, loads of sad tributes, few months ago. Anyway, Arnheim would crush him."

We stared at Richard.

"Dead. He died. Not my fault. Hey, aren't we missing an auction, fellas?"

"Marlon Brando isn't dead," said Perkus, in a voice shredded with fear.

"Sure he is, even Chase knows, he's just too polite to mention it, aren't you, Chase?"

I had no idea either way. But this wasn't what I wanted for Perkus. Our intervention, barely begun, was already too harsh, our reality check too real. "A world without Marlon Brando in it," I began, "would be a far poorer place . . . so I prefer to believe he's alive. Of *course* he's alive."

"Who's alive and dead isn't a matter of belief," said Richard.

"I remember now, he lives on an island . . ." I went on, desperately, "Trinidad-in-Tobago . . . or . . . Mustique . . . ?"

"Everybody lives on some island," said Richard. "Marlon Brando lately inhabits the Isle of the Dead. You could look it up."

"What makes you the authority on who's inhabiting what island?" said Perkus, now summoning fury to cover his trepidation. "You've been looking over your shoulder for months, you only act like you know more than the rest of us, but you're bluffing."

"Bluffing about what, exactly?" Richard Abneg's voice tightened, as it had earlier, when he'd reacted with real discomfort to Perkus's jibe about arrests and interrogations. I couldn't say what was at stake between the two of them, yet I felt the room almost seesaw.

"What's happened to this city," said Perkus. "The tiger, for instance. You can't even catch a tiger. For fuck's sake, you're *eagle-hunted*, Abneg."

"Those eagles and that tiger have absolutely nothing to do with each other."

"Why should I believe you even know?"

"The tiger is . . . not what people think it is. I'd explain it to you, but then I'd have to kill you."

The feeble joke seemed to belittle Richard Abneg's usual ominous aura without quite dispelling it, and so restored a measure of equilibrium to our little company. Perkus's point hadn't been refuted, only bargained with. Now Perkus turned in scorn to the computer keyboard, began rattling. "Good idea," I said, in cheerleader mode. "We don't want to miss our window of opportunity . . ."

I moved into the kitchen and swapped the Van Morrison for Sandy Bull, skipping ahead a few tracks, to where I figured we'd left off. Bull was playing his banjo again, this time a bluegrass version of *Carmina Burana*, calling up a vision of Disney dinosaurs transversing a primordial wasteland. Perfect. The music offered a sense of purpose, of destiny claimed. I wished to lure Perkus back to fugue and, for that matter, join him there myself. Returning, I entered a cloud of expelled Ice fumes, Richard bogarting the joint mercilessly. I plucked it from his lips and passed it to Perkus, who accepted it, puffing distractedly as he typed. "Here," he said at last, his tone petulant. The new screen began to resolve.

It was my first green chaldron. (Like sexual positions or travel to distant locales, I'd begun semiconsciously cataloguing seminal moments, breakthroughs.) With Richard, I leaned over Perkus's shoulder and let it seep into my wide-open eyes and heart. Music and smoke swirled to form a vertiginous cone or funnel of attention, as though we lay at the bottom of a deep well and the chaldron had peered over the top to gaze down at us. The top bid was already sixteen thousand dollars. Three-quarters of an hour remained.

"Christ, look at the price tag on that one," said Richard.

"The green ones are rarer," said Perkus. "Incidentally, Marlon Brando is alive."

"Move," said Richard.

"What?"

"Get up," he said. "Get out of your chair, let me."

"We can't bid," said Perkus. "It's over my PayPal limit. Let's just enjoy this one for what it is."

"Step aside." Richard shucked his tuxedo jacket onto the floor, fumbled off his cuff links and thrust them into a pocket, then shoved his sleeves up carelessly and plunked himself in Perkus's chair and commandeered the keyboard, tackling the Internet as if it were a basin full of sudsy dishes. Perkus passed the joint to me and dithered into the kitchen, his marionette limbs twitching.

"Not only is Marlon Brando dead," Richard muttered into the screen, "but we're going to land one of these mofos tonight. Get me the Hawkman's purse."

"Sorry?"

"It's got pearl bead things, it's right under her ass."

"Are you *sure*?"

"She'd want us to, Chase. Believe me, she can afford it. Go!"

Under Richard's guidance I dug out Georgina's neat, pale-calfskin wallet and, skirting the temptation to learn what wonders I'd find browsing there, handed him her American Express card. The Hawkman never stirred. Richard, typing madly, flinging oaths at the recalcitrant dial-up connection, brought up a fresh window, and fit Georgina's name and digits into online forms. View of the chaldron was blocked, yet I was sure I could still sense its vitality leaching around the screen's boundary. I snuffled at the soggy last inch of joint, waiting. Perkus still hung in the kitchen. Then Richard switched back, and it awed us again. Perkus, perhaps alert to the intake of my breath, snooped around the doorway's edge, sullen but tempted. I watched as Richard, under a new name, UpYours1, committed twenty-five thousand of the Hawkman's dollars to purchase of a vase, that ceramic that was more than a ceramic and yet also so much less: a rumor, a chimera, a throb, a map. We had ten minutes to learn whether it was ours. I had a feeling if it was that it would be living, necessarily, in Georgina's penthouse apartment.

"Now, look." Richard conjured up another screen. "We're online, we don't have to wonder about these things." He narrated aloud from Marlon Brando's Wikipedia entry, *"Final years and death . . . notoriety, troubled family life, obesity attracted more attention than his late acting career . . . earned reputation for being difficult on the set . . .* Okay, skip all that, here, *On July 1, 2004, Brando died in the hospital . . . age of eighty . . . the cause of his death intentionally withheld . . . lawyer citing privacy concerns . . . cremated, ashes scattered partly in Tahiti and partly in Death Valley—"* I leaned in over Richard's shoulder, wanting anything now but to confirm it and strand Perkus in a Brando-less landscape, yet inescapably curious. At that moment Richard hurried back to the auction, to see how Georgina's thousands were holding up—or rather he tried to, and the computer screen went dark. "Fuck!" he yelped.

We turned to find Perkus leaning out his kitchen's back window, a chill wind whistling in around him. "What's wrong?" he asked when he pulled his head in and slammed it shut.

"Your computer crashed or something," I said. "What are you doing?"

"I thought I heard Biller. You had more than two windows open, didn't you? Well, that's what crashes it."

"Did . . . you hear . . . what Richard was—"

"What?"

"Never mind." We stood back while Perkus hurriedly restarted the computer and chased a new connection. Richard, beside himself at the delay, crashed around in the kitchen, igniting another joint's tip on the burner of Perkus's stove. Sandy Bull's banjo urged evolution forward. Richard returned in a new cloud of smoke, waving the smoldering Ice in my direction, and I partook, but maybe we were stoned enough already, or too stoned, yes, unmistakably we were horrendously stoned, our mission curdled, our new Coalition of the Chaldron singed at the edges. Was it worse to tell Perkus that Brando was dead or not? I couldn't decide. Richard Abneg's distress was tangible, too, his gloating dynamism sapped by so many sweaty compromises with eagles, tigers, mayors. A dozing Hawkman no longer prize enough, despite any resemblance. The green chaldron was not only more costly, it was ruining us, exposing our underbellies, whether we were privileged to pay its ransom or not. And now there was no Marlon Brando to redeem us, only chaldrons to salve loss of chaldrons. Perkus brought up the page. The auction bragged a bid of twenty-six thousand. Richard had been topped. Three minutes remained. I felt a green stab in my heart.

Unspeaking now, Richard scrambled to bid. He got it up to thirty-four thousand, a heroic labor of blunt hairy fingers, tooth-grinding jaw visible even through his beard. His white shirt was widely stained under the arms and stank fiercely. The effort took two minutes, more. At forty-eight seconds another veiled bidder drove it to thirty-six thousand, then another, with five seconds to spare, took the jewel at an even forty grand. I think we all three groaned as if gutshot, but it was well covered by Sandy Bull's thrumming music. Georgina Hawkmanaji then punctuated our stunned silence with a long whining exhalation, gleaning disappointment in her sleep. I examined the page, the image there, for any trace of psychedelic vigor I could draw on for repair, but nothing reached me now. Perkus, likely familiar with the effect, spared us, reaching past Richard's numbed hands to click on a box and close the window.

The convocation found its end there, human fragments amid the ashtrays and crumpled rolling papers, Mallomar crumbs, shed evening clothes. The three of us left Georgina in the dark with the screen-saver raccoons, and retreated to the place where we used to thrive, a month or so before, around Perkus's kitchen table. Perkus changed the music, to a band called Souled American, and I didn't know whether it was my imagination or the band's special distinction that they sounded as unspooled as we felt, the bass player and guitarist and singer each absently mumbling their contribution seemingly with no regard for the others.

■

It was after Perkus fished out a dusty, half-filled bottle of single-malt Scotch, twelve-year-old Caol Ila, something Richard had left behind some ancient evening before I'd made their acquaintance, and we began sipping the amber poison from juice glasses, that Richard, uncorking some deeper material from himself as if in reply to the booze, began his disquisition on the tiger. At the start his tone was as diffuse as Souled American's music, so that I almost might have imagined he was singing along. "It's pretty goddamn funny that everyone calls it a tiger in the first place," he said. "Even those of us who know better have fallen into the habit . . . a testament to what Arnheim likes to call the power of popular delusions and the madness of crowds . . ." Perhaps this was Richard's way of consoling us with distraction, as Perkus had before. Yet his words took on the urgency of a confession. "That it's a problem I'd never deny. I mean, it wasn't my fault, but it's become partly my responsibility to deal with it, that's fine, it's the kind of thing I'm supposed to be good at . . ." Neither of us had spoken, let alone challenged him, yet it was as if Richard were negotiating, to persuade not only Perkus and myself but whole invisible balconies of skeptics. "When the Transit Authority began researching ways to build the Second Avenue line, you see, they brought in the engineers who'd built the Channel tunnel, in England—I mean between England and France. They'd built these machines that went underground and burrowed through bedrock. They'd had good luck with them, but ours went a little out of control—"

"You're saying the tiger is a *machine*?" said Perkus.

Richard nodded glumly, and sipped from his juice glass. "A machine, a robot, that's right, for digging a subway tunnel. The thing is, in Europe they had two of them. One started in France, the other in England." He raised and spread his hands to model this for us in the air in front of his face. "Two identical machines, they'd never met, but they went underground and began digging toward each other." His hands progressed downward, toward a meeting point at his chest, clawing like moles at the imaginary earth. "Day and night, just digging that tunnel for months, these two woebegone creatures moving ever incrementally closer—"

"What happened when they met?" I asked. Déjà vu clung to Richard's description; I felt as if I recognized it from some baleful fairy tale or allegorical medieval painting. Our evening had drifted into another register, a fatigued postlude, the air in Perkus's apartment impossible to clear of stale smoke and unnameable regret. Each of us leaned back in his chair as if not conversing but enacting a kind of disconsolate séance, Richard's voice punctuating our trance like a deathbed dictation.

"Well, they were . . . retired, I suppose that's the word for it, when the tunnel was completed. It would have been too expensive to drag them out, so they're buried there together, deep under the ocean, off to one side of the passage. We made a mistake, though. We cut corners when we commissioned our own project. We only had them build a single machine, just digging in one direction, with nothing coming from the other side. I guess the thing got lonely—"

"That's why it destroys bodegas?" asked Perkus.

"At night sometimes it comes up from underneath and sort of, you know, ravages around."

"You can't stop it?" I asked.

"Sure, we could stop it, Chase, if we wanted to. But this city's been waiting for a Second Avenue subway line for a long time, I'm sure you know. The thing's mostly doing a good job with the tunnel, so they've been stalling, and I guess trying to negotiate to keep it underground. The degree of damage is really exaggerated. Anyway, a certain amount of the buildings it's taken out were pretty much dead wood in the first place—"

"That's how urban renewal works," Perkus mused. "You find an excuse to bulldoze stuff so that the developers can come in. Richard's career in civic service is founded on that kind of happy accident."

"Fuck you, Tooth."

I worked to put my mind around all he'd told us. "So the mayor's cover story is that this . . . machine . . . is an escaped tiger? I can't understand why anyone would accept that."

"It's not a cover story, or maybe it is now, but we completely backed into it. After last year, you remember when that coyote wandered across the George Washington Bridge and took up residence in Central Park, and you know, with all this recent talk about displacement of species, including, yes, okay, the fucking eagles, blah blah blah, I guess some old lady saw it and told the news that it was a tiger and the image just colonized the public imagination. It happens that way sometimes, we don't control all this stuff, Chase, no matter how Machiavellian you might think we are."

Was it possible Richard Abneg was somehow mistaken or misled? Might he be unwittingly propagating a cover to a cover, a story he'd been handed himself? "Have you ever actually seen it, Richard?" I asked.

"I've seen footage."

"The *Daily News* had footprints on page three the other day," said Perkus distantly. "This cop was standing in the tiger's footprint, this huge thing with giant claws, it was like ten times longer than the cop's shoe."

"Not footprints, *footage*. Any footprints are a total hoax."

"Doesn't seem like you people have a lot of ground to stand on, calling things hoaxes," said Perkus, refilling his glass with Scotch. His wild eye wasn't wild. It maundered instead.

"I don't know why I ever try explaining anything to you two," said Richard affectionately. He yawned without covering his mouth. "I hate to be the party pooper but I think it's time to extricate the Hawkman from this slough of despond."

I felt a slippage toward vertigo, as though if I allowed Richard Abneg to leave too soon something would be lost. Not my intervention, I'd given up that scheme. But after all we'd come through, we'd arrived at a sort of summit between us, a summit in doubt, even dismay. Who knew how, the name of the treasure we'd sought and lost already seemed hard to recall, the fact of it violently unlikely, yet in that weird quest we'd passed through our everyday delusions, to a place of exalted uncertainty. Perkus, though he might not wish to admit it, had surrendered Marlon Brando. His last layer of cultural armor laid aside or at least suspended. Richard, relinquishing his sinister pretense of confidentiality, had clued us in about the tiger. That he'd done so made me love him. No one pitted themselves against my cherished illusions here, but I felt they should. I needed to carve my way into Perkus's and Richard's good faith by surrendering up some secret, too. I feared to be untouched or unseen.

"I don't . . . I can't really remember Janice Trumbull," I said aloud.

Richard had projected himself from his chair, into the other room. Over the loopy music I heard him rustling in the mound of coats and Georgina, heard her dopey murmur as he got her on her feet and into her heels. I looked to Perkus. He'd passed out where he sat, nose tipped back, lips parted as he silently snored, his juice glass hovering above his banker's-pinstripe lap like a bucket swinging in a well. I freed it from his damply clinging fingers and set it on the table.

"I mean, I feel like I remember falling in love with her, but somewhere after that I can't remember anything at all."

From the other side of the wall came sounds of panting and then chortling, as if in the course of helping the Hawkman into her coat Richard and Georgina had fallen into a clinch and begun dancing again, or perhaps making out.

"Sometimes I can't even remember what she looks like."

The music ran out and for an instant all was calm and silent in the apartment except for a hint of cheeping, like a bird's peep, presumably from Georgina. Involuntarily I pictured Richard running his hands inside her dress, goosing a quick orgasm from her with his clubby fingers, a wake-up call. Hearing this, or imagining I did, I pined for the wrong woman, the clandestine part of my own life. Whatever the facts, after another instant the two of them, fully restored in their evening's glamour apart from Richard's missing bow tie, scooted arm in arm through the kitchen and out, Richard delivering a farewell bow to me as if at the close of a theatrical performance, Georgina only widening her eyes slightly, and parting her lips. They were gone, my confession unheard.

∎

A draft whistled in around the kitchen window frame and I shivered. The digital clock on Perkus's stove read 3:33. I stood and reached for the overhead light's pull string, darkening the kitchen, then helped Perkus gently to his feet, my arm cradling his thin bony shoulders. He shrugged me off. I trailed him into the living room, lit only by his screen saver's treed raccoons, the couch now cleared of the bed of coats, except for mine. Perkus sat again at the computer and clicked up his Web browser, calling up the dumb beep of digits, then the electronic squirt-and-wheeze of a portal's opening. I was terribly afraid Perkus would summon another auction. I doubted I could stand it. But no. He scrolled into his browser's history and refreshed the Wikipedia entry on Marlon Brando. So he'd been listening after all, had only ostensibly stuck his head out of his window looking for Biller to avoid giving Richard the satisfaction of knowing he'd heard. He scrolled impatiently through the page, squinting close to the screen in the dark room, his thin figure in his chair like a lighthouse on some storm-racked shore. He'd been holding his breath, and now he exhaled deeply, ending, to my surprise, in a satisfied snort, even a bitter little chuckle. He pointed and I read over his shoulder. *The rumors of Brando's death circulated in the summer of 2004 and again in early 2005, in both instances triggering a wave of mourning and tributes both on the Internet and in major media outlets* ... At the top of the page, a boxed notice read: *The truthfulness of this article has been questioned. It is believed that some or all of its contents may constitute a* hoax ... *Elements of this article may be deleted if this message remains in place for five days* ...

"You see," said Perkus. "Richard doesn't know everything."

I didn't want to have to try to understand all I'd seen tonight, this perhaps least. Perkus shut down his computer and scuffed through his bedroom's French doors with weary finality. He waved without turning, a lighthouse now crumbling into the sea. "Make sure the door locks when you go." I took my coat and went into the dark kitchen. The rising wind still whistled through the kitchen's back window. I saw that it remained open, just a crack, and as I moved to shut it more firmly I now spotted a black electrical extension cord rising up across the sill, and threaded outside, to drape down into the courtyard. There, below, was Biller. He squatted in a corner of the courtyard, sheltering from the wind, wearing a shiny silver down-stuffed parka with a fake-fur-lined hood, different from the black wool coat he'd worn just this morning, when I'd handed him a hot dog and twenty dollars and confiscated *Obstinate Dust*. (Perhaps I'd financed the new coat.) The cord from Perkus's window trailed to a small white laptop computer, its screen brightly lit, though I couldn't make out whether that screen showed text or images or what. Biller, his back to the window, breath misting in steady bursts from his nostrils, pale moons of his fingernails themselves like ten floating cursors protruding from the darkness of his fingerless black-wool gloves streaming on the laptop's tiny keyboard keenly, unhesitatingly, with all apparent expertise.

■

November 14
Dearest Chase,

I've got some good news and some bad news. Ha ha ha ha ha, imagine please my convulsive laughter. (I read this opening line aloud to Zamyatin, who happens to be running on a treadmill in the room as I type this letter to you, and he found it as hilarious as I did. Moments like these are all we have to savor anymore, please don't begrudge them.) The good news, surely, you will have read in the newspaper and perhaps even seen on some cable news station (except I can't for one instant imagine you bothering with cable television—last I recall you were searching for your remote and failing to find it, then accusing the housekeeper of hiding it in a drawer or throwing it out): we survived the space walk to repair the tile damaged in Keldysh's botched module launch. Better than survived, the space walk was a thrilling success. I myself was even the heroine of the incident, and

Northern Lights will carry on, to drift unmoored in orbit for another day, or month, or however long until we are rescued or choose to destroy ourselves by a deliberate collision with the Chinese mines, which I suspect could happen any minute now, especially if I am judging the Captain's and Keldysh's moods correctly—but pardon me, I was telling you the *good* news! Ha ha ha ha ha ha ha.

Suffice to say no straws were drawn because no one wanted to see Sledge anywhere near the air lock; our dour Captain asserted the leadership he's lately so much abrogated, tapping myself and Keldysh for the walk, Mstislav and Zamyatin for on-board mission guidance, and inventing some kind of make-work for Sledge which did or didn't get done, something back in the Green-house, something to do with Mstislav's doomed reclamation project involving the leaf-cutter bees, those expert pollinators. (We've been ignoring our bees.) I find myself unwilling to bother with the technical stuff, which I'm certain makes your eyes glaze over. Such labors as the forty-eight hours that the walk's mission preparation entailed are wearisome enough to get through, let alone describe for a bored boyfriend. Anyhow, preparation's a poor word. Nothing had or could have prepared myself and Keldysh for the sensations that overcame us upon ejecting from the air lock. Essentially, of falling, like Wile E. Coyote, off a cliff, into a bottomless well of darkness and silent velocity.

We're soaring atoms, Chase, that's what orbit consists of, the inhuman hastening of infinitesimal speck-like bodies through an awesome indifferent void, yet in our cramped homely craft, its rooms named to recall childhood comforts, with our blobs of toothpaste drifting between our brushes and the mirror, our farts and halitosis filling the chambers with odor, we've defaulted to an illusion of substance. Inside *Northern Lights* we've managed to kid ourselves that we exist, that we're curvaceous or lumpy or angular, bristling with hair and snot, taking up a certain amount of room, and that space and time have generously accorded a margin in which we're invited to operate these sizable greedy bodies of ours, a margin in which to reside, to hang out and live our pale, stinky stories. The space walk destroyed all that. (No wonder Mission Control has tried to keep this from ever being necessary.) Oh, the lie of weightlessness! We only feel we're floating because we're forever falling, as in an elevator with no bottom floor to impact. And so, inside the elevator, the human party continues oblivious, the riders flirt and complain and mix zero-G cocktails, or chase bewildered zero-G leaf-cutter bees. Outside the ship, our consoling elevator's walls dissolved, Keldysh and I were two specks falling forever, specks streaming down the face of the night. Ourselves plummeting downward to the gassy blue orb, the gassy blue orb also plummeting at the same mad rate away from us.

Well, after clinging to our telescopic guide-rods in a riot of metaphysical horror for upward of twenty minutes, our eyes locked on each other's while Zamyatin and Mstislav gently beckoned in our ears to explain, please, why we weren't moving a muscle to make the needed repairs to the tile, Keldysh and myself completely mute, we finally managed to bluff ourselves into taking one step into the void, and then another, until like brain-locked automatons we began executing the commands we'd rehearsed. The repair consisted of little beyond the clipping of a hangnail of tile and the application of a sealant (think: Krazy Glue) to the gash the misdirected module had carved into the Den's upper sill. One crumpled signal dish was judged irretrievable; we detached it and let it spin off, down toward the minefield. I think it got through, the reward being, of course, immolation upon reaching the atmosphere—a small blessing of fire sent down in your direction, my Chaseling. My heroism, such as it was, lay in persuading poor Keldysh, who after seeing the dish spiral away, pooped his drawers and reverted to panic, clinging to the tile in a bear hug, to free himself from the ship's exterior and let the guide-rod telescope him home to safety. I had to whisper into Keldysh's private channel for another five minutes or so, the others on the ship all stymied, waiting for us to budge, before I got him to go.

Now, love, for the bad news. A few days after the space walk, Mstislav, in his dutiful way (he's keeping the whole place running!), scheduled checkups for both myself and Keldysh, a routine caution we'd generally neglected for too long. We both came up clean for effects from the walk, but Mstislav seemed puzzled by my white-blood-cell profile. We ran a few successive days' counts, just to be sure we had a meaningful sample, Mstislav trying not to say what he feared he was on the trail of, me gamely offering various bogus notions of female physiology reacting differently to the Greenhouse's oxygen deprivation, joking that Mstislav had gone too long without a lady patient. Eventually our efforts devolved to a sit-down for the ever-humbling medical questionnaire, Mstislav narrating me through a series of self-exams, a drill we'd practiced on the ground but hoped never to see put to use. None of us much like dwelling on the slow erosion of our bodies in this environment, bone-density decay, the pale starved skeletons we've substituted for our old selves. I liked even less what Mstislav guided me toward: acknowledgment that I'd been managing an uncanny pain in my right foot's arch for weeks, at least. Do you remember I said I was having a problem with cramping? That cramp was a tumor, Chase. Funny, huh? Oh, you should have seen the looks on the faces of the Russians, and Sledge. Even Sledge. I think they realized too late that I was a sort of mascot here, their woman. The whole mother-earth thing, unavoidable. Now a good-luck charm with cancer. Not to say, you know, that we don't all still hate one another.

That was yesterday. I'll know more soon, but I doubt we'll be able to much delay a leak to the media, and I wanted to tell you before you learned by other means. (Oh, this is going to be a mess, this is going to be hell.) Behold the onset of my flinty tone. Along with so much else, a soft-tissue sarcoma may apparently drain the exultation from one's prose.

Remember (please remember) the Chinese garden at the Met, that unlikely bit of outdoors indoors? It shouldn't feel so expansive, yet somehow it does. My favorite place in Manhattan, I think. Remember that we went there together, Chase? Did I already ask this?

One of our first days in New York, we were so tired and drunk on sex and the sense of recognition of those early days of our love, and we meandered into the Met, not with any plan, and the suffocating heaviness of those endless European oil paintings made us drowsy and we escaped (I never remember the path exactly, always have to rediscover it) to the Chinese Garden Court, and were nearly alone there, and anyway the gurgling of the water and the rustling of the grasses, the bamboo, seemed to cover any human sound, and we lay down there on that stone that had been chiseled out and shipped from its ancient source and no guard troubled us and soon with our heads tipped together on that dark slate we fell coolly asleep, dozed for who knows how long. Do you remember, Chase? I remember, too, when we woke, and turned to look into the pool beside our heads, and you thought you saw a fish, a little black darting goldfish-type fish, but it was only the reflection of my glasses, a black shimmering reflected shape that had separated, for an instant, from the reflection of my head and from the rest of my glasses, and seemed a separate darting thing, a fish, or a tadpole. Please remember Chase remember please remember, I adore you, my terrestrial saint, my angel wandering avenues, I'm your cancerous angel adrift,

Janice

Then came the weird pervasive chocolate smell that floated like a cloud over Manhattan. At first you thought it was local, you'd passed an unseen bakery, smelled something wafting, chocolate-sweet, stirring cravings and memories both. You'd scan the area, find nothing, continue on, but the smell was with you everywhere, with you in your apartment, too, though the windows were tight. On the street again, you'd see others glancing up, sniffing air, bemused. And soon confirming: yes, they smelled the same thing. It had been downtown, too, someone said, quite nervously. Another said even in the subway. Lexington Avenue sidewalks, normally muffled in regular hostility, broke out suddenly in Willy Wonka comparisons, one passerby saying, I thought of a sundae, another replying, No, syrup on crepes. Or, a tad melancholy: I haven't wanted ice cream like this in forty years. Someone said that the mayor had already given a statement, enigmatically terse, maybe hiding something. The chocolate cloud tugged Manhattan's mind in two directions, recalling inevitably the gray fog that had descended or some said been unleashed on the lower part of the island, two or three years ago, and that had yet to release its doomy grip on that zone. Theories floated in the sweetened breeze, yet no investigation could pin a source for the odor. And yet the scent *was* chocolate, ultimately yummy and silly. It brought merry chocolate comparisons out of everyone remarking on it. The mayor's comment, when you heard it repeated on the news, included as fine a joke as had ever crossed those forbidding lips: he'd called it *the sweet smell of success*.

The chocolate weather came, too, as a moment of relief in a strange, hunkered, hungover time, winter killing. We'd already woken one November morning to the first snow, an overnight inch that glazed every sidewalk and windshield, all the twenty-four-hour markets hurrying to raise plastic tents around their outdoor goods, the citrus and bouquets, the rest of us digging in hallway-closet-floor shopping bags for last winter's gloves and scarves, or else shelling out for on-the-spot sidewalk-stand purchases of same, abandoning hope that the portents of warming were real enough, this year, to thwart this local early-onset frost. No such luck, the wind slapped around the tall corners, tilting citizens into stoic silence under daylight's hastening exit. On the amok calendar's wheel Manhattan found itself damned again to holidays and influenza. So a chocolate mystery reminded us that we all dwelled in Candyland, after all. It was a news item the exact size of our childish wishes: So much for the deliberate terrors advancing on our shores, let alone our complicity with any wider darkness. We were, it turned out, a whole island of crimeless victims, survivors of nothing worse than a cream pie in the face, which, hey, tasted pretty good!

Perkus and Richard and I avoided one another for a week or so after our night of frenzied losses, but I called Perkus on the third morning of the chocolate benediction over the city. That day I was demented with guilty grief, for Janice Trumbull's cancer was the lead feature on all the tabloids, and qualified to run above the fold in the *Times*, at least the War Free copy I'd happened to find abandoned at Savoir Faire, and read over my breakfast cappuccino (which the pervasive scent kept tricking me into thinking was mocha, a beverage I hated). I rang Perkus's phone at one thirty, late enough, I hoped, not to wake him no matter how late he'd been up or what he'd been up late doing—I didn't plan to guess at any possibilities. I was counting on Perkus to divert me from Janice's story, and if I had to tread softly around his own tendernesses, I was willing. Certain words I'd censor. Perkus groaned, though, as if I'd roused him from murky dreams of that item I swore to leave unmentioned. Or else was marooned in his old land of sawdust and sighs, a cluster headache. But he didn't complain, and I didn't ask. He didn't invite me up, either, instead suggesting we meet for a Jackson Hole burger at three.

I slid into the booth, Perkus already there, nattily dressed, hair damped down, face shaved, putting on a good face in a setting he so often treated like an adjunct of his own kitchen, feeling free to lurch in red-eyed, hair like straw. At that hour the restaurant was empty, and the waitress, a zaftig girl with a funny combination of bangs and retro cat-woman glasses topping her sweet bored expression, scurried right over. Perkus raised his finger to preempt her asking, and said, "Two cheeseburgers, deluxe, cheddar, medium-rare. You want a Coke, Chase?"

"Sure."

"Two Cokes."

She obediently scribbled and departed, not speaking a word. Perkus's air was of command and distraction, and I hadn't wished to interfere, but it was a perverse choice for me to join him in one of those mammoth burgers, let alone the slag of fries that came with a deluxe, at this hour on this particular day. In only three more hours I was to be treated to dinner at the restaurant of Le Parker Meridien, a privilege I'd have done nearly anything to wriggle free of. My presence for an evening, or at least the duration of an elegant dinner, had been auctioned off as a premium, at a benefit for one of Maud Woodrow's charities, I couldn't anymore recall which. The night of the auction I'd sat in a ballroom with Maud, at a table with Damien Hirst and Bono and Andrew Wylie, a champagne night, spirits frivolous and self-congratulatory, the named celebrities mostly bidding on and winning one another's offerings, whether fifty-thousand-dollar artworks or the promise of a mention in a song or a film. The whole absurd ritual seemed an excuse for the names on the benefit committee to impress one another with largesse, and I'd believed to the last instant that Maud intended to spare me, to win the dinner with me herself, but, cruelly, she hadn't. I'd gone instead, at the price of fifty thousand, to the Danzigs, Arjuna and Rossmoor, names unknown to me yet reputedly iconic on the social register, names denoting not accomplishments nor even celebrity but rather stewardship of the oldest money, wealth like sacraments, wealth to make Hirst's, and Bono's, even Maud Woodrow's, look silly. The Danzigs, I heard explained, had a staff of two hundred. Staff doing what? I was foolish enough to ask. Staff just keeping things running, was the vague reply. Hiring and firing itself, training new operatives, the several layers between the Danzigs and the world. The Danzigs' money was a kind of nation unto itself.

(That I'd been an item sold at auction, like the chaldrons, only now struck me.)

This was six months earlier, and ever since then I'd been in denial that the dinner in question would actually need to be enacted. How could the lordly Danzigs really care to make an evening's worth of small talk with the child star, the astronaut's beau? Wasn't the point just to win the auction? But no, they were eager. One member of their two hundred, their chief social secretary, I suppose, had contacted me, a few days before, to confirm the dinner reservation. The stupid day had come at last. Even worse, the news of Janice's cancer would surely have reached the Danzigs—they'd likely been briefed over breakfast—ensuring cloying sympathies, over sorrows I didn't relish elaborating. I could, at least, arrive hungry. It would be a little peculiar to down a half-pound fist of ground beef as an appetizer. Anyway, the chocolate odor was very much with me, even as I'd stepped inside this emporium of greasy smells, not much of a complement.

Perkus didn't mention it. He spent a while squinting and shaking his head, even beat on his temple once with the base of his palm. His rude eye careened after our waitress, but she'd gone into the kitchen. I wondered again, had Perkus been dragged down into cluster? Anyway, had I been summoned here for a reason? (I was eliding the fact that I'd called *him*.) I'd been relieved, I thought, to find Perkus not on a mission, myself not a conscript. Yet perhaps his urgency was addictive, and I felt its absence now. My annoyance mingled in a sorry anticipation of dinner with the Danzigs.

"Do you smell it?" I asked finally.

"Smell what? Our meal?"

"Do you have a headache, Perkus?" Maybe his sinuses were blocked.

"No."

"There's a chocolate smell everywhere in the city right now. Has been for days. You must have noticed."

"Oh, that," he said, smirking unhappily. "I guess I have heard it described that way, but no, I don't smell any chocolate. For me it's coming in more as a kind of high-pitched whining sound."

"What are you talking about?"

"Just what I said, Chase. For you it's a chocolate smell, for me, a ringing in my ears. On and off for three days now. Can we just forget about it, please? It kept me up practically all night last night."

"But nobody's talking about any *sounds*," I protested. "Everybody's smelling something sweet, either maple or chocolate . . ." I fished the folded-up section of the *Times*, still in my trench-coat pocket. "It's all over the papers . . ."

Our waitress had arrived, to plant tall Cokes on the mats before us. "You smell it, too?" she said brightly.

She leaned in, smiling at us in turn as she whispered, "It's kind of making me sick, actually."

Perkus squirmed in his seat, crossed his arms tightly, and cinched one knee over the other, knotting himself. "Thank you," he said painfully, staring at the Coke.

"Sure . . . your burgers will be right out."

"*Cheese*burgers."

"Oh, sure. Don't worry, I wrote it down right, Perkus."

He waved her off, and pulled the newspaper section toward him across the booth's countertop, tracking the headlines with his good eye, the other uncooperating.

"You know her," I said wonderingly. For my own part, I couldn't have said whether she was the waitress we always had here or I'd never seen her before. The invisible are always so resolutely invisible, until you see them.

"Sure, yeah."

"You *like* her." I understood it as I said it.

"Whatever."

"No, really, Perkus. Is she—do you want to ask her out? On a *date*?" I enjoyed at least glimpsing his taste. The waitress, in her funny glasses and skirt, made a charming target of Perkus's nerve-wracked attentions. She was womanly enough, if he scored, to snap his spindly femurs like a panda browsing in bamboo.

"Lower your voice."

"Is that why we come here so much?"

He sneered. "I've been coming here a *long* time, Chase."

"Speaking of long times, when did you last have a girlfriend?"

He tried to ignore me, stuck to the paper. "So, let's see about this chocolate odor of yours—"

"No, really, how long?"

He looked up now. "I'm serious, Chase, *shut up*. It's so easy for you, you don't have any idea—" He almost hissed. "I don't want to talk about it *here*."

I showed both palms in surrender. "Okay."

"*And don't you talk to her.*"

"Okay."

I smoothed my expression, but beneath that mask I marveled at the whole thing: How frustrated was he? I thought of something Oona had said, just a few nights ago, when while suspended in her slippery limbs in some kind of interlude or afterglow I'd mentioned how Richard Abneg and the Hawkman had been so grabby, so febrile in their formal dress, that evening in Perkus's rooms. "My theory is you can never over-estimate how much sex the people having sex are having," Oona said. "Or how little sex the people not having sex are having." "The rich getting richer?" I suggested and she'd said, "Yes, and the healthy, health-ier." Then I'd said, "And the—" and she'd put her finger to my lips.

So, how frustrated? Was the Jackson Hole waitress a slow-cooking crush, or only something flitting across his distractible radar? She looked approachable, but I wondered if Perkus knew how to get from here to there. Then I thought of his zany corralling of me, outside the Criterion offices: Perkus knew how to come on. Unless it was that he only knew how to come on to a sort of boyfriend, a gormless disciple like I'd turned out to be.

So did that make Perkus gay? I didn't think so. What hints I knew didn't make him *anything*.

Perkus had been flipping the newspaper's front section over and over again, passing, I assumed, from the chocolate-smell story to the news of Janice's diagnosis, his forehead in a scowl, his lips a determined line. Now he pinned some item with his finger, and looked up. That I'd be made to rehearse the spacewoman's tragedy for Perkus was exhausting, though not as dreadful as contemplating that subject tonight, with the Danzigs. But as it turned out that wasn't the item Perkus had in mind. He rotated the paper to my view. A front-page photograph I'd glossed over showed a polar bear atop a largely melted-away chunk of glacial ice, drifting in a calm open sea, its muzzle raised to howl or bellow at the photographer, who from the picture's angle must have been cruising past on a cutter's deck, or leaning out of a low-zooming helicopter's window. The photograph was cute until you contemplated it. The scribble of ice on which the bear perched was pocked, Swiss-cheesed with melting, the sea all around endless. The bear already looked a little starved. Judging from that ice, it might not have time to starve completely. The War Free edition really depended on how you defined *war*.

"You see that?" Perkus fingered it again so I wouldn't fail to understand. "I *am* that polar bear."

I just looked.

"That bear is me, Chase."

His deadpan look, with even his AWOL eye attendant, defied interrogation. The polar bear was another of Perkus's concerted enigmas: Was this about a doomed species, or was he trying to say that the bear on ice allegorized the existential condition of one such as he— one who, when all others detected an enticing aroma of chocolate, heard instead a high ringing sound? Or was the bear just a description of his dating life, a rebus reply to my question? *Here's my distance from my last girlfriend, and from the prospect of my next*, he might be saying. *As distant as that stranded bear is from the solace of another bear.* Then I recalled Perkus's nebulous rage at Richard Abneg, when we last discussed Marlon Brando: *What makes you the authority on who's inhabiting what island?*

Or was I overthinking? Had Perkus simply awoken, in his usual fierce sudden way, to the plight of bears adrift on ice? Now I would have given anything to hear him talking about Brando or Mailer, *Echolalia* or *Recalcitrant Women*, the invisible black iron prison of our perceptual daydream, or the difference between epiphany and ellipsis, between Chet Baker and a Gnuppet with a trumpet. It was as though I was being punished for each and every time I'd tried redirecting him into a healthier obsession. The only thing less cultural than that ceramic-whose-name-I-did-not-wish-to-pronounce was an arctic bear. I tried to picture Perkus volunteering on some Greenpeace ship, scrubbing tar off a penguin. It was pretty much like wishing he was another person entirely, or dead.

So what did my dull Occam's razor do with the conundrum? I decided my friend needed to get his ashes hauled. A dilemma suiting my own strengths, for once. I could play the tutor, even if I'd have to keep the lessons subliminal to the student. I vowed to set Perkus up. And where better to start than with the large perky waitress whose hipster glasses frames seemed a confession of her susceptibility to nerd celebrities, even shopworn ones like Perkus Tooth. She already knew his name, which had to mean something good. When she arrived with our deluxes I took them from her myself and set them at our places, and said, "What's your name?"

She seemed to know more than his name, knew to glance at Perkus for a kind of permission to speak. He looked sourly into his plate, x-raying his fries, and so she stumbled answering, "I, I'm Lindsay."

"There's nobody here," I pointed out. "You can talk to us for a minute—" I knew how much Perkus wanted me to stop. It was the same amount that it was impossible for me to stop. My project had become compulsive, my premise self-confirming. The more Perkus twitched and recoiled the more he proved his need of an erotic ambassador. "We're harmless, Lindsay, don't worry."

"Oh . . . sure . . ." Lindsay was a little confused.

"How old are you?" I asked her. I gestured at the empty space in the booth beside Perkus, but she didn't dare. "Have you ever seen a Montgomery Clift movie?"

She brightened. "I saw *The Misfits*!"

You're seeing them now, I wanted to tell her. *We're hoping to enlist you into their company*. Instead I said, "Did you know Montgomery Clift was buried in Prospect Park?"

"Can you bring some mustard?" said Perkus stonily.

"Oh, right, you *always* have mustard, sorry!" Off Lindsay scurried to find some. I suddenly imagined what it might have been like for Oona Laszlo, in her glue-girl phase, apprenticed to a little tin god of guerrilla criticism, one not yet tempered by a decade of broadsider's block. Even tempered he was obnoxious.

"Hey, Colonel Mustard," I whispered. "You've really got her dodging bullets. Lighten up."

Perkus only gritted his teeth at me, a cartoon of impotent rage. Lindsay returned with a ramekin of yellow mustard, and then gamely ignored the rotten vibes, which were as undeniable between us as the chocolate smell (unless, that is, you were immune to chocolate smells). "You're . . . Chase Unperson, aren't you?"

"Insteadman, yes, that's me."

"Sorry—Insteadman." Lindsay slapped her forehead. She was shaping into one of the all-time apologizers. Perkus, meanwhile, was having a kind of fit. It was lucky his mouth wasn't full, or bits of beef and bun would have flumed through his nose. "Un—person," he sneezed in bitter hilarity. "Chase *Unperson*!" He still hadn't looked at Lindsay directly, or what would pass for directly in his ambidextrous gaze.

"Funny," I said, trying to absorb and neutralize Perkus's hostility. Lindsay, I could see, was only going to take anything in the air between me and Perkus as her fault. Too late. The default deference in her role as waitress, given the obvious distress in Perkus, would prevail. She shrunk away, giving me a funny helpless smile. Perkus and I were left to the travesty of our steaming mounds of food, spoiled under clouds of chocolate and ill manners, spoiled, really, under Perkus's outright and indignant fury. It helped nothing that we'd been there, in our regular booth with our regular order, so often before. Hemmed in by ghosts of our more innocently garrulous selves, the days of the discovery of our friendship, early September, felt like years ago now. We gnawed the cheeseburgers despondently, under the regime of all we couldn't say.

I looked on Perkus, for the first time, as a creature formed of anger. That was how I'd characterized Richard Abneg to myself, but I'd reserved the judgment for Richard, blinding myself to the essence the two had in common. In truth, there was anger enough to go around. I knew I should ask myself (Strabo Blandiana, in one of his post-needle talks, would have gently insisted I do so) why I made my world out of these kind of persons. Who else struck me as angry in my vicinity just lately? Oona Laszlo, with her acid flippancy. I ached for her. We'd planned to meet up after my dinner with the Danzigs—Oona liked to be more accidental, but I'd persuaded her to be my reward for getting through the evening.

Lindsay surprised me. As she set down our check—Perkus had signaled to her for it even as he wolfed the last bite of his burger, and I'd only unpacked and rearranged my own—she said, "If you guys want to party sometime—"

"Oh—" I began.

She tucked one of the restaurant's cards under my place mat. "Here's my number. Or just, you know, look for me here." I shouldn't have been surprised at all. She was a waitress, after all, on a fading afternoon, and, in the *Of Human Bondage* way of waitresses, she'd grab any ticket out.

Perkus slapped down a twenty, really slapping the table, punctuation to his mute wrath. Lindsay and I both looked up shocked. "Pack up his burger to go," said Perkus tightly.

"Oh, that's okay—" I began.

"*For Biller.*"

"Oh."

On the sidewalk, Perkus turned from me, his glove-less knuckles buried in the pockets of his suit, almost, it appeared to his knees, the white sack containing my leftovers tucked into his elbow. The chocolate wind howled, the early winter still so fierce, the sky darkening at four. I drifted after him, trying to demonstrate we were together on the sidewalk. He muttered, "You're something, Chase, you're really something."

"It's better than not even trying, Perkus. She wants to 'party' with us. Who knows?"

"She thought you wanted her, Chase."

"No, no." I shook my head, but he didn't see it, pressing on ahead toward the corner of Eighty-fourth, toward his building. I didn't really want to keep him outside without a coat for long, but I hurried after. "She could tell you liked her, Perkus, anybody knows that a friend often plays the go-between—"

"Anybody knows *nothing*, Chase. You don't see yourself, you don't see the way women cast their eyeballs at you like a kid shooting marbles on the sidewalk."

At least I'd sparked some irate brilliance in him, I thought, instead of the moribund bovine cheeseburger-chewer he'd been inside Jackson Hole. Perkus couldn't be so intimidated by his waitress, it didn't seem possible.

"You've got women falling out of open windows, out of trees, you've got women on the *moon*, Chase. You don't have any idea how it might be different for me. You actor, you utter *unperson*."

"Now, that's not—"

"How can you fail to see your hostility toward me? I mean, Montgomery Clift? Please."

Hostility? I'd been thinking I'd just uncovered Perkus's. Would I always be just one insight away? Insight was an onion, I doubted there was anything but layers.

"I've been trying to help you," Perkus said. "And this is the way you repay me. Well, you're a hopeless case anyhow. I wash my hands."

Perkus helping me! At least I understood that everything was inside out and upside down. Rather than argue with him like a couple going through a breakup on the street, I elected to silently agree. I was a hopeless case.

"Do you ever look in the mirror, Chase?"

"Sure," was my idiot reply.

"How convenient that you'd mention Montgomery Clift to her. You *resemble* Clift, you know. *Before* the accident."

Perkus somehow managed to make this seem a warning, or even a threat. In his view every Clift, I suppose, was scheduled for a face-rearranging encounter with a windshield or dashboard. There being no happy medium between innocence and jaw-smashing, ruinous disenchantment. Now I felt my own hostility around me like a burred skin. Also I tried on my despair. For Perkus, I was cast permanently as fool. Maybe I was one, I'd had to consider it before. Yet I'd always preferred to think

I was a harmless fool, at least. Who knows, maybe I'd been lasciviously poaching on my friend's burger waitress. I might be that irresponsible, it seemed to me now. In point of fact I was reeling, rudderless, without a compass, high on phantom chocolate and infidelity, ignoring the phone, voice mail piling up, in deranged avoidance of the Janice cancer crisis. I ought to be stifling tears at a press conference somewhere, giving evidence of my loving support in this crisis. Perkus was surely right to be mad. I must be acting out.

We stood at his entrance, in a penumbra of stubbed butts from the previous night's sidewalk smokers. A single half-full martini glass stood perched on the curb. Inside, a tuner was refurbishing Brandy's piano, the plinked notes groaning sharper as he tightened its bolts. I offered Perkus the card on which Lindsay had scribbled her digits. He didn't budge hands from pockets, only glared. He wouldn't even go for his key until I was safely away, and so we hovered in stalemate, me in a coat and scarf, Perkus shivering in his suit jacket, its two buttons pathetically done up, covering nothing. The white sack containing my burger—Biller's burger—rustled in the crook of his arm.

"See you later," Perkus said at last.

I nodded at that sack, making small talk. "So how is old Biller, in this cold?"

"He's fine."

"He could always build a bonfire out of your books," I joked.

"Actually, I think Biller got a bed in a rooming house," said Perkus, with a dryness evidently restraining sarcasm. "He's not selling books on the street anymore, he got a job on the Internet."

"I've seen him at his computer. He looked like a real wizard."

"When was that?" he said, scowling. Our fight wasn't over. I was still under suspicion of all sorts of skulduggery—rustling waitresses might be the least of it.

"Some night," I said, not wanting to specify. "Out-side, in your little alley."

I saw I'd only fueled his suspicions. Yet I also saw him shiver. Though I wore a coat, I too felt the wind ripping at me. Actually, I felt horrendous, like I wanted to lie down.

"Don't you have anywhere to be, Chase?"

"Not for a couple of hours." I might as well have begged for an invitation inside.

"Then go home," he said acidly.

"Of course, sure, hey, uh, what are you doing for Thanksgiving?"

"Nothing, out of respect for Sacheen Littlefeather." He abruptly pulled out his keys and went through the door, taking my cheeseburger with him.

Some member of the Danzigs' staff arranged a limousine to pick me up at my apartment. The driver needed to have my doorman ring me twice, as I'd fallen into a toxic slumber with the early nightfall, my rooms dim as midnight, and I'd lapsed back to sleep between the ringings, then staggered out into the lobby, through the frigid margin of outdoors, and into the backseat of the feverishly overheated limousine. There I wiped my running nose on my coat sleeve and watched the snail trail of smear saturate into the coat's black wool, wondering how long it had been since the coat had been drycleaned and what layers of filth its dark elegance might be bearing around, feeling myself a skeleton or ghost, a being of no substance draped in a grimy cloak. By the time I found myself delivered to the lobby of Le Parker Meridien, I felt bullied, bruited about by staff and handlers, like David Bowie in *The Man Who Fell to Earth*, an incomprehensible film Perkus had weeks before insisted I watch, a treatise on luxuriant self-pity that now felt terrifically relevant. I said I thought I was expected at Seppi's, the French restaurant off the hotel lobby, but the concierge told me I was expected at Norma's instead.

"Isn't Norma's just a breakfast place?"

"It's open for you tonight, sir."

Ironically, I hadn't shaved or showered, failing to do for billionaires what Perkus had done on account of a hamburger waitress whom he couldn't even bring himself to speak with—that is, primp. Or maybe it wasn't ironic, since Perkus, in his feeble and conflicted way, was trying to make an impression, while I was just collecting my due, going through my regular paces. I saw everything in light of Perkus's contempt, helplessly heard my self-loathing narrated in his scorning tones.

So the Danzigs had paid to have the place to themselves, impressive, I suppose, except it had probably cost a tenth of what they'd spent to secure my presence. The windows of Norma's were shuttered, a dim light glowing from within. Escorted inside, I found Rossmoor and Arjuna already seated at a large round table in the restaurant's center, spotlit like the set of a one-act. Each nodded and smiled as I approached, and neither rose.

"Mr. Insteadman," said Rossmoor Danzig. "Truly an uncommon pleasure." Rossmoor, leaning into the table's light to reach for my hand with a chubby paw that extended from what appeared to be a maroon pinstriped pajama top, at first seemed a giant cherub, a scruffy grimacing infant in gigantic black-framed glasses and mad-flowing hair. Massive as his head was, his hair and glasses made it look small. Like me, the cherub needed a shave. Taking that flabby hand in mine, I felt woozy, dislocated, still stuck in my nap and even further behind, in my sidewalk conflagration with Perkus, his burger-girl's phone number still nestled in my pocket, my tongue thick with afterthoughts. I'd need to collect myself, find some way to summon my charm to the occasion—a measure of charm, if not fifty grand's worth.

"The feeling is mutual," I said robotically. "You've . . . ensured we'll . . . have the time to ourselves."

"I don't like eating at restaurants that are *open*," he said. "We've got a four-star chef in our basement, we never need visit a restaurant at all. But there's a specialty here I thought might amuse you." Rossmoor Danzig pronounced this word *spesh-ee-ality*. "I really do hope it will. It amuses me very much."

Rossmoor Danzig wasn't young, much less a homunculoid infant. He was old, his skin parchment, wrinkled and powdery, his magnified orbs eggy in their scrotal sockets, yet his barge of hair seemed naturally, even obscenely, thick and dark, barely salted, the stubble on his chin also mostly dark. He did wear, as I got a closer look, pajamas, top and bottom. They were beautiful pajamas, but still. Figures flitted at my vision's edges, outside our table's golden circle: waitstaff working after hours, slaves of weird opportunity. I wondered what they made of us. I had to remind myself it wasn't midnight or three in the morning, but an ordinary dinner hour. All around outside this derelict brunch place Manhattanites dined, and waiters worked. Due to my haze and the winter light I was marooned in time. I couldn't keep from wishing we were at Seppi's instead, or some other restaurant teeming with ordinary happenings. Trapped alone with the Danzigs, I felt claustrophobically remote from life's mainland, like, yes, a polar bear adrift on an ice floe. (I couldn't quit rehearsing my blown encounter with Perkus. I wanted a retake on our afternoon, a chance to say I understood everything he felt.)

"Ross doesn't eat anything except breakfast," Arjuna Danzig explained painfully. Rossmoor's wife seemed designed to compensate for his oddity, dressed with elegant simplicity, black high-necked dress and pearls, hair upswept, eyebrows sculpted into arches as persistently surprised as her eyes were infinitely weary, her olive skin a ghost of the exotic beauty her name had seemed to promise, all the rest of her defeated, folded neatly in its sarcophagus of makeup. Rossmoor was a desiccated toddler, age floating unfixed; Arjuna's fifty-some years were pinned to her like a police-artist's sketch, or an archaeologist's reconstruction of flesh on an unearthed hominid's skull. Years were all she had. She bore them patiently. Well, years and billions. I'll admit she was a woman I might be seated beside at a party and flatter with half-assed remarks for hours, then not recognize next time we met. Now, in my state, and with no one to turn to apart from those waiters skittering through the outlying gloom, I felt reliant on Arjuna Danzig to protect me if the gargoyle in pajamas turned feral.

"At a certain point, Chase, I determined I didn't have to eat anything I didn't care to," said Rossmoor. His self-regard was like a grand pipe organ visible in the air between us, which he played with shameless gusto. "And I don't care to eat anything but breakfast. I eat it three or four times a day. Once a year I do a weeklong grapefruit-juice purge, again, simply for the pleasure it brings me."

"That's enough of that," said Arjuna.

"Arjuna doesn't countenance mention of poop," said Rossmoor, merrily taunting. "We have such a number of toilets in our home, Chase, that you could go without flushing for a month if you liked. Conversely, my dear wife will frequently flush an empty toilet, just out of nervous energy."

"I . . . I've done that myself," I said stupidly.

"Have you? That's interesting. It must be commoner than I'd realized." Into the following silence, as if into one of Noteless's chasms, my morale plunged, so Danzig's next gambit was a life preserver. "You'll notice we're without menus, Thespian!"

"Uh, yes."

"I've taken the liberty of ordering for you the great *speciality*"—there it was again—"of the house. I wonder if you've heard of the 'zillion-dollar frittata'?"

"It, uh, rings a bell."

"Prepare to be amazed. The dish entails six eggs, one whole Maine lobster, and ten ounces of Sevruga caviar." Danzig liked to enumerate every digit of his wealth: eggs, ounces, toilets, zillion-dollar frittatas eaten at fifty-thousand-dollar tête-à-têtes. Would we count turds afterward?

"We'll share it," I said, in fear. Despite barely touching my three o'clock cheeseburger, I couldn't locate my appetite. The prospect of caviar swam before my eyes like oily black phosphenes.

"No, no, it's entirely yours," Danzig assured me. "I'll derive pleasure watching *you* enjoy it. Arjuna's not eating, I think, and I'll be having French toast, which incidentally is superb here. And needless to say a round of mimosas for the table."

"*Needless to say*." Had I said this aloud? I ought to check my sarcasm, unless it sounded only in my head's echo chamber. I fluttered fingers at the waiter, my arm seeming too heavy to lift. "Actually, I could use some coffee—"

"Certainly!" Danzig got one of those phantasms hopping to it. "And music, music," he said. "Being a man of the theater . . ."

"I'm sorry?"

"I presume that as a man of the theater, you'd want there to be accompaniment, a soundtrack of some kind." Had the evening fragmented to non sequiturs? Did I miss some transition? "Perhaps you'll dance with my wife, she's an outstanding tangoist. I can't keep up with her!" Arjuna's cheeks reddened with shame, her gaze riveted to some distance. Had Danzig secured a suite in the hotel? What privileges did he think he'd won at that auction?

"I . . . I thank you, please forgive me if, uh, I have to take a rain check, I'm sure you'd be a *lovely* dancing partner . . ." As I stammered out these words, silent hands deposited a cup of black coffee (tiny oil rainbow swirling at its center) at one corner of my vision, a flute of juice and champagne (orange seeds swirling at the bottom) at the other, then pushed my bread plate aside and swept a fuming calamity across the table and under the spotlight, filling my view. It was as though someone had dissected a creature whose fleece was pallid egg, to reveal a scalded skeleton of lobster and spilled vitals of glistening caviar. The dish's oval tray resembled a medical basin, its contents seeming to stretch and bloat before me. I crossed my legs and reclined in my chair, my senses churning. "I . . . uh, I haven't had such a great day," I heard myself say. "I got some terrible news . . ." It was the last thing I'd meant to discuss. "Someone I love . . . very much . . ." I tested the coffee cup with my palms, but it was too hot to dare sip.

"Yes, we know all about it," said Arjuna Danzig, her eyes brimming. "You poor, poor man."

"We want *you* to know it's a wonderful thing, what you're doing for this city," said Rossmoor. "People sit up and notice a thing like this. I want you to be assured that Mayor Arnheim *personally* appreciates it."

"He does?"

"Oh, certainly. He'll find some way of conveying his gratitude. For the time being, we're conveying *ours*."

"She's got cancer," I said helplessly, as if they might not have completely understood. "If they can't find a way to bring the crew down, she might die up there."

"Oh, she'll be all right," said Rossmoor. "It's *you* we need to worry about. You must take care of yourself."

"I'm cheating on her. I have a lover."

"Well, that's fine, too," said Rossmoor benevolently. "You mustn't tell anyone, of course. But anything you do is just fine with us."

I looked to Arjuna, who only nodded her sympathy.

"She's got a tumor in her foot," I said, wanting it to mean something to them, something more than it meant to me.

Arjuna Danzig took my hand. "Perhaps it was the space walk," she suggested, with gentle solicitude.

"The space walk?"

"Well, it can't be sheer coincidence," reasoned Arjuna. "First, a *walk* in space. Next . . ." She appeared sorry to say it aloud, but after a moment's silence, reluctantly connected the dots. "Next a cancer in her *foot*."

"I'm not sure a space walk works the way you're thinking." At that moment my levees were breached again by the uncanny chocolate smell, catalyzing with the egg and lobster medley already fogging my sinuses. I staggered out of my chair and backward from the table, out of the golden circle, frittata steam rising into the cone of spotlight. "Do you . . . smell . . . that?" I asked.

"Smell what?" said Arjuna.

"He means the chocolate," said Rossmoor.

"Yes, yes, a kind of chocolate smell," I said. "It's been happening for days—"

"I *told* you!" said Rossmoor to Arjuna.

"For me it's been more of a *tone*," said Arjuna, sounding truly puzzled. "It just began again, now that you mention it, a kind of ringing—"

I was cheered to think Perkus wasn't completely alone. I'd find a way to let him know. But now I had to flee the mingled odors, flee Rossmoor's silk sleeves and toxic munificence, Arjuna's pity. "I'm sorry," I said. "I have to go, I'm not feeling well . . ." Invisible waiters rustled nearby. I envied their simple, anonymous lives. "Please," I called into the darkness, "please . . . get me a taxicab." I flagged with both hands, struggling for balance, as if

229

a cabbie could somehow see me here, and veer inside from the street. My eyes misting, the table before me fragmented into kaleidoscopic glints. "Sorry—" I said again.

"It was lovely seeing you," said Arjuna.

"Stay strong!" woofed Rossmoor.

12

Enduring a flu alone in an apartment has always included a certain psychedelic aspect, it seems to me. But it is a psychedelia of the body, not the mind. A sustained, sapping fever is a reeducation in the true weight of a blunt human collection of arms and legs, of a lollipop head wobbling on a woozy neck, and in the sensation of a throw pillow's scrape against ribs as sensitive as a lover's lips. To taste, in that condition, Tom Kha Gai, a white cardboard quart of which may be easily summoned to your door, there handed over by a Thai delivery boy who's left his bicycle with the doorman downstairs, is to feel coconut-sweet chicken and tomato broth flood your ravaged pipes as succor, the soup replacing lost spinal fluids directly with each mouthful. The distances between bathroom and couch, then back to huddle within womb of mattress and duvet, becomes an epic slog, full of feeble triumphs. Comfortably arranging for oneself a clean glass of water, a paperback or magazine, and a television remote, a magician's feat. Crossing a room to lift a ringing phone's receiver, an Everest ascent.

I was sick for a week and a half. That first night I just managed to drag myself home and call Oona Laszlo to cancel, even as I fell into a teeth-chattering swoon. Oona wasn't vastly sympathetic, told me to find her when

I felt better—at that point I still credited my illness to the events of the day before. It all seemed mixed up with cheeseburgers, champagne, and chocolate, at least for the first twenty-four hours, which I spent mostly shivering over my toilet. After I'd racked myself dry, the sickness decamped from my gut and percolated outward, to the very ends of my fingertips and eyelids, which felt thick and sodden as ravioli when I shut them over my poor eyes.

Oona did pass through on the second day, but she wasn't much in the way of a nursemaid, and I was hardly company. She didn't remove her coat, just unloaded a batch of recycled magazines, *Vanity Fair*, *People*, *The New York Observer*, onto the couch, where I lay cocooned in a stained blanket, surrounded by half-finished mugs of Theraflu. In the wavery depths of my fever I recall monologuing to her all about chaldrons, unburdening myself totally, but I'm not convinced she was really present for the confession. I might have been babbling at Oona-phantasms, perhaps not even speaking aloud. On the fourth day I'd begun feeling stronger, possibly hungry for the first time, and capable of self-pity, and I rang her number, mildly surprised she hadn't checked up on me a second time, after witnessing my early dejection.

"You sound better," she said uncomfortably.

"I'm *horrible*," I said.

"Look, Chase, sick isn't my thing. You should call your friends."

On that chilly note we ended the call. I'd have liked to think she meant we were something more than friends, though nothing in her tone had encouraged me to think she meant anything but less. Perhaps she'd only visited the first time to be sure I wasn't malingering. I'd never even been inside Oona's apartment and now I wondered whether she'd be inside mine again. All I had to show for my illicit love was wrinkled magazines, and the copy of *People* had turned out to be a poison pill, containing a one-page piece on Janice's diagnosis called "Adversity in the Sky." I left it untouched on my couch. Oona must have spotted the item herself, and what she meant by bringing it into my apartment I couldn't guess.

Perkus didn't find me, but Susan Eldred did. The occasion was the arrival in her office of the first finished DVD copies of *The City Is a Maze*. When Susan learned I was sick she used her lunch hour to visit, showing no fear of taking away my infection, bearing in roast lentil soup and a jar of a remedy she swore by, a mossy-smelling horse tablet called Wellness Formula. (These reminded me exactly of what Strabo Blandiana might prescribe; in the next days I'd choke down as many of the pills as I could stand.) Along with the early copy of Von Tropen Zollner's film, Susan also brought a cache of Criterion booty, the cheeriest items, she claimed, on their list: William Powell and Carole Lombard in *My Man Godfrey*, a British romance called *I Know Where I'm Going!*, and what Susan advertised as "Godard's only musical," *A Woman Is a Woman*. This was the fifth or sixth day of my quarantine, my strength returning, and Susan struck me as a vision of what a sane, female version of Perkus Tooth might resemble: you didn't have to be mad to care for mad stuff. Maybe Susan would stay and ladle me soup and educate me on the outer reaches of the Criterion list, and I could forget Perkus and Oona both. My self-pity was opening to a more acquisitive phase (sometimes, reinstated in my body by illness, in the grip of weakening fevers I woke to paradoxically vital erections), but Susan Eldred had a fiancé, as did Janice Trumbull, a fact everyone knew. So I let her get away unmolested.

I watched the effervescent *My Man Godfrey* first, then I tried *I Know Where I'm Going!* But I started the second feature at the wrong hour, my fever tending to peak toward midnight, and the movie, which seemed to concern a woman who was trying to leave one island and go to another, and a man who was afraid to enter, even in daylight, an ancient stone tower, struck me as dreamlike and terrifying, not a romance at all. At the climax, if I wasn't actually dreaming, a man frantically rowed a minuscule boat at the edge of a whirlpool, thanks a lot, Susan. All the film lacked was a bear on a floe. The next morning I ejected the disk and put it with the others in a drawer (I was relieved to have skirted the Godard musical). I only paused to glance at Perkus's liner notes for *The City Is a Maze*, which began: *As Leonard Cohen tells us, "there is a war between the ones who say there is a war and the ones who say there isn't." Equally, according to Iris Murdoch, "the bereaved have no language for speaking to the unbereaved." For denizens of the country of Noir, such protests delineate the incommensurable rift or gulf between those doomed to patrol the night country and those moored in daylight, a coexistence of realms, one laid upon the other as veneer. This irreconcilable doubleness may be credited to dictates of the Production Code, but is also grounded in the fecund versatility of the studio system, where crew, actors, and even sets were employed in hasty alternation to the task of depicting the fates of both doomed and undoomed, bereaved and unbereaved. Many of the studio pros help-ing realize Zollner's exemplary nightmare had been, weeks before, shooting a romantic comedy on the same row of facsimile New York brownstones as* The City Is a Maze, *one featuring the same lead players, among whom Edmond O'Brien, for one, gives no evidence of having read to the end of the script to see his character's fate . . .*

Oh, I missed him, and his ridiculous language. I wanted to hear Perkus speak it again, everything revealing its opposite, everything incommensurate and *ir*reconcilable and *un*bereaved. In the same spirit, we'd been too briefly chaldroned, and now were unchaldroned. Was it better to have loved chaldrons and lost, or never to have loved them at all? And what came after?

In this interval I barely saw a newspaper, but I gath-ered that the chocolate smell cleared up without expla-nation. Also I heard that the cold front wouldn't budge, the slate skies winter-locked, and that the tiger wrecked a York Avenue temple gymnasium where aging Jewish men played pickup ball every Monday and Wednesday in a game that had been regular for thirty years. The following day the mayor's office unveiled a Web site for tracking the tiger's movements, and recommended it to those seeking forewarning of traffic tie-ups and subway cancellations. All this came to me while flipping channels, and when I passed over a news station I never lingered. I avoided news and newspapers because I feared getting word of Janice's heroic self-biopsy, and what it would reveal. I learned anyway, from breaking-news crawls at the bottom of my screen, that she had a malignant cancer in her foot, and spreading to other regions. That plans were under way for a course of improvised chemotherapy, using what they had on hand in *Northern Lights*' medical supplies. Possibly an attempt would be made to launch a small rocket filled with better meds past the Chinese mines, into orbit, where the Russians could grapple it into the space station. Failing chemical intervention, there was talk of the possibility of a desperate surgery, even amputation.

In my head I composed tormented letters, but I'd been warned that Mission Control would refuse their delivery, so I never put a word on paper. I screened my calls. The only news I wanted, finally, was outside my window: that the birds still attacked their routes around the spire, those pathways to nowhere that seemed to articulate my own invisible urgencies. The birds couldn't interpret the stone, but by their proximity they could seem to define it, adore it, abide with it. That was as near to a sense of valuable work in the world as I could imagine myself having. Only I would need, when I was well again, to make sure of what my own church spire should be. I knew the plan for Chase Insteadman was that I should wait for Janice. Yet something nearer at hand, some person or artifact, some situation or scene, was calling. I didn't know whether I was bereaved or unbereaved, but I wasn't bereaved the way I felt I ought to be.

Richard Abneg and Georgina Hawkmanaji came on Thursday. I was almost well. They learned not from Perkus (who might be oblivious, so far as I knew) but from Maud Woodrow, whom I'd telephoned just hoping for some breath of gossip in my loneliness, not because I hoped she'd visit or even be particularly sympathetic. When I'd then been contacted by Richard I explained I was really fine, but he said Georgina insisted they look in. The two of them arrived just before noon with a caterer's roasted turkey and some sides, shocking me. Richard seemed to think it was incredibly funny, and maybe it was. He wore an expensive Burberry coat, unmistakably new, and after he helped Georgina out of her own he went into my wardrobe and found wooden hangers for them both. The Hawkman helped me set a small table, scooping sweet-potato mash and creamed spinach from plastic quarts into rarely used serving bowls, gravy poured into a coffee mug, and dusting off a batch of cloth napkins I'd forgotten I owned. We even switched on the television to catch the end of the Macy's parade, the kooky giant balloons, supermen and Gnuppets and unrecognizable new personae bobbing through the sleety canyons, the kids toughing it out in the cold.

"May I ask, what does that represent?"

"That represents SpongeBob SquarePants, Georgie."

My appetite suddenly savage, I was, yes, thankful, wildly so, to have the turkey's inexhaustible flesh before me, ate white and dark in a gravied pile together, felt myself plundering the bird's life forces, stripping it free of the obedient skeleton. Recovering with each bite,

I felt a teenager's strength and greed rising in me. Richard laughed. They ate, too, more decorously, though threads of dry breast lodged in Richard's beard until Georgina picked them out, and gossiped absently, remarking on items of paltry interest in my apartment, which was revealing, truthfully, only in its hotel-ish anonymity, order, booklessness.

Something in the parade caught my eye, a golden-swelling outline among the balloons filing down Broadway. The distracting balloon wasn't the focus of the shot, which framed instead a swollen Spider-Man, but trapped behind the blue-and-red superhero that golden shape bobbed in and out of visibility between the lamp-posts, its vinyl skin peppered with sleet and confetti. The balloon, I was fairly certain, was meant to depict a chaldron. My mouth, I think, fell open. Anyway, my eyes widened, chewing stopped. Richard Abneg followed my attention to the television screen, and before I could speak he'd already raised a finger to his lips and shook his head to silence me, even while raising his brows and rolling his eyes to acknowledge that yes, he'd recognized it too. This petition wasn't threatening or duplicitous; rather, his look conveyed hope I'd keep it from Georgina in the manner of an indulgence between hen-pecked husbands, as if Richard were a sworn quitter sneaking a cigarette.

Georgina made a visit to my bathroom and Richard immediately leaned across the turkey's carcass to whisper an apology. "I'm trying to get her mind off those things," he said. "She just gets too worked up, it's not healthy. You'd be amazed, there are little reminders,

238

hints of them everywhere, once you know what you're looking for."

I was amazed. "You've been bidding in auctions?"

He frowned annoyance. "Just a couple of times. The supply's dried up at the moment."

"You haven't won?"

"Nope. But, you know what? Stay tuned. The Hawkman's accustomed to getting what she wants. Shhhhh." Georgina had returned, closing off further questions. Yet I'd had answered the one question I never meant to ask, had avoided even framing. Phenomena I'd in some way been hoping were circumscribed within the Eighty-fourth Street apartment, within Perkus's computer or broadsides or ravings, weren't. Even when I—and Perkus, possibly—ignored them, chaldrons, for instance, went on being chaldrons. For some people, apparently, they were a way of life. I'd be forced to make my peace with the fact.

13

It wasn't as though I didn't know where Oona lived.
I'd dropped her at her building's entrance in a taxicab
more than once. So on the first day I felt completely well
I put myself thoroughly together, shaving, flossing, even
patrolling my nostrils for vagrant hairs and lint-rolling
my winter coat and my scarf, then conveyed myself to
her address, on a bright cold Monday afternoon, the
first in December, as if turning up for an audition for
entrance into her rooms. Oona's building had no doorman, and after spotting O. Laszlo on the buzzer's direc-
tory, I declined using the intercom, wanting to ensure
she at least had to look me in the eye. A tall young
woman with a tall silky dog appeared as I stalled at the
intercom, and in my well-ordered state she showed no
hesitation holding the door open for me, even before
I smiled for her. So I was inside. The lobby was con-
summately ordinary, the building's old bones renovated
into timeless blandness, but I felt a prickle of revelation,
as though crossing some secret boundary or limit,
Manhattan's hidden panels sliding open to my gentle
pressure. My week of fever might have been a price paid
in advance for passing so easily into forbidden territory:
I felt transparent, had even shed an authentic pound
or two, my pants riding looser on my hips. I'd revved

myself to make this run at Oona's door, but now, past first defenses so easily, my mood turned slinky, elliptical, possibly even ellipsistic. I sort of wanted just to poke around the corridors a bit.

Or do something else. We rode the elevator together, the door-holding woman and the pony-like dog and I, and I could see she wanted to ask who I might be in her building to see, and that she hoped it wasn't a woman prettier than herself, or any woman at all. And she was awfully pretty, in a way I didn't have to take personally, copper hair in unkempt ringlets under her felt cap's earlaps, her profile, once she'd unwound her scarf so I could see it, elegantly long, an imperial snout to match the dog's. She had an unneurotic attractiveness, or so I could tell myself. I could also tell that she liked me without knowing who I was. This made me want to be someone other, even entertain the scoundrel fantasy. Perhaps this was what I was really for, after all. And New York, a puzzle trap for anonymous encounters. You might find no pity to spare for the child star, but I'd known this feeling too rarely. I'd always had to be dutifully myself, even while shirking any other duty. Now, for the eternity of an elevator's ascent to the eleventh floor, I had another idea. The copper-haired woman presented a path between my schizoid fates, Janice Trumbull in the sky and Oona Laszlo behind a door on the floor the elevator's red numbers now lazily counted off. The dog had this woman to himself, I could see from his assuming posture. He slept in her bed. I felt I could probably handle the mute furry rival, and that otherwise nothing else stood between me and escape, not only from my women but from larger confusions I'd wandered into these past months. I only had to think up another name to go by. Kertus Booth. Then the doors opened to the eleventh, and I stepped off, fantasy bursting like a soap bubble. I went straight to Oona's door, and rang the chime there.

A man opened the door, a sandy-haired, sallow man with acne-burred cheeks and a boneless, indolent quality to his shoulders and hips, seeming not fat but shoddily put together or unfinished, his age hovering nebulous between twenty and forty, and with an expression vaguely drunken and irritable at once. Dressed in a tan polo shirt and brown corduroys, loafers without socks, he was small, too, but not in the pumpkin-on-stick-figure manner of Perkus Tooth or Oona herself, more like a golem made by someone running low on clay, who'd therefore cheated at both proportion and detail, leaving legs, arms, and fingers stubby, nose indistinct, lips nonexistent. As he widened the door he recognized me, unmistakably, and with only mild surprise.

"Oh!" he said. "I thought you were sandwiches."

I couldn't find my voice to reply. The door-opener's smile was like a line drawn in wet sand with a stick, pale doughy eyes not joining in. At last he said, "Just a minute," and turned without inviting me inside. He didn't close the door, just called out, "Oona," without raising his voice, and traipsed back the way he'd come, down an antiseptically white corridor, toward a wide-open room. I followed.

Oona or some previous owner had renovated the apartment clean of molding, or of any furnishings older than a decade or so, the lines around windows and doors as clean and square as a Chelsea gallery's, the blond floors polished slick, and bare of carpet. The minimal shelves stood free, and were loaded with books sporadically bunched in spine-wrecking slouches, or laid sideways to begin with, and boxed and unboxed manuscripts, the walls undecorated apart from the images Oona had tacked around her work site in temporary and slipshod fashion, most of them letter-sized color printouts, some with e-mail headings intact, others pages seemingly heedlessly razored out of art books. The windows were shaded with Japanese paper, the afternoon's bright-angled sun glowing through, filling the space with ambient radiance, the ceiling speckled and streaked with light.

Oona's desk was a simple table, brushed metal like a refurbished medical or laboratory surface, on which a gleaming laptop sat, a bright steel spider enwebbed in external components—speakers, drives, printer, wireless keyboard and mouse, and with Oona hunched over it, thin black wires running to her ears, a daylight vampire in her regular crow's black. The door-opener preceded me into the large bright room, then seated himself silently in a red leather chair against the farthest wall, as though returning to some penitential observance, seemingly wearing an invisible dunce cap. Oona sensed my presence, an extra ripple in the room's stillness, removed earbuds, and turned in her chair. She wore the mysterious glasses, but plucked them off into a vest pocket when she spotted me. Then immediately stood.

"Excuse me." Oona went out of the room, through another corridor, presumably to the more domestic quarter of the apartment, bedrooms and bathroom, though I wondered how warmly furnished they could be, by the standard of the room in which I stood. Oona's work site, now that I was free to examine it, was festooned with photographs and drawings of a host of excavated pits, precisely dug holes in the ground, at various locations, among buildings, or in woods, or by the sea, or in one case islanded by a suburban industrial park's circular drive. A couple I recognized as views of *Urban Fjord*. Others were labeled *Local Chasm*, *Demapped Intersection*, *Former Landmark*, *Erased Atrocity*. The varied attractions of Laird Noteless. The sculptor stared from another photograph, silver torrent brushed back over his skull, wild unmanaged eyebrows atop drillingly dark pupils, deep-lined cheeks, hands in pockets or behind his back, impossible to tell as the coat he wore buttoned to the top showed no hint of form, was instead a light-destroying blob filling the frame on three sides, his head like a sculpture itself mounted on the black Rorschach of coat, dour sentinel overseeing his works.

I continued this close inspection for a full minute or two. It was as if I'd come for this purpose, Oona's failure to greet me a consent that I should absorb the scene at her desk. I felt alone there, though technically I wasn't, being in the company of one who'd melted into the limbs of his padded leather chair—had the chair been dun-colored everywhere, like him, instead of firehouse red, he'd be impossible to notice: *Blurred Person*. I did feel some whisper of déjà vu at our arrangement, but I placed it soon enough—Susan Eldred had stepped out, left me not completely alone in her office once, a few months ago. So perhaps the man who'd come to Oona Laszlo's door was Oona's version of Perkus Tooth. He certainly lingered in a kind of ellipsis. But I not only found him unthreatening, I wasn't interested. I had no room for another recursion, for human Chinese boxes, Perkuses hiding inside Oonas hiding inside Perkuses. What was next—would the pale-brownish man in Oona's red leather easy chair turn out to have a Biller of his own, and so on? Forget it. Forget him, he was nothing, and evidently content to be. It was Laird Noteless who bothered me. Had he replaced me in Oona's life? Her desk looked like a shrine.

Something held me from stepping nearer, to see what words I could read from her screen. I suppose I wasn't alone, after all. Then, as I hesitated, it blinked off. The room, lit by that flood of sun through the handmade paper over the windows, seemed to pulse, to brighten around that spot of dark in which I now saw myself reflected, the shape of my coat outlined against the clean white walls, not entirely unlike Noteless's photographic portrait. I could also see the figure behind me. He'd left his loafers on the floor, and tucked his bare feet up to sit cross-legged on the leather cushion, and though I couldn't be certain I thought his eyes might be closed. I wouldn't have been shocked to hear him snoring. There was no sound from the corridor down which Oona had fled.

The buzzer sounded. I turned in alarm, though I should have expected it. The dun-man unfolded from his seat and padded down the hallway to the intercom, where he buzzed a sandwich-delivery person into the lobby.

Shortly he'd exchanged a wad of dollars for a plastic sack, which he plopped at the foot of the red chair, then retook his cushion, his economy of action suggesting an especially weary distillate of Zen observance.

"I don't think she's coming out," he said. His smile bore an air of wan complicity. "Would you like a half? It's spa tuna on wheat."

"No, thank you," I said.

"Do you mind terribly—?"

"Please." I said. He leaned into the bag on the floor and unwrapped his sandwich. I left.

On the street, I felt stripped of all intention, as if shunted outside my own skin. The bright day was already falling to early December dark. I hailed a cab, though it was walking distance, really. It was always so much easier to find one going downtown, like falling out of bed, or out of the sky. I might have fallen out of the sky I was so insubstantial, had so little relation here on Earth, if Lexington Avenue qualified as Earth. Had I even seen Oona? Barely. I'd spent more time with the woman and dog in the elevator. Even more with Oona's washed-out man. But it wasn't any particular person I dwelled upon as I bumped across Eighty-sixth Street, to Second Avenue. Instead I considered the fate embodied in New York apartments. Perkus Tooth was utterly a creature of Eighty-fourth Street, that labyrinth of broadsides and collections, the walls bearing a decade's patina of smoke and old music and conversation. What if Perkus were to be freed into a clean space like Oona's? Might he take a breath and write something new, something that mattered to him? (With that state-of-the-art computer he'd stand a better chance of winning a chaldron, if nothing else.) Conversely, Oona's jittery susceptibility, it seemed to me now, might be exemplified in those bare walls, that Teflon floor. Anyone's portrait might be featured next, to colonize the place as completely as had Noteless and his potholes: a disgraced governor or bishop, a rehabbed rock star or wide receiver, a vindicated scapegoat, a mass killer. No wonder she didn't want me around the blank slate of those rooms. The ghost writer was too totally permeable.

Why she didn't see that this was what we had in common—this was the only thing I didn't understand.

14

Yet for all I felt bankrupt and stranded that day as I slumped back to my empty turret, a Rapunzel unbeckoned from below, not even raving sick and feverish anymore, just as natty clean and straight of posture and pointlessly deferential as I'd been before I'd ever met Perkus Tooth or Oona Laszlo, too noble to pursue strange redheads in elevators, not noble enough to live out my scripted role as Janice Trumbull's betrothed, rather somewhere hopelessly between, I was, in fact, about to be rescued. As if they'd been testing me, Perkus and Oona gathered me back into the strange consolations of their company just before I petulantly flunked out of it.

In other words, I only had to stare at my telephone for a day and a half to will it to ring. It was Perkus who called, the following night at nine, but as if by miracle or design, Oona was in tow.

"So, where have you been?"

"Hello, Perkus."

"You were sick? Why didn't you call?" I knew him well enough to hear how his tone of grievance contained both an apology and a commandment to pretend our Second Avenue street squabble had never taken place.

"I was barely able to lift the phone. There was nothing anyone could do, I just had to sweat it out."

"Why don't you come over now?"

"Well—"

I was surely going to be convinced, but my sulkiness hadn't quite dissolved. Then, behind Perkus, Oona's voice chimed in to dissolve it. "Come on, Chase, get with the program!" As if I'd already missed an appointment.

"We're hanging out," said Perkus, now with a shade of chagrin, or even pleading, as if he really needed my presence to buffer Oona's. Women, I began to think, embarrassed him per se, made him feel goofy or uneasy, when they didn't make him furious. "It's not the same around here without you."

Well, it wasn't the same around *here*, either, I wanted to joke. I did feel I'd vacated my life somehow. Instead I told him I'd be right over. Needless to say.

Doing so, rushing back to Eighty-fourth Street, I was steering into a storm's eye. Things in Perkus Tooth's apartment could never be as they were, because they'd never been any particular way for more than two evenings in a row, really. Nevertheless, I was to briefly reenter a dream I'd idealized. One of life's oases, those moments that come less often than we want to believe. And are only known in retrospect, after the inevitable wreck and rearrangements have come.

That first night I was shocked to arrive and find them on Perkus's living-room floor together, Perkus cross-legged like a kindergartener, scissors looped on thumb and forefinger as he browsed half-mangled magazines, Oona kneeling on folded knees, squinting at scraps of text, forgoing her glasses, I guessed, in anticipation of my arrival. They had a broadside in progress between them, one in the late manner, made entirely of collaged elements, devoid of Perkus's distinctive scribbled hand, Oona resuming her glue duties—perhaps I wasn't the only one who'd gotten nostalgic around here! Yet they'd only settled, so far, on a single image, smack in the center of a large sheet of drawing paper: the newsprint photo of the polar bear on his raft of ice, which Perkus had latched onto during our last visit. The image, raggedly clipped free of surrounding text, now sat smeared and wrinkling in an excess of rubber cement, worse for wear, bordered by the mute page. Oona's hair was rubber-banded up into two blunt, irregular ponytails, as if to make an extra joke about my discovering the pair in their childish arrangement on the carpet.

"Hello, Chase Insteadman." She grinned up at me wryly and lowered her voice to a laconic drawl, as if playing the sheriff in a satiric Western.

"Hello, Oona."

"Haven't see you in a while."

I suppose we weren't counting that curtailed encounter in her apartment. It now seemed totally unreal. "Too long," I said keeping it noncommittal.

"We're making a poster," she said. "For old times' sake, while trying not to, you know, *feel* old."

"Yes, I see."

"It's on the theme of isolation," she said. At this Perkus tilted up one goonish eye, and one severe. "Excuse me," Oona corrected. "It's on the theme of bears."

"Why feel the need to choose?" I said.

"Great point." She slugged Perkus on the arm. "Bears *and* isolation."

In my conception Perkus and Oona were enemies or contestants, yet I'd never known what was at stake. Now Perkus was wholly caught up in Oona's ironic frolic, or frolicsome irony, whichever it was. He seemed cowed and catalyzed at once. I wondered if Oona was thrilled to reclaim her place as his Tweedledee, if the nostalgic gesture hadn't opened some door into discarded possibilities, taking her by surprise. She might have set out to please Perkus just to please (and unnerve) me, then found herself pleased, too.

Or perhaps this was my projection. I might be crediting to Oona the thrill of relief I felt to reenter the Eighty-fourth Street sensorium, to hear Perkus's strange music (if I asked what was playing he'd surely pretend to be shocked I didn't know it), to step into his arena of exhaled fumes, knowing that soon enough I'd exhale plenty myself (I'd absentmindedly catalogued the presence of a fresh row of joints on the kitchen table, and one, half smoked, tipped into a tray), to see his information hectically distributed across the living-room afghan, a puzzle whose pleasure was its insolvability, to find myself restored to my small shelf in his collection. It had taken just one disinvitation to make me glimpse exile.

Perkus tried to fit a clipping containing a paragraph of small type into the white expanse surrounding the bear photo. Over his shoulder, I read: *Perhaps such secrets, the secrets of everyone, were only expressed when the person laboriously dragged them into the light of the world, imposed them on the world, and made them a part of the world's experience. Without this effort, the secret place was merely a dungeon in which the person perished* . . . The way he shifted the clipping from spot to spot, intently evaluating, then rejecting, each position, suggested Perkus was trying to believe in the worthy coexistence of those words with the conundrum of the bear, almost as if hoping that the paragraph could comprise a rescue, make a bridge or raft back to the mainland the bear could hop across to safety. But no, the new element fell short, no matter where he placed it, and so Perkus swept it into a pile of others that lay to one side and behind him. I scanned the other tatters, until my eyes lit on a recent clipping from *The New Yorker*, a Talk of the Town describing the city's tormented infatuation with Janice Trumbull's medical saga. At this I turned away, not wanting to know what else might be auditioned to fit the theme of *bears and isolation*.

"Light up a smoke, if you want," said Perkus, the eyes in the back of his head telling him I'd shifted back toward the kitchen. "We've got more on the way, actually," he added. "Watt should be coming around any minute now, just so you know."

"Waiting for Watt," said Oona, in singsong, not looking up from the old magazine she browsed. She unfurled the centerfold from a crackling thick copy of *Playboy*, circa the early '70s at the latest, given the model's coy mascara and bobbed hair, and the Technicolor wrongness of her aureoles. "Who'll tell us what's what. And sell us some pot."

"Oona only comes around here to score," said Perkus cheerily, at last daring to jab back. "I no longer hold that against her."

Foster Watt did come and lay out his wares, though not before we'd attempted to use up the last of the present supply. The poor pot dealer was shivering, still locked into his uniform of red vinyl jacket and no head covering, despite the cold, and he must have felt, coming into that kitchen, that he'd stepped onto a vaudeville stage. We were so high we finished each other's lines like the Marx Brothers, even if the result was mostly a verbal version of a game of exquisite corpse. Perkus offered Watt a fresh-brewed cup of coffee, and Watt took it and struck a pose of claustrophobic cool by the door while the three of us slavered over his open case of goods, running our reddened and hysterical orbs over the rainbow fonts that differentiated the plastic boxes crammed full of fertile buds. Oona kept surprising me. I'd thought she flinched from direct encounters with the drug trade, but she seemed positively exuberant to see Watt, who enlarged the pool of victims for her global mockery.

"Hindu Kush . . . ooh, that's too exotic for me . . ." she said. "What's this, Giant Tiger? Are you trying to frighten your customers, Foster?"

"Yeah," said Watt absently, though it was hardly meant as affirmative to her question. Conversationally, Watt was a Magic 8 Ball. It was merely a question of which answer would come up. "Yeah, I got a few new things, good stuff."

"Ice," said Perkus. "Where's the Ice?"

"Have I ever let you down, Perkus? I've got plenty of your favorite."

"Giant Tiger, Gray Fog, Two Eagles," Oona listed. "Very, uh, *topical* selection, Foster."

"People are digging Two Eagles," said Watt. "You ought to try it."

Perkus hoarded all the Ice he could find in the sample case, built a little architectural stack of five Lucite boxes at one corner of his table. Oona went on listing brand names. "Northern Lights, Chinese Mine . . . what's next? Lonely Astronaut? Do you make these up yourself, Foster? Because no offense, but somebody's really cribbing a lot of this material."

Watt didn't even trouble to shrug, just ignored her. I suspect she'd lost him at "topical." Oona couldn't let it go, though. "Somebody needs to get some of their own material," she said again pointedly, as if she were a professor offering a plagiarizing student a first warning. Watt took it lightly enough. Yet even after he left, bearing away a large stack of our pooled twenties in return for eight of his Lucite containers—Perkus's five portions of Ice, a couple of the old standby, Chronic, which vanished into Oona's purse, and one Northern Lights I purchased as a morbid souvenir—Oona circled back to the topic. "Don't you think Watt isn't playing fair, Perkus?"

"I don't have the faintest idea what you're on about."

"Tailoring his material to his audience like that," she said. "It sort of breaks the illusion, don't you think?" She kept calling it "material," though it seemed to me an odd word for names snatched from the headlines.

"What illusion?" Perkus rolled a joint while he contended with her.

"That, you know, there's an ancient and mighty *marijuana tree* somewhere in South America called

254

El Chronic, named that by some Mayan priest a thousand centuries ago, for its special properties of transubstantiation—you know. It just doesn't seem right some skanky Irish kid from Chelsea Clinton or wherever it is Watt lives to rename this ancient essence 'Balthazar' or 'Derek Jeter' just because he has a laser printer and a captive audience."

"I don't think it's Watt," said Perkus slyly, seeming to take her concern seriously. "He's just a middleman. I think it's someone else giving them names. Maybe actually even a Mayan priest, one who's just, you know, keeping up with the news."

"Then it's him I want a word with," said Oona. "Can you get the Mayan priest's beeper number?"

"So," said Perkus, the key word signaling he'd become interested at last, had found something he could work with, "maybe we've got the polarities reversed. It's crucial we remember to question basic assumptions."

"Polarities reversed . . . how?" The hungry mind supplying this query was my own. Perkus's paradoxes were just what I'd been starved of, no matter that they gave me a dangerous sense of reality slippage. I'd become an addict and needed replenishment, as much as Perkus had needed Watt's visit.

"What if *The New York Times* is getting its material from Watt's brand names, rather than the other way around?" said Perkus. At this, his revelatory eye exulted, though we'd no time to linger on the point—Perkus had reminded himself he had a sort of front page of his own to consider, an edition in progress. "Maybe the bear is enough," he said to Oona, musingly. "Maybe the empty border around the picture says something nothing else could ever say . . ."

"We might not even need the bear," said Oona.

■

That first night of reunion, and the ones that came after, turned out to be episodes hinged in the middle. A brief frigid walk back to my building and Oona and I were at it. Actually, that night we started in the fluorescent glare of Perkus's hallway, like teenagers escaping a party, hands invading outfits, knees interlaced, sagging to the wall until our breathing got too slow and regular and we contained ourselves, shoved out through that subset of Brandy's smokers drunk enough not to realize they were freezing, then teetered together, hips eagerly jostling, to my apartment. Our December fucks made what had come before seem like glimpses, tourist views from some highway pull-off—now we abandoned the car and climbed the guardrail and built a hut in that landscape below, where no one could see, to dwell for a while in a place from which, when we climbed out woolly-eyed and helplessly grinning afterward, we were astonished to find any highway so close, it was so primeval.

This wasn't the sort of thing I was inclined to examine for causes, a gift horse, a windfall of sex like I'd known just a time or two before. I didn't want to think my own intensity drew in any measure on what I'd turned from: Janice's weird crises, off away in space. Oona and I pursued expression of something that had zip to do with anyone else, I tried to believe it desperately. As for what anyone else might judge, that was obvious, and irrelevant. However this chance had come, we'd taken it. We didn't discuss it—after leaving Perkus's place we barely spoke. If I was looking for causes, there might be one. A few hours with Perkus and all Oona's mordancy was bantered out of her, and my need to play the dopey straight man used up, too. All talk could fall by the wayside.

We weren't a secret from Perkus, though we kept our hands to ourselves in his company. I didn't know whether Oona had spoken to him privately, or if our state was obvious after that first night. Perkus granted it, no more. Nothing said in hearing of all three, that might be the rule. He did acknowledge the fact to me alone, one early evening in the middle of the month, he and I under way at Watt's product while Oona slaved to meet a deadline, her panicking editor having pleaded for some chapters, some evidence of progress on the Noteless book. But Perkus only arrived at the subject indirectly, as a passing remark during an alienated disquisition on what he called "pair bonding."

"So, it's not one hundred percent a received notion," he began, as if a topic heading had been announced, or revealed on a banner only he could see. "I mean, I always used to feel critical of anyone who fell into pair-bonding, like they were failing the test of reimagining all the basic premises."

"What basic premises?"

"The basic premises of existence," he said impatiently. "But then, really, if you pay attention to animals, there's *tons* of pair-bonding. I was thinking about Abneg's eagles."

"You're saying, basically, birds do it, bees do it, even the, uh, Chinese do it . . ." I could never remember the finish of that lyric.

Perkus revealed no sign he took this as mockery. I'd merely shown I grokked. "Exactly! In that context, you really can't blame people, can you? I mean, it tends to happen, even when you think you're in one kind of arrangement, some other group or affiliation, but then members of your group keep sort of *defaulting* into these pairs . . . I guess you should never be surprised, huh?"

"I'd say no." Was I falling into some trap?

"Like Abneg and the Hawkman," he mused. A fuming joint between his knuckles, Perkus studied the wending smoke as if casting distantly for a second example, though it was certainly near enough at hand. "Or you and Laszlo. It's the most natural thing in the world, I don't know why I should be in any way surprised. Janice Trumbull is out of reach, and so far as the animal part of you is concerned, she might as well not exist. She's only an idea, a whisper in your forebrain. The rest of you was howling like one of those eagles for a mate. And so then came along Oona Laszlo. Like dancing, you look around the room, and take a partner."

"I don't think eagles howl," I said. I took none of this personally. Oona and I were too ecstatic these days to be damaged by Perkus's addled paraphrase. It was only interesting to hear him find a way to let me know he knew.

"We'll see about that," he said humorously, rising to his shelves. He dug out the tall blue *Field Guide to*

North American Birds of Prey. "There's something else I want to check anyhow."

"What's that?"

"Whether eagles are monogamous."

Oh, Tooth. I watched him hunt in the book, as if it really held the clue he needed. It didn't. That clue served as a bookmark in a P. G. Wodehouse *Jeeves Omnibus* on my bedside table: the wrinkled card on which Lindsay of Jackson Hole had scribbled her phone number. I didn't dare mention it. That project had too much calamity in it, and I was selfishly willing to let Perkus go unlaid to keep the peace I now enjoyed. So we'd explore the dating profile of apartment eagles instead, or lapse into some other subject even more imaginary and arcane. Why was Perkus so determined to be sexually lonely? I asked this question of myself, not him.

■

One of these nights I came in and found them back at their nostalgic samizdat, organizing what looked like a finished project, in piles on the living-room floor. Someone had done some photocopying, and Perkus had apparently resolved the conundrum of the polar bear by creating two broadsides: one with only the bear, the other with the bear almost blotted out with a proliferation of other clippings, text excerpts, and illustrations (including, I noticed, at least one scientific diagram explaining *Northern Lights*' possible procedure for docking an unmanned scow of medical supplies). Somewhere between these two lay the truth Perkus wished to unveil. The photocopies had none of the grandeur of his famous broadsides, arrayed in painful evidence throughout the apartment, but I was impressed that the edition even existed. Evidence of outside destinations for Perkus, other than Jackson Hole, was always startling, he was such a creature of that apartment. But that was the least of it, for now he and Oona were pulling on their winter coats, preparing for an old-school postering run. I found myself enlisted, after a quick smoke.

"Look out for the graffiti patrol," said Perkus, once we'd bumped out into the cold streets with our freight of posters and masking tape. "They travel in black vans. Arnheim's quality-of-life initiatives are no joke, ever since Gladwell and his fucking *Tipping Point*." (Here was another of Perkus's sacred enemies; I recalled one early rant blaming Gladwell for the "commodification of whim.") Once Perkus declared this, black vans seemed to be everywhere, though if these held quality-of-life police they looked to me to have bigger fish to fry. Oona, unruffled, capriciously taped a poster, one of those in which the bear was jumbled over with other stuff, around a lamppost. Mostly, though, our trouble was we couldn't find places to put the things. Perkus exhorted us to find construction sites, but the blocks between Second and Third Avenues didn't have any of these. "This whole town used to be one big claptrap collage," Perkus complained. "Nobody even removed posters, they were in too much of a hurry, they'd just layer them over with other stuff. Sometimes somebody would rip away a chunk and reveal seven or eight different layers, and I'd see something I put up six months or a year earlier resurface in a new context . . ."

It was cold for reminiscing, but I didn't want to let him down too abruptly. "That was a . . . certain amount of time ago," I said. "And a little farther downtown."

Oona went on affixing posters wherever she could, her breath billowing steam as she warmed herself with the effort, her scrappy winding dance with the dispenser making her resemble a kind of bat in her black layers and loose hair. I felt I should take her example, but it seemed to me the bear-only version, which was what I carried, when bound to a lamppost looked far too much like a "lost dog" flyer, only one lacking a phone number and the promise of a reward.

"This way—" Perkus whisked us from block to block, searching, I think, for the door into 1988 or there-abouts. In lieu of this we slapped a desultory photocopy on a bus shelter or two, always lowering heads guiltily at the sight of passersby, ordinary Manhattanites whom I couldn't keep from suspecting we'd typically meet at book parties or gallery openings—me and Oona, that is. But tonight we were enveloped in Perkus's cloak of banditry. We should have been smoking cheroots and sporting eye patches. Whatever reputation Perkus might have once conjured for himself by his vigilante disserta-tions, these present scraps of visual noise couldn't have been more meaningless on these walls if they'd been gum wrappers. The meaning resided in our gesture, silly as it was. Or there was no meaning. I began stuffing our posters into trash cans when the others weren't look-ing. I would have liked to set them afire to warm our hands, but I suspected that might have finally drawn some quality-of-life-enforcement attention.

Circling back to Perkus's at last, bankrupt of post-ers due to my illicit disposals, speaking with chattering teeth of the coffee Perkus was about to brew, we found ourselves confronted at his doorstep not by the usual Brandy's drunks—it really was too chilly tonight—but by a weird sentinel presence planted in our path. He wore a long leather coat with a floppy buckle, a thick-ribbed purple turtleneck rising from inside the coat's wide col-lar, and an absurd imperial fur tower of a hat, under which glared the whites of his eyes in a mask of dark-ness, making him resemble Orson Welles as Othello. But that mask wasn't blackface. We all had been primed by Perkus to be met by some figure of authority, and Biller's new costume looked anything but secondhand. He might have been deputized to arrest us, if the mayor's graffiti squad had been configured on a Blaxploitation theme. Biller was famously boycotted from the building, but it was hard to imagine Perkus's neighbors challeng-ing him now. Somebody had laid out some money to dress the homeless man this way. Then I remembered that Biller wasn't homeless anymore. The other day Perkus had been trying to explain Biller's weird new apartment, where Biller lived, Perkus said, "with forty or fifty dogs." I chalked the dogs up to exaggeration, and forgot about the apartment until now.

Before I could express my surprise, Perkus and Biller embraced, Perkus vanishing for an instant into the larger man's clasp. "Come inside, it's too cold," said Perkus. "You want some coffee, Biller?"

"That would be nice." His voice was still gentle, even meekly hesitant, but now you imparted to this gentleness a certain majesty, a noble restraint. The clothes made the man.

"You're looking fantastic," said Perkus, sweeping us all inside. If there was a grain of overcompensation in Perkus's heartiness with Biller, I assumed this had less to do with any guilt toward the silent wandering figure than a relief that the timing of Biller's appearance would blot out contemplation of the lame broadsiding session. (In fact, we'd never mention it again.) "So, you know Chase and Oona, don't you?" Perkus asked belatedly. Well, Biller did or didn't, but he nodded, taking us in together as Perkus's introduction had suggested, *Chase and Oona*.

Indoors, we defrosted our paper-cut fingertips around stingingly hot mugs while Perkus prompted Biller to explain his new good fortune, the respectability he'd attained through the strange backdoor of his laptop computer, or explain it as well as he could, anyway, to us Internet primitives. Biller sat, his shiny leather coat and monstrous hat shed, resplendent in his purple sweater, commandingly patient with our stupidity. Had we heard of Yet Another World? No?

It was difficult to explain, and it didn't help that Perkus tried to help Biller paint the picture while plainly not grasping it himself. Neither a video game nor an online community, exactly, Yet Another World was, in itself, only a set of templates and tools, "a place with stuff," in Biller's words. "A place where you can do things." You might go there to build a virtual house, to furnish it with the virtual objects you liked. Much of it, according to Biller, was pretty much like the world out here—homes, with belongings inside. You also made *yourself*, there behind the screen, and the self you made was something Biller called an "avatar." Again, many visitors to Yet Another World settled for realism in this regard, their avatars little more than digitally prettified versions of their usual selves, spines a little straighter, waists narrower, tits bigger, and so on. Many were content to shamble through this potential paradise in cliques of sexy avatars browsing virtual shops and cruising or flirting, as in a mall. "Man is born free," Perkus offered, "and everywhere is in chain stores."

Things got a little more interesting in other precincts, Biller went on to indicate. It was this infinity of possible selves and possible neighborhoods, the total and endless expansibility of Yet Another World, which gave it its magnificence. Deviants and avant-gardists could build neighborhoods as solid, in their way, as those of the suburbanites—kingdoms of barter, Dada, or rape, castles of chaos. Grown-ups masqueraded as children, men as women, and so on. Others created inhuman selves, gorgons, strolling penises, pornified Gnuppets. All ethics were local, and endlessly up for negotiation. Declaring whether Yet Another World was or wasn't a game might be as difficult as declaring whether life was.

While I was mesmerized, Oona showed her typical impatience once she'd grasped the concept. Like a Noteless chasm, she'd glanced into the unusual thing and now wanted to get back to business, or have a drink and get laid, or whatever. It wasn't that Oona wasn't interested in infinity—she was, only just *briefly*. Possibly it was her ghostwriter's instincts that made her wish to break the frame of the Escher drawing Biller and Perkus were elaborating before us, and examine it for fingerprints, find the human gist. "Biller," she interrupted, "if you don't mind my asking, how did all this admittedly marvelous virtual Communism buy you a real ocelot hat?" It was just like her to have nailed the breed of fur.

Biller understood her question perfectly, but he had to forage for language that would elucidate it to us one-worlders. "There's a certain kind of stuff people like to collect," he said. "They call it 'treasure.' It's different from the other stuff in there, it isn't easy to make. There's a limit on how much you can make, and it takes a long time, people don't like that. So you can buy someone else's treasure, or you can steal it—"

"That's what *you* do!" said Oona, exhilarated. "You're a virtual thief. I love it."

Biller shook his head, not insulted, just moving at a slower pace and unwilling to be hurried. "I manufacture treasure, and sell it. I'm a craftsman."

"You mean you sell it to virtual people?" asked Oona.

"Real people," said Biller. "They pay real money."

"You've done awfully well for yourself."

"I make good treasure. People pay a lot."

"That's what he was doing all that time in the alley," said Perkus. "Making . . . virtual . . . treasure." He seemed to find it pitiable.

"You mean you're gainfully employed," said Oona, not concealing disappointment, either. Here her radar for scandal wasn't so unlike Perkus's romance of dissidence—each was a little unthrilled at a secret life consisting of dull industry. Admittedly, this was some-thing we all three had in common, for I'd surely done nothing in life except duck a day job.

Before Biller left he jotted down his new apartment's address so Perkus could contact him, explaining that there was no telephone. Then he asked to use Perkus's computer. We all shuffled in, assuming that we'd get some glimpse of Yet Another World, but after Perkus transferred his phone line, Biller instead logged on to the city's Tiger Watch Web site. The monster had last been seen two days ago, on Sixty-eighth Street by a couple of Hunter undergraduates, rustling beneath an opened metal grating at a work site. There had been no casu-alties or damage, and the site ranked risk of an attack tonight as Yellow, or Low-to-Moderate. Biller sensed we were watching over his shoulder.

"I like to check before I go out."

"That's fine," Perkus assured him.

"Do you want me to set up an alert on your desktop? It blinks if the code goes to Red."

"That's okay. I'm not online enough for it to matter."

"Can you show us your . . . World?" said Oona.

"This computer's too slow," said Biller. He retopped his head with the ocelot, and was gone.

"I don't want to worry anyone," said Oona half an hour later, seemingly apropos of nothing, "but Biller's little wonderland might eventually bring about the destruction of our universe."

"Huh?" We'd been smoking marijuana, I'd been scheming on shifting Oona and myself out the door, shifting our evening to a more physical plane. Perkus had been auditioning CD tracks for us, airing rock groups he claimed as precursors to or missing links between other rock groups I'd never heard of. And I was confused before Oona had even spoken. When these evenings dragged into epics, I sometimes wished I could keep Perkus in better focus. Oona's ferocities frequently nudged him to the margins here on his own main stage. But I had no option of asking her leave in order to be alone with Perkus, so I'd opt instead to remove her and myself. There were rewards.

"Have you heard of simulated worlds theory?" she asked both of us. "It's something Emil Junrow was working on before he died, I actually wrote about it in *I Can't Quite Believe You Said That, Dr. Junrow*."

"Sure, I've heard of it," said Perkus, voice conveying a defensive uncertainty. "What's that got to do with Biller?"

"If you understand it, you must realize that the likelihood is that we'll be shut down once we develop our own virtual worlds," she said, plainly mocking. By using the word *understand* she meant to say she knew that Perkus, and certainly myself, didn't.

"Please explain," I said.

"Simulated worlds theory says that computing power is inevitably going to rise to a level where it's possible to create a simulation of an entire universe, in every detail, and populated with little simulated beings, something like Biller's avatars, who sincerely believe they're truly alive. If you were in one of these simulated universes you'd never know it. Every sensory detail would be as complete as the world around us, the world as we find it."

"Sure," said Perkus. "Everybody knows that." He tried to dismiss or encompass Oona's description before she could complete it. "It's common knowledge we could be living in a gigantic computer simulation unawares. I think science established that *decades* ago, for crying out loud. Your Junrow was—huh!—behind the curve on that one."

"Right, right," said Oona slyly. "But here's the point. If we agree that the odds are overwhelming that it's already happened, then we're just one of innumerable universes living in parallel, a series of experiments just to see how things will develop. You know, whether we'll end up destroying ourselves with nuclear weapons, or become a giant hippie commune, or whatever. There might be trillions of these simulations going on at once."

"Why couldn't we be the original?" I asked.

"We *could* be," said Oona. "But the odds aren't good. You wouldn't want to bet on it."

I didn't protest to Oona that we *felt* like the original, to me. I knew she'd say that every fake universe would feel like the original, to its inhabitants. Yet everything around me, every tangy specific in the simulation in which I found myself embedded, militated against the suggestion that it was a simulation: the furls of stale smoke and gritty phosphenes drifting between my eyes and the kitchen's overhead light, the involuntary memory-echo telling me one of the rock bands Perkus had played was called Crispy Ambulance, a throbbing hangnail I'd misguidedly gnawed at and now worked to ignore, the secret parts of Oona Laszlo I'd uncover and touch and taste within the hour, if my guess was right.

"The problem," she continued, "is that our own simulated reality might only be allowed to continue if it were either informative or entertaining enough to be worth the computing power. Or anyway, as long as we didn't use too much, they might not unplug us. That's assuming there remains some limit on that kind of resource, which all our physical laws suggest *would* be the case. So the moment we develop our own computers capable of spinning out their own virtual universes—like Yet Another World—we become a drastic drain on their computing power. It's exponential, because now they have to generate all of our simulations, too. We wouldn't be worth the trouble at that point, we'd have blown the budget allocated to our particular little simulation. They'd just pull our plug. I mean, they'd have millions of other realities running, they'd hardly miss one. But, you know, too bad for *us*."

"By 'they' you mean God, I guess." I was surprised to hear myself use the word.

"Let's agree to call them 'our simulators.' "

Now Perkus looked truly terrified. His good eye withdrew, his kooky one reeled. "*What should we do?*"

"I don't think there's anything we can do," said Oona. "Except, if possible, keep our simulators really entertained." With that she gave me a look. Lecture over. Something else to begin.

■

How did Perkus occupy himself, when Oona and I left him alone those December nights? Richard Abneg and I used to see him through to the dawn, until one or all of us were dozing in our chairs. Oona and I, on the other hand, typically whipped Perkus and ourselves into a frenzy, then vamoosed. I felt an extra pang this night, discharging him into the wake of Oona's provocations. Her merry nightmare of simulated worlds was too much the sort of thing Perkus would gnaw over.

Yet he never seemed to begrudge our going. I wondered if Perkus might be bidding on chaldrons all alone, in the dark, after hours. He still hoarded Ice, used other name brands for social smoking. I could so easily picture him, padding in his socks to the CD player to insert the Sandy Bull disk, then lowering the lights and leaning his head into the cowl of the screen's glow, fingers puttering without angst or undue wishfulness, all possessive lusts dispelled in past attempts, only entering a perfunctory bid for what he no longer imagined he'd win, content to seek the remote embrace of that inexplicable ceramic other—the only variety of pair-bonding Perkus Tooth allowed himself, so far as I could tell. Was this picture real? Who knew? Chaldrons, like Lindsay the waitress and whether Marlon Brando was alive or dead, had joined the list of things we no longer mentioned. Our silence on those subjects was just part of the price we'd paid to enter this oasis, this false calm that had carried me, carried all of us, if I can be trusted to speak for the others, to nearly the end of the year, to the day in late December when things changed again, that irreversible day which began with the mayor's invitation arriving in the mail.

15

I culled it from the mass of junk in my brass mailbox on my way out that morning. Who knew how long it had spent there—I checked that box once a week or so, and then just to bundle the pointless catalogues and credit-card offers into the building's handy recycling bins. The creamy rectangular envelope, my name and address hand-calligraphied, HIS HONOR JULES ARNHEIM embossed in the upper corner, had some mass or density that tugged downward, and so slipped from the garbagy sheaf, and into my attention, almost as in a card trick. For all that it telegraphed importance, I tucked the envelope into my coat's inner breast pocket to open in the taxicab, worrying I'd be late. Then I forgot it there for a little while, disconcerted by the early hour and already regretting my awkward mission.

The previous Wednesday I'd emerged from the shower to find Oona with her head cocked, punching impatiently through the messages piled on my answering machine, whose digital readout had been blinking Full for a few days already. She turned to offer a crookedly sweet smile, unashamed at her prying. I suppose I was transparently hapless in this regard: Oona could feel confident she was my only secret, so what would she be prying after? She'd restored the volume so the messages were audible; the voice of my old publicist Foley leaked from the machine while Oona's finger hovered over the Next button.

"You've got to do something about this," said Oona, with an uncommon air of sympathy.

"About what?"

"You need to go out once in a while and represent," she said gently. "It's your only job."

Oona tapped past the blipping first syllables of the last few unheard messages, the bulk of them Foley's greeting, repeated in descending tones of resignation. I'd certainly known it was Foley's calls I'd been ignoring, even after I lowered the machine's volume. Janice's diagnosis had brought a raft of media requests, mercifully channeled through my lecture agency. After so long having nothing for me, I suppose they might be a little frustrated I wasn't pouncing on these fresh opportunities. What I couldn't fathom was what Oona thought she was doing nudging my denial's manhole cover and peeking underneath.

I toweled my hair, convenient cover. "I'm not an expert on decaying orbits or foot cancer, you know. They want me to wring my hands and talk about how much I love her."

"Well, that's easy then, since you do love her."

I stared. I didn't know why Oona insisted on it, but I was less sure of my love each time she did. Perhaps that was her reason.

"I'll help you sort through these if you like."

"I think if you hit Delete twice it erases them all."

By the time I was dressed she'd cleared the machine, but had also written out, on a lined yellow pad she kept

in her coat pocket, a list of the outlets requesting interviews, then begun crossing out the majority of them.
"Don't bother with these . . . this you've already missed
. . . look, Chase, you should at least do the *Brian Lehrer
Show*. It isn't sensational or hysterical, there's nothing to
be afraid of. The whole city tunes in to WNYC, you get
a lot of bang for your buck."

"What if I want . . . no bang?"

"We all have to do our part." Oona's encouragement
was strangely tender, like a cornerman exhorting a jittery boxer back into the ring. I found myself not wanting
to let her down. If it was for Oona, I could talk about
Janice once or twice, exhibit my heartbreak and confusion. No one would ever known how little I remembered, and if I wanted details I only had to read the
newspaper.

"Call your friend Foley," said Oona, tearing off the top
sheet, on which she'd heavily circled the radio invitation
she favored. She left it beside my phone, then reloaded
her pockets and tugged her skinny leather gloves over
her knuckles. "Bye for now."

"Foley's not my friend," I said. "She's my publicist."

"Okay, call your publicist."

"You're my friend."

"I'm your whatever."

It wasn't the twenty-minute segment of airtime to
which I'd consented that unnerved me now. I could call
on old vocal prowess; for me, voice-over had been the
least difficult task in performance, while embodiment
was the more esoteric art, and I was rusty. A voice issuing in the void could claim anything and persuade easily

enough. If Brian Lehrer or his staff meanwhile wished to see through me, let them feel welcome. I'm sure they'd had bigger fakes than me on the premises. But once I'd heard where WNYC was headquartered, in the Municipal Building on Centre Street at Chambers, at the mouth of the Brooklyn Bridge, I realized I hadn't been so far downtown since the gray fog's onset. I didn't think of myself as afraid, nor a recluse like Perkus. I just figured I hadn't happened to go. But this morning I was afraid, perhaps an intimation of the evening to come. Foley had said she would meet me at WNYC's offices and I was glad.

Wouldn't you know it, giving flesh to my fear were distant sirens. You could hear these anywhere in the city, but they took on a different cast at the perimeter of that cloud bank that had settled on the island below Chambers. I glimpsed the fog's rim in the crooked canyons from the windows of my cab. It swallowed daylight right up to the bridge's on-ramp, hazy tendrils nestling into the greens around city hall. At that I recalled the envelope in my breast pocket, my fingers drifting in to confirm its presence, but too late, I'd arrived. I passed through the Municipal Building's airport-style security, emptying pockets of change and keys for bored men in uniform, then rode the elevator twenty-five floors to meet my small public fate.

Foley found me at the station's glass doors and ushered me in. The show was to consist of me and a female cancer doctor, an oncologist who'd been consulting with Mission Control on Janice's case, and who greeted me a little coldly, I thought. We'd been seated at our microphones and prepped a little, supplied with drinking water and shown the Cough button, when Lehrer came in, trailing more of his staff, and Foley too, and made an apology: we weren't going to go on the air after all, had been bumped. Those sirens weren't irrelevant, something had happened, close by, and the station was shifting to live coverage, on the street. A man, one of the money people, instead of showing up at the offices of the brokerage house where he worked, had thrown himself and his briefcase into the giant excavation for Noteless's memorial. It was all unfortunately too easy to do, creep close to that site, under cover of the gray fog. Lehrer explained all this in a wryly consoling voice I now realized I'd heard a hundred times before. "I suspect we'll be seeing more of this as winter comes in," he told us. "I think it's that much harder to report for work down under that cloud every day when it's so cold." The doctor and I stood, rendered dumb. Everything about this confused me, but I didn't want to take up anyone's time. I felt I should be the apologetic one, sorry for my own dispensability, as though I'd let down Lehrer and Foley, Oona too. Yet confirmed in my own suspicion that I was generally a filler item, useful only on slow news days.

Foley led me downstairs to share a cab back uptown, shaking her head. I felt affectionately toward the small, intent publicist, making such effort always to keep her needless professional distance, forever on my side in any misunderstanding or disappointment, as though my cause was righteous or just, or was a cause at all. This absurdity, that Foley cared more than I did, kept me from ever knowing how to make conversation with her, despite all fondness. So I committed the discourtesy of opening the creamy envelope in front of her there, in the cab's backseat. *Jules Arnheim / Requests the Presence of You and Your Guest / At His Residence / For a Champagne Dinner / In Celebration of the Holidays*. A separate tiny envelope, stamped, for RSVP, slipped out into my lap. The party was two days before Christmas, eight days from now. Despite the engraved elegance of the paperwork, the whole thing smacked of imperial impulsiveness. Arnheim was known for commanding celebrities to his table at whim.

This was a surprise. I recalled some prediction from Rossmoor Danzig, a mention of the mayor's gratitude. But that whole episode was like a cameo in fever. So it was as if my own illness had arranged to introduce me to Mayor Arnheim. Anyway, I must have concealed my amazement well enough from Foley. Her face fell. She thought I'd been shunning her calls because I'd wandered into fabulousness. Realms a mere PR girl daren't imagine. I had no way to explain how wrong she was, that I'd in fact stumbled into squalor and marginal romance. I shouldn't mention Oona and I couldn't describe Perkus. Foley dropped me off at my door, so we could both forget the errand's conundrum, my near miss with publicity. I was only relieved. That part of my life could go on without me for all I cared, was as distant as the space station.

■

I had to kill a few hours before I could descend into my well of squalor and romance again. What I failed to note was how those sirens in the fog had sounded a note of disaster that cold morning. I was diverted from contemplation of harbingers by Christmas decorations on Second Avenue and the mayor's invitation burning a hole in my pocket all through the day's empty hours. I'll confess I did feel a little fabulous about it. I became fixated on taking Oona to the mayor's, flaunting our secret affiliation in a semipublic place from which I could be positive the media would be banished. Nobody was as guarded as Jules Arnheim, never more so than in his private domain. I wanted to present this fun to Oona in person, like a Valentine. Yet I knew she was hammering at her chapters and wouldn't reward interruption. I also expected she'd find me at Perkus's later if I was patient.

The phone rang an hour or so after I'd appeared at Eighty-fourth Street myself, but it wasn't Oona. "It's Abneg," Perkus reported to me, holding the receiver aside. "They're in a cab a few blocks away. He says Georgina's having a craving for burgers, he wonders do we want to meet them at Jackson Hole?"

There was only one possible reply. I wasn't worried, Oona could find us there easily enough, at that restaurant which was like an annex to Perkus's kitchen. We grabbed our coats—even Perkus had at last admitted winter's irreversibility, and dug out of his closet a moth-eaten maroon stadium coat, half its wooden-peg fasteners missing, and a black captain's cap, which made him resemble an Irish folksinger or terrorist. We were just downstairs and in the building's doorway when we felt the crack and shudder beneath our feet, a wrenching seizure in the earth below the tile of the corridor, the foundations of the building, the pavement of the street.

I don't know if there was truly a roaring sound or if it was merely the disconcerting roar of silence that followed, an instant afterward.

Whatever had snapped beneath the world, beam or bone, wasn't in our imagination. The cars crawling up the street each braked, and the piano inside Brandy's halted too, the sing-along stilled. Then, as we stood trying to fathom it, a bubble of laughter and mock-shrieks erupted within the bar, the uncurious singers only relieved to be alive, and the piano resumed its strolling tune, and a ragged harmony of voices resumed, too. The cars picked up their crawl. Perkus and I rounded the corner of Second, hungry and habitual (and yes, freshly stoned).

Neither of us spoke, and in that heartbeat's moment of bogus imperturbability, like the interval before blood wells in a deep-sliced fingertip, it seemed not impossible we'd take our booth at Jackson Hole and never mention it. Except the gaudy burger joint had just an instant before been demolished, the building wholly wrecked from underneath, the recognizable shards of exterior window frame and signage and also the chrome-and-vinyl booths and bar and stools of the interior sagging together, under the crushing weight of the roof and the yellow-painted brick of the upper stories, into a groaning trench, a ragged black smile in the concrete that was meant never to betray us, with tiny waterfalls of pulverized drywall like chalk trickling into the corners of that new mouth. Stepping up entranced with others on the sidewalk, Perkus and I found ourselves transformed into first members of a mob of rubberneckers, gathered at the outskirts of a crime or disaster, the nearest layer of the concentric amazed staring from windows and out of stopped vehicles. Then the sirens came, as if replying to those in the morning's fog, and converged on us where we swayed stupefied in the blossoming dust.

Richard Abneg and Georgina Hawkmanaji joined us there, milling in that human amoeba of gawkers as it was brushed back from the scene by policemen and emergency medical workers, though at its outer edge the collective creature grew grotesquely huge, and throbbed, livid and possibly dangerous, faces lit from underneath by sparking red-and-yellow flares that had been laid like sticks of dynamite at the feet of barricades. I'd read of this, an unintended consequence of the city's Tiger Watch Web site, that hundreds with vicarious investment in the activities of the predator, citizens superstitious or worshipful, others disbelieving, seeking to confirm conspiracy explanations for the shutdowns and ruin, others armed with cameras or concealed weaponry, others hoping to pillage wrecked stores, all had been flocking in increasing numbers to the coordinates of reported sightings, their numbers growing, their response times unnervingly sharp. Then again, by any outward measure Perkus and I were part and parcel, members of the Tiger Stalkers' Union.

Richard, when he and Georgina located us, linked each of his arms into one of ours, breaking the spell of disaster a little, divorcing us from the spectating group mind. He and Georgina were bundled into their cold-weather finery, returning, I suppose, from another of their endless sequence of formal occasions. Richard, since meeting

Georgina, seemed to have shelved his irreverence toward ceremony.

"Hey," Richard said. "I talked to a cop, he says they're pretty sure it tunneled back uptown. We aren't likely to hear anything about survivors for a while yet. It's pretty cold out here—maybe we ought to get something to eat?" He spoke embracingly, as though escorting mourners from a graveside, toward the consolations of the wake. "This'll be waiting when we get back, it's not going anywhere."

"Did this happen because of us?" said Perkus hollowly. "In another minute we would have been inside."

"Don't be ridiculous," said Richard.

"I think if I don't eat a meal soon I will vomit," said Georgina. "Please. I'm sorry."

"Isn't there another place around here for a burger?" said Richard. He must know he risked hamburger heresy. It might be worth the grievance if it drew Perkus back from the brink of total identification with the mauled restaurant. There'd be no cheeseburger deluxes originating there anytime soon. As for any further losses, we were numbed, unable to think. Or at least, if Perkus thought of them, he didn't speak.

I said, "We could go to Gracie Mews." I worried about missing Oona, but then again, unlike Richard Abneg, Oona was hardly likely to come browsing for us in this mad scene.

Now it was Georgina who clutched my arm. "Please—anything." She really did look a bit green. Actually, there was an unhealthy sheen of agitation to the Hawkman and Richard Abneg both, as though it had been too hot in their taxicab, or they'd been making out in it. By the time we'd nudged Perkus out of his spell enough to filter out of the crowd, walked to First Avenue, and gotten ourselves seated under the grilling fluorescents of the Mews, I saw they were both perspiring, their eyes raccoonish. Richard's blustery good cheer, which I'd taken as concern for Perkus's fragility, now seemed to me an almost frantic heartiness in response to the disaster. "This looks really bad," he chirruped. "There's certainly fatalities this time out!" He might be overcompensating, out of some sense of culpability.

Or was it in fear? Perhaps Richard felt Perkus's guess had been off by a degree, that the tiger had come not for Perkus but for him. That absurd epithet Perkus had thrown at him, *eagle-hunted*—maybe tiger-hunted, too. Yet, how absurd and solipsistic. I'd begun to do Perkus's thinking for him. As if the tiger had had to be hunting someone in our company, and it was only a matter of figuring who! As if it had to be hunting any one person. As if it was a tiger after all, and we hadn't been given another explanation. Yet there must be some reason Richard and Georgina were so agitated, in contrast to Perkus's zomboid numbness. I suppose I too might have seemed out of kilter, to the others—it was as if we'd all just climbed out of that crater, rather than merely wandering up to its periphery.

So we ordered and ate. The Hawkman consoled her nerves by gobbling the bowlful of dill halves our waiter plunked down to keep us while we waited for our meal. I didn't point out to her that someone else might have wanted one. Instead I borrowed Richard's cell phone, and dialed Oona's number. When I entered the last digit and hit Call, the screen announced CALLING/OONA LASZLO.

"Oona's in your phone?"

"Oh, sure."

"I didn't realize you even knew each other."

Of all things, this snapped Perkus from his daze, just to snipe at my innocence. "You're like the ultimate amnesiac American, Chase. You never can imagine anything actually happened before you wandered along." This attack, both rote and gratuitous, was surely Perkus at his most mediocre. Under the circumstances I cut him slack—I had no reply to his jibe, anyhow.

I got Oona's voice mail, as expected, and told her where we'd ended up. (Oona never answered her phone, that I'd seen. Just checked it constantly.) And she must have been near, for this brought her, so quickly that she beat the Mews' kitchen, by a whisker. Our four burgers slid onto our place mats just after she'd crowded in between Georgina and Perkus. Oona signaled to the imperturbable waiter that she'd take one too, then added, "Medium rare."

"Hello, Oona," said Richard, a neutral greeting, devoid of clues for me to examine. "You haven't met Georgina, I don't think."

The women managed a polite introduction, even as the Hawkman drowned her plate in ketchup and jammed a bouquet of fries into her mouth, still trying to outrun disaster's appetite. Only now did it occur to me how by making the call, and then blurting the surprised question that elicited Perkus's scolding, I'd widened the circle of conspirators—mine, and Oona's—to include Richard and Georgina. This felt natural, in a life-during-wartime sort of way.

Seeing the company assembled here for the first time—four of us with our burgers, and now came Oona's, too—I believed I was seeing my present life complete for what it was, or what I wished it to be. Like a foreign correspondent in a zone of peril, a Graham Greene protagonist, I was secretly thrilled that chaos had rearranged a few things. I had my people around me. There might be undercurrents of the undisclosed between us at that table—Oona's ignorance of chaldrons, say (but then again, like the readout on Richard's phone, nearly anything might be known to all but me), or the extra reason, quite beyond milk shakes, which I knew, but couldn't risk saying, that Perkus might have to mourn the demolition of Jackson Hole. Yet these hesitations didn't outweigh the solidarity of our team. That we existed against a backdrop of baffling and indistinct dangers gave us our shape.

Then again, utterly negating all this camaraderie was the gasp of jealousy I'd felt at spotting her name on Richard's phone. This made me want to assert my place, at any risk to our secret. So I reached across the table and took Oona's hand. She didn't pull it away, but while I held it she wouldn't meet my eyes. After a moment I let her go. I'd at least conveyed my unguilty pleasure at her arrival. Who knew I'd take such crazy comfort in the leavings of catastrophe? I might be giddy that something of my own had come along, to rival Janice's melodrama.

"At least it's on a Second Avenue axis, that's the good news . . . maybe we should have been fueling the fucking thing with hamburgers to keep it underground . . ." Garrulous Richard carried on, and meanwhile the women seemed to be getting along splendidly over their burgers, Georgina buzzing through hers, using the bun to swab ketchup, Oona mostly tiptoeing around her own. Their talk was largely dropped names, the filling in of degrees of social separation, always fewer than you'd expect. I thought of them in those terms, as if I were a member of a frontier wagon train: "the women." They shed grace on our table by fitting together so disparately well: the Hawkman towering above us, Euro-exotic and impeccable, despite her frantic chowing, and Oona, so raven-like and quarrelsome, a rib of Manhattan torn out to make a woman.

It was—surprise!—Perkus I felt concerned about. Here we were, his whole support group (I didn't want to include Watt or Biller or Susan Eldred or anyone else right now in my desert-island fantasy), yet he'd shrunken to near-invisibility in our midst. Wrong restaurant, for a start. He fingered his burger like a skater toeing thin ice. Then, just as I'd alighted on my worry, ready to study him for minute indications, Perkus was on his feet. "We have to go." One eye was out the door, the other pleaded with us. "I have to go."

Sure enough, we went. Hand it to us, we at least understood we were a support group. Or lieutenants. Like that, we abandoned the meal, whisked back out into the cold, our visit to my own preferred restaurant unceremoniously interrupted—I wondered what it would take for me to burnish my favorites into myth like Perkus had done with Jackson Hole. Would he find another place? Well, we were rushing out partly to see what he would do, to follow the plot of his fixations. I glanced back, projecting embarrassment onto my regular waiters in the Mews, but they bussed our unfinished meal as implacably as ever, scooping tips into apron pockets, enduring the curse of the twenty-four-hour restaurant, which by definition required machines, not men, for its operation. So they'd become machines, more expert and obedient than the unruly tunneling thing that had surfaced from under Second Avenue.

The site had evolved rapidly in our absence—most of all by becoming a "site" (or possibly a "zone"), by revealing the unnerving readiness of a familiar street to be revised in martial strife, like a gentle friend suddenly enlisted in war, then returned decorated, missing limbs, and with a hundred-yard stare. The tiger-oglers had been stretched to a wide quarantine, across Second and the intersection of Eighty-fourth, by police barricades now manned by officers in vigilant pairs, who spoke only to one another, mercilessly snubbing the barrage of citizen inquiries. Behind them, the crater and the surrounding street blazed white, lit by emergency spotlights that had been cranked into position to facilitate specialists crawling over rubble, perhaps sounding within it with stethoscopes for Morse tapping or cries. Within the cordon ambulances blinked, ricocheting amber off upper stories. Dust cycloned through the klieg lights, up into the strobe and shadow.

We flanked Perkus, taking his cues. This was his precinct, his inquiry to make. He made none, but as we craned our necks for views through the rows of heads, all with their breath steaming as they muttered rumors or perhaps prayers, another bystander, a fiftyish woman with a leashed terrier clutched in her arms and shivering as it eyed us, a neighbor of Perkus's perhaps, leaned in and announced, "If you live close by you're safe now. It never strikes in the same place twice."

Perkus only peered at her, the dog now growling low in its throat, perhaps at his suspicious eye. But Richard, patroller of civic logic, stepped up.

"Sorry?" he said. "What's that you said?"

"The tiger doesn't return to the same place twice, everyone knows."

"It can't fail," Richard declared with instant exasperation, as if she weren't with us. "The human brain is sick with superstition." I was just glad he hadn't come out with "old wives' tale."

"Are people dead?" Perkus asked bluntly, ignoring both dog and Richard.

The woman shrugged, grudging to be pushed beyond the prophetic range of her first remark, into dull specifics. "Some got out, they were talking to the news." She nodded to the opposite side of the intersection, where two vans with satellite dishes on ladders had staked out an operation. "Two dead upstairs, and a girl from the restaurant, I think." It was as if her syntax had collapsed into the spontaneous grave along with the bodies.

"What girl?"

Again the woman spoke with a nod of her chin. "The Korean at the deli, he knew her."

We raced to the Korean, who stood measuring the spectacle, sheltered inside the flapped plastic tent covering his bins of produce and bundles of psychedelically pink-and-orange carnations. He'd seemingly been at his beer stash, cheeks red, eyes shiny, and also had a few rehearsals in his answer to Perkus's question. "Lin-*Say*," he reported, tsk-tsking as if we'd failed to pay attention the first dozen times he'd memorialized her. "A nice girl. A very nice girl. Came in every day, always smoke Camel Lights. I used tell her, 'When you gonna quit?'" He shook his head at the fine irony he'd dispensed, though it seemed to me second-rate, cribbed from a war movie.

We milled back into the traffic-stopped intersection, toward the cordon at the vent of Perkus's block. It was too clear what it meant that the ambulances didn't bother leaving the scene. Despite their authoritarian light show, those ice-cream trucks of death couldn't do any more for Perkus's murdered infatuation, his crushed crush, than could a keening Greek chorus, or a moaning witch doctor. Our group, fortunately, was stupidly silent—I prayed Richard wouldn't claim some memory of Lindsay, just to have something to say. For my part, I'd stay mum. How could I possibly explain to the others when Perkus had disclaimed any interest in her? He'd only treated her like a waitress. It now seemed awful to me that we'd bundled off to Gracie Mews, but I consoled myself with the reminder that Georgina had been a blood-sugar desperado. It wasn't as if we'd have accomplished anything more out here in the chill and confusion, where our team now threatened to unmoor, each member to drift off like a bear on his or her own floe.

Oona lagged behind us, inspired by the Korean's remark to bum a cigarette of her own from a passing stranger. I'd never seen Oona smoke tobacco before, but given the precedent of her secret eyeglasses, I wasn't too taken aback. Her personality had serial quitter in its DNA. Georgina hung back, too, while Richard and I tried to stick at Perkus's elbows, as if our friend were a drunkard. Perkus seemed to want to go home.

Eighty-fourth Street's traffic was stopped, too, and pedestrians were funneled by police to an entry point between two barricades on the north sidewalk, where many who approached were turned away. We waited our turn to meet the troll at this bridge, a towering grim older cop who spent as much time conversing with the radio Velcroed to his shoulder as with any mere citizens. "Street's closed," he informed us. "Use Eighty-fifth to get to Third." Each player on this stage of chaos had a line or two they were made to deliver ad infinitum, while we, the audience, filtered among them, gathering these coupons like stamps in an album.

"I *live* here." Perkus almost whined, the cop's size and clout reducing him to pipsqueak protest. I wanted to register my own claim of access, but couldn't find the words.

"All of you, or just him?" The cop asked for Perkus's identification, in order to check his address. Perkus handed it across numbly. The cop then sorted us out from him, the rest of us presumed guilty, rabble to be considered singly and subsequently, if at all. And before we could make any proper farewell, Perkus had been eased through the funnel's mouth. We four watched him go, his shoulders rounded with the burden of acquiescence to the larger forces, the alteration of his street into dystopian tableau, his personality made tiny by his dealings with the cop. What else he carried on that gaunt-slumped frame, what sway the tiger's close strike might have over his free associations, or the significance to his heart of the loss of Lindsay or that which she'd so ungrudgingly emissaried to his table, I feared presuming. On the sidewalk beyond, a clutch of Brandy's patrons, not more than one or two likely to be legitimate residents of the block, had spilled out to watch the cop's operation from behind his back, many with drinks still in their mitts. No fair, I thought.

16

The ruinous night had more to give. Richard and Georgina led us in retreat to a wine bar up Second Avenue, a place for grown-ups (and therefore, to me, usually invisible) called Pangaea. It was as if we were intent on dishonoring the occasion, as if one bottle of wine could drive the scent of catastrophe and sorrow, the ozone singe of an acetylene torch cutting in twisted rebar, from our nostrils. Yet after a perfunctory glass of Barbera the other couple quit the place, and it was then that Oona and I tumbled into a grotesque conflict. Like a member of an ensemble still working from an earlier draft of the appointed script, I'd clung to my fancy idea about the mayor's party, and I now produced that creamy invitation from my pocket, slid it across the candlelit table between us.

"I've got one of those," Oona said.

"You do?"

"Funny, isn't it?"

"I was hoping we'd go together." I winced at hearing myself reproduce the tones of some minor courtier, or possibly those of Ralph Bellamy in a movie belonging to Cary Grant. Oona's hunched and hunted posture suggested she felt uncomfortably public with me here, and that, in turn, seemed relevant to my dim proposal. Our skulking, I'd notice, was for Oona a highly local matter: West Side or Inwood okay, the East Side distinctly not. The mayor's address was on Fifth Avenue. I'd pleased myself thinking she meant to spare me bad publicity, rather than avoid embarrassment with her friends. I could be wrong.

"I'll be bringing Laird Noteless," she told me. The unspoken insinuation I couldn't keep from hearing was that she'd be sorry to see me there at all. The name she'd spoken revived an image of that shrine she kept over her desk, glowering Noteless and his portentous potholes, and threatened to give fly to every fearful accusation I'd kept partitioned for weeks simply out of gratitude that Oona would see me.

But I began coolly enough. "That reminds me, something happened downtown, I never had a chance to mention it with all this stuff. I don't know if you heard, a man killed himself by jumping into Noteless's memorial pit. As a result I never got to go on *Brian Lehrer*."

Everything I mentioned annoyed her. "That happens from time to time. It's just one of those stories they like to make a big deal over. You know how many suicides there are in this city?"

"You mean . . . more than one person has thrown themselves into his memorial?"

"The memorial, and other things he built. If you build bridges people throw themselves off those, too."

"I'm surprised there's such a big hole downtown," I said. "I was under the impression Noteless just got that commission."

"You're mistaken. Excavation started down there a long time ago."

Sure, sure, I was always mistaken. To be so was my great role, my Lear. Only I was less Learian than Othelloish at the moment. What was rising in me wouldn't be so curtly swept aside whatever the mistaken facts surrounding excavations, fog, or suicide. I felt the sort of jealousy that wants to ruin all the things it doesn't understand, because they suddenly made a picture of conspiracy. "This isn't your usual piece of ghostwriting, is it?" I spoke as if I knew a remarkable amount about her regular work. At the moment I couldn't recall the name of her raped power forward or defrosted Everest climber, but I fished up the one name that offered itself. "What is it about Noteless that's so different from, say, Emil Junrow?"

"One important difference I can think of is that Emil Junrow has gone to meet his maker, whom he incidentally always referred to as the Flying Spaghetti Monster."

"Does Noteless chase you around the desk like Junrow?"

"Oh, no, Noteless, strangely enough, employed hand-cuffs and chloroform." Oona's sarcasm was keyed precisely to the level of my righteousness, her tone ferocious enough to convey how little she cared to be questioned. We might ascend to a screaming match by this method, my accusations lucid while her chosen words remained all spaghetti monsters and other non sequiturs.

Seeing the trap, I was nonetheless doomed to the jealous interlocutor's task: I needed to hear her deny *something*. "Why would you go as Noteless's date? Is he some kind of extra boyfriend?"

"I'm not Laird's plus-one, he's mine. And here's the funny thing: you don't need an extra boyfriend when you don't have one in the first place. Next time you spot our waitress, flag her down. I don't like it here."

The waitress had been keeping her eye on me, I'd happened to notice (that might be something Oona didn't like about the place), so I extended my hands and made a scribbling motion on an invisible notepad. "Why am I not your boyfriend?" I said. I knew it was abject, but there's something about me, I like to think, that can carry off an abject line.

"That's too easy: because I'm not your girlfriend." She rolled her eyes at the ceiling, meaning outer space.

We'd reached another accustomed juncture: Oona pouring cold water on my romancing by means of a disconcerting allegiance to my fiancée. The waitress slipped a bill under the candlelight, and not wishing for Oona to pay, I slapped down a pair of twenties as if to trump it. One of many trumps I now intended to make. I wouldn't think about Janice, or Noteless, instead turn my disadvantages, the whole night's wretchedness, into adamancy, and opportunity. "Fair enough, but I'm your *something*," I said slyly, quoting Oona to herself.

"For now we'll leave it at that."

"Let's say I wanted to change the world all around."

"Make day night, black white, that sort of thing?" She spoke distractedly, fidgeting into her coat.

293

"Why don't we go back to your place?" I said. Oona only looked at me, but her crooked smile, lip caught on her teeth, might have admitted for the first time that I'd once appeared in that apartment. She let me guide her to the street again, to where it was cold and the only thing to do was to begin walking briskly somewhere. I couldn't tell whether any of the people on the sidewalk were special visitors drawn to the neighborhood by the tiger's attack. If so, they did nothing to give themselves away. We were two blocks north of it all. I didn't think about Perkus, alone in his apartment. I meant to do some pair-bonding. Oona fell into step beside me, clearly on a bearing for my building, not so large a victory as I craved.

"Why can't I visit there?" I pressed.

"It's a workplace, not a fuck place, that's all." She liked to use this word often. "I didn't get where I am today fucking in my workplace."

"Do you have some other—'fuck place'?"

"Yes. Your apartment."

Though this qualified as a sort of happy thought, my cascading emotions glitched again. "Who's the strange small man you eat sandwiches with?" The words spoke themselves, my desperation couched in a feeble air of impertinence.

"Is that a Zen koan? I eat sandwiches with a wide array of strange small men."

"The one in your apartment that day—I mean, your workplace. Is he some kind of Noteless research assistant?" My brain was like a tongue exploring a cold sore.

"I call him He-Who-Is-No-Larger-Than-a-Breadbox. You have nineteen questions left."

"He must have an actual name."

"That's true. If I tell it to you will you shut up?"

"Sure." Now that it was too late I hoped this deal we'd struck could be convivial. I wanted to shut up, truly I did, and I'd be glad to think she knew it.

"His name is Stanley Toothbrush."

"See, now you're definitely making fun of me, because that's idiotic." It was as though she'd read my thoughts the afternoon I'd invaded her office: that the indistinct little door-opener might somehow be Oona's equivalent to Perkus.

"Stanley would be awfully hurt if he heard you. You've no idea how often people laugh in his face."

"Toothbrush . . . that's just a little hard to swallow."

"No more so than stuff you swallow every day."

This puzzle given air, we entered my building and rode the elevator in silence. Who could pull off a credible jealous outburst in this incongruent atmosphere? So just through my doorway, into the dark of my rooms, I cornered and kissed her, leaving the lights off. Was I as hungry to have her in bed as I suddenly felt, or was I faking one agitation into another? Oona's lips and hands were cold, and I was aware of the fragility of her little body in the winter. Her frame wasn't strong enough to drag around a coat heavy enough to warm her. I pushed up her sweater and even her nipples seemed cool in my lips. We tripped over ourselves to my bed. I hadn't had a significant amount of wine but it appeared we might be drunk on the tiger's kill. The shades were raised so moonlight streamed in and outlined our limbs cinematically, an effect which doomed my brain to distracted ponderings at key moments. If Oona was a raven, then her armor of irony was all feathers, as delicate, as crucial. Nobody wanted to imagine a bird without feathers. She couldn't be blamed, had shrouded herself in this life, in this world, the only way she knew how. So anything she inflicted on me was on the order of a helpless defense against this disarranging urgency I couldn't possibly be alone in feeling. (I had a gasp or two from her now for proof.) We'd only been cast in roles, and I could forgive any witty tactics. I should go deeper into my part, not slacken for fear of being foolish. In this I drew on everything that was obvious about women and intellectuals as well as everything I knew in my art.

First I pushed Oona to one extra brink, after I had nothing left myself, used my mouth, everything I knew in that other art. Her orgasms shuddered through her to her eyelids, her skinny knees and elbows swimming together as though she fought upstream, a froglike convulsion, while she glanced at the nearest blank wall, her gaze trying to deny what the rest of her confessed. When at last we lay cooling and destroyed, heads twinned on pillows, I spoke, bearing in mind that actors were more at home in their emotions than many who might be smarter in other ways. The key would be to forge a language so direct, so irony-immune, that it cut off Oona's typical avenues of escape. "I'm with you now," I said. "There's no one else. I don't love anyone else."

"You don't know who you love."

"You, you, you."

"You're confused. I'm a suitable secret, if you also have a glamorous dying astronaut. Without her, you'd see clearly that I'm a creep."

Oona's voice was small and steady in the dark. From this angle my window was half blocked by the Dorffl Tower, the bar of moonlight running across our naked bodies, to the curtain of shadow bisecting our stomachs. I'd have had to crane around to see my church spire. The birds were elsewhere at night. I figured they found shelter in another place, together or separately—tabulate this with the other mysteries.

"Why do you say she's dying?"

"Isn't that the story? My mistake, if not."

"I hadn't—" I couldn't finish, my grandiose offering broken apart, shattered from underneath as a building might be wrecked by a burrowing tiger, by levels of despair opening within me. I mourned the passing of a restaurant; the premature death of an eager-to-party waitress named Lindsay, whose phone number in fact lay within reach, still bookmarking my bedside Wodehouse; the exile of Perkus Tooth from the pair-bonding I so yearned for on his behalf; the incommensurate, irreconcilable, unbereaved nature of all human relations, particularly the local sample now on display in my bed; I mourned too the collapse of my script, the skit of avowal I'd scripted while we fucked, and had vowed to enact afterward; I mourned it all except for Janice, who seemed remoter from me than ever. Perhaps the poisonous failure of my love had grown in her, and was now threatening to murder her, an abscess mimicking a tumor. In space you were meant to die by vacuum. I was the vacuum.

"I'm extremely tired of this conversation," said Oona without mercy. Certainly she'd heard the shallows in my breathing as I strained not to weep. "If you love me, go on loving Janice. That's what I need you to do."

"I don't know if I can."

"Pretend."

"I'm having a crisis of authenticity."

"Well, I wouldn't, if I were you."

"What do you mean, you wouldn't?"

"I just wouldn't recommend that type of crisis for a person in your position. You've got little enough authenticity to spare, I wouldn't use up any of your precious supply on a crisis."

Before I knew it Oona was dressed. Some nights she stayed, others crept away, but she'd always before hovered in our afterglow at least a while. I'd driven her away. I scrambled to don pajama bottoms, looking to dignify the early exit, mask it as normal.

"Do I have any questions left?"

"Nineteen," she said, rather tenderly now. "I keep my promises."

"A few weeks ago, did you happen to notice either a sweet chocolate smell or a high ringing sound?"

"Neither," she said. "I was busy working."

"Okay," I said. I padded after her as she retraced the path of our strewn clothing, finally to the still-dark entranceway where she reclaimed her coat and heels.

"Anything else?" she asked.

"Are you really going to the mayor's with Noteless instead of me?"

"You have your own invitation. I'll see you there. It's just a dinner party."

"Not a date."

"Not a date." Every word Oona gave me before slipping away was generosity, drops of water in the desert. "I don't date old men. Not around Christmastime, anyway. Too depressing." The light from the outside corridor fell in around her as she readied her escape, casting her in doorway silhouette. I crossed my arms over my naked white chest, feeling the typical humbleness of the shirtless and barefoot before the dressed. At that moment, out of that vulnerability, I understood my assignment. What Oona had asked of me was simple, only I'd refused to understand until now, believed her arcane or perverse. The answer was love. My job was not only to endure and thrive in the impossible situation but to make myself into a kind of chaldron, to generate a love field broad enough to enclose our fear. This was no time for parsimony. If my love was enough to reach Janice in orbit it would ipso facto cover Oona as well, and anyone else who needed to feel it, most particularly Perkus in his desolate rooms. I had nothing to protect or defend. I only had to do my job. This is what Oona wanted me to know, I was sure of it. I uncrossed my arms, stepped into the light so she could see the tender face that had just fitted itself between her thighs. All the talk since was like wind rattling the windows, outside of what mattered.

"You can bring someone, too, you know," she said.

"I'll bring Perkus," I said. "He needs to get out more often."

■

December 18
My darling Chase,
Now comes the winter of my discombobulation. Of course we have no winter here, it's always cold out and filthy hot sweaty moist oxygenless inside, but hey, I notice the pages flying off the calendar, Santa's loading his sleigh! Hope he gets through the minefield okay! We've reverted to believing in Santa, Chase. Don't tell me different. Saint Nick is one of the cultural touchstones up here, something Sledge and I and the Russians can all get behind, whereas E. Bunny and T. Fairy are too American apparently, hence comprise terra incognita. As is, come to think of it, terra! But we believe in mythical things here, like Earth and Santa. After all, we have invisible enemies—CO_2, cancer, gravity. So heck, why not invisible friends?

Each bout of chemo is worse than the last. My days ("days") a dull cycle of recovery until I'm strong enough to suck the poison again. During my latest bouts of helplessness I've been installed in the Nursery, which in a kind of moron pun has become a sickroom, and everyone aboard's a nurse now, all too adept at tapping one of my veins and inserting an IV, not to mention swabbing my puke from where it's drifted into my hair and so on. I suppose we're enjoying a faint resurgent solidarity, at last obeying Mission Control psychiatric guidelines that we gather for meals and meetings every other day.

The Captain is a captain again, his melancholic depression no contest for my cancer—yes, I feel like a winner, Chase. I may have bought a lottery ticket out of here, as it happens, and once in a while Keldysh or the Captain can't keep from peering at me with a sympathy that includes a trace of morbid fascination at the strange journey I've managed to undertake from within our orbiting stasis, and perhaps even envy for my possible destination (Mstislav is too devoted an attending physician ever to reveal such a sentiment, and Zamyatin, the angry cosmonaut, too much of a bastard). It's almost as if I've broken a pledge we'd made to one another and to our audience on Earth: that we'd live forever here, mascots of futility.

Most astonishing of all, though, is the effect on poor Sledge. The dawning signs of this transformation we credited to circumstance: with Mstislav giving so much of his time to my care, the Greenhouse was neglected, worse than usual, I mean, and so Sledge began to grope his way out of the Attic back into a share of his old duties, tending the wheatgrass and cabbages and hives as if he'd never abandoned them, and really producing some miraculous results. Sledge is a more instinctive and sympathetic gardener than Mstislav, something we all, perhaps even Sledge, had forgotten. Without even appearing to try he's reversed a degree of the CO_2 slide. He's also a better cook. The two roles are intertwined. He offers me broths of freshly harvested sweet-potato greens and baby bok choy, and though the air we breathe in here is itself a kind of broth, I sip them gratefully.

There's more. You'll say he's got some kind of vampiric jones for suffering, but Sledge has become a tender companion in my worst hours, vigilant over my fevers, an entertainer when I can bear entertainment. Whether in stoicism or hostility, we'd long since quit sharing personal stories up here, but during quiet hours when everyone else is sleeping and the toxins inflaming my veins won't let me rest, Sledge has been disburdening to me tales of collegiate mayhem in the Pacific Northwest, at Evergreen College. How a pale secret fag (did I just let that slip?) made his way first amid those blustery, sunburned hippie biology majors, then here to patriotic doom with me and the Russians, God only knows. If half the amount of crystal meth and threesomes he claims in his youthful annals are factual, sleepy old Sledge truly belonged in the Warhol Factory. Never underestimate anybody, Chase (I think you often do).

I know, my foolish darling, how you like to root for improbable heroes on unlikely quests, so I'll make you party to a secret. Sledge has been sneaking leaf-cutter bees out of the Greenhouse, one at a time, in a mason jar. It's his wild theory that their stings immunize against cancer, and so once or twice a day, on top of my official poisons, I roll up a pants leg and allow Sledge to bully a bee into injecting its venom into my shin. The dead bees he then lines up on the Nursery's doorjamb, facing outward, their dry little feet affixed with rubber cement so they won't drift. Fifteen or twenty now, keeping vigil while I nod. If the Russians have noticed, they've said nothing.

I'm sparing you, sparing us both, my pining evocations, refusing this time to rhapsodize on your appetite for pastry, the slightly ashy skin of your earlobes, any days spent failing to rouse ourselves beyond your bedroom threshold, or other days wandering museums, gazing in indoor fountains, startled by the sight of our own innocent faces in rippling pools. None of this. If I beckon you to remember me, Chase, I fear you'll slip to some image of another, for I suspect I'm beginning to dissolve, can barely remember myself anymore. But I remember you, Chase, I really do. I see you before me, like that mute Greek chorus of bees.

Your lost one,
Janice

17

The first globs had begun drifting to earth three hours before the mayor's party, not so much flakes as frost-spun jigsaw chunks rotating themselves into view as if an invisible examiner were hoping to puzzle them together on arrival. None of these were pure six-pointed specimens, those famously symmetrical and fingerprint-unique ski-chalet-wallpaper darlings, instead rough amalgams of three or four or six that had clotted together somewhere above the city, assembling into eerie contours, snow-cartoon images of docking spacecraft or German coffeemakers or shattered Greek statuary. This advance wave melted so smoothly it was as though ghosts slid through the wet pavement's screen to some realm below. Then, abruptly, the stuff quadrupled and began to lodge, the ghosts denied entry to the subterranean world, too many to welcome there, their bodies heaping uselessly against the former portal.

Then suddenly the drifting globs had gone torrential, bidding to replace the windless air itself entirely with white material, undertaking a crazy campaign to outline every contour in Manhattan, each sill and rearview mirror, each knuckle of crossing-signal plumbing, each midget newspaper dispenser, all the things too dumb to scurry through the cold. Perkus and I, we'd dashed from our taxicab, which had plodded its way down Park Avenue to Sixty-fourth Street, its tires chewing along the echo-deafened streets. The steps of the wide, curved stoop of the mayor's town house had been scraped and salted; our footing confident, we took them two at a time, eager to get out of the suffocating clots of white that swarmed into our noses and clung to our lashes, and though we'd both have denied it, each buzzing with adrenaline at the occasion of the party. Perkus, the practical one for once, wore a black toque decorated with a knit patch depicting the Rolling Stones' lips-and-tongue logo, something likely exhumed from deep in his collection, its wool everywhere pilled and knobbed, like a scalp showing beginnings of dreadlocks. I'd had to pray he'd stuff the hat into his coat pocket the moment we were through the door. For myself, I'd been vain about my haircut, left my head bare, and so had meltage trickling through my sideburns and behind my ears for the party's first half hour.

Now we mingled in the mayor's vast parlor, a scene of glowing golds and browns against monumental windows showing blizzard, backdrops blue and silent as aquarium views. We'd entered into a scrum of arrival, another type of blizzard, guests busy emptying flutes of Prosecco and vodka shots and trays of tiny sushi and blini shopped among us by the catering staff, all of us tabulating faces we knew and others we recognized, all awed beneath a thirty-foot-high plaster scrollwork ceiling painted and lit to resemble buttercream icing on an inverted wedding cake. Richard Abneg and Georgina Hawkmanaji stood in one corner pleasantly receiving admiration as though they themselves were the gathering's hosts, Richard in his renovated elegance, shined shoes where he'd have ordinarily flown Converse high-tops as his freak flag, even his beard trimmed closer than I'd seen it, exposing a disconcerting chinlessness; Georgina lordly and tall, her dress an unrevealing cone of black, her silver earrings and piled hair imparting aspects of Gothic Christmas tree. I also saw, at a first survey, Strabo Blandiana (no surprise, he knew everyone), Naomi Kandel, Steve Martin, Lou Reed and Laurie Anderson, David Blaine, and Richard's co-op-board enemy and my sitcom mom, Sandra Saunders Eppling, accompanied by a graying distinguished man who was not Senator Eppling. Mayor Arnheim had decorated his party with a cultural crowd, for the holidays. I couldn't find Oona and Laird Noteless, but my search was compromised by trying to keep tabs on my own "date."

Perkus had treated us to the airing of another secret costume for the occasion, a purple velvet suit, the velvet either intentionally "crushed" or badly stored and in need of pressing—I really didn't know which—over a crimson shirt and matching tie. I thought it would be simple to follow the purple velvet, but Perkus flitted after someone or something, his thin shoulders vanishing sideways through some brief entranceway through the crowd that shut to me as simply as subway doors. I'd lost him. Assorted pleasantries imposed themselves, a round of reintroductions that wouldn't make the next round any less necessary, followed hard and fast by those ever-more-dire condolences for Janice's sickness. I gulped Prosecco, too much right off the bat, trying to keep from screaming in their faces that though I appreciated their good wishes I didn't have cancer, personally—that in fact *every possible human tumor* was geographically nearer to us, here where we stood, than Janice's, and didn't they find that odd? And incidentally, had they seen a doctor themselves anytime lately?

I remembered my vows, though, to disburse a field of love to enclose all within my range, which certainly should include the walls of this parlor. Oona might be watching, after all. So I gathered their well-wishes and their sadness to me, took their hands in mine, and thanked them. If you plumb into a person's eyes at an occasion like this one, you can usually spook them in a moment or two, and be done. The trick was not to try to break the circuit too soon but to wait, until they'd had their tiny fill. Trying to manage the migration of my gaze elsewhere from the persons it should be attending, I felt like Perkus even as I searched for him, an acolyte to his brand of double and wandering vision.

A young man in a tuxedo and obnoxiously slicked-back hair was suddenly before me, putting a finger in my chest.

"Chase!"

"Yes?" Now I recognized but couldn't place him.

"How do you like the script?"

He was one of that pair of "producers" that had tried, so long ago, to enlist me in their dream project. The role of my lifetime, they'd promised.

"I didn't get it," I said.

"I love it, you didn't *get it*. There's nothing *to get*, Chase!"

I felt irritated, even beyond my anxiousness that Perkus had slipped free of my caretaking. "I mean it never arrived, I never received it."

"That's a good one, you're a riot, Chase. Just keep on doing what you're doing—"

Then I heard Perkus's voice, in full harangue, rising out of the gregarious babble: ". . . rock critics are like little animals that live in holes . . . they defend themselves by scraping up fortifications of dirt and shit and regurgitated food . . ." Someone must have introduced him as a former famous *Rolling Stone* columnist, so Perkus was elaborating his standard defense. I tipped up on my toes to locate him. Perkus stood not far off, his back to me. He addressed his spiel to Mayor Arnheim, who looked to be listening. It was the first time I'd seen the mighty billionaire in person. I tried to believe he was nothing more than another graying operative in a suit, but like other truly powerful men Arnheim seemed a bit of gravitational sinkhole, a place where other men's hopes had gone to die. His eyes and teeth gleamed with bonus luminosity, his stance and posture arranged to support an extra density. Arnheim might in truth be many men crushed together, like a diamond.

"Excuse me," I said to the wolfish producer. "I've got to go . . . over there."

"Talk later?"

"You bet," I said to brush him off.

I elbowed in toward the mayor, in time to collide with a shortish thirtyish attractive blonde in tense eyeglasses, who though well dressed seemed unfestive, no guest. I could feel agendas humming around her head, as though she were checking prioritized lists in the very air. Though her glance sliced me into a pie chart, I assumed we were on the same side here, had come to chaperone and disentangle. I'd be happy to get my introduction some other time. I edged Perkus from the mayor just as the blonde, recovering from our little tangle, power-pointed Arnheim in another direction.

"Come with me, my little purple friend," I said. "Help me find Oona."

Perkus held an emptied Prosecco flute—a first warning I should heed, since he always refused Richard Abneg's fine red wines, and I doubted he could hold the stuff—and now waved it overhead as if toasting or blessing the whole crowd. His mood was already electric, though it might have nothing to do with meeting the mayor. "I'll help you find Oona, sure," he said. "But after that we have to go talk to Russ Grinspoon. I just saw him come in."

"Russ Grinspoon the singer? He's here?" I thought of Grinspoon as the lamer half of a well-forgotten seventies smooth-rock duo, Grinspoon and Hale. I was surprised Perkus much cared.

"He's Manhattan's arts commissioner," said Perkus chidingly. "You of all people should know that. He's at Arnheim's elbow at the gala openings of museum wings and restored opera houses and so on."

"Is that how you see me?" I asked. "A hack among hacks?" A snippet of "The Night Takes Back What You Said," the act's early, Dylanesque hit and one tolerable song, ran now through my brain. Grinspoon was the guy doing the high lilting harmonies, not the "genius" one who'd written the lyrics—sort of the girl in the act, I'd always thought. But then by some lights I was probably the girl in Insteadman and Tooth. "I resent your notion of me as a specialist in superficial occasions." No tone of irony was enough to secure my protest, not here.

Perkus was after bigger game than my pride, anyhow. "Forget what you know of his music," he said. "In another lifetime Grinspoon hung out with the Semina Culture guys in L.A. He was an extra in that Monte Hellman movie I was telling you about, *Two-Lane Blacktop*. He's actually one of only two actors to be directed by *both* Morrison Groom and Florian Ib, the director of *The Gnuppet Movie*."

"I know you're going to tell me who the other one is."

"Marlon Brando," he said with maximum satisfaction.

So the game was afoot. Tonight, I gathered, we'd attempt to penetrate one or several vital questions, pertaining to Marlon Brando's aliveness or lack thereof, his Gnuppet interlude and its sinister importance, as well as Morrison Groom's suicide: Faked, or Not? I felt involuntary jubilation and horror. Here was what I'd conducted Perkus into this midst for, unknowingly. I was an instrument, and among my duties was to resound with excitement at mad quests I couldn't comprehend. Semina and Hellman, for instance, were names I hadn't retained, but they carried with them a scent of summer, of Perkus as I'd first met him, and a time when, I now realized, my life changed totally. I'd never pass a pop quiz, yet these obsessions felt as rich to me as sexual pursuits, and hence it seemed perfectly appropriate that Perkus had bargained one for the other.

"I'm amazed that Arnheim's not more wary of letting a Brando mole like Grinspoon this deep into his organization," I teased. "Seeing as how Brando's about to topple Arnheim for mayor of New York. But I suppose that's the typical arrogance of power, to taunt a rival by stealing his people."

Perkus put his finger to his lips to silence me, his severity seeming to ratify even my looniest implication. Meanwhile, his mugwump eye was busy elsewhere.

"Okay," I said, before I lost my chance, seeing Perkus eager to reel off along his own foggy trail. "But Oona first." I wasn't going to let him off my leash, but I couldn't bear to think of Oona and Noteless working this room unpatrolled by me. In my mind's eye they looked as complacently coupled as Abneg and the Hawkman.

Then, as though I'd really needed him for my dowsing rod, Perkus took my elbow and steered me right into them, the party opening like a door. Noteless stood, tall and imposing as in one of his iconic photographs, shoulders square in loose black linen, face crevassed with significant doubts, hair a platinum flume. I had to admit I saw why the man had gone into sculpture. Oona, at his side, was the bird perched on the alligator's fang. In a room where we all frolicked with bubbly wine, she'd somehow cadged a perfect-looking twist martini.

Perkus dashed the silence. It turned out he had a program here, too. "So, I've been wanting to speak with you, Laszlo," he said.

"Yes?" said Oona. They hadn't seen each other since the tiger's destruction of Jackson Hole. I'd barely seen Perkus since, and not once at his place. Eighty-fourth Street was still cordoned while the city engineers measured structural damage beneath the blocks adjacent to the crater. He and I had met for a couple of feeble, pot-deprived encounters at Gracie Mews, Perkus giving my haunt a desultory audition.

"I've been thinking about what you were saying about simulated worlds," Perkus launched in. "About the simulators shutting us off if we started running our own simulations, because it might use too much juice . . ." For Perkus every meeting was only tabled, every ruling merely given a continuance (for this reason, if no other, Marlon Brando could never die).

"Right, sure, what of it?" Oona slurped at her martini, awfully blithe about apocalypse. That might be because she shepherded apocalypse in gelled human form through the world at the moment, and for her living presently took His dictation. Noteless, maker of chasms, swayed gently, perhaps tracking Perkus's eye, his whole looming form like a nudged metronome. The party seemed to have receded around us, or perhaps that was only my sensation of its unimportance, the mayor and all the flies in his web of no relevance now that I had Perkus beside and Oona before me.

"Here's my second thought," said Perkus. "The fact that we develop simulations of our own only drains their computing power if the way they simulate is to make everything exist *whether we look at it or not*. If, on the other hand, the simulators only trouble to put stuff where we're going to look at it, then the amount of effort and energy is exactly the same."

"I don't get you," said Oona.

"It's like this. Picture a man in a library. The books are all blank, until he picks one out. Then the simulator—or whatever—fills in that book, only for as long as he leafs through it, inscribing the minimum number of words, just in time for his eyes to meet the page. If he drops that book and selects another, the simulator's efforts go to making *that* book exist. But the preponderance of the library is a bluff, just a lot of book spines that wouldn't even have titles if you didn't look too closely."

"Probably the man only goes there because he thinks the librarian is hot," said Oona.

"The point is, Biller's computer universe might not make any difference to these guys at all. Our little simulated brains have got to be paying attention to *something*. Who says it's any harder for them to put some virtual-reality gobbledygook in front of our eyes than it is to, I don't know, persuasively cobble up a visit to the Cloisters or a cheeseburger deluxe."

"I've personally never found the Cloisters persuasive in the least," said Oona. "I don't care how old it's supposed to be."

I now had another wave of my straddling-universes feeling. Perkus and Noteless could meet each other, yet they were forever apart, impenetrable essences. Only I had the freedom to dabble in each of their realities and feel the native absurdity of their simultaneous distance and proximity. Who needed computers to simulate worlds? Every person was their own simulator. But give him credit, Noteless didn't flinch at Oona's witticisms, or Perkus's non sequiturs. His eyes only flared as if he thought the Cloisters might make a nice locale for a monumental pit. And then tilted forward to issue a non sequitur of his own: "Potemkin villages."

Oona and I were silent, demurring to the gnomic imperious, while Perkus blurted, "Yes, that's it, Potemkin villages, exactly."

"What's that supposed to mean?" asked Oona.

"Potemkin villages, you know—huts and bonfires and flocks of sheep, false fronts, stage sets, like they used to fool Catherine the Great," said Perkus impatiently, before returning to his main thread. "So, I was thinking it might even be cheaper on the computing power, because a simulation of the Cloisters or this room or whatever has to obey certain dictates of time and space, all our different impressions have to be brought into alignment, whereas from what I've gathered about a virtual space like Yet Another World, it's sort of rubbery and expansible, full of jump cuts and glitches. So, maybe that would be easier, since no one's expecting smooth continuity."

"It is only our wishful senses that give continuity to chaos," said Noteless ominously.

"That's amazing," I said. "Because I was just about to say the exact same thing." Standing in Noteless's shade had brought out a twitchy, hectoring humor in me. I'm taller than most men, and when I look up at one, it makes me feel like Bugs Bunny. Or perhaps I was sick of watching Noteless burn holes in Perkus with his eyes, wanted the great man to know I was his proper rival, the one to hate. "You really ought to give virtual reality a chance, Mr. Noteless."

"Ought I?"

Oona's glance said I'd better squelch this impulse, but I had one more jape in me, at least. "A place like Yet Another World might be a terrific opportunity for one of your installations. Without applying for a permit you could insert the Grand Canyon between Seventy-second and Seventy-third Streets, and no one would be in any way inconvenienced."

"I don't work in pixels," intoned Noteless, with the self-regard of a Stella Adler student declaring he refused to consider commercials. "I work in stone and soil."

"Like a rock critic," I suggested. Now all three stared, and I shut up. I'd at least gained my share of Noteless's scorn. Before I could screw myself deeper into this hole—call it *One-Man Fjord*—a member of the catering staff intruded to announce that dinner was served, and we should feel free to move into the dining room, and to take any seat we liked. Aroused from my fixation, I saw the guests had been trickling away for a while now.

"Let's go," said Perkus, instantaneously frantic. His radar had gone off: he meant to sit near enough to interrogate Russ Grinspoon, and I felt I should sit near enough to monitor Perkus.

"Your date needs you," said Oona, with the relish of a savored line. Noteless ignored us, returned to his mental aerie. I gave her one look I hoped could say I contained as large a love as she'd ever require, but that obviously no love could encompass Laird Noteless, then let myself be swept off in the direction the party was flowing, helpless Alice to Perkus's Red Queen.

■

Yet Another World wasn't the only reality that was expansible. Money had its solvent powers, could dissolve the rear walls of a nineteenth-century town house to throw a dining room into what must have been the backyard, under a glass atrium that now worked as a blizzardy planetarium. Admittedly, the effect was thrilling, and the guests fell into a nice hush as they sorted out into seats around the six circular, candelabra-lit tables. Perkus, true to my guess, made a beeline for a far table where I now spotted Russ Grinspoon, albeit a demurely suited, balding, and goateed rendition of the singer I remembered. He still had the languor of a congenital sidekick (it takes one to know one), and I could restore his frizzy reddish halo of hair and Nehru jacket in mind's eye easily enough. Perkus grabbed us two places beside him, and then seated himself in the middle. I followed, distantly aware of Oona and Noteless taking places in the room's opposite corner.

Grinspoon played our table's host, I suppose in his role as the mayor's man, shaking hands, kissing the ladies, remaining standing until the chairs were full. I couldn't tell whether this was something planned or not, but at the table to our left Richard Abneg took a similar role, while at the mayor's table the small steely blonde still acted as Arnheim's usher and protector. Only after this ritual settling did Grinspoon turn to Perkus Tooth, a curious expression on his face, and under cover of the jocular roar and babble that now rose to the snow-mad skylights to drown out any soft-spoken comment, said wryly, "What are *you* doing here?"

"Oh, you know each other?" I said.

Grinspoon wrinkled an eyebrow, and let a beat pass. "No." I understood he meant he'd simply heard his freak alarm go off—purple velvet over crimson didn't make it too hard—and that it amused him to find someone like Perkus here, where Grinspoon himself was accustomed to defining the perimeter of the outré. He offered his hand to Perkus, then me, and it was droopy and soft as an empty glove. "I haven't had that pleasure." We said our names, and Grinspoon looked at me a moment longer, and said, "Right." But it was Perkus who interested him. "You want to get high?" Grinspoon said, not whispering, relying that others were engaged elsewhere, showing the assurance of a veteran of a hundred such evenings.

"Sure!" said Perkus.

"Okay, but down, boy. We're going to have to wait until after the appetizers." With that, Grinspoon turned decisively from us, to the guests at his right, leaving me with Perkus, who seemed totally gratified but also mastered, as if in some preemptory maneuver, by Grinspoon's offer. All his verbal imperatives stifled for the moment, the stuff I imagined he'd been saving to tell or ask a man who, however unimportant an artist himself, had been directed by two men *who'd also directed Brando*. Perkus was a little beside himself, in the glittering room, recognizable faces everywhere, and the throne of power, too. When he found his tongue again he began

317

yammering disjointedly in my ear, charting associations the party's inhabitants and scenery held for him, and I trusted myself to appear to be listening even as I phased him out for my own relief. I felt bad, almost, for overstimulating Perkus. I'd ushered a kind of Rip Van Winkle from the gentle bed of his fantasies to this harsh tableau of real fame and influence, and jarring a sleepwalker incurs responsibility.

It was all I could do, though, to keep from craning my neck at Oona's far table. As Russ Grinspoon had implied, this getting-to-know-you interlude, while only wine had been poured but no plates set down, would be an impolite moment to break from our table. Later, in the rhythm of such things, we could browse between the tables. I had a good excuse for going over to Oona's. Sandra Saunders Eppling was seated there, and it was in the nature of male-to-female etiquette, as well as the duties of a sitcom son to a sitcom mom, that I should approach Sandra for the reunion scene I could safely guess many bystanders quietly anticipated. Oona and Noteless were chatting with Sandra now.

First we had to eat what now appeared, tongues of eggplant and bell pepper rolled into a juicy little vortex or eye at the center of a plate spattered with pesto, and then depart the table in the flurry as these dishes were cleared, following Russ Grinspoon, who'd ever-so-suavely placed his fishy hand on the bare shoulder of his rapt listener and asked her to excuse him, explaining that he'd promised to show me and Perkus a certain rare vase in Arnheim's collection. Out we went, incredibly, easily, through the maze of tables and up the mighty staircase, afraid to touch a polished banister too wide for mortal hands, on steps so plushed by carpet that our footfalls felt ungravitied, so that we might have been ghosts, or snowflakes, riding an updraft instead of settling to earth where we belonged. In a dim, swank study at the top of the stairs, walls lined with leather-bound sets, storm-giddy windows overlooking the top of the greenhouse roof and, within it, the dinner party we'd vacated, Grinspoon sparked a ready joint.

"You're the cat with the astronaut gig," said Grinspoon. He was nothing if not an aging, red-haired hepcat, his freckles sunburned at Christmastime. I might be predisposed to dislike him because his present career echoed mine, only with the difference he'd just pointed out. His job was just to preside, while I had to play Janice's fiancé.

"Yes."

"And you—just along for the ride?" He gave the joint to Perkus.

"I like to keep my eye on this kind of thing," said Perkus coolly, taking the pose of the first hard-boiled detective to crash a scene in purple velvet. I recalled him telling me I could "learn a lot" from my vantage amid the privileged. He drew on the joint and blew a gust toward the bookshelves. "You worked with Morrison Groom, didn't you?"

"Funny you should mention that name," parried Grinspoon. "It doesn't come up so often these days." He smirked as if despite his words he'd been expecting Perkus's question, as though he knew what I didn't: that Perkus and I had really come here to enact this weird interrogation in a room apart. I hadn't even smoked yet and the party seemed to be melting away into some more essential reality of Perkus's devising—this one, unexpectedly, a detective movie starring a crapped-out '70s star whose songs had been used, I believed I now remembered, as the soundtrack to a Robert Altman film about young orderlies at an old-age home, who ducked into broom closets to get high just as we were doing. Or possibly I remembered wrong. Perkus would tell me later. For now he passed me the smoldering joint.

"Actually, I'm working on a piece," said Perkus, as if this explained anything. A piece of what? I received an involuntary vision of the name "Morrison Groom", clipped and pasted beneath an ice-floe polar bear.

"None of those movies made any money," said Grinspoon.

"That doesn't mean anything."

"No?" Grinspoon shrugged. "Okay."

Game, set, and match, Grinspoon. Perkus would have to organize his indignant feelings into some more impressive foray. "Any one of those unprofitable movies is worth all the rest of the films you appeared in put together."

Grinspoon showed his palms, a Nazi officer so decadent he was pleased to surrender. "Sure, but I was never much of an actor." With this he winked at me, the fucker. "You didn't dig *Bartleby Rising*?"

"You were in that?"

"I'm Bartleby's boss." Grinspoon now peered through his fingers to mimic spectacles, and pursed his lips like

320

Scrooge. "Guess you missed it, huh?" Grinspoon kept mutating his appearance and affect, as though sensing, and wishing to mock, Perkus's investment in matters of authenticity. He was rather obligingly monstrous, I thought.

"I wasn't curious. Florian Ib's comedies are everything that's wrong with Hollywood since 1976. At least George Lucas made *American Graffiti*. Ib should be forbidden from working with humans. He was better with Gnuppets."

"See, that's the difference between us," said Grinspoon. "To me they're pretty much the exact same thing." He gestured for me to return the joint to him, even as he glanced to check the progress of the party below.

"*Humans and Gnuppets?*" asked Perkus with alarm.

"No, no," laughed Grinspoon. "Groom and Ib. But hey, man, I'm not an expert on film, like you."

"Groom and Ib are two opposed principles."

"I was thinking more of the joy they each took in a plate of carbonara, or a drunk hooker. Actually, I used to wonder if under that Santa Claus beard and beer belly, Florian might actually *be* Mo, hiding behind an assumed name."

"What?" Perkus's response was electric, one eye riveted to Russ Grinspoon, the other pleading with me to attend this emergency.

"You've heard the rumor that Groom's suicide was staged, right?" said Grinspoon. "Nobody really believes coyotes could drag a corpse away and chew off all identifying features in twenty-four hours."

I was happy not to have another/suck at the joint, for this evening was already dangerously distorted, the mayor's home colonized by the magic zone of Perkus's kitchen. How was it possible that Grinspoon could so acutely push Perkus's buttons, molest his sacredest theories? Well, I watched Perkus gather himself, summoning forces reserved for a crossroads like this one. His first instinct was to outflank Grinspoon. "Sure, that's common knowledge. But Groom wouldn't waste his time on the kind of stuff Florian Ib's been doing . . ." Then, despite himself, he turned the possibility over. "Though it would certainly explain why Brando would appear in *The Gnuppet Movie* . . ."

I didn't want Brando's name spoken here. Russ Grinspoon would say he not only was dead but had never been alive. Mercifully, Grinspoon pinched the joint's tip dark, then used it to point through the layers of glass and snow, to where I now saw the whole party with its attention turned to the mayor's table. Arnheim stood speaking. We'd been missing a toast. I couldn't see Oona's table from here.

"I gotta get down there and make a show of things," said Grinspoon. "Hope the stuff is good to you boys. Enjoy." Though we'd be returning to the same table, Grinspoon seemed to be offering fair notice that the present conversation wasn't to be continued downstairs.

"Mr. Grinspoon?" It was strange to hear Perkus default to this formality, addressing the hipster Grinspoon. But I saw clearly now how Perkus wasn't really any kind of hipster at all. He was too grimly intent on his pursuits to waste time in such poses. The other difference was rage. Grinspoon had none, was breezy to his bones.

"Yep?"

"You mentioned . . . a vase?"

"Oh yeah, one more flight, in the stairwell, look all the way up. It's really cool, especially if you're" — Grinspoon made one more face for us, fingers wriggled in front of his eyes — "stoned."

Back at the landing Perkus sprinted up the next wide staircase, into the muffled dark. Grinspoon turned the other way, to redescend to the party. I stood between, my mind coursing with marijuana confusion and possibility, my body paralyzed. Grinspoon turned and beckoned to me in my helplessness.

"You've got a part to play downstairs too, I think. Have you met the mayor yet?" He checked my glance backward, up that stair. "Don't worry, he's a big boy, he won't get lost."

"I'm not worried," I said. What if I'd wanted to see the vase, too? Somehow cowed, I didn't speak, but followed Grinspoon down the main staircase. A part of me wanted to monitor Oona and Noteless, but also, more prosaically, I was really eager now to greet Sandra Saunders Eppling. The pot smoke had brought up some well of sentiment inside me, for that lost time in my life when I had a simple avocation, to go each day to the cheesy set of *Martyr & Pesty*, that Potemkin village, and pretend that Sandra was my mom. I wanted to meet the mayor, too, and to talk to Richard and Georgina, to know their news. I missed them. They seemed entrenched in a daily world I missed, too. When was the last time

I'd gossiped about anyone's sex life? Meanwhile, Perkus was gone. He was the birds, the party was the tower. So what if I'd glimpsed both worlds—to which did I belong? I was a middling figure, a dabbler, much like Russ Grinspoon, who'd been directed by Groom and Ib and didn't see much difference, who could decorate a variety of scenes. Like him, I went downstairs.

■

Straightaway I was prisoner of my plate's arrival, roast brown glistening something. I dutifully spread it around my plate, while Perkus's sat at his empty place beside me, glistening and cooling. Wineglasses emptied and were filled, the party at a boil, and I leaned across Perkus's vacancy to join the niceties at my own table until fair excuse came to abandon it. The pot I'd smoked—it was very good pot—meant I relied on the purely sonic aspects of friendly talk to stand in for comprehension. Had anyone asked me to give the topic of the conversation I'd entered, let alone the names of the speakers, I'd have been reduced to clucking like a chicken. Grinspoon turned his back to me, plainly unconcerned at Perkus's long absence. In that I took my cue from him again. When one or two others had broken from their seats to commune elsewhere, I was up like a shot to cross the room, and from a place behind Oona's chair leaned in for an embrace with Sandra Saunders Eppling. I hoped my movements weren't as raw and hungry as I felt.

Sandra's features had long since taken on a kind of ageless flensed quality, but when I drew her to my chest I felt with a guilty shiver the brazen torso that had been the uncomfortable object of fantasy for my on-set self as well as for so many teenage boys on the other side of the television screen (I'd spent my life since as the involuntary recipient of such confessions). Could it really be that Sandra squirmed into my embrace as she stood, as if to be sure I knew what she still had? Or was I sexualizing what shouldn't be, because of the proximity of Oona? Whichever, it was the case that in retrospect this instant was the one where the evening or I began to disintegrate, so that all I'd recollect from this point on was a series of particulate elements strung incoherently in the void—the first of these being the disconcerting volumetrics of Sandra's breasts, the second her voice maternally pronouncing my first name, introducing me to her evening's (totally uninterested) companion, then inquiring, as she would have to do, after Janice's health. I waved her off with a gesture designed to imply a burden beyond speech.

"And have you met ... ?" Sandra had forgotten Oona's name, a fact she didn't trouble to conceal, off-loading the task of introductions with the candid indifference of an air kiss.

"Oona Laszlo," I said. "Selfless autobiographer. I'm a fan."

"Mr. Insteadman," said Oona, barely playing along. Noteless sat stiff and remote, his chair pushed back from the table so he could evaluate the room for possible demolition.

"So you've met my mom."

Sandra took this as incitement to lean in, again, it seemed to me, lasciviously. "Oh, Chase, you never write, you never call, you never visit . . ." I clutched her waist, fishing for jealous reaction, and registered her unsteadiness on her heels. Drunk Sandra and I verged on reviving that treacherous sentimental fiction of *theater* people, and I was already disgusted with how we appeared through Oona's eyes. I took it out on Oona's silent friend. "And have you met Laird Noteless, Sandy? He's the living master of dystopian public sculpture." *Dystopian* was a Perkus word I'd fished up—I was probably too cowardly to insult Noteless as myself, but I could do it if I pretended to be Perkus filleting some cosmic mediocrity.

Sandra knit her brow, exaggerating sobriety. "But of course. I sit on the board of the memorial, Chase."

"Ah!"

Now Noteless grumbled to life. "There's nothing dystopian in my work, young man." My borrowed dart had found its mark. "In point of fact, I operate strictly on what Robert Smithson termed an *atopian* basis. That is to say, my work attempts to erase received notions or boundaries, and hence to reinstate the viewer in the world as it actually is, without judgment."

"So if a viewer were to, say, stumble into one of your holes and break his foot, henceforth that would have to be considered a *strictly atopian* broken foot."

"You must forgive Chase," said Oona to Sandra Saunders Eppling, as if she were the one who should feel affronted. "He's sensitive on the subject of injured feet lately."

"I am not." My voice struck me as issuing from some place other than my body, and sounding rather bratty, too. Perhaps it was my inner child.

"Excuse me," said Oona to the others, as she stood and swept me from the group there, into the zone between tables, now occupied by milling bodies exploiting the lull before dessert. Since this departure was what I'd most have wished to have happen, it wasn't difficult for Oona to accomplish. I smiled at her to show it was a happy thing, however coerced.

"I spotted you lads sneaking off upstairs like the band at a wedding." She mimed a sniff, as if catching the tang of smoke on my jacket. I doubted she could, but since her guess was right I gave her the point. Anyway, I felt proud to be stoned, at that exact moment. Oona and I had shed our dates and stood paired in full view of the party, a total fulfillment of my childish yearning. Go figure: I'd only had to set free my brat for him to be instantly gratified! That I'd also cut Perkus loose to some macabre, unauthorized quest in the mayor's private rooms, I pushed out of mind. I further decided I didn't need to apologize for insulting Laird Noteless.

"See that blizzard outside?" I asked, fluttering my fingers to indicate the blue fever overhead. "That's how I feel *inside*, when I see you."

"Would a cup of coffee help? Because I promised to drag you over to meet Arnheim, and I think I'd better quickly, before you get any further unspooled."

"You know Mayor Arnheim?"

"We've met a few times."

"He knows—about us?"

327

"Don't be idiotic. He knows I know you, that's all. People see us talking, Chase."

"Why does he care about meeting *me*?"

"The things that escape your notice, Chase—it isn't always the case that you've escaped theirs. You're a public person."

"Now you're going to remind me of my duties."

"You used to remind me of them, not so long ago."

I glanced back. The chair beside Russ Grinspoon was empty. "He'll want to meet Perkus, too." I overlooked the fact that, technically, they'd met at the start of the party. "We should wait."

"Nobody here cares about Perkus." Oona left this blatancy between us, her gaze merciless. It seemed to demand I grant how distant we were from broadsides and glue pots.

"I'd better find him." My resistance was meek.

"Have a coffee with the mayor and then I'll help you find him." It made the reverse of the deal I'd struck with Perkus at the party's beginning, but I doubted I'd amuse Oona pointing out this symmetry. What I liked about the present situation was how it didn't include Noteless. I nodded.

The party had broken out beyond espresso and biscotti. Cigars, banned in public places, were the order here. Borne around in silver boxes, surprising numbers of us found no way of refusing, including many of the women. The mayor himself gave grandiose lessons on the pruning of a cigar tip, and the proper method of lighting one. Oona and I crashed the golden circle and were made to join in the corrupted smoky revels, which

328

seemed to place us above the law and a little out of time, too, the ultimate luxury. In front of Oona and what had become a number of other female observers I was pleased to demonstrate that even in my state I knew well enough how to handle one of the leaf-stinky things, though I had to remind myself not to suck the fumes to the far tendrils of my lungs as I had the pot smoke upstairs. Chairs were now pulled away and rearranged, our corner a pocket drama within the larger room, consisting of Arnheim and Insteadman and any number of women, and I was glad that Oona was seeing me this way, and that Perkus was away elsewhere for the time being. Only that same blonde, the professional watcher at the mayor's hand, didn't seem at all charmed by me.

I didn't care. Jules Arnheim was all he was cracked up to be, fully manifesting power's great refractive tendency. I found him almost impossible to regard directly, he was like a black hole or a blot on my vision in the shape of a small Jewish man, yet I could enjoy the gravitational warpage effects, the way we all seemed denser and more luscious in his presence. I couldn't actually hear my voice, except as a kind of damped trembling echo in the wake of his pronouncements, which emerged in cigar gusts, between flame blasts from his silver lighter.

"Chase Insteadman."

"Mr. Mayor."

"I like the way you do things."

"What things?"

"You keep the faith."

"Thank you."

"You bring honor to this city."

"I do?"

"We learn from your example."

"You're very kind."

"Keep an eye on this one, ha ha ha ha ha." He threatened Oona with his cigar, turning the ember downward. The mouthy part glistened, so gross and juicy it might have been politer, actually, to point the fiery end. "She's a troublemaker."

"I'll do that, Your Honor." I liked the way Arnheim seemed to place her in my care, and hoped she was listening. I realized, a happy surprise, that I was better off with Oona in public groupings tonight. Here we exchanged complicated glances, intimations of the layered parts we played in each other's stories, and I could enjoy knowing we were a conspiracy. Off alone, as we had been in the room's center, with no one listening, Oona was free to inform me we were nothing.

"We mustn't let Janice Trumbull die up there in space," said the mayor, with surprising directness, even bullying force.

"Well, we're all doing our best."

"I hope so."

"She is quite sick," said Oona. Sympathetically, it seemed to me.

"That doesn't mean she has to die," said Arnheim. He seemed to insinuate this outcome was in our power, adding to my sense of a man accustomed to nudging galactic bodies in and out of orbit with gesticulations of his furry eyebrow.

Into this arena came a disturbance, someone or thing moving at cross-purposes, without deference to the

330

postures and attitudes that made us all like a painting of Dutch burghers around the mayor's table. Perkus, shooting in like an unanticipated and hence uncontrolled galactic body in his velvet and red, emergency colors, his high narrow forehead and flop of hair a semaphore flag of panic. At this gathering he was akin to a tiger erupting from beneath the pavement, I saw it now. What had I been thinking, bringing him? I'd already fitted myself so naturally to the mayor's company that our renegade jaunt upstairs with Grinspoon seemed implausible at best.

Well, this group did what Dutch burghers would have done: pretend he was invisible, and reformat the table to push me to the outside, forcing me to cope with him, like an antibody. My cigar was no help, I was back in Perkusland, while Oona went on dwelling in the exalted domain of Arnheim.

"You have to see it." Perkus plumped down beside me in a loose chair.

"See what?"

"Grinspoon's dope must have been Ice." He spoke in a hoarse stage whisper, only no one listened besides me. "The mayor's got a chaldron upstairs, a real one, and zowie, that thing just *pops*!" Curled fingers springing outward, Perkus mimicked eyes bugging from head, not a far reach for him. Under the pressure of his excitement his vocabulary defaulted to Maynard G. Krebs.

"You're sure it's not just some Ming vase with a nice glaze on it?" I offered my soothingest tone, but behind it I'd caught his thrill like a fever. After all, if chaldrons were attainable wouldn't the mayor have one? Maybe it

331

was my brain that had a nice glaze on it, Prosecco and Grinspoon's pot, but I wanted to see for myself.

"Oh, I'm sure. Come and have a gander yourself."

"I don't want to cause a stir," I said, as evenly as I could. "We can't both go running upstairs again."

"You go. The thing's burned into my retinas anyway. Did I miss the coffee?" Perkus spoke from the corner of his mouth, we both did, like spies, whether our words were secrets or not.

"I'm sure they'll pour you some."

"Look up," he said. "When you're at the top, look up."

I didn't think of what havoc Perkus might invent downstairs in my absence. There was only the havoc of possibility he'd seeded in my head as I edged from the partyers and then skipped up the wide silent staircase. Past the landing and the entrance to the study where Grinspoon had parked us, up the next flight and into the dark. I ran out of steps, ended holding my breath at the floor of a conical turret streaked with shadow and reflection, facing numbers of doors and corridors at the topmost landing. Then recalled Perkus's instructions and tilted my head. Two beacons loomed high overhead: another skylight, this one a mere hatch to the sky, possibly no bigger than a manhole, its pitched sections of glass flurried with snow. And, in a recessed nook in the turret's curved wall, well beyond reach, tucked within a neat glass vitrine and radioactively shimmering with oil-slick rainbows, the chaldron.

■

I backed against the wall, craning upward, stretching to get the whole of it into view, though the angle was impossible. It sure did "pop." The real thing retroactively obliterated the recollection of our eBay encounters. More than diminished, these were overwritten, turned into rehearsals, premonitions of a future encounter: this. What the chaldron revealed now, that no image could ever reproduce, was its sublime and superb *thingliness* (again this word came unbidden). Perkus had been merciful, I now saw, leaving me to ascend here in solitude, to permit me first contact unmediated. I didn't want to talk. I didn't want to share. Like Georgina, I fought an urge to shed my clothes.

Time, among other things, was destroyed. I don't know how long I sagged there, feeling the cool plaster through the shoulders of my suit, a Saint Sebastian in continuous ecstatic surrender to the one ubiquitous and unceasing arrow of the chaldron streaming toward me from above. My vision was irritated by the portion of the form I couldn't see from that angle, a minor failing, but it was perhaps this which kept me grounded in the everyday fact of the party downstairs, and my duties there. I'd say I pulled out of my trance for Oona, except that this healing and encompassing chaldron seemed to catch up and resolve within it the fact of Oona, too. That she was so nearby didn't hurt. I could bring her to see it. Maybe we'd fuck on this landing, in this light. In the chaldron's holistic force I also saw that Perkus's apparently schizophrenic inquiries all led to the same place, whether I could follow them or not. They sprang from the certainty that a thing as splendid as the chaldron could be hidden, hogged, privatized by the mayor and other over-lords. This theft in turn described the basic condition of Manhattan and the universe. Whatever Perkus mourned or beckoned from the brink of vanishing—Morrison Groom and his fabulous ruined films, Brando, the polar bear and Norman Mailer, ellipsis, every thwarted gasp of freedom—all were here, sealed for safekeeping, and at the same time so healthy their promise grinned from the container.

I'd never been drawn to conspiracy theories, not being smart (or high-functioning autistic) enough to nourish the mental maps they demanded. This, however, was uncomplicated: the chaldron belonged not to Arnheim but to everyone (which was to say, probably, especially, exactly, to myself and my friends). On this thought, I broke away to rush downstairs, an inevitable step in my assignment, the unwrecking of the world. I didn't miss the chaldron now that I'd seen it. Like Perkus it was burned into my retinas, but also into my brain, giving instruction.

How perfect, that the whole consortium was in atten-dance tonight. As I breached into the party again Perkus attached himself to me, and I simply nodded, to let him know I knew what he knew. Then I pointed us to the table where Richard Abneg and Georgina sat. Richard would manage the intricacies here, know how we should cope with the reality of a chaldron coming to light in the nest of power, where he'd negotiated his own career. If Richard's radical origins made him a kind of long-term mole, a one-man sleeper cell in the Arnheim administra-tion, then this was the moment he'd been waiting for.

His lifetime's slide into compromise could be redeemed in an instant.

Their table's population hadn't dissolved so much into wider circulation in this dessert-and-cigar phase. They sat formed into one convivial group, including Strabo Blandiana, Naomi Kandel, and David Blaine, with Richard dominating the conversation. ". . . these floor-length urinals, all arranged in somber rows, and everybody pissing in silence, the Stonehenge restroom was a more holy scene than Stonehenge by far, I'm telling you . . ."

His audience was rapt, including Georgina. The two seemed to have receded into some glow even deeper than sexual satiation, though I couldn't give it a name. Was Richard some bore who told this story everywhere? Perhaps *Stonehenge restroom* was a trigger phrase, a code Richard Abneg had to let drop each time he mingled in the world of wealth and privilege, until the time he heard the reply come back to him, the shrouded reply that would foment revolution. I had Perkus, here at my side, to blame for the plague of overinterpretation that left me feeling that Richard was trying to communicate something to me personally: much of my whole life had been a kind of Stonehenge restroom, a cartoon of depth, in the shadows of some large truth before which I'd balked.

Well, I had a code word to lay on Richard in return. I had to get him away from the table, though. Strabo Blandiana was obviously party to chaldron manipulations, but he was too much a pet of power to be trusted. Naomi Kandel, too, though I liked her. She was a sieve

335

of gossip. I thought of how in my earlier innocence I'd mentioned chaldrons directly to Maud Woodrow and Sharon Spencer, and shuddered. I trusted no one with whom I hadn't smoked Ice. I leaned in and asked Richard if I could have a word with him. He saw Perkus at my shoulder and scowled, but excused himself. The table's others looked us over and shrugged, returning to other talk.

"I would have come over, but I saw you two consorting with that eagle hugger, Epping."

"Sandra," I said, hoping to humanize her. "My mom. She doesn't mean any harm."

"I had to hire a licensed ornithologist to get a few keepsakes out of that eagle hatchery that was once my apartment. He went in dressed in a suit of leather armor."

Perkus leaned in, impatient with our small talk. "So, there's a chaldron upstairs, Abneg."

I saw Richard make the same conjugation I'd done, so recently. Automatic skepticism couldn't hide what went deeper than curiosity, straight to appetite. He first had to put up a front, though. "Funny you should say that, Tooth. Because looking at you, I was thinking you'd come *dressed* as a chaldron, and I was going to have to explain how it wasn't Halloween."

Perkus never seemed more valiant than when faced with Richard's or Oona's glibbest mockery. "It never snows on Halloween, even I know that."

"So you were just rummaging around in the mayor's belongings and you happened to come across this . . . chaldron?" In the hitch in his speech I saw how, like me,

Richard had tried to control thoughts of chaldrons by censoring the word. Uselessly.

"He's got it mounted on a high shelf, out of reach," said Perkus. "It's a tricky spot, on a curved wall. We're going to need an extension ladder." His leaps to the next implausible thought would have seemed more outrageous if they didn't anticipate my own.

"What are you guys, the Marx Brothers?" said Richard. "Stay cool, for fuck's sake, and let me have a look at this so-called chaldron before you start burgling."

"Should we include Georgina?" I suggested, excited to restore the whole team. This was strategic as well as generous: I wanted to gather up Oona, too, and I remembered how the two women had bonded at Gracie Mews.

Richard Abneg darted a look back at the table, where Georgina remained caught up in glamorous attentions. She seemed to feel his eyes, and glanced back. He smiled at her, but shook his head at us. "No, no shenanigans for the Hawkman tonight," he warned. "I'll go. You two keep a handle on yourselves."

I wanted to remind Richard he was the first to bring Bolshevik rage into this pursuit—to propose seizing the chaldrons of the rich. I suppose then he hadn't had Arnheim in mind. But my tongue was clotted with smoke and drink. Anyway, Perkus, looking not in the least hurt about *Marx Brothers* or *shenanigans*, with full faith in the persuasiveness of what awaited, gave chaldron-spotting instructions. Then, putting finger to lips, extra admonishment to good behavior in his absence, gait revealing the eagerness I'd likely also displayed, Richard slipped upstairs.

The decadence that mobbed around us now seemed worse than random, the scrollwork ceiling itself, the wide shadowy stair, the four walls, all a pen for conspirators, villainous overbidders. How many of them hoarded chaldrons at home? I'd never look at Strabo Blandiana or Steve Martin the same way. (Grinspoon I couldn't quantify—either he'd betrayed the trust of the chaldron controllers, or was a conspirator so secure he felt free to taunt us.) I wanted to round up the catering staff for protection, make them a proletarian corps, radicalizing them instantly with a glimpse of chaldron. The selfishness I'd felt upstairs turned itself inside out, for an instant. Then reversed again. My little gang was fine. I didn't want to share so promiscuously. I only had to tell Oona, immediately. Again I dragged Perkus, against the grain of the party, which seemed arranged to deny us movement in the mayor's direction. Some music had been started, and it floated overhead, chunks of oppressive jazz. I lowered my head, ignoring shouted greetings, shunning the call of my own decorousness for once.

I found myself at a juncture where I could neither advance nor retreat, but did catch Oona's eye. I motioned for her to join us where we stood, aware my gesticulations had become wild, yet willing to play Perkus's card, and let my clownishness protect me from any suspicion.

"You found your friend," she said when she reached us. "Was he rolled up in a rug somewhere? Because you both look a little wrinkled and flustered, if you don't mind my saying so. Also your eyeballs are pink. Hello,

Perkus." She waved at him as if swabbing a dirty pane between them. Without Noteless nearby Oona had gone into her chipper routine.

"Listen, Oona, have we ever discussed chaldrons?" I honestly wasn't sure.

"I never figured I'd be very good with chaldrons," she said. "Though I've never been asked in the pluperfect before, I'll admit that. When you put it so charmingly, I might have to reconsider."

"What?"

"I'm sorry—little boytrons and girltrons, cleaning their poop trails and teaching them alphabeticals, isn't that what we were discussing?"

"Seriously, Oona. We found one."

"I think you can get a medal for that, if you redeem them at a police station."

Perkus interrupted. "Forget it, Oona, it isn't your kind of thing." The old petulance between them was always near the surface. "I could have told you not to bother, Chase."

"Ah, more boy games, I should have known." Now she feigned hurt. I saw we couldn't win with Oona, not in our present condition, doubly or triply intoxicated. She'd only take pleasure in running rings around us. Since Richard had excluded Georgina, I couldn't precisely argue Oona's point. Mind's-eyeing Abneg alone with the prize, my suspicion now forked: What if, holy smokes, it was *Richard* we shouldn't trust? He'd co-opted to the mayor everything placed in his care— what kind of fools were we, after all? That we had Georgina in our clutches might be our only insurance. So we needed to take the Hawkman hostage—that's how far I'd gone down this slippery slope, before Richard rejoined us, and a hungry, Rasputin glint in his eyes told me all I needed to know about his allegiances. The party erupted in laughter and applause, and for an instant I thought we were being mocked for our transparent plotting. But no, some unseen voice had dragged the room back to toasting. Under cover of huzzahs we resumed skulduggery. Oona was meanwhile our bewildered witness.

"You should leave this to me," Richard began.

"Not on your life." Perkus had spotted the thing tonight, as he had to begin with, and was in every sense our spearhead into chaldrondom.

"I've got an in here."

"We don't need an in, we need an extension ladder."

"How the fuck do you imagine you're going to—?" Richard left the implication open.

"I'll go upstairs," said Perkus. "None of the other guests knows me."

"Forget guests," said Richard. "Don't you think Arnheim has security staff in this joint?" Involuntarily I turned my head to examine the room, bringing a sneer from Richard for my lapsed discretion. The catering staff, moments ago my prole army, now struck me as Secret Service operators, prepared to drop their cloth napkins and pull out Glocks.

"Calm down, Chase. I'll figure out something."

"I am calm!"

Already the guests spilled disastrously out through the front hall, to filter back toward the grand parlor.

Some lined up for their coats, others settled in with an after-dinner drink for more talk. A few had even camped on the bottom steps, blocking the way upstairs. We'd never recover the privacy we'd enjoyed in our little solo raids. Our mission needed, probably, Spider-Man.

"You're in this cabal, Richard?" asked Oona. "I'm impressed. I was thinking these two were just high on something." We tried to ignore her, and failed. "What exactly are you subversives bent on? You've got me curious, though I'm sure the answer will be woefully disappointing."

Richard scowled at Oona, but addressed Perkus. "When did you decide *the more the merrier*, Tooth? Because, no offense, but we've got no time to waste persuading Madam Skeptic here."

"Ask Chase," shrugged Perkus.

Richard gave me the stinky eyeball. "Why don't you and Oona shove off, Chase. Make a drunken distraction in the far room."

"I'm not drunk!" I was stunned Richard could favor Perkus in a pinch.

"Not only drunk, but somewhat famous," said Richard. "You're no help."

How clownish had I become in their eyes? Was I blackballed from the Chaldron Club for Men? At that moment another element overtook us: Georgina Hawkmanaji appeared, with Sandra Saunders Eppling in tow. Both looked drunk on some plot of their own, an eagle armistice, perhaps.

"Darling, Sandra would like to say something to you."

"Richard, Richard . . . this has all gotten out of hand. When I saw you here, with dear Chase . . . I thought, I'm just going to march over there and—" Sandra used her body, bombing into Richard's unwilling embrace. "Come back to the building, sweetheart!"

Richard's eyes took on a trapped-animal cast. I remembered his injunction against drawing Georgina into chaldron-hunting, and kept my tongue. Maybe I could sweep Oona upstairs, somehow. Make some coupleish reason that we needed to visit some private room together. And there, rifle closets to find a ladder, or some suction cups. Only Oona and I weren't meant to be a couple. At that instant I turned to find Laird Noteless helping her into the sleeves of her coat. The whole party, now that I noticed, was being helped into its coats. A member of the staff, an attractive girl in a tuxedo and ponytail, with an apologetic-lustful gaze, held my own coat and scarf, waiting for her chance to dress me in them. Just then the idiot *producer-with-no-script* hailed me with a grin and a beckoning wave. I waved back, miming helplessness to cross the room. It wasn't so hard to mime.

"They say the streets are becoming impassible in the storm," said Oona. I must have been staring at her with the dumb helplessness I felt. Forget Secret Service: my coat and scarf were as fatal to our plans as a Glock. "The limousine drivers want to go immediately. Apparently the taxicabs have given up already. The limousine drivers want to go home to their families."

"We didn't come in a limousine," I said stupidly.

"Ask Richard and Georgina to give you a ride in theirs."

Noteless guided Oona by the shoulders away from our group which was no longer a group, Richard leaning in to Georgina as he extricated himself from Sandra Eppling, whispering something I couldn't hear, others with names I couldn't recall jostling in to make farewells, clotting around us as they fitted into their dressy coats and oohing and ahhing at the gusts of cold as outer doors were pried open against the battering snow. I saw Grinspoon now, shaking hands like a politician, bearing away whatever forbidden knowledge of Brando and chaldrons he possessed. I watched Oona and Noteless go. Noteless was taller than me. We were the two tallest men in the vicinity. It didn't mean I knew his secrets. Or that he had any. I felt sick. The girl gentled me into my coat. I turned to find Perkus, but he was gone. My eyes knew where to search before I was conscious of the thought. I sighted him, just barely, sprinting alone upstairs into dark. With Richard and Georgina and a tide of guests I streamed out to the frigid blue transformed city, wet static hazing every personal screen, all objects and persons nearer than they appeared, all of us impossibly vague to one another as we laughed and sneezed into the backseats of limousines, leaving him behind.

■

January 8
C.,

Severed-foot disposal in a pocket biosphere is really a daft problem, one I hope you never need face, love. We considered air-lock ejection, a sailor's funeral, but to send my pedal appendage spinning down to Earth, or worse yet, to trigger a mine, seemed florid, flamboyant, a bit of a flambé, and not in the least flame-retardant, even if we wrapped it in a foil boot. (If we had a thousand feet among us, a millipede's supply to lop off and defenestrate, maybe we'd kick our way out of this crate!) So we opted for a somber burial in the Greenhouse, under the shade of the tallest of the mangroves, though in truth it meant a slightly watery grave after all, stuff seeping up through the muck to swallow the foot, bubbles of mud detaching and floating among us during our tiny, foot-size ritual observances. Sledge, having scooped up the dead bees from the shelf in the Nursery, embedded these in the gunk to form a ring of bee emissaries, the better to passport the foot into whatever afterlife it deserves. Keldysh recited a poem in Russian, Mstislav made a joke about Gogol, then we sealed up this weird stew with cheesecloth mesh, as we do the rest of the topsoil, to keep it from absconding in the zero-G.

Afterward, back to work or to moping in our various private nests. I'm not so much an occasion, anymore, for renewed bonhomie. My ailment is another ambient backdrop now, another machine falling apart with no parts to replace the scrapped ones, another grim dispatch from the various quadrants of the deadly dull but not yet quite deadly enough condition our condition is in. My cancer is a mood. We all of us up here have our moods.

Now a part of me will never touch Earth again, Chase.

Happy New Year!

Footloose,

J.

18

Perkus was gone. By the time February rolled around, the blizzard's traces down to those last blackened rinds in gutters, each marking a spot where some ambitious driver had made mountains uselessly digging out around their wheels, I'd long since quit my ritual visits to Eighty-fourth Street to search for him. The condemned buildings on his block had nothing more to show me. The neighbors of Brandy's Piano Bar might be able to rest at last, the place shuttered, its noisy smokers flitted elsewhere, except Brandy's had no neighbors anymore. The inhabitants of Perkus's building, as well as two others on the block, had all been dislodged at once, to who knows where, the apartments of families and friends, I suppose, to await the city's settlement for the tiger's ravages, the machine's or beast's assertion of eminent domain over what had been their homes. The block wasn't even fascinating or appalling by then, the darkness in those windows not ominous or intense. Around the corner, Jackson Hole still made a rather dramatic crater, but these were merely uninhabitable buildings, destined to come down and be replaced with something newer, and soon they'd be hard to remember. The city had moved on. Nothing there matched my own ominous intensity, certainly, as I pushed to the edges of the police barricades to cruise them for trace meanings, and soon enough my feeling faded. Perkus was gone, and I couldn't mourn it the way I had before, at least not by creeping around his street.

Perkus was gone. By the last part of January, Oona and I had settled into yet another version of our stilted routine, and not mentioning Perkus or the circumstances of his going was a part of it. It was as if Oona and I had met through some other common friend, or picked each other up at a bar. If our career as secret lovers had always had weird denominators, Perkus now became part of that murky undertow, the stuff Oona and I left unspoken. She was deep in the finishing throes of Noteless's book, on a crash publication schedule, in order to be in stores concurrently with a ceremony at the hole downtown, at the end of the spring. Without Perkus's apartment as a rendezvous point, and forbidden from calling lest I interrupt, I mostly ended up waiting at home until she'd exhausted herself writing and felt she needed some reward. I knew just how she liked her martinis now, and had a perfect one waiting for her when she came sighing through the door bragging of how many pages she'd batted out. But she wasn't looking for conversation, and I managed not to press her on sore points, mostly. My encounter with Noteless at the mayor's party seemed distant history, part of the Perkus era, last year. I'd satisfied myself well enough that they weren't lovers, but Oona had established something too. By squiring the artist through the party and leaving in his car she'd cemented me in my subsidiary place, forging our present odd equilibrium. I loved her in my bed, but I kept my mouth shut about it.

One day I whined that I couldn't leave my apartment for fear of missing her. "You should carry a cell phone like everyone else," she said. "Then you wouldn't worry."

"Perkus doesn't carry a cell phone."

"Like regular people. If he did carry one you'd be able to call him, wouldn't you?"

"But you never call me."

"I might if you had a number."

"I don't like the whole rigmarole, everyone going around . . . talking . . . everywhere."

"You don't have to talk anywhere you don't want to."

"I guess I'm old-fashioned."

"Sort of like the word *rigmarole*."

The next morning, before sharing breakfast at the Mews—a rarity, these days, that she'd linger for breakfast—we ducked in at a newsstand and Oona bought me a disposable mobile phone, with a hundred minutes built in before the thing expired. She entered its digits into her Treo, then handed the little plastic implement to me. It barely weighed anything. "There you go," she said. "You don't have to do anything else, just carry it around. If it rings, it's me. The Oonaphone."

Nice, but the Oonaphone never rang once. I waited at home with the martini makings—I had nowhere else I wanted to go.

Something else happened then. With Perkus gone, and Oona systematically depriving my heart's hopes, I pined deeply for Janice, even if I couldn't know who I was pining for. Maybe I pined for pining, for the notion of love itself. I read and reread the letters, the wealth of them from before her sickness, the few that had come since. Guiltily, I found I loved most not the Janice I was supposed to love, my onetime fiancée on earth, then heroically launched on her mission, nor even the brave professional of the first months after the Chinese mines had trapped her and the Russians in space. No, I loved the deranged astronaut of midwinter, resigned to the space station's degeneration and perhaps to dying. The less of Janice I got, the more I cherished her. Any past was like the church tower, gray and mute, bedrocked in mystery. Her scant words now were like the birds, who when they circled into view took my breath away. The flock had never quit, returning to soar at kooky angles even in the tailing last flurries the morning after the blizzard and Arnheim's party.

Perkus was gone. Midway through the month of January, before I'd completely quit pacing the periphery of that quarantined block of Eighty-fourth Street, I had an idea I was investigating his disappearance, though I could hardly report what outward form, if any, my investigation took. I made a pretty lame detective. One of my forays was to call Strabo Blandiana and get an appointment. I couldn't imagine a way to interrogate Mayor Arnheim or Russ Grinspoon, but Strabo Blandiana was within reach. The Chinese medicinalist was implicated in the first moments of Perkus's errancy, if that was what it was, the first encounter which eventually led up the mayor's staircase. I wanted to see the evidence of the framed photograph in his treatment room and weigh for myself Strabo's awareness of any plot. Likely I sensed that Strabo would treat any question kindly, and also as symptomatic. When I say I made a feeble detective, I mean that I was as willing to be cured of my case as to solve it.

Yet even anticipating Strabo's soothing, nothing fully prepared me for how much of a rebuke his tranquil offices could be to my disquiet. I came in stamping off snowmelt, my rattling taxicab's horn-honking pinball course through glistening, trafficky intersections fresh in my ears, and wrought up with recalled images of Strabo at Arnheim's dinner, among (fellow?) conspirators. Through the door, at the sound of his chimes and sight of his receptionist's smile, I was ashamed. To arrive here in a state was to fail Blandiana's test as his longtime client, to suggest I'd gained no peace from all his needles over the years. So before Strabo even appeared I aligned myself, using breathing methods learned in these same rooms, and began dreaming of a time when I'd never known the name Perkus Tooth.

Inside, on his table, any shred of fear was converted. Though in his turtleneck and impeccable razor-cut Strabo could easily be cast as a Bond villain, it was impossible to find him sinister when he turned his Buddha searchlights on your distress. Who needed chaldrons? The light was in yourself. That was possibly the lesson of his tenderness. Though more gift than lesson, with all the reproach lesson implied. You were forgiven even for being inadequately tenacious in your peacefulness. We all slipped. And, as if to reinforce the self-chaldronizing principle, the framed print was gone from the wall at the foot of his bed. Wearing Strabo's painless needles, mind settled into a fine drone, I gazed up at a dun-colored page of Sanskrit instead.

"You took it down," I said when he came back for me.

His look in reply was sweetly puzzled.

"The . . . vase photograph you had there."

"Oh, yes, that's true. A few patients found it over-stimulating."

"You took it home instead?"

"I donated it to a charity auction."

"Ah." Material things were only ever passing through his relaxed fingers.

"Truthfully, I get too many gifts from patients."

"What charity?"

"Médecins Sans Frontières." Strabo never shed a dew-drop of impatience with irrelevant questions, yet also conveyed a sense that such exchanges stood in lieu of personal work that waited to be done. So I let him per-form his usual mind-meld, his stunt of empathy. With-out intruding or naming names, in elegant paraphrase, Strabo Blandiana informed me that I should quit won-dering whether to love Oona Laszlo or Janice Trumbull, that the task instead was simply and unquestioningly *to love*. Of course. Then, as ever, he added that I obviously hardly needed to be told, that I contained this knowl-edge within myself and had evidently already been act-ing upon it, and that Strabo Blandiana as my friend was proud of me and confident in my talent for self-care. A cynic would have asked why he didn't take his show to

Las Vegas. Me, I strode back out into the cold chaos of Manhattan believing myself a sunbeam in which all who wished could bask.

Whether I searched for him or not, Perkus was gone, and I was tired of searching alone. I'd made one attempt to enlist Richard Abneg, two weeks earlier, on New Year's Eve. This was just ten days since the mayor's party, and all the traces felt fresh, the blizzard's drifts still reshaping the streets, albeit crusted and steadily blackening. Richard and Georgina took pity on me and called me to spend the evening with them in Georgina's penthouse, knowing (because I'd complained) that Oona had avoided me on Christmas, rightly suspecting she'd do it again. I was something especially pathetic in the way of third-wheel bachelor companions—there being not one but two women I was divided from, on that night when any couple is meant to be together. Richard and Georgina made the evening easy for me, ordering in excellent Chinese, tilapia medallions with spicy green chilies and Napa cabbage, eggplant with ground pork and green peas, then putting on some old black-and-white movies, consoling ones, Jimmy Stewart as a rube outwitting large numbers of sophisticates.

Between features Richard took me into their bedroom and cracked a window and we got high. Richard didn't seem to want Georgina to know. He rolled a joint out of a box of Chronic and at first I didn't think anything of it. We exhaled into the chill whistling breeze and it seemed to me the smoke was all blown back inside, that its perfume would draft to Georgina, several rooms away, but I didn't point this out. I was just grateful to be where I was. From the high penthouse window distant party noises rose to find us, sweetly harmless at this distance, though I hoped we'd shut the window before the appointed hour, not hear the popping of corks, the commemorating hollers. I didn't want to think of the year's end passing with Perkus's whereabouts unknown. The smell of the dope was commemoration enough, and I grew wistful. In return for Richard and Georgina's kindness in not mentioning Oona or Janice, I could have left another name unmentioned, but the impulse was too fierce. Though I'd brought Perkus to the party, I wanted Richard to feel as responsible as I did.

"Where do you think he's gone?" I said, handing over the joint, and waving off any return.

Richard shrugged. He reached through the window opening to stub the remaining quarter-joint against the outer sill before replying. "I wouldn't drive myself crazy over it," he said. "He'll reappear right when you've given up."

"I keep visiting Eighty-fourth, thinking I'll see him haunting the block," I said. "Other tenants are at the barricades sometimes, pleading for access to stuff they left inside. That apartment was Perkus's snail shell. I can't picture him surviving naked."

"He's resourceful, Chase. You'd be surprised." The words might be hopeful, but Richard's tone was curtly dismissive. It only made me want to push him.

"Have you talked to the mayor's people? After all, he was last seen at Arnheim's town house—"

"That's where he was last seen by *you*," said Richard irritably. "I'll bet he was last seen elsewhere.

He's a grown-up. Anyway, Perkus's name wasn't on the guest list. What do you expect me to do, barrel into Arnheim's office and say, 'Did anyone cleaning up after your party find a one-eyed rock critic dressed in purple, because one's gone missing'?"

"You're being deliberately callous."

Richard's sneer said *What else is there to do?* I had no answer. "Let's go in," he said. "She's probably wondering what we're up to."

"What if he got away with the mayor's chaldron?" I whispered. It was a possibility too terrifying and thrilling to speak aloud.

"Listen, Chase. No fucking chaldron talk tonight, okay? It isn't good for Georgina. That word's verboten around here."

It struck me as peculiar and maybe suspicious that Richard had declared martial law. We'd lost Perkus, and now the crippled Fellowship of the Chaldron might be suspending the civil rights of one of its remaining members. "Does Georgina know you've made that decision for her?" I said, managing to get honestly indignant on her account, though I knew I was up against the tyranny of coupledom—what Perkus would have called "pair-bonding." I reminded myself I'd met Georgina several times before Richard laid eyes on her, and that we'd all lusted for chaldrons democratically together.

Richard had judo for my righteousness. "Have you had a look at her?" He cupped his hand, low at his own slight paunch, and raised his brows, waiting for me to understand. Then he couldn't wait. "You haven't noticed she's not drinking, I guess—"

"What? Wait, *really*?"

"Use your eyes."

"When—?"

"We're pretty sure the very first night. She's three months along, but she's built so flat there you can already see a bulge, like a sweet potato." I heard a crazy wondering pride in Richard Abneg, a dreaminess that had colonized his patented tone of worldly grousing. In conquering the exotic ostrich-woman, seizing her from the bracket of privilege, that now-epochal night at Maud and Thatcher Woodrow's, something else had conquered Abneg in turn, an unaccountable human possibility.

So I went in half tripping and gathered Georgina in an embrace, making a joke about my dimness and self-absorption in not noticing sooner, and insisting that no matter what the date happened to be, we really ought to open some champagne. Richard uncorked another Châteauneuf-du-Pape instead, but he did pour an aggressively protective thimbleful for Georgina, who didn't blink at being stinted. Her mood was implacably mellow, as though bodily exalted by pregnancy, shifted to some elevated plane, past the flushed-and-vomity phase. (And indeed, I could make out the sweet potato she was sporting.) By contrast I felt Richard smoldering as he shifted around the room, ruminating through his beard while replacing one DVD with another and crushing white cartons slimed with sauce into a trash bag, his impregnator's pride mingled with something more ambivalent and turgid. Our talk of Perkus felt incomplete, usurped by the news of the Hawkman's pregnancy. Whatever was disgruntling Richard, I knew what I felt

354

it should be. I wanted Georgina to hear about Perkus, too, before they sealed themselves in parental solipsism and forgot the floe-stranded polar bears of the world. My passive-aggression took form as the last thing I'd expected to hear myself delivering this night, a toast.

"Here we sit . . . in this city of apartments . . . in one of the most superb examples anywhere . . . such a perch you enjoy, Georgina! We're lucky souls, aren't we? And you're bringing along a little Hawkboy, who'll some-day need an apartment of his own . . ." In my muddle I couldn't remember whether Richard ever called Georgina "Hawkman" to her face. And I'd awarded them a boy child, with random confidence. "I'll go home to mine tonight and give thanks, though by comparison it's a tawdry shoe box . . . yet what a thing it is to have a place, any place at all, in the great conglomeration of apartments making up this mad island . . . so let's drink, too, to our friend Perkus who's been cast out in the cold, who's lost his purchase on Manhattan . . ." I aimed at Richard's weakness, real estate. By harping on apartments I'd remind him he'd lost one, too. I couldn't have known, though, how exactly I probed a sore point.

"What are you driving at, Insteadman?"

"Nothing, just thinking of Perkus, on this night of blessings."

Georgina asked. "I fail to understand. What has happened to Perkus?"

"Richard didn't tell you? After the blizzard, the city condemned the tract of apartments around the Jackson Hole disaster. We don't know where Perkus ended up." I was restricted from saying the rest: that his actual

355

departing gesture was to throw himself at Arnheim's chaldron, on all our behalves.

"That's terrible. Richard, did you know about this?"

Abneg bore a hole in me, his gaze like a cigarette ember knocked off onto a sleeve. "Perkus was just playing out the string in that place to begin with," he said, his tone hard-boiled. "He was on borrowed time."

"What's that supposed to mean?" I asked.

"Look, nobody's entitled to live in a rent-controlled apartment forever. I protected him as long as I could. He was past his time, that's all."

Past his time? The era of Mailer and Brando? I tried to grasp Richard's implications. "Protected him exactly how?"

"Protected literally. You don't think he'd have been able to afford that apartment if he'd lost his sixty-year-old rent control, do you? Did you imagine Perkus was actually the legitimate holder? Wanna know why his name wasn't on the buzzer? Because he and I pried off the old linoleum nameplate reading *E. Abneg*."

"Who's E. Abneg?"

"Funny you should ask. Ephraim Abneg—my father. That pad was my college graduation gift, at the rent, in 1988, of seven hundred and forty-six dollars. I think it's gone up a hundred bucks since then. I set up Perkus in the sublet when I bought my place. A new management company bought the building five years ago and harassed all the rent-stabilized tenants out with the old trick of not cashing their checks and then suing for nonpayment, so I've had to personally wade in and fend off all sorts of shit just to keep him installed there, including a definite abuse or two of the power invested in me by blah-blah-blah. The point is, it wasn't going to last forever, Chase."

It was as if I'd just wandered into the big city from the boondocks, and was forever to be the callow newcomer. Everyone else's friendships had provenances I couldn't begin to trace, let alone compete with. Also, I might be stoned, and reading too elaborately into Richard's outburst, but it puzzled me how eager he was to view the tiger as an envoy of real estate destiny, an impartial (if regrettable) agent calling in the city's old debts. At this instant, though, I only wished to rebottle the pressures I'd uncorked in Richard, which looked to wreck the evening. I felt I'd rewarded Georgina's hospitality poorly. She now reached out to stroke Richard's arm, to draw him back to her special corporeal calm, that oasis in her which they'd created together. But Richard wasn't pregnant, she was—just as this wasn't his glorious penthouse, but hers. If apartments were fate, what about Abneg's?

"I didn't know you'd put yourself out like that," I said placatingly. "Still, just because Perkus was on borrowed time in that place doesn't mean we shouldn't worry about his going up in smoke entirely."

"You're the one who raised a toast to *apartments*," Richard snarled.

"This is irrelevant," said Georgina, her tone of correction gentle but absolute. "You must try to do something from within your offices, Richard."

"What makes you think I *haven't* done something from within my offices?" asked Richard darkly, though his words were plainly chosen to skirt a lie. "Though

357

some would defend the right of an adult to fall off the radar in this town without necessarily conferring with the fucking authorities."

"You must find your friend," said Georgina. The clarity of her statement suggested a simple parallel with Richard's fussing to keep her from red wine, pot smoke, and chaldrons, a posture that plainly hadn't escaped her. If Richard Abneg was a protector now, he should protect.

With that we turned to Jimmy Stewart, who always knew when he was a protector. Stewart set about rescuing a gun-ridden town without carrying a gun, but before Marlene Dietrich could be won over, the Hawkman was fast asleep, her stockinged feet drawn up and tucked to one side. The love seat on which she'd been sitting formed a plush catcher's mitt where she sagged, so Richard and I finished the movie before he gently guided her away to bed. Somewhere in there midnight had tolled, but sealed in our turret we'd been blessedly unaware.

When Richard returned to where I waited, where the tube's blue glow provided the only illumination over Georgina's spoils, her Arp and her Halimi and her several Starcks, I couldn't read his expression but figured in any event it was time for me to go. But Richard said, "Do you want one more smoke?" It was then I had my big idea.

"That's Watt's stuff we were smoking before, wasn't it?"

"Yeah."

"So you're on his safe list?"

358

"Sure, and I can guess what you're thinking, but I haven't called him in months, that's an old stash."

"Okay, so call him now."

"Tonight? Are you kidding?"

"He's a drug dealer, he's working, I'm sure."

Richard used his cell, entering his digits into Watt's beeper. The dealer confirmed immediately, so Richard dialed down to Georgina's doorman, to prepare him to expect the late visitor. I sat with Richard and waited in sullen silence, our last grab at camaraderie apparently spoiled by my detective work. Fortunately, our wait wasn't long. Watt was such a pro.

"You remember Chase Insteadman," said Richard grousingly, once Watt was settled in and his case of wares clamshelled on the coffee table between us.

"Sure, Perkus's friend. I used to love your show, man."

"Thanks. Listen, speaking of Perkus, when's the last time you heard from him?"

Friend or fan or whatnot, Watt had an ingrained dislike of questioning, and retreated to generalities. "I do a lot of business," he said. "I don't keep a log or anything, fellas, and if I did—"

"Right, you wouldn't share it with anyone," said Richard, glaring at me. "We're all grateful for that."

"He's missing," I said. "But we know he calls you a lot, and we were just wondering if you'd heard from him in the past ten days or so. Or if you'd gone to visit him anywhere apart from Eighty-fourth Street."

This brought a scoffing laugh. "Brother never budges from his crib." The burst of rococo dialect seemed a response to being asked to discuss Perkus in his absence, as though Watt had until now expected Perkus to emerge from the shadows of Georgina's apartment, hence had still been on best behavior. I found it touching that the dealer had a special edition of himself tailored to please Perkus Tooth. It was more proof Perkus existed, at least.

"He's budged now," said Richard. "The city condemned his building."

"Oh, *shit*," said Watt. "Tiger?"

We both nodded. My eyes fell to the rows of Lucite boxes, with their gloriously ugly multicolored font: URBAN JUNGLE, TIGER'S CLAW, GIANT PAW PRINT. SABER-TOOTH, these nestled in alongside CHRONIC and the other usual names. Watt noticed me looking. "Kind of a craze lately," he said, with the air of one making a helpless excuse. "Can't sell enough, which just goes to show, you know, what I've always heard. People do love them some fear."

"You've always heard that, huh?" said Richard. I felt the sarcasm was aimed in my direction. Certainly Watt took no notice.

"Listen, Foster," I said, waving off the matter of his tiger-centric line of goods. "What about Ice?"

"Got plenty of that." He shifted aside the top layer, the new names, to show me, even as he shifted his own register back to that of salesman. "Never travel without the old standbys."

"I meant what's *different* about it? Because you must be aware it has some special properties."

"They've all got special properties," he said, again resorting to platitudes. "Just depends what you're in the mood for."

This concerned Richard, too. He'd journeyed with me to the crossroads of Ice and eBay. He made a sour face, then summoned his full authority. "Here's the thing, Foster. You're not in any kind of trouble with us, we've just got a simple question. *The names change*, right? You don't really have access to a hundred different grades of pot, you couldn't possibly. That's fine, you need to keep things interesting for your clientele. We just want to know if there's something about Ice in particular that's different, or if any of your other clients are reporting any special effects from it. This might or might not have something to do with Perkus's disappearance, we don't know, but we'd appreciate an honest answer."

"It's real popular," Watt stalled. Under pressure he shrank to a Nielsen-rating view of his trade. Ice was a smash pop hit, like Coca-Cola or Adidas, like *Martyr & Pesty*. Maybe Watt could retire on the residuals from it. What else was there to consider?

"Do you switch the labels?" I said, barely containing my impatience.

"Seriously?"

"Yes, seriously."

"Sure, I switch them around. There's usually about three or four different grades. Chronic and Ice, that's the same dope. Same as AK-47 too, usually. Ice used to be called Bubonic for a while, then someone told me what that means. Anyway, I'm not even always with the same supplier." He squinted at the red digital glow of his beeper. "No offense, but you picked out what you want?"

"It doesn't . . . mean . . . anything—?"

Nothing left to be defensive about, Watt could afford to show his own impatience. "Some smoke sweet, some a little skunkier. They all get you high, or you get your money back."

I'd felt a creeping sympathy for Watt, summoned up into the lap of luxury to find himself good-and-bad-copped by surly customers, but now his rap was only infuriating. "How much Ice have you got?" I asked, in blatant defiance of his confession that the brand meant nothing. I couldn't refuse that knowledge, but I could try to keep it from Perkus, if I ever had that chance.

Watt found four of the Lucite boxes labeled ICE. I had Richard empty his wallet to help me afford them, then we discharged Watt back into the first morning of the new year. Richard and I smoked some—there wasn't anything else to do—and in the fading hour as we sat together I felt that though we didn't speak of it directly, he'd both forgiven me the clumsy zeal of my investigation and made it clear the lengths he could (and, mostly, couldn't) go in assisting me. He cared about Perkus, had for years before I was on the job. Georgina was pregnant. The two facts seemed balanced one against the other. If there was yet something else lingering unsaid, I chalked it up to the feeling Richard Abneg was always wanting to impart, that he had responsibilities I couldn't imagine.

So Perkus was gone. It was all I thought about that January, except when I thought about something else, or nothing at all, watching my birds circle, munching eggs alone at Gracie Mews, trudging through refrozen slush to catch afternoon matinees on Eighty-sixth Street, all the prestige pictures that clung to one screen on the East Side and one on the West, waiting for Oscars to give them immortality or at least get them into the black. Days spent waiting for Oona or for not-Oona, it was always a toss-up. It occurred to me that I worried about Perkus because the case of his vanishing was simple, as opposed to the two women I should be troubled over, one present in absence, the other the reverse, or something like that.

Perkus was gone, Perkus was lost, and I spent weeks wandering in circles, but before that, for one instant, I'd actually been thrilled inside my fear, even proud. It was the first afternoon following the party, when, thinking I'd visit and at the very least hear some wild tale of his ejection from the mayor's residence, I found myself approaching the barricade at Eighty-fourth Street to find policemen everywhere, their lights blipping and radios crackling with the fizz of a fresh emergency. My initial thought was that it had something to do with the blizzard, and in a way it did. The streets everywhere were stopped in white, every hard edge rounded or heaped into softness, lanes empty apart from sanitation plows scudding their blades, groping for the buried asphalt. The sky, its white and gray pressed claustrophobically near the day before, now gaped infinite blue, as though awestruck at what it had belched out onto the city.

When I got to the limit and saw the senior detectives, weathering the cold in their knit caps, filtering in and out of Perkus's very entranceway, there came one thrilling moment when I was sure he'd done it. The cocky fool stole the mayor's chaldron! And oh, what confirmation of the treasure's value, that fuzz swarmed in all directions, even helicoptering overhead, and had had to set up a cordon! The story I told myself in those brief seconds of misunderstanding veered from disbelief to giddy terror: Had he outsmarted them, or was he caught? Would I be implicated? You can think a lot in a microsecond, a fact I never seem to notice except when I'm all wrong.

"Who are they looking for?" I asked, cagily, I thought, of the nearest cop at the barricade where I stood, in a tramped-down section of snow. Very little of Perkus's block had been shoveled, but there were several places where it appeared a flare had burned down through the drifts during the night. God, they'd really been on him almost instantly, I thought. I hoped he'd never returned here with the chaldron at all, but was sealed with the treasure in fugitive ecstasy, in some unguessable neutral site.

"Step back from the line, sir, thank you."

"Did they already apprehend him?" The cop I addressed had a face like a bowl of pudding someone had thrown his features at, and they'd barely stuck. The features claimed experience, attitude, cynicism, but the medium in which they'd embedded was impossibly raw and blank.

"Uh, I'm not at liberty to discuss cases with you, sir. Are you a resident of one of the buildings here? If not, I'll have to ask you to go on about your business."

"I'm a regular visitor to one of the buildings, that one. I'd like to go say hello to my friend, if you don't mind."

"Your friend's not in that building, sir. This whole area is unsafe to occupy. Our orders are to clear this area."

Perkus's dwelling, holy diorama of possibility and encounter, had been bureaucratically shrunken to a mere area. The police presence had nothing to do with Perkus or where we'd been the night before, that was just my lowly brain connecting the nearest available dots. When I sorted out my confusion, I learned it was the weight of the snowfall and the erosion of street salt on the century-old foundations accessible within the Jackson Hole crater that brought about the wider damage which made Perkus's building, and the others, unsafe. The word *infrastructure* came to mind. This city was always on the brink, hardly needing an excavating tiger's help to fail.

So Perkus was gone. The Ice I'd bought with Richard's money, on New Year's Eve, I sunk deep into my freezer, where I thought it belonged, though that January I could have kept it as consistently frozen on my windowsill. But if that cache of Lucite boxes could be a kind of homing device, it was Perkus I meant to call home, not pigeons.

19

Perkus Tooth had twenty-four hours alone in the apartment before Ava arrived. Biller kept close tabs on all the vacancies there and said it was the best way. The intended result being that the dog would take him for granted, detect his traces on the floors and walls and in the bed and then unquestioningly settle in as a roommate. So Perkus spent the first night on the surprisingly soft bed alone, half awake in the dark, and up to pace the rooms at first light. He dwelled in the space alone just long enough to posit some conjunction between his new self, shorn of so many defining accoutrements, dressed in an ill-fitting, lumpish blue-and-orange sports sweatshirt with an iron-on decal name, presumably of some star player, his right temple throbbing with cluster, a really monstrous attack, its eighth or ninth day in a row now, ebbing steadily in its fashion but still obnoxious, yet also, somehow, his brain awoken from some long-fogging dream, with a blind spot in sight, yes, but peripheral vision around the occlusion's edges widened, refreshed—some conjunction between this new self and the apartment in which he'd strangely landed, the apartment which had been fitted, like his body, with hand-me-downs, with furnishings and decor that would be rejected even by a thrift shop. The presumption being if he puzzled at the weird decrepit paintings and prints hung over the decaying living-room set, the framed *Streamers* poster, or the blue-period Picasso guitarist sun-faded to yellow over the non-working stove in the dummy kitchen, he should be able to divine from his surround what sort of person he'd become since the last time his inquiries turned inward. (That as opposed to issuing from a resolute self, to interrogate a malign and slippery world requiring constant vigilance.) Who he was seemed actually in the meantime to have slipped Perkus's mind.

Yet no. The rooms weren't going to tell him who he was. They weren't his. This was a dog's apartment, only the dog hadn't come yet. Biller had explained to him that though it was preferable that Perkus keep himself invisible, he had only to call himself a "volunteer" if anyone asked. The real volunteers had come to a tacit understanding with those, like Perkus, who'd occasionally slipped into the Friendreth Canine Apartments to stealthily reside with the animals. Faced head-on with the ethical allegory of homeless persons sneaking into human-shaped spaces in a building reserved for abandoned dogs, the pet-rescue workers could be relied upon to defy the Friendreth Foundation's mandate and let silence cover what they witnessed when they entered the building. Snow and cold only made sympathy that much more certain.

Perkus, for his part, hadn't encountered another soul in the hours he'd been installed in the apartments, had only gazed on minute human forms picking along drifts on the Sixty-fifth Street sidewalk seven stories below, through immovably paint-sealed window frames, the city a distant stilled terrarium. This corner of York Avenue, where Sixty-fifth abutted the scraps of parkland at the edge of Rockefeller University, formed an utter no-man's-land in the winterscape. There might only be dogs living in the apartment buildings for several blocks around, that's how it felt to Perkus. Biller informed him he shared the building with three other human squatters among the thirty-some dogs, though none on his floor or immediately above or below him. Perkus felt no eagerness to renew contact with his own species. He listened at the walls, and through the spasmodic barking imagined he heard a scrape of furniture or a groan or sigh that could be human, but no voices to give proof, until the morning when the volunteers began to come to take the dogs for walks, calling them by name each at their individual doors, praising them as "good boy" or "good girl" on their way out to use the snowdrifts as a potty.

Even those voicings were faint, the stolid prewar building's heavy lathe and plaster making fine insulation, and Perkus could feel confident of remaining undetected if he wished to be. When clunking footsteps and scrabbling paws led to his threshold, his apartment's unlocked door widened to allow the dog inside to take occupancy, Perkus hid like a killer in the tub behind the shower curtain, slumping down to sit against the porcelain's cool shape. He heard Ava's name spoken then, by a woman who, before leaving her behind, set out a bowl of kibble and another of water on the kitchen floor, then cooed a few more of the sweet doggish nothings a canine lover coos when fingering behind an ear or under a whiskery chin. Perkus had never lived with a dog. But much had changed just lately, and he was open to new things. He couldn't think of a breed to wish for but had an approximate size in mind, some scruffy mutt the size and shape of a lunch pail, say. The door shut, the volunteer's footsteps quickly receding in the corridor. Perkus had not done more than rustle at the plastic curtain, preparing to hoist himself from the tub, when the divider was nudged aside by a white grinning face—slavering rubbery pink lips and dinosaur teeth hinged to a squarish ridged skull nearly the size of his own, this craned forward by a neck and shoulders of pulsing and twitching muscle. One sharp white pink-nailed paw braced on the tub's edge as a tongue slapped forth and began brutalizing Perkus's helpless lips and nostrils. Ava the pit bull greeted her roommate with grunts and slobber, her expression demonic, her green-brown eyes rimmed in pink showing piggish intellect and gusto, yet almost helpless to command her smacking, cavernous jaws: from the first instant, before even grasping his instinctive fear, Perkus understood that Ava did her thinking with her mouth.

The next moment, falling back against the porcelain under her demonstrative assault, watching her struggle and slip as she tried and failed to hurtle deeper into the tub after him, he saw that the one front paw with which she scrabbled with was all she had for scrabbling, as she braced and arched on her two back feet: Ava was a three-legged dog. This fact would regularly, as it did now, give Perkus a crucial opening, his only physical edge on her, really. Ava slid awkwardly and fell on her side with a thump against the tile. Perkus managed to stand. By the time he got himself out of the tub she was on her three legs again, and flung herself upward once more, insisting that boxy skull, with its smooth loose-bunching carpet of flesh, into his hands to be adored. Ava was primally terrifying, but she persuaded Perkus pretty soon that she didn't mean to turn him into kibble. If Ava killed him it would be accidental, in seeking to staunch her emotional hungers.

Those first days were all sensual intimacy, a feast of familiarization, an orgy of, yes, pair-bonding, as Perkus learned how Ava negotiated the world, or at least the apartment, and how he was to negotiate the boisterous, insatiable dog, who became a kind of new world to him. Ava's surgery scar was clean and pink, an eight- or ten-inch seam from shoulder blade to a point just short of where he could most easily detect her heartbeat, at a crest of fur beneath her breast. Some veterinary surgeon had done a superlative job of sealing her joint so she appeared a creature naturally like a muscular furry torpedo there, missing nothing. Perkus couldn't guess how fresh it was or whether Ava's occasional stumbling indicated she was still learning to walk on three legs— mostly she made it look natural, and never once did she wince or cringe or otherwise indicate pain, but seemed cheerfully to accept tripod status as her fate. When she exhausted herself trailing him in this manner from room to room she'd sometimes charmingly sag against a wall or chair. More often she leaned against Perkus, or plopped her muzzle across his thigh if he sat. Her mouth closed then, as it rarely did otherwise, and Perkus could admire the pale brown of her liverish lips, the pinker brown of her nose, and the raw pale pink beneath her scant, stiff whiskers—the same color as her eyelids and the interior of her ears and her scar, and the flesh beneath the transparent pistachio shells of her nails. The rest, albino white, with a single, saucer-sized chocolate oval just above her tail to prove, with her hazel eyes, she was no albino. More usually, that mouth was transfixingly open—even after he'd persuaded himself she'd never intentionally damage him with the massive hinged trap full of erratic, sharklike teeth, Perkus found it impossible not to gaze inside and marvel at the map of pink and white and brown on her upper palate, the wild permanent grin of her throat. And when he let her win the prize she sought, to clean his ears or neck with her tongue, he'd have a close-up view, more than he could really endure. Easier to stand was her ticklish tongue baths of his toes, anytime he shed the ugly Nikes, though she sometimes nipped between them with a fang in her eagerness to root out the sour traces.

Ava was a listener, not a barker. As they sat together on the sofa, Ava pawing at Perkus occasionally to keep his hands moving on her, scratching her jowls or the bases of her ears or the cocoa spot above her tail, she'd also cock her head and meet his eyes and show that she, too, was monitoring the Friendreth Canine Apartments' other dwellers and the volunteers that moved through the halls. (As Perkus studied the building's patterns he understood that the most certain proof of human visitors, or other squatters, was the occasional flushing of a toilet.) She listened to the fits of barking that would possess the building periodically yet felt no need to reply.

Perkus believed this likely extended from the authority inherent in the fantastic power of her own shape, even reduced by the missing limb. He guessed she'd never met another body she couldn't dominate, so why bark? She also liked to gaze through the window, when he moved a chair to a place where she could make a sentry's perch. Her vigilance was absolutely placid, yet she seemed to find some purpose in it, and could spend an hour watching the street below without nodding. This was her favorite sport, apart from love.

Ava let him know they were to sleep in the bed together, that first night, joining him there and, then, when he tried to cede it to her, clambering atop him on the narrow sofa to which he'd retreated, spilling her sixty or seventy writhing pounds across his body and flipping her head up under his jaw in a crass seduction. That wasn't going to be very restful for either of them, so it was back to the twin-size mattress, where she could instead fit herself against his length and curl her snout around his hip bone. He grew accustomed by the end of the second night. If he didn't shift his position too much in his sleep she'd still be there when dawn trickled in around the heavy curtains to rouse him awake. Often then he'd keep from stirring, ignoring growing pressure in his bladder, balancing the comfort in Ava's warm weight against the exhausting prospect of her grunting excitement at his waking—she was at her keenest first thing, and he suspected that like him, she pretended to be asleep until he showed some sign. So they'd lie together, both pretending. If he lasted long enough, the volunteer would come and open the door and Ava would jounce up for a walk at the call of her name (and he'd lie still until the echoes of "Okay, Ava, down girl, down, *down*, down, that's good, no, down, *down*, yes, I love you too, down, down, *down* . . ." had trickled away through the corridor).

Though the gas was disabled, the Friendreth's electricity flowed, thankfully, just as its plumbing worked. Biller provided Perkus with a hot plate on which he could boil coffee, and he'd have a cup in his hand by the time Ava returned from her walk. He imagined the volunteer could smell it brewing when she opened the door. Coffee was the last constant between Perkus's old daily routine and his new, a kind of lens through which he contemplated his own transformations. For there was no mistaking that the command had come, as in Rilke's line: you must change your life. The physical absolutes of coexistence with the three-legged pit bull stood as the outward emblem of a new doctrine: recover bodily absolutes, journey into the real. Perkus's reckoning with Arnheim's chaldron had catapulted him into this phase, the night of the blizzard and the loss of his apartment and the books and papers inside all manifestations of the same watershed encounter. He held off interpretation for now. Until the stupendous cluster headache vanished into last traces, until he learned what Ava needed from him and how to give it, until he became self-sufficient within the Friendreth and stopped requiring Biller's care packages of sandwiches and pints of Tropicana, interpretation could wait.

The final step between them came when Perkus assumed responsibility for Ava's twice-daily walks (he'd already several times scooped more kibble into her bowl, when she emptied it, having discovered the supply in the cabinet under the sink). On the fifth day Perkus woke refreshed and amazed, alert before coffee, with his cluster migraine completely vanished. He'd clambered out of bed and dressed in a kind of exultation to match the dog's own, for once. He felt sure Ava hoped he'd walk her. And was tired of hiding. So he introduced himself to the volunteer at the door, and said simply that if she'd leave him the leash he'd walk her now and in the future. The woman, perhaps fifty, in a lumpy cloth coat, her frizzy hair bunched under a woolen cap, now fishing in a Ziploc of dog treats for one to offer to Ava, and who'd certainly earlier discerned his presence by any number of clues, showed less surprise than fascination that he'd spoken to her directly. Then she stopped.

"Something wrong with your eye?"

He'd gone unseen by all but Biller for so long, her scrutiny disarmed him. Likely his unhinged eyeball signified differently now that he was out of his suits, instead in this homeless-man garb, and featuring a two-week beard. To this kindly dog custodian it revealed that Ava's spectral cohabitant was not only poor but dissolute or deranged. A firm gaze, like a firm handshake, might be a minimum.

"From birth," Perkus said, referring to something he'd never mention in any other setting, but pridelessly needing to establish his competency here. He smiled at her as he said it.

"It's cold out."

"I've got a coat and boots." Biller had loaded both into the apartment's closet, for when he'd need it.

"You can control her?"

Perkus restricted himself from any fancy remarks. "Yes."

On the street, fighting for balance on icy sidewalks, Perkus discovered what Ava's massiveness and strength could do besides bound upward to pulse in his arms. Even on three legs, she rode and patrolled the universe within scope of her senses, chastening poodles, pugs, Jack Russells, even causing noble rescued racetrack greyhounds to bolt, as well as cats and squirrels foolish enough to scurry through the zone. Ava only had to grin and grunt, to strain her leash one front-paw hop in their direction, and every creature bristled in fear or bogus hostility, sensing her imperial lethal force, which required no trumping up, no Kabuki enactments of coiling to pounce, no theatrical snarls. On the street she was another dog, with little regard for Perkus now except as the rudder on her sailing, their affair suspended until they'd returned indoors. That first morning out the glare of daylight stunned Perkus, but also fed an appetite he'd had no idea he'd been starving. The walks became a regular highlight, twice a day, then three times, because why not? It was only a minority of female dogs, he learned, who bothered with marking behaviors, those scent-leavings typical of all males. Ava was in the exceptional category, hoarded her urine to squirt parsimoniously in ten, sometimes twenty different spots. Biller brought Perkus some gloves to shelter his exposed knuckles but also cover the chafing of Ava's heavy-woven leash, that ship's rigging, in his landlubber palms. Perkus learned to invert a plastic baggie on his splayed fingers and deftly inside-out a curl of her waste, to deposit an instant later in the nearest garbage can. Then inside, to the ceremonial hail of barking from the Friendreth's other inhabitants, who seemed to grasp Ava's preferential arrangement through their doors and ceilings.

Ava's volunteer—her name revealed as Sadie Zapping—poked her head in a couple of times to inquire, and once pointedly intersected with Perkus and Ava during one of their walks, startling Perkus from reverie, and making him feel, briefly, spied upon. But she seemed to take confidence enough from what she witnessed, and Perkus felt he'd been granted full stewardship. Now the two gradually enlarged their walking orbit, steering the compass of Ava's sniffing curiosity, around the Rockefeller campus and the Weill Cornell Medical Center, on a bridge over the FDR Drive, to gaze across at the permanent non sequitur of Roosevelt Island, defined for Perkus by its abandoned TB asylum to which no one ever referred, certainly not the population living there serviced by its goofy tram, like commuting by ski lift. "No dogs allowed," he reminded Ava every time she seemed to be contemplating that false haven. Or down First Avenue, into the lower Sixties along Second, a nefariously vague zone whose residents seemed to Perkus like zombies, beyond help.

Yet far more important than any human map, Perkus learned to which patches of snow-scraped earth Ava craved return, a neighborhood circuit of invisible importances not so different, he decided, from his old paces uptown, the magazine stand where he preferred to snag the *Times*, or East Side Bagel, or the crater formerly known as Jackson Hole. Perkus never veered in the direction of Eighty-fourth Street, though, and Ava never happened to drag him there. His old life might have rearranged itself around his absence, his building reopened, his places waiting for him to reinhabit them — but he doubted it. Equally plausible to him, if also unlikely, the tiger might have razed everything he'd ever known. The creature, which Richard Abneg had claimed was a machine operated by the city, might have been on a Perkus-eradication course to begin with. Perkus accepted this possibility with equanimity. The breadth of the city's mysteries that had begun to reveal themselves to him were beyond taking personally, even if they occasionally sought out a personal victim like himself or the Jackson Hole waitress, Lindsay. Occasionally he missed a particular book, felt himself almost reaching in Friendreth toward some blank wall as though he could pull down an oft-browsed volume and find consolation in some familiar lines. Or glance at an old broadside to recall some epiphany he'd gained, publicized to the street corners, and then forgotten. Nothing worse than this, he didn't miss the old life in and of itself. The notion he should cling to a mere apartment, he found both pathetic and specious. Apartments came and went, that was their nature, and he'd kept that one too long, so long he had trouble recalling himself before it. Good riddance. There was mold in the grout of the tiles around the tub he'd never have gotten clean in a million years.

Perkus had let go of things more dear than apartments. His encounter with the mayor's chaldron spared him such simplicities: an apartment was only a container for bodies, after all, while a chaldron was a container for what under duress he'd call *souls*. And Perkus had only ever possessed a chaldron by wanting one, and then lost the only chaldron he'd even seen by seeking to possess it. Meanwhile all along their true source had been near at hand to begin with, sometimes no farther than his kitchen's rear window. Perkus, who'd lived for as long as he could remember snared in such perplexities, the existential equivalent of an impossible object, stuck forever in parallax view, its different aspects irreconcilable, could only afford mild surprise at how the events of this winter had overturned him. It was on these long walks with Ava, dog flaneur, when he began to allow himself to muse on the implications, but never resentfully. Gratefully. He felt grateful to still live anywhere in Manhattan. If Ava could thrive with one forelimb gone, the seam of its removal nearly erased in her elastic hide, he could negotiate minus one apartment, as well as with the phantom limbs of conspiracy and epiphany and ellipsis that had always pulled him so many directions at once.

20

He'd spent that whole night right there, huddled at what came to seem the bottom of a well of dark, as though rather than climb to this point he'd fallen, and the snow-covered skylight and the glowing chaldron in its nook were two portals above, representing his only hope of escape. The mayor's carpeted stair was thick enough to make a comfortable perch, and he chose the stair that split the difference between his need to be as near as possible to the chaldron and to find an angle of view from which the least of its form was obstructed by the underside of the shelf on which it sat, then settled there, fully expecting to be interrupted, rescued, arrested, or assassinated.

But no. Mayor Arnheim never arrived with a flock of policemen or some dark-suited private force, the modern equivalent of Pinkertons. Nor did Richard Abneg or Chase Insteadman or even Georgina Hawkmanaji come. Nor his dangerous new acquaintance Russ Grinspoon, who'd said such disturbing things about Morrison Groom. Nor his cunning old protégée Oona Laszlo, no surprise in that. The mayor's astounding chaldron had no appreciator besides himself, and Perkus Tooth began to wonder if it had only conjured him into being to provide itself with an imaginary friend, he felt so invisible and unknown there through the passing hours. The party sounds were long gone from the foyer below. The irreverent clangor of a catering staff sealing up and loading its materials soon followed. Abandoning him in silence there. He centered the chaldron in his vision, a matter, paradoxically, of turning his head to disfavor the rebellious eye. Then steeled himself to ignore the portion he couldn't see, the imperfection of its outline. What was ever perfect? The form pulsed in his vision, beaming concurrence with his most reconciled thoughts, absolving all failure. To abide was not to compromise. At this Perkus fell deeply asleep.

He woke in early-morning light flooding the stairwell, his neck sore where it had rested crookedly against the curved wall. A woman stood on the stair above him. The mayor's aide, Chase had pointed her out at Arnheim's table.

"Hello," she said.

"Hello," he replied.

"I wondered when you'd wake up," she said. "My name is Claire Carter, by the way." How long had she stood there? Was he caught? If so, at what?

"So, I'm Perkus Tooth," he said.

"We know."

"You do?"

"You came with the actor," she said.

"Yes." He glanced up at the chaldron. In the bright light its unearthly radiance was a little blanched. He wondered whether it would have caught his eye in this light. A ridiculous thought. A chaldron was a chaldron, immeasurable and bright. Yet here Claire Carter stood, just beneath one, and either totally oblivious or uninterested. This weird fact imparted some of the chaldron's force to the woman herself, whose corn-husky-golden Dorothy Hamill was backlit to a halo like a solar flare, while her rectangular glasses pitched back to Perkus letterboxed, fish-eye-lens impressions of his own sorry form. Beneath those reflections her own features were precisely serene and nonjudgmental. The mayor's woman had brought with her no cops or Pinkertons, apparently not fearing him, and she presented nothing for Perkus to fear—not, anyway, apparently. He felt his presence had been lightly tolerated in the stairwell overnight, nothing worse. That "they" knew his name suggested he wasn't just some phantasm the chaldron had dreamed up to keep itself amused or adored.

"How—"

"There was a single checked overcoat left behind," she said. "In its pocket was a woolen hat with a distinctive patch featuring bright red lips and tongue. Security found you on the tape, walking in."

"Ah." So this was the sense in which he was known, by cultural iconography Claire Carter was apparently too young to identify. Perkus could imagine spadefuls of earth dropping onto a casket where everything that had ever been relevant to him was being quietly buried.

"Your coat is waiting downstairs."

"You don't care that I broke in?"

"You didn't break in," she pointed out. "You stayed."

"You don't want to know what I'm doing here?" He began to feel taken lightly. He didn't know how he wanted to be taken instead. His heart beat wildly.

"What are you doing here?"

"I'd like to speak with Mayor Arnheim, please." He stood, gathered himself, joined Claire Carter on the landing so that she no longer loomed above him, smoothed real and imaginary lint from the front of his velvet, hoping she knew it was intended to be wrinkled. Perkus decided he wanted her to understand that he was fundamentally a *dandy*, a word he'd never precisely applied to himself before but which he felt might pardon his spending the night on the fourth stair from the top. She should consider herself lucky he didn't have a pet lobster on a string, though that reference was likely beyond the compass of someone who couldn't identify the Rolling Stones' logo.

"He's not here."

"Isn't this his home?" Now he detected himself growing uselessly huffy, as though he had some higher ground attainable in this situation. He couldn't quit trying to make an impression, however, since Claire Carter, with her implacable, nearly mechanized mood of bright efficiency, made him feel invisible.

"The mayor entertains here, but he's got an apartment he prefers."

"Did you spend the night here?" Perkus asked. He found himself suddenly stirred by the notion of the two of them alone in the town house together through the long hours of the night, the chaldron really a sort of sexual beacon.

"The mayor's been very generous in letting me occupy the in-law apartment downstairs."

"Are you lovers?"

"Not that it's any of your business, but no." She appeared unoffended, but regarded him with fresh curiosity, ticking the golden bowl cut of her head sideways like the second hand of an alert clock. Impressively, in meeting Perkus's gaze she never once took the bait of tracking the wrong eye.

"I've got a question for him about . . . that vase up there."

"The chaldron, you mean? Jules couldn't tell you much about that."

"You know what it is?"

"Sure. I gave it to him. I don't think he's glanced at it twice."

She gratified each question with a little surplus of revelatory value for which he couldn't have thought to ask. Yet the ease of this exchange felt slippery and corrupt, as though she were toying with him. He preferred to find the question that would make Claire Carter balk. "Where did *you* get it? Did you buy it on *eBay*?"

"My brother gave it to me. Do you want to have a look? I think you'll be surprised."

At last Perkus could quit trying to make an impression, or to calibrate the nature of this encounter, for he was surely still asleep on the stair, and dreaming. Or perhaps the dream had begun long before. "Who's your brother?"

"Linus Carter, you may have heard of him. He's the designer."

"Designer of what—chaldrons?"

"That and all the rest of it, yes."

"The rest of what?"

"Yet Another World."

"I would very much like to see it, yes."

He followed her through the door at the landing, to find himself surprised, if surprise were still possible, by a curved stair leading up inside what he'd taken for a thin outer wall. Deep-set windows in the turret allowed just slivers of blue above gouts of snow, evidence of the storm Perkus had nearly forgotten. They climbed the steep curled stair in single file, the ascent of her tiny, pear-shaped buttocks before him a transfixing vision, as though one by one a chaldron's effects were transferring to Arnheim's Girl Friday.

The room at the top was large enough for the two of them and a chair and small desk, nothing more, making with its single window a kind of lookout or observation room. Perkus thought it would be a spectacular place to get some clear thinking done, to write a broadside or two, but he'd no sooner entertained the thought than Claire Carter unbolted a midget-size door at the level of her waist, swinging it inward, to disclose how it backed to the high nook below which he'd thirsted and pined through the dark hours, before passing out. She reached in and slid the box containing the chaldron onto the floor between them, revealing, among other things, a small power cord, trailing off to a transformer plugged in a socket at the rear of the nook. The thing inside looked watery and nebulous, its glamour and force completely spent in the bright sunlight that suffused the little attic study. Perkus saw immediately that what stood at his feet wasn't anything as definite as a ceramic, let alone one of some perfect and unearthly density, was less, in truth, than the photograph he'd admired in Strabo Blandiana's office or the pixel-dense lures he'd ogled on eBay. This chaldron was a hologram, and when Claire Carter switched off the tiny laser at the bottom of the vitrine it blinked out completely. The vessel had appeared so ineffectual that this seemed nearly an act of mercy: last one out, please turn off the chaldron.

"Looks more impressive at night, doesn't it?"

"Yes, yes, it does. Is there any chance I could get a cup of coffee?" Until the last possible instant Perkus had felt in the grip of an exalted confusion. Even as she debunked chaldrons, Perkus's encounter with Claire Carter had taken on some of a chaldron's strange ambiance. With the hologram's switching off, though, deflation set in. Perkus had begun to recognize the first glimmerings of a cluster prodrome, the inevitable aura preceding a really major headache. Caffeine was his first line of defense, at least the first available—he couldn't really ask whether any of Grinspoon's roaches had happened to be still lying in the mayor's marble ashtrays. The snow's sideways glare that attacked him through the windows everywhere he turned was possibly implicated, bright-angled light being one of several typical migraine triggers, along with dark chocolate and Richard Abneg's infernal red wines. Perkus kept his shades drawn low for a reason. There was nothing to do about it now but cope. He dreaded going out into that sunshine.

■

Linus Carter, though famously camera shy, was real, not, as rumored, just the name behind which some consortium of geniuses had hidden themselves. She should know, since she grew up with his brilliance overshadowing hers, Linus being three years older, though he was also so physically and emotionally immature that they were mistaken, and in some sense mistook themselves, for twins. Certainly they trusted each other more than anyone else, their parents, or the Dalton kids who treated them both a bit like freaks for their closeness, and for their lack of interest in the gossip and status games that defined the place. College divided them only a little, her Harvard, him MIT, and both places ones where they could shake themselves free of the unspoken expectations of the Manhattan castes they'd instinctively set themselves apart from. It was a matter of money, always money, and so when she came back to the city it was in the employ of media conglomerateer Arnheim, then several years from his run for the mayoralty, and if you'd mentioned that possibility it would have seemed a joke. Her first job, for which she found herself scouted before summa cum laude graduation, and working for Arnheim meant that money was never again going to divide Claire Carter from anything. It wasn't even that he paid her so well, as that she'd put herself right up against money's large and impassive flank, under its vast scaly wing. As a matter of fact, when some of the really hugely trust-funded kids who'd shit on her and Linus at Dalton resurfaced these days, spaced-out on boards of corporations they didn't even know whether they owned, she was usually running rings around them, telling them what to do. And when Linus came back to the city with his big idea and needed capital investiture to get it started up, she could take care of him, too, introduce him to the right people.

She explained all this in the town house's big kitchen, where they sat on stools at a marble counter, over coffee—cappuccinos from a machine that took a little cartridge of coffee under a lever and spat them out perfectly, brimming with foam on top. The device's brief guttering productions shattered the dawn's eerie silence. Perkus would have preferred for purposes of headache prevention a bottomless mug of traditional black, but was too polite to say anything. He sipped the hot foam and ignored the background of approaching migraine and listened to what Claire Carter appeared compelled to explain to him as his reward for camping out beneath the hologram. It seemed that her shy and kooky older brother had written all the design protocols for Yet Another World in secret, while working for a Menlo Park company whose contract claimed any idea he originated as their own, and so he'd quit and moved to their parents' apartment, sleeping in his old room like the unsocialized loser he perhaps felt himself to be, and let five months tick by watching TV Land reruns of *Square Pegs* and *Martyr & Pesty*, only afterward whispering to Claire that he was sitting on a gold mine but couldn't afford the tools to dig with. She set him up with investors, not Arnheim himself but a rich-beyond-rich pajama-wearing Hugh Hefner wannabe, no disrespect, named Rossmoor Danzig.

Two years later three million souls worldwide, a number doubling every six months, conducted some part of their daily lives in the elaborate and infinitely expansible realm that had sprung from Linus Carter's generous parameters, this pixel paraphrase of reality which welcomed role-players, entrepreneurs, sexual trollers, whatever. You could play by Linus's rules or write your own, invent a self unlike yourself, invent a nation for yourself and your friends: Yet Another World made room for it all. A separate economy, originating within the game, had leaked out into the wider world, as players seeking to accumulate in-game wealth and sway by shortcut rather than diligence began hoarding and trading on the small number of unique and unduplicable treasure items Linus had ingeniously tucked into the corners of his world. In a system where any kind of artifact, six-dimensional, invisible, antigravitational, whatever its designer could imagine, was not only possible but replicable ad nauseam, these scattered few objets d'art, known as *chaldrons*, were capable of driving players insane with acquisitive frenzy. For all the anarchy Linus loosed, he'd kept this one means of playing God: a monopoly on the local equivalent of a short supply of Holy Grails. To protect his symbolic economy from inflation, Linus also designed a few expert subroutines for rooting out and destroying any counterfeits put into circulation, a NetBot goon squad.

So the chaldron quickly became the supreme symbol of the game's elite. To know someone who could get you access to a chaldron wasn't bad, so you could spend time communing with the thing, but to own one was far better. The items, fundamentally imaginary though they might be, had begun trading in the "real" world for hundreds then thousands of dollars. No one had yet determined what the ceiling might be, since the hordes of new players arriving every day drove the ratio of chaldron-to-player scarcity continually through the roof. Among players without so much disposable income the objects had nearly a religious aspect, and in some precincts of Yet Another World a community of caretakers, often calling themselves "knights," had united around the cause of protecting and honoring a single chaldron, forming consortiums of purpose out of what had been a polymorphous libertarian playground.

Linus's cartel needless to say added a layer of menacing mystique to his legend as the game's creator. His subsequent fear of irrational chaldron fetishists who might think of him as Chapman did Lennon drove him deeper into seclusion. That, in turn, fueled rumors of his death and secret replacement by a corporate clone, or of his fictional existence from the start. Poor Linus had never been terribly comfortable on the outer side of a computer's screen to begin with, and now, despite a phenomenal success as others would quantify it, he was miserable. Claire was his lifeline and even she didn't know what he did with most of his days, though she'd had some reports he wandered his own invented landscape hidden inside an anonymous and humble avatar, perversely dedicating himself to trying to persuade other players of the unimportance of chaldrons in a universe where anything else was as free as oxygen and daylight. As a thank-you to Claire for all she'd done (putting aside the argument that by helping him incorporate she'd wrecked him), Linus had presented her with the hologram that had attracted Perkus's interest, as well as, inside the realm of Yet Another World, a treasury of ten chaldrons of surpassing quality, hidden in a high and impregnable redoubt. She'd visited this castle and checked her priceless stash once or twice, though, really, she was sorry to say, virtual reality just wasn't her cup of tea. So her virtual treasures sat gathering virtual dust. The way things were going, she'd be able to put future kids through college on the things.

■

"Is Linus by any chance a client of an acupuncturist named Strabo Blandiana?" Perkus interrupted. He'd been reminded of that framed poster, Blandiana's gift from a patient.

"Yes," said Claire Carter, looking mildly surprised. "I sent him there. I've been visiting Strabo for a couple of years. Why do you ask?"

"I met him at the party last night," said Perkus, hedging.

"Everyone knows Strabo."

"I guess. Miss Carter, may I ask you why you're telling me all this?" Perkus had a theory on this subject, actually: he figured he reminded Claire Carter of her brother. Under her glossy surface she had a soft spot for helpless brainy boys. That was to say, too, that despite the gulf between her yuppieish dress-for-success manner and Perkus's bohemian shambles, she identified with Perkus herself. Being a human being, she sought vindication for the choices that had made her lonely: hence the effort spent to convince him she wasn't just one of those moneyed Dalton kids. No matter how it looked now, she was an outsider. Claire Carter, Perkus recognized, was from the we-nerds-run-the-universe school, and wanted Perkus to flash the secret hand signals back to her. *Square Pegs* indeed. Perkus had known this vibe before—the rock critics, always asking him to recite the pledge of allegiance of the Elite Despised. He'd tended to decline politely, just as he now didn't mention to Claire Carter that he'd never been able to rouse his sympathy for anyone who'd gone to Dalton no matter how sulky they felt about it.

The other possibility, that she was wildly lying to divert him, would seem to have been shut down completely with the blinking off of that laser. Perkus had thrown a lot of himself, too much, down a rabbit hole leading into no Wonderland whatsoever. He'd been pathetically chasing video-game booty. The exhaustion of it was only beginning to set in, along with the cluster headache. He'd sucked the dregs of his cappuccino, uselessly—hoping for that fey foamy beverage to do anything to thwart his massive impending migraine was like bringing a poodle to the beach and siccing it on Melville's great white whale. Perkus's vertiginous sexual interest had vanished, too, somewhere in the course of Claire Carter's narration. He remembered now where he'd heard her name before: Richard Abneg hated this woman, saw her as the symbol of the destruction of the city's soul. She was certainly an ace disenchanter.

Her reply gave no nod to his theories. "The actor's got a lot of fans around here," she said, reverting to her special robotic bluntness, totally unsentimental once the topic migrated from her Seymour Glassian brother.

"We're aware you're a favorite of Insteadman's. His story keeps a lot of people enthralled, you know. This is a difficult time in the city."

So, it was all about Chase Insteadman after all. And: everything Perkus suspected was true. Perkus had suspected so much, so extensively, for so long. But it was different to have a thing confirmed. "I'm not so sure Chase realizes it's a story." Perkus could barely believe he'd said this aloud. Again, he experienced the conviction he was dreaming, only Claire Carter was the least dreamlike gorgon he'd ever encountered.

"Well, we all get lost in our roles sometimes. Mr. Tooth, you'll have to excuse me. I see you've finished your coffee, and I do have to get to work."

So, was this how it happened? When you finally penetrated the highest chambers of power and gazed into corruption's face, was it neither beautiful nor terrifying, but merely—Claire Carter's? Apparently so. And her attempt to enlist his consent was so paltry, so half-assed, that it seemed she assumed she'd gained it in advance.

"Chase Insteadman is my friend," he said weakly. He wondered what there was left to defend or protect. Nothing, most likely.

"Yes," she allowed.

"That much is real." Even as he said it, he felt the foolishness of turning to this woman for confirmation of what was or wasn't real. Now the white whale of his headache broke to the surface and swallowed him completely. Around the penumbra of his blind spot he saw that a man had joined them in the room, a valet or Secret Service agent of some kind—needless to say, Claire

Carter hadn't relied on luck or goodwill to protect her in the town house alone with a party-crashing weirdo; how ludicrous to imagine she would. Maybe he was the one who'd pored over the security tapes and spotted him entering the party with Chase. Now he carried Perkus's overcoat and hat, holding them at arm's length as if about to burn contaminated items in a bonfire. Perkus accepted the garments and staggered from the kitchen, toward the foyer. With cluster in full blossom, he had nothing further to fear from the glare of the fresh snow. He was even curious to see the extent of the storm that had, so far as he could tell, completely silenced the city. Claire Carter didn't escort him out.

■

He'd have walked the twenty blocks home in any event, since the migraine nausea would have made a cab ride unbearable, but there wasn't any choice. The streets were free of cabs and any other traffic. Some of the larger, better-managed buildings had had their walks laboriously cleared and salted, the snow pushed to mounds covering hydrants and newspaper boxes, but elsewhere Perkus had to climb into drifts that had barely been traversed, fitting his poor shoes into boot prints that had punched deep as his knees. His pants were quickly soaked, and his sleeves as well, since between semi-blindness and poor footing he stumbled to his hands and knees several times before even getting to Second Avenue. Under other circumstances he'd have been pitied, perhaps offered aid, or possibly arrested by the quality-of-life police for public drunkenness, but on streets the blizzard had remade there was no one to observe him apart from a cross-country skier who stared pitilessly from behind solar goggles, then a few dads here and there dragging a kid or two on a sled. If they saw him at all they probably thought he was out playing, too. Nobody would have any other reason to be making their way along impassible streets so early the day after. Not a single shop was open, their entrances buried in drifts.

When he met the barricade at the corner of Eighty-fourth, he at first tried to bluster his way past, thinking the cop had misunderstood—*of course* they were letting through the residents of the buildings on the block, even if other pedestrians had to make their way the long way around. But no. His building was one of three the tiger had undermined, and the snowstorm had finished the job. He talked with neighbors he hadn't spoken to in fifteen years of dwelling on the same floor, though gripped in the vise of his cluster headache he barely heard a word they said, and he couldn't have made too good an impression. *You need to find someplace to sleep tonight*, that was a fragment that got through to him. *They might let you in for your stuff later, but not now. You can call this number* . . . but the number he missed. Then, as Perkus teetered away: *Get yourself indoors, young man.* And: *Pity about that one.*

Now, as he made his way through the snow to he knew not where, what engulfed Perkus Tooth, as completely as the headache engulfed his brain and the snow the city, was the sense of cumulative and devastating losses in the last twelve hours, since he'd allowed himself to be lured to the mayor's party, by Chase Insteadman, and upstairs, to see the hologram, by Russ Grinspoon. All of it felt terribly coherent and scripted, down to the last sequence, when Claire Carter, if that was even her real name, had spun out her story just long enough to allow the cluster migraine to eclipse him totally, only then booting him out into the streets to find his apartment barred. For she'd surely known. The tiger was a city operative, hadn't Abneg confirmed it? Perkus couldn't think straight, but you didn't need to think straight to put such simple facts together. Claire Carter and the forces for which she was a mere spokesperson, a bland front, had evidently meant to smash him, and she'd chosen to flaunt the fact by how she toyed with him for the last hour or so. She was, he saw now, a member of the we-nerds-will-destroy-you-so-thoroughly-it-will-leave-you-gasping school. Under the power pantsuits, she was part of that inexplicable generation subsequent to his, the Trench Coat Mafia. Arnheim probably surrounded himself with them, autistic revengers, like Howard Hughes insulating himself with Mormons. Seeing him in the teeth of his ruination, Claire Carter had even told him the whole plot, like Goldfinger with Bond strapped to the death ray.

Being Perkus Tooth, he blamed the nearest cultural referent he could find: I smoked dope with a man who went from being directed by Groom to being directed by Ib and couldn't tell the difference! What a fool I am. That joint was probably laced with *essence of mediocrity*, a substance that gave you a solo career as feeble as Grinspoon's once he'd parted ways with Hale, and made its imbiber hallucinate that sublime chaldrons were only video-game fodder. For now that Perkus had begun to distrust one assumption he had to question them all. Chaldrons were something else. Maybe Claire Carter didn't even know, though at the same time he was certain she was trying to throw him off the hunt. Linus Carter might have glimpsed their form somewhere and based the crappy decoder ring in the cereal box of Yet Another World on what he'd glimpsed. Nothing was necessarily so simple. Hah, as if it even outwardly claimed to be!

Chase Insteadman was his friend. Chase Insteadman was an actor and the ultimate fake. A cog in the city's fiction.

The tiger was destroying the city. The tiger was being used by the city to un-home its enemies.

Chaldrons were real and fake, as Marlon Brando was alive and dead.

Mailer, almost destroyed by gravity, walking with two canes, and complacently resigned to Provincetown, vacating the fight.

Richard Abneg worked for the city and the eagles were therefore a wild force from elsewhere. Richard Abneg might be a key to something, if Perkus thought about him coherently enough, impossible in this snow and cluster. Abneg, inside and outside at once, self-consciously corrupted, a hinge on the door between the old city and the new.

Oona Laszlo, Perkus's own Frankenstein creation, mocking him always. She carried the tang of betrayal and sellout. One thing to dash off with your left hand memoirs of abused point guards, but Oona carried water for that middlebrow *Times* darling, Noteless. Nothing worse than what Perkus liked to call too-late modernism. Clever Oona had written herself into a bed of lies. Perkus only pitied Chase for being so much under her thumb, and excommunicated her now in his mind.

He thought, too, of friends lost to time, who'd left their traces in the Eighty-fourth Street apartment: the mad bookseller D. B. "Bats" Breithaupt; George, the art restorer from the Met; Roe, Specktor, Amato, Sorrentino, Howe, Hultkrans, other names he'd misplaced, the good faith implicit in convivial uncompromising evenings now stranded in amnesiac mists. *Where are my friends?* If he could see all his friends again, the apartment or chaldrons wouldn't matter.

Somewhere, far off, a urine-stained bear bellowed (did polar bears bellow?) on a sun-blasted floe, seeming to ask what did *anything* in the city have to do with what was real?

■

All of this occurred on Eighty-fourth between Second and First, as Perkus made his staggering way across the traffic-barren intersection. He'd begun walking in the center of the streets, in the gully the early plows had made. To cover a block's distance required a sort of heroic effort, but Perkus wasn't in a state to savor the exertion of his own will so much as he observed himself from a fascinated distance, like a creature in nature footage, one of those bears spied on from a biplane window, or a crippled caribou strayed from the herd into an unwelcoming landscape. His books and CDs and videotapes were okay. The building hadn't fallen, they remained indoors, waiting for him. It was as if the apartment represented the better part of him, the brain in archive, and it didn't so much matter what happened to the exiled scrawny body that now noticed the wetness of cuffs and sleeves beginning to clumpily freeze in the chill wind. Nonetheless, discomfort gusted his sails to a nearby port: Gracie Mews. A twenty-four-hour place, the coffee shop hadn't bowed to the storm, its waiters taking turns scraping and chopping at the sidewalk through the night to keep at least a symbolic pathway open, though a customer would have to clamber over a hell of a lot of other unshoveled snow to get to the area they'd cleared. Well, Perkus did the clambering now. He plunged through the door of the Mews and, though he could barely see his hand in front of his face anymore for the breadth of his blind spot, smelled coffee, tureens of it, the good stuff.

Despite his appearance they welcomed him into a booth, recognizing a friend of the actor's, or anyway one of their few likely customers under present weather conditions. Perkus had about forty dollars in his pocket—good thing he hadn't been able to hail a cab. He ordered a poached egg, if only to have something to try to center in his vision, a peg to drink coffee around. Drink coffee he did, though it was too late. Cluster had risen like a sea over his head. Perkus was now (at least) triply divided from the world, riven by loss and snow and the imposition over his senses of that state of half-life which would have kept him from even noticing the restoration of those other things.

He told himself he was waiting in Chase Instead-man's place for Insteadman to come, but after the first hour or so of nodding in and out of a psychedelic caffeinated coma right there in the booth, he admitted to himself that he couldn't really imagine the former child star budging from his apartment in this stuff for love or money. It wasn't as if Chase knew he was here. Perkus would have to go from the Mews eventually, back out into the cold. The obvious thought was to find his way to Chase's building, if he could manage it by memory, crippled by migraine. Yet the more he lived with Claire Carter's taunts the less eager he was to face the actor soon. Associations with the Mews gave him cause to meditate on the actor's part in things, the changes that had crept over the city and Perkus's life since late last summer, since their meeting in Susan Eldred's office at Criterion.

Perkus lived as much inside a conundrum as he did a city. At any given moments the conundrum presented itself in some outward form, a vessel or symbol. Chase Insteadman might be the thing that had come along to replace chaldrons, which had themselves probably replaced some other emissary pregnant with undisclosed messages—Gnuppets, say, or Marlon Brando, Perkus couldn't always say which was the preeminent form conundrum took at a given time.

Unlike Brando or any of the others, however, Chase Insteadman had presented himself at Perkus's own door, offered himself as a friend.

Perkus had been readying himself to tell the actor what he knew: that his life was a lie, an entertainment.

That there was no beautiful heartbreaking astronaut alive overhead, dropping sad notes from space. Perkus had been astonished that Claire Carter had let this secret be confirmed. Yet why fall into such a simple trap? There must be more. There was more. Why explain Yet Another World so laboriously to him? The answer lay in plain sight: Claire Carter wanted Perkus Tooth to consider the extent to which *he lived as much in a construction as Chase Insteadman.*

Perkus held to one ethos above all, a standard drawn from early drug episodes, Ecstasy, mescaline, one memorable day a silver tray heaped full of psilocybin-mushroom tea sandwiches, crusts trimmed by a friend steeped in WASP manners, as with companions he experienced side-by-side plunging in and out of brief dazzling revelation, while others lurched into bad trips, negative worlds, needing to be retrieved: don't rupture another's illusion unless you're positive the alternative you offer is more worthwhile than that from which you're wrenching them. Interrogate your solipsism: Does it offer any better a home than the delusions you're reaching to shatter? Perkus, operating from a platform of cultural clues arranged into jigsaw sense, had gone years certain his solipsism was a pretty good home. Plastering the city with broadsides, he'd done his best to widen it to let passersby be drawn inside, so sure he was of its grounding in autodidactic scholarship and hard-won ellipsis.

Now, all certainty had fled him at once. If a man found himself consoled inside a virtual chalice, wasn't he possibly a virtual man? Maybe Perkus's Manhattan was as fragile a projection as Yet Another World, crafted by an unnamed maker or makers as erratic and helpless as Linus Carter. Did he want to destroy it? The city was a thing of beauty, however compromised at its seams, however overrun with crass moola, however many zones were hocked to Disney or Trump. Claire Carter had done the impossible, inspiring in Perkus a yearning sympathy for anyone who kept this mad anthill running, even developers throwing up vacuous condos in place of brownstones, or the sorrow-stricken moneymen working beneath the gray fog. They were all pitching in, and who was Perkus to let them down if they liked reading about Janice Trumbull on their folded-over front page as they stood crammed into the IRT? Perkus's present bit of business, she'd not-so-subtly implied, might be to keep the actor happy, like a spear-carrier on the Met's stage who was really the lead tenor's rent boy or coke dealer. Did that mean jolting Chase from his astronaut dream? No, don't accuse any other person of functioning as a Gnuppet unless you are ready, like Brando, to walk onto the set without pants to prove what you've got underneath, to show that no hand has climbed up your shirt to operate your hands and head and to speak through your mouth. Sleepwalkers, leave other sleepwalkers alone! Here was how extensively Claire Carter had destabilized him: Perkus Tooth now knew he might be a Gnuppet, though operated by whom he couldn't say.

So he couldn't face Chase Insteadman, at least not yet. He wouldn't know what to say to him.

This fugue wasn't instantaneous. On a more tangible plane, the Mews' waiters eventually took away the yolk-curdled remains of Perkus's egg, swabbed with a string mop at the slush as it unclung from his velvet cuffs and from between his shoelaces, and refilled his coffee five or six times. They must love that ritual of refilling, either that or feel their customers got a kind of macho charge from emptying so many cups, they gave you such a shallow coffee mug at these places. A noisy couple of customers, a chortling example of pair-bonding at its most self-congratulatory, had come and gone what might be hours ago. At last, from within his zone of self-erasure, his chalk outline, Perkus's raging bladder signaled the risk of soaking his pants right here in the booth. For an instant he calculated that it might pass as more melted snow, then decided he'd haul himself to the Mews' bathroom. When he returned he found his place cleared, a check on the table, decorous dinerese for the old heave-ho.

If not to Chase's, where? Richard Abneg? The eagles had preempted that destination. He had no idea where Georgina Hawkmanaji lived. Oona? Hah! Perkus might as well return and appeal to Claire Carter for shelter, that's how low his regard for Oona Laszlo had sunk.

No, there was only one inevitable haven, and as in a merciful desert vision the information Biller had jotted on a scrap of receipt on Perkus's kitchen table appeared before him, oasis in a blind spot: Biller's new street, the dog apartments, Sixty-fifth near York. Not the numerical address, but he didn't need that, from Biller's descriptions he'd surely be able to stake out the volunteer walkers crisscrossing the lobby with their leashed clientele.

His warming and elliptical passage of hours within the Mews had served another purpose, allowing more

402

streets to become negotiable, though still the city's official life was charmingly on hold, giving way to the goofy storm-trooperish skiers, and kids in bright plastic saucers. Perkus tried and failed to remember doing such a thing himself. On a snow day he'd have been indoors with a pile of Kurt Vonnegut Jr. In Dell Pocket editions—he could still see *Cat's Cradle* in red, *The Sirens of Titan* in purple, *God Bless You, Mr. Rosewater* in blue, fox-blond pages softened by his eager thumbs. Cluster couldn't drag him deep enough into half-life to blot from mind's eye the beacon of those Dell Vonneguts.

Biller was the one he needed now. As though Perkus had been keeping Biller in the bank, feeding and strengthening a daily soldier accustomed to Life During Wartime. Well, here, trudging sickened in the snowdrifts like a Napoleonic soldier in retreat from Moscow, Perkus was adequately convinced. *There is a war between the ones who say there is a war and the ones who say there isn't.* Perkus had gotten complacent in the Eighty-fourth Street apartment. Time to go underground. Biller knew how to live off the grid, even in a place like Manhattan that was nothing but grid. Even better, Biller had an encampment in the enemy terrain of Yet Another World. Biller could tell him what he knew about Linus Carter and chaldrons—now Perkus would be patient enough to listen to what had always seemed a little pointless before. With the virtual realm seeming to have penetrated Perkus's city at any number of points, Biller was the essential man, with means for survival in both places. They could compare notes and pool resources, Perkus preferring to think of himself as not yet completely without resources. Perkus laughed at himself now: Biller was like Old Man McGurkus in Seuss's *Circus McGurkus*, who'd single-handedly raise the tents, sell the pink lemonade, shovel the elephants' shit, and also do the high-wire aerialist act.

In this manner, dismal yet self-amused, Perkus propelled his body to Sixty-fifth Street, despite the headache's dislodging of himself from himself, working with the only body he had, the shivering frost-fingered blind stumbler in sweat- and salt-stained purple velvet.

He trailed a dog and walker into the lobby, catching the swinging door before it clicked shut, one last act of mastery of the mechanics of outward existence, and then passed out in a melting pool on the tile just inside. Biller would later explain that a volunteer had sought him out, knowing that the tall black man in the spotted fur hat functioned as ambassador for the vagabond entities sometimes seen modestly lurking in the rooms of certain dogs, and that this tatterdemalion in the entranceway was nothing if not one of those. So Biller gathered Perkus and immediately installed him in what would become Ava's apartment. It was there, nursed through the first hours by Biller's methodical and unquestioning attentions, his clothes changed, his brow mopped, his sapped body nourished with a simple cup of ramen and beef broth until it could keep down something more, that Perkus had felt his new life begin. It was a life of bodily immediacy, after Ava's example. Perkus didn't look past the next meal, the next walk, the next bowel movement (with Ava these were like a clock's measure), the next furry sighing caress into mutual sleep.

Biller, attuned to this, minimized, when Perkus brought it up, any talk of Yet Another World. Sure, he knew about chaldrons. They were the crème de la crème of virtual treasure, and people had quit trading them for any accumulation of virtual anything—tracts of land, magnificent architecture, sex slaves, other treasure. They only changed hands for dollars now, and quite a lot of those. But Biller reminded Perkus that if you cared about Yet Another World there was a lot else to care about besides chaldrons. And yeah, he knew the legends of Linus Carter, but so what? Every place had a creator. What made Yet Another World interesting was that it had thousands. You didn't have to pay any attention to the wishes of the originator of the place if you didn't care to—a creator who might, after all, be the last person to know what was really going on. Still, Perkus saw Biller's ears perk up when he told him about the castle hoard of chaldrons Linus had bestowed on his unimpressed sibling. That fact did stir the imagination. Putting the subject aside, Biller promised he would help Perkus set up an avatar, a persona on Yet Another World, if he wanted one. Somehow, at least through January and into February, they failed to get around to it. There was no computer in Ava's apartment.

Biller wasn't a hanger-outer. He had his entrepreneurial paces to go through, and his altruistic ones, too, which included checking in with Perkus and, most days, dropping off edible donated items of food and new clothes he thought might fit, most recently a pair of heavy and useful tan work boots. Otherwise, he left Perkus and Ava alone. When Perkus was drawn unexpectedly back a step or two into the human realm, it was Ava's former walker, Sadie Zapping, who drew him. Sadie had other dogs in the building and still troubled to look in from time to time, always with a treat in her palm for Ava to snort up. This day she also had a steaming to-go coffee and a grilled halved corn muffin in a grease-spotted white bag which she offered to Perkus, who accepted it. This being not a time in life of charity refused or even questioned. She asked him his name again and he said it through a mouthful of coffee-soaked crumbs.

"I thought so," said Sadie Zapping. She plucked off her knit cap and shook loose her wild gray curls. "It took a little while for me to put it together. Me and my band used to read your posters all the time. I read you in the *Voice*, too."

Ah. Existence confirmed, always when you least expected it. "Broadsides," he corrected. Then he asked the name of her band, understanding it was the polite response to the leading remark.

"Zeroville," she said. "Like the opposite of Alphaville, get it? You probably saw our graffiti around, even if you never heard us. Our bassist was a guy named Ed Constantine, I mean, he renamed himself that, and he used to scribble our name on every blank square inch in a ten-block radius around CBGB, even though we only ever played there a couple of times. We did open for Chthonic Youth once." She plopped herself down now, on a chair in Ava's kitchen Perkus had never pulled out from under the table. He still used the apartment as minimally as possible, as if he were to be judged afterward on how little he'd displaced. Meanwhile Ava gaily smashed her square jowly head across Sadie's lap, into her cradling hands and scrubbing fingers. "Gawd, we used to pore over those crazy posters of yours, or broadsides if you like. You're a lot younger-looking than I figured. We thought you were like some punk elder statesman, like the missing link to the era of Lester Bangs or Legs McNeil or what have you. It's not like we were holding our breath waiting for you to *review* us or anything, but it sure was nice knowing you were out there, somebody who would have gotten our jokes if he'd had the chance. Crap, that's another time and place, though. Look at us now."

Sadie had begun to uncover an endearing blabbermouthedness (and even when not addressing Perkus she'd give forth with a constant stream of "Good girl, there you go girl, aw, do you have an itchy ear? There you go, that's a girl, yes, yessss, good dog. Ava, whaaata good girl you are!," etc.) but another elegist for Ye Olde Lower East Side was perhaps not precisely what the doctor ordered just now. Perkus, who'd preferred to think he was in the manner of a Pied Piper, influencing a generation following his, didn't really want to believe that when his audience made itself visible again it would resemble somebody's lesbian aunt. He sensed himself ready to split hairs—*not so much Lester Bangs as Seymour Krim, actually*—and thought better of it. He was somewhat at a loss for diversions, however. He couldn't properly claim he had elsewhere to be. Sadie, sensing resistance, provided her own non sequitur. "You play cribbage?"

"Sorry?"

"The card game? I'm always looking for someone with the patience and intelligence to give me a good game. Cribbage is a real winter sport, and this is a hell of a winter, don't you think?"

With his consent, the following day Sadie Zapping arrived at the same hour, having completed her walks, and unloaded onto the kitchen table two well-worn decks of cards, a wooden cribbage board with plastic pegs, and two packets of powdered Swiss Miss. Perkus, who hated hot chocolate, said nothing and, when she served it, drained his mug. He'd gone without marijuana now for more than a month, and alcohol (never his favorite anyhow), taking no stimulants besides caffeine and sucrose, both of which the hot chocolate provided in a rather degraded form. The game Sadie taught him was perfectly poised between dull and involving (so any talk could be subsumed to concentration) as well as between skill and luck. The first few days Perkus steadily lost, then got the feel of it. Sadie sharpened, too, her best play not aroused until she felt him pushing back. They kept their talk in the arena of the local and mundane: the state of the building, which had its own minor dramas involving the bureaucratic management imposed by the Manhattan Reification Society versus the pragmatic hands-on knowledge won by the volunteers themselves; the state of the streets, which had borne another two-inch snowfall, a treacherous slush carpet laid over the now seemingly permanent irregularities of black ice wherever the blizzard had been shoved aside; the ever-improving state of Perkus's cribbage; above all, the state of Ava, who thrived on Sadie's visits and seemed to revel in being discussed. Perkus could, as a result, tell himself he tolerated the visits on the dog's account. It was nearly the end of February before Sadie told him the tragedy of Ava's fourth limb.

"I thought you knew," she said, a defensive near-apology.

He didn't want to appear sarcastic—did Sadie think Ava had told him?—so said nothing, and let her come out with the tale, which, together with her age and the names of her former owners and other facts Perkus couldn't know, Sadie had spied in Ava's paperwork upon transfer to the canine dorm. Three-year-old Ava was a citizen of the Bronx, it turned out. She'd lived in the Sack Wern Houses, a public development in the drug dealers' war zone of Soundview, and had been unlucky enough to rush through an ajar door and into the corridor during a police raid on the apartment next door. The policeman who'd emptied his pistol in her direction, one of three on the scene, misdirected all but one bullet in his panic, exploding her shank. Another cop, a dog fancier who'd cried out but failed to halt the barrage, tended the fallen dog, who, even greeted with this injury, only wanted to beseech for love with her tongue and snout. Her owner, a Dominican who may or may not have considered his pit bull ruined for some grim atavistic purpose, balked at the expense and bother of veterinary treatment, so Ava's fate was thrown to the kindly cop's whims. The cop found her the best, a surgeon who knew that she'd be better spared cycling the useless shoulder limb, its groping for a footing it could never attain, and so excised everything to the breastbone. It was the love-smitten cop who'd named her, ironically after the daughter whose terrified mom forbade their adopting the drooling sharky creature into a household that already made room for two Norwich terriers. So Ava came into the Friendreth Society's care.

"She's got hiccups," Sadie pointed out another day, a cold one but then they were all cold ones, toward the end of February now. "She" was forever Ava, no need to specify. The dog was their occasion and rationale, vessel for all else unnameable Perkus Tooth and Sadie Zapping had in common. Anyway, it was her apartment, they were only guests. He spotted the start card she'd revealed, the jack of clubs, and shifted his peg two spaces—"Two for his heels," she'd taught him to say.

"Yeah, on and off for a couple of days now." The dog had been hiccing and gulping between breaths as she fell asleep in Perkus's arms and then again often as she strained her leash toward the next street corner. Sometimes she had to pause in snorting consumption of the pounds of kibble that kept her sinewy machine running, and once she'd had to cough back a gobbet of bagel and lox Perkus had tossed her. That instance had seemed to puzzle the pit bull, yet otherwise she shrugged off a bout of hiccups as joyfully as she did her calamitous asymmetry.

"Other day I noticed you guys crossing Seventy-ninth Street," she said. On the table between them she scored with a pair of queens. "Thought you never went that far uptown. Weren't there some people you didn't want to run into?"

He regarded her squarely. Sadie Zapping's blunt remarks and frank unattractiveness seemed to permit if not invite unabashed inspection, and Perkus sometimes caught himself puzzling backward, attempting to visualize a woman onstage behind a drum kit at the Mudd Club. But that had been, as Sadie earlier pointed out, another time and place. It was this attitude that made her the perfect companion for Perkus's campaign to dwell in the actual. The perfect human companion, that was, for on this score no one could rival Ava.

Perkus played an ace and advanced his peg murmuring "Thirty-one for two" before shrugging and pulling an elaborate face in reply to her question. "We go where she drags us," he said. "Lately, uptown." This only left out the entire truth: that at the instant of his foolish pronouncement a week ago, enunciating the wish to avoid those friends who'd defined the period of his life just previous, he'd felt himself silently but unmistakably reverse the decision. He was ready to see Chase Insteadman, even if he didn't know what to say or not to say to his actor friend about the letters from space. Ever since, he'd been piloting Ava, rudder driving sails for once, uptown along First Avenue to have a look in the window of Gracie Mews, searching for Chase. Never Second Avenue—he didn't want to see the barricaded apartment building (regarding which Biller had promised to give him notification if it either reopened or crumbled into the pit of its foundations). Only as far as the pane of the Mews, never farther, and never inside the restaurant, just peering in searching for the actor, of whom he found himself thinking, in paraphrase of a

Captain Beefheart song that hadn't come to mind in a decade or more, *I miss you, you big dummy*. And Perkus yearned for Chase to meet Ava. The two had certain things in common: root charisma, a versatile obliviousness, luck for inspiring generosity. The hiccuping dog could tell soon enough that they were on a mission, and pushed her nose to the Mews' window, too, looking for she knew not what, leaving nose doodles, like slug trails, that frosted in the cold.

21

When Perkus began his herky-jerky dance, I worried. For Ava always responded, cantilevered onto rear legs and hurled herself with the single forelimb like a unicorn spear in the direction of his clavicle. Yet somehow Perkus always caught her, forepaw in his open palm like a ballroom partner's clasp, and though he staggered backward at her weight, cheek turned to the hiccuping barrage of tongue-kisses she aimed at his mouth and nose, and though the record skipped on its turntable at the thud of his heels, and though other dogs in the neighboring apartments began a chorus of barking protests at the ruckus, he made it all part of the same frenzied occasion, the song, the one he had to hear twelve or fifteen times a day, and which when he heard he simply couldn't sit still. The song was "Shattered," by the Rolling Stones. His current anthem. He'd found both record and player ten days before when on both Sadie's and Biller's encouragement he'd begun rummaging through other dogs' apartments besides Ava's. "A dog doesn't need a stereo, Chase! There's all sorts of terrific stuff, they stock these apartments from auctions of the contents of abandoned storage spaces, I learned. Go figure! People dwindle to the point where they move their stuff into storage, then vanish entirely, this happens all the time, that's the kind of world we live in."

I didn't force the implicit comparison to his own vanishing, nor the dwindled state he now seemed to occupy, nor the question of what had or was to become of his own possessions in the Eighty-fourth Street building. Other tenants had presumably been allowed to enter and reclaim at least a few valuables by now. But Perkus waved his hand. "I've got everything I need. Anyway, I suspect the management company has seized this opportunity to purge their rolls of all rent-controlled sublets like mine." I tried pointing out that Richard Abneg, the city's specialist in tenants' rights, might continue as his guardian angel. "Hah! He couldn't even keep his own apartment." (All accounts of subway excavation devices apparently forgotten, the tiger and the eagles were for Perkus the same thing.)

If anything, Perkus seemed to feel he'd been liberated: Eighty-fourth Street couldn't fire him, he quit! A lifetime's collection of books and CDs couldn't hold a candle to this one serendipitous vinyl talisman, fetched from a Labradoodle's apartment, which now stood in for all he'd ever known or lost or cared for, even if it happened to feature a gouge that rendered "Miss You" unplayable. "Of all records, Chase, *Some Girls*! It was in a clutch of the most horrendous crap, J. Geils Band, Sniff 'n' the Tears, the kind of albums you'd use for landfill. Look at this." He insisted I admire the original die-cut cardboard jacket of the Stones LP, the band members' lipsticked and wig-topped faces camouflaged among those of Lucille Ball, Raquel Welch, Judy Garland, and Marilyn

Monroe. "You can tell it's the first pressing, because right afterward they had to withdraw this jacket—the Garland and Monroe estates sued. It's incredible how much this music is steeped in the ambiance of the New York City of 1978. It's as much a New York record as *White Light/White Heat* or *Blonde on Blonde*." Well, I only half followed this, but I was glad to hear him back tracing tangible cultural clues, this being one thing that made him recognizably himself, under the sports warm-up jackets and other homeless-person outfits, and in the smoke-free-motel-room environs of Ava's.

Only, as I learned over the course of a few visits, Perkus wasn't really tracing his tangible cultural clue of *Some Girls* any place in particular, so much as worrying it like, yes, a dog with a bone. "Sh-sh-sh-shattered!" he'd declare, resetting the ancient player's coarse stylus at the start of the track, which was, even before Perkus's appropriation, already more a rant or riff than a proper song, its froggy, mocking guitar figure only a setting for Mick Jagger's giddy nihilistic kiss-offs, *success success success, does it mat-ter! This town's been wearing tatters. Look at me!* Round and round man and dog danced, one nearly as tall as the other, man urging the refrain on the dog as if wishing to teach her the lyrics, or at least the key word, *I've been SHAT-tered!* The dog loudly hiccuped, as if that might be her version of the same thought.

If dancing to the song was a kind of enactment, a show for me, it wasn't a deceptive one. Rather, it was a show of what he'd really come to since I'd seen him last, and of how he honestly spent his time between my visits to him here at the Friendreth: in Ava's arms. There were no books or magazines or newspapers in evidence, and no television or computer. Biller had offered Perkus a laptop and he'd refused, "Shattered"'s microcosm of 1978 being as far as Perkus wished to descend into any virtual world. The rest was Ava. Ostensibly for her sake, Perkus wasn't willing to visit my apartment or any restaurant. He ate mostly garbage from cans heated on a hot plate, or takeout sandwiches Biller or Sadie Zapping brought around, a step down from the bagels and burgers he used to lower into Biller's alley, but not too far. He made quick exploratory raids on the other canine apartments, then retreated to Ava's. He made do. Stripped of Eighty-fourth Street's rituals and amenities, Perkus's agoraphobia stood revealed—except for the ceaseless rounds with Ava, far beyond her bathroom needs and during which he braved the cold in layers of inadequate synthetic sweatshirts and Windbreakers until I bought him a secondhand woolen coat and told him it was from my own closet. In truth, my own would have been absurdly large on him; he must have known this, but said nothing. Perkus claimed that their itineraries had reverted, after the day he'd contacted me at the Mews, to Ava's preferences, usually to the waterside, man and dog leaning into winds that swept up and down the East River, man and dog gazing across at archipelagoes of industry and construction, the perimeters of boroughs as effectively distant as the clouds scalloping overhead, man and dog moving along icy walkways in silent communion with traces vivid to them alone, not apparent to others.

February was as cold as January, maybe colder. The snows never melted, the city never breathed clear. That day Perkus reappeared I'd spotted the dog first, obscene cherry nose, twin coxcombs of spare flesh dripping from each corner of its grin, gusting breath steam onto the diner's glass. Then the apparitional figure, bulky hooded sweatshirt pinned beneath a satiny baseball jacket, out-size dungarees hugely cuffed, over tan work boots showing a line where, soaked by slush, street salts had marked their high point in residue, like the tidal deposit of sea-weed on a beach. Professional dog walker? No, worse. Homeless snow survivor, now tapping at the restaurant window, campaigning for me to emerge with a dollar to crumple in his gloved hand, or to get my leftovers to-go, in a doggie bag but not for Doggie. Despite bulky ragged dress the raving figure was small statured and possibly inconsequential, but the pit bull seemed threat enough. Then the person's features, miming talk, made them-selves known to me. The next instant Perkus plucked off his hood and startled me a second time, the hair that once swept back so proudly from his widow's peak now cropped raggedly to inmate length, a half-inch from his skull everywhere.

Sadie Zapping had cut it. It was part of her regular duties in the Friendreth, to carry a pair of round-tipped scissors to trim obtrusive and untidy growth around the eyes and ears and anal glands of the shaggier residents, and so when between cribbage hands Perkus had com-plained that he needed a haircut she'd whipped them out. Perkus introduced me to the woman he called "Ava's

417

friend Sadie" the second or third time I came to see him there. We met in the lobby, her "Hello" more grunt than word as she aimed a tall black poodle out into the cold. I don't think she was possessive of Perkus's attention so much as gruffly worried that he'd broken the boycott on his former life. That, or she'd been banking on a card game that afternoon.

Didn't Perkus want to see Richard Abneg? I wanted Richard to see Perkus and assess the situation, but I advanced this suggestion with an air of fun. The Three Musketeers should ride again. No. Perkus seemed distrustful and disappointed after seeing Richard in the lap of power, and the lap of the Hawkman. I told him about their pregnancy. This brought a cast of wistfulness to half of Perkus's face—his divergent eye could never sit still for looking wistful. But even that look implied Richard was only more deeply compromised, lost to us. (Nothing in Perkus ever suggested any awareness we'd all been babies, once. You couldn't get here from there.) Perkus remained obstinate. He'd prefer I didn't mention him to Abneg.

Oona? I wasn't foolish enough to try. I didn't want to subject him, or myself for being here with him, to the risk of her scorn. More and more through February, as she pushed deeper into Noteless's book, Oona had been daring me to view myself as her toy or tool—letting herself in after I'd given up and fallen asleep (I'd volunteered my apartment key, and cleared her with my doorman), blotting my wounded questions with urgent kisses, then departing before morning light. There was something almost depraved in her exhaustion, her bloodshot eyes, her grim fits of lust, and I'd have felt sorry for her if she'd given me the slightest opening. She never did.

In this, their refusal of my pity, she and Perkus again reminded me of each other. I snuck in as much food as I could, and made him swear not to give it all to Ava. Her head wasn't much below the level of the kitchen table there, and sometimes with a plate of something in front of him Perkus would begin on some line of fevered free association and begin waving his hands and she'd plop her jaw on the table's edge and begin tonguing the food sideways off his plate, three-bean salad, French fries, baba ghanoush, anything. Since he never reprimanded her, she showed no compunction. If the food came to her, why not? It was her place. By the time he'd wound up his rant Perkus's plate might be empty, and he'd scrape it into the sink as if satisfied. I parachuted other care-package items into his life: a gift bag from a Condé Nast party, which I knew contained a bar of soap, a T-shirt, and a scented candle; a pair of rabbit-fur-lined leather gloves; a gold filter for his plastic one-cup coffeemaker (he'd been rinsing out, air-drying, and reusing the Melitta paper filters, a thrifty practice likely absorbed from Biller, but which saddened me); and a Sunday *New York Times* just to remind him his old enemies in the line of middlebrow reality placation were still in business, hoping to rile him back into curiosity about the life of the city. One day I reached into my coat pocket and found the Oonaphone, the old disposable cell that had never once rung. I thrust it on him, with its charger, and made him promise to use it in an emergency, or even just to let me know he was ready to have me help him transition back into himself—anything. He looked at it curiously and shoved it in a drawer with some other plastic objects he wanted to protect from being gnawed for dental exercise. I told him I didn't remember the phone's number anymore, but I'd try to find out. He raised his hand from where it scoured at Ava's seashell ears, signaling me to stop. "Dogs don't need numbers," he said.

"You're not a dog."

"I know, Chase, but I'm living in their building. I was telling Sadie this just the other day, I think we should pry the digits off the apartment doors. The dogs have means of knowing when they're at the right door."

"Did Sadie agree?"

"She said it was fine if I wanted to waste my time that way, but that she'd kill me if I removed the buttons from the elevator, which I also suggested. In retaliation I told her I wanted her to find us a deck of playing cards without numbers, just the pips. It's healthy for our animal minds to be able to count them at a glance, as easily as we tell the kings from queens, to eschew unnecessary symbolic languages."

Wasn't it autistic savants—Asperger's types, like those rock critics from whom he wished to distance himself—who counted scattered things at a glance? Well, anything could be reversed in Perkus's system. He who'd once layered his own linguistic chatter onto the urban environment's screen now seemed to hope to peel such stuff away to reveal preverbal essences, Platonic forms. I suppose he'd decided in favor of the unadorned polar-bear broadside, if he even recalled that old conundrum. If anything, in Ava he seemed to have located his own personal polar bear in distress. Only rather than rescue her, he'd elected to merge with her, here on the floe of the Friendreth Apartments.

Despite the injunction, new objects did appear in Ava's rooms from time to time, not all of them things dogs needed, some even laden with symbolic language, thanks to Perkus's raids on the other apartments. One day I found him with a volume of Franz Kafka's stories, a pale green paperback called *The Great Wall of China*. Perkus seemed to regard the item as a portent, like the Rolling Stones record. "I hadn't read Kafka since I was a teenager, Chase, it's incredible what I'd forgotten or taken for granted, it's like he's reading your mind! These storage-space people are a previous vanished tribe of New Yorkers, trying to make us understand something, if we'd only listen." Perkus launched into narration from the first story, called "Investigations of a Dog"— apparently it was Ava's mind that Kafka was reading. *"How much my life has changed, and yet how unchanged it has remained at bottom! When I think back and recall the time when I was still a member of the canine community, sharing in all its preoccupations, a dog among dogs, I find on closer examination that from the very beginning I sensed some discrepancy, some little maladjustment . . . that sometimes, no, not sometimes, but very often, the mere look of some fellow-dog of my own circle that I was fond of, the mere look of him, as if I had just caught it for the first time, would fill me with helpless embarrassment and fear, even with despair . . .* Wait, listen, Chase, this part's amazing, he gets to the heart of Ava's ambivalence about other dogs: *We all live together in a literal heap . . . nothing can prevent us from satisfying that communal impulse . . . this longing for the greatest bliss we are capable of, the warm comfort of being together. But now consider the other side of the picture. No creatures to my knowledge live in such wide dispersion as we dogs, none have so many distinctions of class, of kind, of occupation . . . we, whose one desire is to stick together . . . we above all others are compelled to live separated from one another by strange vocations that are often incomprehensible even to our canine neighbors, holding firmly to laws that are not those of the dog world, but are actually directed against it.* You see, Chase? Kafka's pointing us to what I couldn't know until I met Ava, that a domesticated animal isn't some wild free thing that happens to be living indoors. Thanks to years of interdependence it's permanently fixed on a grid of human concepts, a microcosm of our own incoherent urban existence. Dogs are canaries in our evolutionary coal mine!"

"I never realized Kafka was such a Communist," I joked.

He blinked away contempt for my wit. "I used to find it tragic that we turned these pack animals into paranoid hermits," he said. "Now, living here, I see that dogs *like* having their own apartments." Perkus was explaining himself, I thought but didn't say. "What's astonishing about Kafka is that reading this you're suspecting he's never even met a dog and at the same time it's the greatest handbook to living with one I could ever imagine!"

This might be Perkus in a perfect nutshell, taking Kafka as a resource guide to pet ownership. "Does he say anything about how to cure her hiccups?" Ava's hiccing seemed to be getting worse—or perhaps I should say more persistent, since it didn't appear to bother the indomitable animal.

"She's fine," he said. "At night they go away so she can sleep. I hug her around the chest and sort of squeeze them away."

"Is that prescribed in Kafka? Maybe we should take her to see Strabo Blandiana." I teased, but again, it was Perkus I wanted to have Strabo take a stab at. Maybe the medicinalist knew the right points for a needle to enter the human body and trigger self-awareness, pride in one's appearance, as well as species pride, the desire to rejoin the human race. Then I felt ashamed for preferring Perkus's Beau Brummell phase to his present guise as a Staten Island garbageman—it wasn't as if the first had been geared to impress others or me personally, or signaled any high regard for the opinions of the human race. What had drawn me to Perkus was his absence of any calculation, except in figuring how to persuade me of his next urgent theory or ephemeral fact.

Still, I worried about his health. I'd already snuck aspirin and floss into his bathroom. He boasted he was cluster-free since the hallucinatory and epochal headache that, with tiger and blizzard, had ushered him to this new life. He didn't smoke pot—it was now as if he'd never smoked pot. I didn't ask if ellipsis had departed him, too. Who was I to judge that he looked hungry, hunted, harrowed? Maybe being out of his apartment had only revealed an underlying truth, and I, fatally callow, had romanticized his former appearance. One thing

I was sure of, Perkus's temples looked flattened, dented, without the disguise of floppy hair. Once he'd had only the wrecked and reckless eye. Now his whole cranium looked imbalanced to me, though possibly this was birth trauma, a forceps impression. Perkus *had*, after all, gotten from there to here like the rest of us. But where was he going?

■

It was after the next snowstorm that I uncovered the fact that Biller and I weren't Perkus's only lifeline at the Friendreth anymore. The temperature locked in again, the skies white so that we could feel it coming for a day or two. Korean markets and bodegas and building superintendents everywhere had given up trying to pry up the baked black crusts on either side of narrow-carved walkways, and now laid down a desultory path of salts hoping to preserve just that width they'd struggled for. Only a couple of inches fell overnight, nothing more. By morning it was done and in the bright daylight you might feel you'd been largely spared, after that warning sky. Except now it was March and you felt something was wrong, or anyway different. Winter had stayed. Everyone joked about the weather, and the joke they joked was "Everyone does something about the weather, but nobody ever talks about it," and it wasn't funny.

The snowfall, though negligible, slowed the city into depression, a ceremonial plummet like a flag at half-mast. You could travel where you liked but people called in sick and battened themselves at home. I really only knew this by osmosis since the people I knew mostly had nowhere to go, by privilege or otherwise. But I ran into Susan Eldred, from Criterion's noble offices, in her snow boots outside the Friendreth's door, just leaving. I was arriving with East Side bagels, miraculously still a little hot in their paper sack. This was two in the afternoon—still, thanks not to Perkus but to Oona, my idea of first thing in the morning. (Perkus rose with Ava and the dawn for the first walk and first coffee of the day.) Susan and I looked at each other rather stupidly at first, as though we'd been caught and now had something to justify or confess.

"We must be calling on the same dog," I joked, trying to dispel the air of needless guilt.

"Perkus has been bugging me to round up some stuff for him," Susan explained, as if she had to. "Nobody's going into the offices because of the snow, so I figured this would be a good day to drop by."

"Bugging you how? Does he call?"

"He's called a couple of times but honestly what lit a fire under me was when he showed up in the offices last week with Ava."

"Well, I'm relieved he's making the effort," I admitted.

"I'd do anything for him, actually," said Susan Eldred, with helpless sincerity. I filed it away as her promise if I needed it. It was too cold to shift to small talk, and so, in some embarrassment, I think, Susan moved past me on the sidewalk. I went inside.

"Were you hiding the fact that you're in touch with Susan Eldred from me?" I asked after we three had devoured the bagels.

"Why would I do that?" Perkus said distractedly. Ava mounted his back and tongue-bathed his nape as he reached to the floor to display to me a new prize, which appeared to be a shabby boxed set of VHS tapes, decorated with constellations of stars and a giant disembodied eyeball in black and white.

"Did you call her on the cell phone?" A quick scan had revealed the Oonaphone's charger, trailing from a socket on the kitchen counter.

"Sure."

"I didn't know you ever used it."

"That's what it's for, right?"

"Why don't you ever call me?"

"I don't have to call, you just appear." If he'd meant it as anything but a flat observation this might have seemed fairly hostile, but clearly the subject simply didn't engage him. Once he'd welcomed me into the Friendreth my visits became predictable phenomena, regular as cribbage matches and Ava's bowel movements. Perkus was engaged with deeper inquiries, into less obvious subjects. His tone left open the possibility that Perkus felt he was the one doing the caretaking in this friendship, but also that if I wanted to think it went the other way, he wouldn't object. Far more important was this ancient black VHS cassette he now slipped into the '80s-vintage Panasonic television with built-in player that had been integrated into Ava's living-room ensemble.

"Where'd you get that thing?"

"From a Labrador. Dogs don't need VCRs, Chase!"

"I doubt anyone needs them lately."

"You do if you're going to play VHS tapes," he said, speaking as if to a child. "Can you stay for a bit? I've got something I want to show you, it's less than half an hour long. Ouch, Ava! Ava, down now, get down, that's a good girl, Ava, Ava down!" Ava, hell-bent on Perkus's neck and ears as he crouched, nibbled and tongue-scrubbed him with increasing ferocity. Perkus, often surprisingly forceful with the dog, now gripped her one forepaw and twisted her onto her back, rear limbs cocked and twitching in submission while she writhed the mighty worm of her torso and neck under Perkus's wrestler hold. I prayed for the dog never to exercise her full powers on him in return, having no doubt who'd prevail. Perkus seemed to whisper something directly into Ava's mouth, then, still pinning her, returned to blandly pitching his discovery to me. "You might already have seen this, these shows are a part of the collective unconscious. But that's the nature of this kind of material, Chase, it falls into the category of what D. W. Winnicott calls 'the unthought known.' You absorb a thing like this before you've assembled the context necessary to grasp it." Ava hiccuped violently.

I lifted the package from the floor. A four-tape set, *Rod Serling's THE TWILIGHT ZONE: The Platinum Collection.* By process of elimination I determined the tape Perkus had inserted was Season Three. "More salvage from the storage-space people?"

"No. I spotted it in Eldred's office, but she'd taken it home. I've been drooling after this item for years, it's surprisingly scarce. CBS had to delete it, because they hadn't gotten permission to include "An Occurrence at Owl Creek Bridge.""

427

I tried not to let on that I had no idea what he was talking about, feeling more generally disgruntled that he'd presume to blow my mind with something as commonplace as *The Twilight Zone*. "I used to watch these things on late-night TV," I said, though I couldn't recall a thing beyond the opening narration, Serling seeming to mock his own stiletto delivery, which I mocked now. *"There is a fifth dimension—"*

"The easiest way to pass as a spy is to tell everyone you're a spy," Perkus pronounced gnomically. He loosed Ava, who twisted to her feet and began nosing at the box in my hands. "Once they think you're a fool, you get away with anything."

"Are we going to watch 'The . . . Incident . . . at . . . Al's Creek Bridge'?" I knew I'd gotten it wrong.

"No, we're going to watch 'The Midnight Sun.' "

"Is it about Japan?"

"No. Be patient." Perkus held his forefinger to the VCR's Fast-forward, which apparently needed to be continuously pressed, and not only moved with the speed of a man crawling across the desert but mimicked his groans as he died of thirst. I intertwined my fingers beneath Ava's throat, keeping her corralled with me.

"Wait, I just guessed: it was directed by Morrison Groom, before he was famous." I tried not to allow too sardonic a pronunciation to this last word.

"It wasn't directed by anyone important." Perkus had his selection cued, and now put on a kettle for more coffee.

I grew more peevish by the minute. At three in the afternoon the light outside wasn't impressive, but it was daylight, sun fracturing off the fine new powder, however firmly Perkus kept Ava's curtains drawn. This wasn't one AM, we weren't in the mental theater of Eighty-fourth Street, we'd smoked no Chronic nor Blueberry Kush, let alone Ice, and I wasn't positive Perkus could enthrall me with creaky tapes of old television episodes this time around. The surround was just too tragically shabby and irrelevant to me all of a sudden. If Perkus couldn't see he'd tumbled, I could. He'd misplaced the old heartbeat of his dissidence, wasn't cutting across the grain of anything except himself (or so I thought at that moment). I wasn't totally unaware that my judgments mingled with an irrational sense of betrayal that he'd summoned Susan Eldred, that the Friendreth apartments were turning into as much of a revolving door of acquaintances and contacts as his old apartment had been. I might have been smarting over his remark about the predictability of my visits, but for the first time I felt disappointed in him. Perkus's ascetic phase had no more rules than had his libertinism—he made calls on mobile phones, watched old TV shows, and who knows, probably sneaked a joint now and again, only wouldn't share it with me. I felt we were headed for our second fight (after "The Incident Concerning the Jackson Hole Waitress") and I didn't mind. I was glad now it was Susan Eldred and not me that had said aloud that she'd do anything for him. Right now I wanted to do nothing.

So what did I do? The day's light graying behind those curtains, I joined Perkus on Ava's couch, each with our fresh cups of coffee, and dutifully watched "The Midnight Sun," from *The Twilight Zone*'s third season, on glitchy, burping videotape. Ava wedged herself between us to sit bolt upright regarding the television screen as if it were a window, her head darting at the blocking of the characters, growling once when a man holding a pistol pushed his way through a door (you couldn't quibble with her prejudices), otherwise hiccuping at regular intervals.

■

The episode was set entirely in a New York apartment building. (I felt Perkus glance at me with satisfaction at this hint of relevance, but I ignored him, wedded to the grudging line I'd drawn in the sand: I'd watch it, but refuse to marvel over whatever he wanted me to marvel over.) The city is nearly abandoned, due to an end-of-the-world heat wave, Earth's orbit declining toward the sun, which never exits the sky—hence the title. The few who cling to existence in the melting city, namely a young female painter (a Village bohemian in a 1950s sense) and an older woman in her building, are dependent on failing air-conditioning and a failing Frigidaire, which houses what may be the last pitcher of water in Manhattan. The man with the gun, at whom Ava snarled, is a thirst-maddened desperado who breaks in and swigs down this treasure, a scene played by the sweating women as if it were an allegory of rape. Then, thirst quenched, the intruder apologizes and departs in shame. The heat, reaching a peak, murders the older woman and causes a painting to melt off a canvas. Only after the young painter also collapses does the tale reveal its characteristic twist: she awakens from what is revealed to be a nightmare to find with relief that the sky is dark, the air cool, and outside, snow is falling, but relief gives way to the next horror—the Earth is moving away from the sun, not nearer to it, and Manhattan is locked in a fatal deepening freeze.

That I followed this narrative is a blooming miracle, however, as throughout our viewing Perkus was unable to keep from voicing a filibuster of interpretations. The twenty-odd minutes of black-and-white fable gave him innumerable opportunities to persuade me that Rod Serling was the zero point for the pure themes: Cold War fear! Conformity! Alienation! Collective and consensual delusion, the leakage of the dream life into the waking! *The Twilight Zone*, Perkus explained, was news that stayed news (I took this as rebuke of my gift of the Sunday *Times*), in this case speaking volumes about the true nature of the unnatural winter the city had been enduring. Perkus had Kafka for his veterinarian, Serling for his meteorologist.

"Remind you of anything?" he insisted afterward, scurrying to halt the tape's progress to the next immortal episode.

Remember, I'd done television, too much of it. I mostly had just pitied the actors, forced to work on such an impoverished set and to be sprayed with glycerin between takes. Then again, these were pretty feeble actors.

"Lots of things," I said. "What things did you have in mind?"

"The state of . . . everything. Your life, mine, the state of the weather."

I played dumb. It couldn't be a crime merely to exaggerate the role Perkus cast me in always. "Sure, it's been a little cold. You think despite how it feels, it's actually hot out?"

"Many things helplessly produce their own opposites." Sensing my resistance, he half swallowed this manifesto line. I saw him squint, too, to keep his dodgy eye from embarrassing him. "I think I'm losing you."

"It all feels a little plotty to me," I said, dead set on disappointing him. "I was never one for plots."

"Too bad, since you're in one."

"The newspaper is the news, too, at least on the day it's published. Did you read about the crane collapse on Ninety-first? They think Abneg's tiger might be to blame."

"Fuck Abneg's tiger, and fuck the newspaper." Perkus began swearing, invoking Richard's style. "The *Times* isn't the commissar of the real, not anymore, not as far as I'm concerned. It's the cover story."

"Well, that's easy for you to say, Perkus. You don't have to rely on it, like I do, for updates on your personal life!"

"Why are you yelling?"

I had gotten a little ventilated, without noticing. I felt tide-swamped with provocations: the serial bulging of Ava's ribs as she hiccuped under my hand; the moldering smell and tawdriness of the Friendreth generally; the fine grounds the gold filter hadn't kept from ending in the bottom of my cup and on the carpet of my tongue; the unrelenting March weather, which seemed to prove some arcane fact my loopy friend Perkus held over me like a threat, as though he could be right and I could be wrong about everything; that neither Perkus nor Oona ever called me on the phone—I was somehow a principle taken for granted, as much an item of decor in Perkus's circle as I had been the chunk of handsome furniture at wealth's table; that Mission Control hadn't received a communication from Janice or *Northern Lights* generally for almost three weeks. Once upon a time Janice had peppered the newspapers with affectionate updates I guiltily speed-read; now I guiltily scoured the papers daily for hints of her existence which refused to appear. All of this seemed irreconcilable data, yet the ultimate provocation was the way Perkus arched his eyebrows at me as though I was supposed to grasp it as a whole.

"Janice might be dead," I blurted, seeking his sympathy. "And I'm in love with Oona."

"Have you ever found yourself exhausted by a friend whose problems simply never change? Here, Ava." Perkus rattled her leash and she sprang from the couch to the door—her transitions, from placidity to avidity, were like jump cuts. Then he began bundling himself into outer layers I'd mostly purchased for him. Despite the uncanny truth *The Twilight Zone* episode had revealed, he'd protect himself from the cold outside. Perkus's selfish certainties took my breath away. Yet I had to grant the distinction: he was, if nothing else, a person whose problems were never exactly the same twice. There is a war, I thought, between the ones who stagger from chaldron drunkenness to cohabitation with a three-legged pit bull, and those who try to keep up with them. I was losing the war. Chaldrons, for instance: Would they ever be mentioned again, or had they slipped from his scheme? Was it my duty, as I'd earlier assumed, to suppress uncomfortable facts, or was I somehow the stooge who couldn't keep all the essentials in his head? I didn't mind jigsaw puzzles, but this one seemed to have no edge pieces. *Marlon Brando is dead!* I wanted to shout after him as he departed, leaving me there alone in Ava's digs.

I think!

I said nothing, as footfalls of man and dog waned to silence in the corridor. So much for the fight I'd planned. I was no match. Perkus's transitions were as rapid as Ava's, and if he was applying tough love it was fairly tough. On the other hand, his mysterioso style left my pride some wiggle room. Sure, I replied to Perkus's absence, I *have* been exhausted by those people whose problems never change. Good thing there's none of those around here! My own bedevilments seemed dynamic enough to me. If I stuck around and changed the subject I could pretend we'd never tangled. Only I might have to praise Rod Serling to get back in Perkus's graces. That's when I located my pride—I fled.

◾

Well, if I'd felt betrayed by Perkus consorting with Susan Eldred, it was only a warm-up. I didn't wander round to the Friendreth for three days after, making an interval of self-containment and restored private routine, like I'd established when Perkus went missing. There wasn't any Oona to distract me, either. She counted the days to delivery of the Noteless manuscript.

In this vacuum I reacquainted myself with the afternoon movie theaters of the Upper East Side, a good place not to think about the weather among other things. I scared myself, one day at the old United Artists on First Avenue and Eighty-fifth, imagining that a low rumble on the film's soundtrack was the scraping of the mechanical tiger's excavations beneath the theater—of course, it was only the noise of an army of Orcs grinding into battle, silly me.

At home after that endless afternoon movie I recalled the moment of worry, and took it as an intimation: if one of us was being hounded by that tiger, it probably wasn't me. So I rushed to my computer to pull up TigerWatch, to make certain the Friendreth hadn't been destroyed. It was the first time I'd ever condescended to visit the Web site, which had struck me previously as a sop to public prurience at misfortune, rather than an upstanding service. Anyway, I'd prided myself on having the inside scoop from Richard Abneg. What I found allowed me to breathe easy. At last reports the tiger was off the map of my companions entirely, in Spanish Harlem. But the scare made me want to overlook dignity's boycott, and see Perkus. This was the very day Oona had said she'd be putting the book on her editor's desk. Rather than waiting for whatever degree of celebration she'd deign to share, I elected not to be such a slave, or anyway such an obedient one. So it was a curiously mingled pride and pridelessness that saw me headed back out into the fresh night.

I heard Oona through the door to Ava's apartment. She was in the midst of a self-lacerating harangue, in what I thought of as her single-malt voice. Sure enough, a bottle of twelve-year-old Oban sat between them, its gold essence at the halfway point, its discarded paper wrapper and shards of lead-foil cork wrapper on the table beside Oona's handbag to prove the bottle's halfwaying had been accomplished just now. Seeing an intoxicant other than coffee inside the walls of the Friendreth was as startling as seeing Oona (intoxicant to me). I'd come to think of the place as a rehab facility, though Perkus would have said, *Dogs have no use for the twelve steps, Chase!* But I hadn't regarded it as my own hiding place from Oona until seeing it stormed by her. Oona and Perkus each held juice glasses, full with more than a finger, and smiled up at me guiltlessly. Perkus, curiously, held a small hardcover book in his lap, as though using it as a handy shield to protect his genitals. Ava knelt beneath Oona's chair, head craned adoringly upward, obviously enthralled by that wiry, fitful little black-clad poppet, or Gnuppet, with the maniacal, winding voice. I knew Ava well enough now to gather she'd developed a quick crush. The dog might have been starved for female companionship, too. I was. Oona all at once called out a kind of Mickey Spillane urgency from me, I wanted to kiss her and take her away from there and I wanted to hit her for being there in the first place. And for getting Perkus drunk. And for knowing where to find him, and coming to find him instead of me. And. And. And.

Well, Oona was beating herself up, and quickly let me understand the occasion. "Oh, hello, Chase. We're having an Irish wake for the greatest book I ever wrote or will write. I called it *Pages from a Void*, though I guess I figured that title was never going to fly with the sales force. Still, I like saying it aloud."

"The editor didn't love it?" I stepped in and shut the door behind me.

"Oh, the editor was always sure to hate this book. I didn't get where I am today, Chase, relying on the integrity of a New York publishing syndicate. My mistake was imagining I had Noteless at my back. I thought the joke was on the editor for signing up a nihilist absolutist who's made a career of treating the hand that feeds him like a plate of gravy fries. I climbed inside this project, I channeled that mofo's tar pit of an aesthetic and served it to them chilled. Excuse the mixed metaphors, they're strictly a symptom of alleviation from Laird's black tunnel of suffocation and silence. I mix my metaphors so I know I'm alive. I mix metaphors, I fall down, no problem. Speaking of which, help yourself, darling."

At this word Perkus couldn't meet my eye. I took the opening and dug in Ava's shelves for a glass, then siphoned off as much of the Scotch as it would hold, preventative measures. "So Noteless bit *your* hand instead? With or without his dentures?" I slugged back half of my bitter cup at one go.

"It turns out Laird was ready to commence licking asses instead. Just my luck to hook up with him at the moment his integrity plummets into one of his so-called bottomless 'sculptures.' Not luck, really. I was typecast. Noteless and Catherine Hamwright, that's the editor, they hatched a scheme to sell him like everybody's sinister uncle who's really a barrel of laughs, another Emil

Junrow, or the Edward Gorey of urban sinkholes. They were hoping I'd write *Did You Really Say What I Think You Just Said, Mr. Noteless?* Apparently, I'm who you enlist when you're selling out in this town. Perkus here hasn't said anything but I can tell he thinks this is my just deserts—my *comeuppance*, to use a Chase Instead-man word."

Oona's tiny bullets flew everywhere. Was I really notorious for my archaicisms? I'd taken worse blows. She'd earned only a little grace with me for using the word "darling"; I still wanted to know how she'd come to be here. She and Perkus never seemed like friends to me, no matter what they claimed. They seemed half enemies, half conspirators, relishing snickering complicity I was too innocent to share. Perkus, for his part, did show a wily, red-rimmed satisfaction at Oona in her amphetamine cups, but only from the vantage of his own. I'd never witnessed Perkus really bombed on alcohol before, but it seemed his recent bout of clean living made him a very cheap date. He swayed on his chair, with only the book for ballast. I suppose the dog's life had been a bit less enthralling than he'd wanted to admit. I just wished I could dislodge him from his perches so easily as Oona.

"It's really the best thing you've done?" I asked.

Perkus raised his eyebrows at her challengingly, as if he knew of something else lurking in a drawer somewhere, but still didn't speak. In his dog's haircut, lips softened by drink, he looked more and more the bit player from *One Flew Over the Cuckoo's Nest*.

"Absolutely."

"So forget what this editor thinks. It'll get published somewhere else."

"You don't understand, it's all written in the imperious voice of Deepster McHole-in-the-Ground. I steeped myself in his sources, and then spit them back out—it was like writing a graduate dissertation, something I've spent my life avoiding." It wasn't enough to mention sources, Oona had to begin listing them in a deliberate drone. "I read Deleuze and Guattari, I read John Gray and E. M. Cioran and Bernhard's *Correction*, I read Mike Davis and Donna Haraway and John Baldessari, I read Ballard and Baudrillard, and by the way, I don't care what anyone says, Ballard's just Baudrillard without the *u-d-r-i*. I practically memorized *The Writings of Robert Smithson*, for god's sake, which is the exact equivalent of ordering a month's worth of meals at a restaurant where John Cage is the chef."

"Good for you," said Perkus, finally piping up. His voice was clotted, the words surfacing each like a bubble through a pot of oatmeal. I forgot for a moment which was his abstruse eye—both seemed to curl toward unseen dimensions. "A secret masterpiece is always best. It changes the world slightly. Everyone should have one, like one of those simulated worlds you were talking about, or an Ant Farm."

Oona guffawed. "When I write my masterpiece it won't have so many boring machines in it. That's boring as in '*What do we do with all the soil this boring machine has piled up?*'"

I'd never put Noteless and Abneg's tiger in conjunction until that instant. I looked at Perkus, sure he'd make the same leap, but either this was too obvious or I was no longer the target for his arched eyebrow. He was elsewhere. Ava whined and hiccuped quietly where she crouched below, but he seemed not to notice her, either. It was the longest I'd seen him go without caressing the dog since I'd come to the Friendreth. How predictable, my confusion: I was never able to appreciate one of his phases until they were vanishing, assuming wrongly I'd have a little while to get used to things. But this was Perkus's trick, he shed orientations like skins. Yet he'd seemed so permanent when we met. Bogged in stasis, writer's block elevated to a principle. I'd have to relegate this paradox to my growing pile of impossible questions, like why he and Oona Laszlo periodically shrugged off their enmity and converged, or whether Laird Noteless's holes and the tiger's were aspects of the same phenomenon, like Groom's and Ib's movies. I was sure of one thing: if Perkus wasn't interested anymore, I refused to be. He could shrug off skins, but I wouldn't wear them. Besides, I had an easy question: What was that book in his lap? I had it confused with Oona's supposed masterpiece. But I knew enough not to embarrass myself—unpublished manuscripts weren't bound in cloth and boards.

Oona answered for him. "That was my ticket of entry to this dog museum," she laughed. "Perkus had me buy him a book on my way over here. I guess he and his new friend don't darken the doors of Barnes & Nobles."

It figured. Perkus had turned each of us into a version of Foster Watt, on call for the supplies he needed. Susan

Eldred was his dealer in celluloid, Oona text. I'd been entrusted with nothing more cultural than bagels.

Perkus stirred himself from the mire to say, "Yeah, but you bought the wrong book." He pushed it into my hands. *Immaculate Rust*, by Sterling Wilson Hobo. A volume of poetry, fifty or sixty pages, largely white space, strewn with paltry syllables. *I never peeked / behind your bogus ducks / and lilies to see / the cogs and wheels concealed / or / everywhere your glamorous / falsified apples* ... "I asked for *Obstinate Dust*, by Ralph Warden Meeker," Perkus continued. "How hard could that have been?"

"This looks about the same," shrugged Oona. "Just mercifully shorter."

"Hobo is a charlatan," said Perkus, mustering energy for the dismissal. "A third-rate W. S. Merwin."

"I got confused," said Oona. "You're lucky I didn't come back with *Adequate Lust*, which is a how-to book. I might have written it, I forget."

"Why not rely on communiqués from the storage-space people?" I said bitterly. "Anyway, didn't you already give *Obstinate Dust* a go?"

"I wanted to try again," said Perkus through a slurp at his glass. He felt no need to justify his whims. Why should he? He couldn't imagine my regard for him was tipping into ruin. I felt he was a fraud, making theater of acquiring weighty books he'd never read.

I finished my glass and poured another, to catch up and to salve the aggravation of their banter. At this Oona showed a glance of panic, fearing her self-commiserating bottle would be drained without her help. She refilled not

only her glass, but Perkus's, seeming to incriminate me
for rudeness. Ava wedged her cranium under my hand.
She barely hiccuped at all, deferentially minimizing her
presence, trying not to be displaced. With the prompting
of the dog's heightened instincts, I sniffed a lie in the air.
There was a name for the flavor of mixed dislike and
intimacy between Oona and Perkus. The two were exes,
I was positive, no matter what I'd been told. So I added
sexual jealousy to my roster of hurts and mysteries. It
was simpler to manage, and blotted out the others, at
least with the help of Oona's Scotch. The evening blun-
dered forward this way, until Perkus went into the back
to urinate or lie down, I didn't ask, Ava abjectly trotting
after him. I demanded to know how Oona had ended up
in the Friendreth, and heard my sibilants hiss.

"You weren't home, so I called your cell, you idiot."

"The Oonaphone," I said stupidly.

"Right, the Oonaphone."

"You never call in the daytime."

"It was a special occasion, as you can see. I was making an afternoon booty call. Imagine my surprise."

"I was at the movies."

"For five hours?"

I didn't care to say what effort had been required to
topple Saruman and Sauron.

"Well, it hardly matters, since you gave your phone
away."

I brushed aside this line of inquiry, which was making
me look foolish when I wanted to be fierce and prosecu-
torial. I was full of wild thoughts and convergences. In
my brain Sterling Wilson Hobo was to Ralph Warden

Meeker as Florian Ib was to Morrison Groom. Or maybe they were all the same person! Was Noteless involved in designing the tiger? But if paranoiac interpretation was a skin Perkus had shed and I'd involuntarily assumed, it fit awkwardly. If I thought I was close, I was nowhere at all. The secret lay outside my understanding. Oona Laszlo might have my existential puzzle's edge pieces hidden on her person somewhere, but I'd never make her admit it. I could only formulate bizarre accusations: for instance, that Oona was preventing anyone from reading Meeker's *Obstinate Dust*. This was obvious, since she'd tricked me into chucking one copy into *Urban Fjord*, and then pretended to forget the title when Perkus requested a second. What information was hidden in those pages? If that was idiotic, at least it was fancier than accusing her and Perkus of having been lovers. I felt sure something fancy was going on.

"Is there something you and Perkus aren't telling me?" I kept my question vague, to invite any confession that might want to produce itself.

"What makes you think it's one thing?" she teased. "Perkus and I might be not telling you completely different things. Why assume we've gotten our stories synced?"

"There are times when I think he's trying to warn me about you."

"I'd have returned the favor, but unfortunately by the time you and I met you'd already fallen completely into his clutches."

At that point I did something regrettable. I used the only articulate weapon I had at my disposal: I threw my

443

body at her. I'd been at full attention since the phrase "booty call" anyhow, rigid with intent in the one part of me capable of sustaining a clear thought. Maybe it could impart one, too. If I fucked Oona right, she might take my distress seriously at last, and blurt in the throes of ecstasy an explanation of why I'd felt so much more alive and at the same time so disassembled, so out of joint, since that day I'd walked into Perkus's Eighty-fourth Street kitchen and seen her, since the time seven months ago when I'd fallen into *both* their clutches.

Oona was drunk enough that I could push her around easily, and soon enough we worked together on the same project. By the time Perkus and Ava strolled back into the kitchen I had Oona raised against the wall, her hands clutching my ass, though our pants were still on.

"Ava and I are going out," said Perkus, marble-mouthed with drink and embarrassment. I turned to see him grappling to clip the leash to Ava's collar, fingers evidently as anesthetized as his tongue. If I was the friend to Perkus I wanted to believe I was, I'd have insisted he not go out into the slippery night alone in that state. Let's all walk the dog! We could have linked arms, like companions on the Yellow Brick Road (I knew which among us had straw for brains, and Ava made a nice Uncowardly Lion). Nobody spoke before he was through the door.

Nobody spoke after. Oona and I shut ourselves into Ava's bedroom, shamelessly. Without comparing notes, the general thought was to finish before Perkus and the dog returned, but that was self-delusion. Somewhere in our throes we heard man and dog clunking and careening in the kitchen after their jaunt. Perkus made a show of cleaning up after our party and broke a glass in the sink. He bumped the stereo's needle, making an agonized amplified scrape, finding the starting point of "Shattered." Played the song to the end, then again, man and dog creaking the floorboards with their dance. Oona freed some groans while Mick Jagger covered our noise, but no revelatory exclamations or confessions. Soon the clunking and grappling on both sides of the bedroom door settled to silence. The light peeking underneath was switched off, and I heard Ava's couch springs squeak as man and dog settled there together. My splitting of our foursome into the two couples I preferred had been decisive.

■

In the earliest light Oona staggered up to use the bathroom and stayed there a while, running water at the sink, gargling and spitting and so on. I took a turn after. When I emerged she'd dressed again, to stand waiting by the bed, an apparition in the granular light. Through my head-pounding sobriety I could see what I'd only smelled the night before, the layer of Ava's white hairs that decorated the sheets we'd been sleeping and sweating upon. Oona's glance, eyes pickled in regret, told me she wasn't willing to slip back into that bed. The hairs already clung everywhere to her black clothing, so stark and abundant it was as if she was hoping to pass back through the front room in a pathetic dog costume.

"Buy me breakfast at your Mews," she whispered hoarsely. "Just don't force me to talk or think about anything, I couldn't possibly."

"Okay."

"Whatever I might have said last night I take it all back," she said.

"You didn't say anything."

"I take it back anyway."

We tiptoed through the front. Man and dog spooned on the couch, Perkus on the inside track, his back to the cushions, Ava nestled into the C of his stomach and knees with her spine, three legs fetally tucked, upraised snout against Perkus's collarbone. Perkus still wore his corduroy pants and woolly socks, his muddy boots pried off just at the couch's corner. Both slept with mouths drool-leakingly wide, eyes squeezed as if actively braving harsh light. There was none. Perkus might be the only person who'd keep his front room more firmly sealed against sunlight than the place where he usually slept. Oona and I didn't stop to let our eyes adjust. We were self-sickened, wreathed in shame, certain we'd violated this place. There was no fucking in the Friendreth. If the dogs could keep themselves one to an apartment, what excuse did we have? We slipped through the unlocked front door, clicking it shut behind us as carefully as we could. On the other side we exhaled.

"Wow, listen to those hiccups," said Oona.

"Yes, Ava's got a bad case," I said.

"That's not the dog, Chase."

I put my ear to the door. She was right.

∎

March 19

C.,

Forgive glitchos, I type in the dark. The screen's back-lighting's shot, too. One of the leaf-cutter bees is crawling on my face, drinking sweat — hard not to interpret it as a mosquito and swat it away, but they'll sting if incited and I've had my requisite bee stings for the week already. We've all taken to negotiating this lightless humid labyrinth in bare feet, or bare foot in my case, mostly in underwear or pajamas — if we had little enough motivation to impress one another with personal grooming before, the last is gone — and when I wedged my one foot below Keldysh's console, to write you this letter, I stirred some growth both vine-tangled and mulchy, and up rose the vivid, unmistakable smell of fresh unfiltered apple cider, the kind with a simple label, from Vermont or Connecticut. It can't possibly be apple cider.

It's been a while, Chase, but I won't apologize now for that. I've got more to tell than I'll manage. Systems began domino-falling, one failure catalyzing another, mid-February. At some point Keldysh persuaded us to create a rotation of diagnostic maintenance shutdowns, isolating each in turn: climate, navigation, communications, orbital tracking, plumbing, and so on. Hardly attractive, but no one came up with a credible Plan B. Everything went swimmingly (some words are treacherous — what I'd give for a swim!) until the last time we switched off the central-core light banks, ten days ago now, and they wouldn't come back on. They still haven't. (Picture a Russian flipping a switch repeatedly, frowning in the dark.) We're rationing the backup

447

generator's delegated functions, so we're down to what illumination Sledge's bio-spectrum grow lights can shed, as he places them here and there, a farmer rotating crops throughout the station. Keldysh warns this may be our last communications packet; he scheduled us each a one-hour session on the sole functioning keyboard—no luxury of writer's block today! While morale is low, we have a kind of camaraderie at last. I suppose a similar peace may be gained by prisoners sharing death row. This is no time for settling scores. However, I want it on record, right here and now, that I never ever stole anything from the fridge, anyone else's leftovers, or the Captain's birthday cake.

Though black humor is the only functioning humor here, I didn't quite have the nerve to ask if I could take Zamyatin's keyboard hour. I suspect it'll go unused, a symbolic silent communication, an aria of cosmic null-music to foreshadow the chorale the rest of us will soon chime in with. Zamyatin commandeered a landing module and kamikazied himself out of the air lock yesterday. As expected, he sparked one of the Chinese mines, making a tiny missing tooth in the dynamite smile that pins us on the far side of home. No one was certain what (more) was wrong when Klaxons sounded, but Keldysh inventoried the missing lander, and on doing a head count and finding Z. absent we rushed to the Library's south window, which gives a panorama of Earth through a coy lace veil of mines, a view we usually avoid, just in time to see him flare and burn. We cheered wildly. It isn't as though Zamyatin's bid could be whitewashed as other than suicide—he'd have been baked Alaska on reentry into Earth's atmosphere even if he had negotiated the mine layer. That would have been a purely symbolic triumph, where this we could call taking one for the team.

And then there were five. Our remaining lives are in Sledge's hands. What little remains of them. I suppose our remains will be in his hands, too, in the sense that the whole of *Northern Lights* is being given over to the gardens, now expanded from the Greenhouse to wherever Sledge can get something green to cling or take root and get busy swapping our exhaled breath for something worth inhaling. So when this last brave stand collapses, and we asphyxiate in one collective heap, there'll be no one left to give us interstellar funerals—instead we'll rot in the dark mossy grotto we've left behind. At least we no longer fear starvation, as Sledge is always ladling up some horrible fruity or rooty stew—there's plenty of spare biomass to consume, now that Sledge has been invited to turn the whole station into a throbbing wet garden. The ironies are rich. Trapped in the infinite cold of space, we bake like Russian mafiosi in a steam room. Technology expelled us from Earth's garden and then, having shot its wad, gardening is left to take over. Similarly, runaway growth is eating me from within, yet Sledge encourages a runaway growth that may prolong my life, allowing me to die longer. The station has a kind of cancer, we smell it in the corridors everywhere, and trip over new growth every time we touch our blind appendages to the walls. As a girl, Chase, I always did get tubers and tumors confused.

Ordinarily, I'm exempted from my turn helping

Sledge shift his banks of grow lights from one position to the next, but one day recently I was feeling vital
and bored shitless enough to give it a go. In zero-G the
task doesn't involve any lifting, obviously, and even a
one-footed lady can be useful nudging the arrays around
corners and helping Sledge reorient them in a new zone.
Sometimes in all this dark it's pleasant to cling to those
few yellowish lights, too. This day Sledge confessed to
me the basis of his mastery of indoor agriculture: he
once single-handedly ran the most profitable indoor
marijuana farm on the whole island of Manhattan. The
operation was tucked inside a four-room apartment on
the Upper East Side, unknown not only to the authorities (kept off the scent by elaborately rerouted utility
accounts, the massive electrical bills thrown to other
addresses like a ventriloquist's voice into a dummy's
body) but to even the closest neighbors, who regarded
Sledge as an innocent, forgettable fellow tenant in the
large and anonymous building. Sledge described it generously, the rooms teeming to the ceilings with bud-heavy
green stalks, the floor cabled with water sprinklers, the
walls lined with foil reflectors to maximize the ripening
effects of the solar-spectrum lamps, the stereo chattering NPR—talk radio to cover the drone of the daytime
light banks, and classical music to give the plants a
cultural heritage through the cool damp night. In one
large closet he kept what he called the "mother plant,"
a grotesquely thickened and practically pulsing rope of
marijuana from which he cloned seedlings, a fine-tuned
specimen of THC. The result he spliced from her was
the highest high-end "one-toke dope," or so he bragged.

He'd made himself and several confederates wealthy from the operation before a paranoid inkling triggered a violent two-day fit in which he completely disassembled the farm and eradicated its traces. It was those skills that now turned our once-shiny space station into a steamy green bacteria-funky lung. I suppose I am Sledge's mother plant, the improbable thing he keeps alive in an unnatural cramped space.

I don't know why I'm wasting so much of my keyboard time paraphrasing Sledge's tale, except that it was as if I'd visited the place myself. We're prone to transporting visualizations now, in our darkened station, not to mention vivid olfactory hallucinations like the apple cider presently rising to my nostrils. The Russians talk about their childhoods incessantly, when they talk at all. Mstislav, drifting in the dark like a dreamer in a sensory-deprivation tank, has spontaneously offered several wistful accounts of cutting his bare foot on a sickle while pursuing a goat, and while we've many creatures roaming the station now that the Greenhouse doors have been thrown open, I'm fairly certain there's no goat on our roster. For me, it isn't juvenile pastoral to which I revert, but moments between us, Chase, daydream flashes I prefer not to believe I've cobbled out of wishful thinking and damp air. (Did you know we can't even properly gaze at the stars, now? Our breath fogs any window we turn to. We're moisture, Chase, we're returning to dew.) I know I've got a lot of gall questioning your existence when it's my own that's so transparently dubious, or dubiously transparent, or something. But you never write, you never call, ha ha ha. So each time

I roam the corridors of the Met in my imaginings, seeking that Chinese garden where our cool thrilling birdlike kisses were exchanged, finding that oasis of stone and fern and skylight, bowing my head to see our twinned reflections in the rippling pool there, the museum and the Chinese garden and the mirror of water grow clearer and clearer while you begin to pale, I see only myself and a shimmer beside me, you're nothing now but an urgent elusive talisman, an object glimpsed but unseen, a fish's lure in the deep, a reason to go on living. And I do that, Chase. At someone's command, and I prefer to believe it is yours, my friend, I go on living.

Love,
J.

22

Hiccup-afflicted, Perkus began to oscillate like his own eye, as though some internal compass was being again and again jostled out of its usual operation. Or perhaps it was more as if a needle was bumping on a scuffed LP, like his salvaged copy of *Some Girls*, and skipping from track to track. Not that Perkus had ever seemed particularly compassed—it took the onset of hiccups to make me see the relative continuity of his earlier passages. Now he reeled. He'd revive his old mode of whirlwind intertextual eurekas, citing Mailer's *The White Negro*, Seymour Krim calling Lenny Bruce "the Jazz Circuit Hegel," the expulsion of Richard Hell from Television, *The Man Who Was Thursday*, the aphorisms of Franz Marplot, Colin Wilson on Gurdjieff, Dennett's theory of mind-as-computer, Borges's "Doctor Brodie's Report," a Cassavetes appearance on *The Gnuppet Show*, all in a flurry, relying on shorthand—a glimpse of turrets in mist where once he would have drawn a whole castle in the air before me. Or he'd launch a manic exposé—something to do with Claire Carter, the mayor's right hand and Richard Abneg's bête noire, having a nerd-king brother who'd invented chaldrons— but run aground, mutter into his fist, begin discoursing on the progress of Ava's bowel movements mid-sentence, or otherwise, before gaining any momentum, lose his way. If his arguments were once brakeless vehicles he could ride a mile or two before veering into a ditch—a listener climbing aboard if they dared—now they seemed compacted on arrival in one of those junkyard car-crushing machines, recognizable for their former purpose but undrivable.

Then he'd reverse himself, plunge into the newer vein, aping Ava's doggish absolutes, renounce proliferating interpretation and context, all the cultural clues. Too much news or manufactured opinion was distraction from the deeper soundings to be conducted at a level of pure experience: Ava's sniffing walkabouts, the corroded jape of Keith Richards's guitar, the juicy platonic ideal of a pastrami sandwich he'd isolated at a coffee shop on York Avenue. And the weather, he was devoted to the snow and cold, the uncanny force of it, as he was to the legend of the tiger, his own personal destroyer. He preferred what defied or needed no explanation. "Alan Watts said you mustn't concern yourself with information from outside your immediate village. People, like dogs, make demimondes for the purposes of sensory sanity. Nobody—that's *no body*—really believes in the news from beyond the boundaries of their neighborhood or pocket universe. Manhattan is one of those, you know, a pocket universe." These harangues I'd begun to think of as the Friendreth Purities, though really they'd begun earlier, with the floe-borne polar bear, whose profundity had shamed a broadside into silence. Now he published a daily War Free edition of the mind. What a dog couldn't know wasn't worth knowing.

Whatever the pursuit, I was his student again, reenlisted. It was as though we'd wasted time enough on misunderstandings of a personal nature. Perkus seemed in a hurry, too eager for our connection to resume his sporadic cruel needling. Apparently I gave him something Ava or Sadie Zapping couldn't. He had their ears, but mine were more attuned to Perkus's vocabulary, his field of reference, even if he claimed he wished to vacate that field. Biller was invisible, so far as I could tell, and Sadie treated me as an incidental presence, when we overlapped. Oona didn't turn up in the Friendreth again. The Oonaphone was silent, or used secretly.

First, though, it had to be admitted that he *had* a chronic case. When I saw him the first time, two days after Oona and I had made our dawn escape, Perkus was covering his mouth, belching once or twice, or pausing in his speech, turning his head—covering, in other words, any way he could, rather than confessing the situation. At last a sonically undeniable *hiccup*, the world's most onomatopoetic utterance, brazened its way from his lips while Perkus faced me directly, nowhere to hide.

"Runs in the family," I suggested.

He glared a little warning to me not to get too cute. "Not Ava anymore."

"Have you had them continuously?" I didn't add, *since that night*.

"On and off." He breezed a hand to dismiss the topic, but even as he did I saw him clench and swallow, stifling another.

"Trouble sleeping?"

"No," he lied.

Her hiccups shed, Ava thrived, though it couldn't be just my projection that she seemed more orderly, less bounding, as though the dog were every much as concerned as I was, fearing she'd somehow sap Perkus's energies now that he'd taken her malady upon himself. Their relationship had entered another phase (I don't know why I should find this remarkable, knowing Perkus). Ava seemed to pride herself on deferentially coiling at his feet, energies banked until Perkus made a grab for her leash or beckoned her to the dance. She'd never climb his back now, never hurl herself between his knees to trip his steps to the door. She stole less food from the table, perhaps only because she'd observed how rarely Perkus finished a meal anymore, losing interest in trying to fit in bites of egg-and-cheese or pastrami sandwiches between his grunting contractions, and how certain it was he'd push a substantial remainder her way at the end. It was as if Perkus had been training her, but when I asked he denied it, said he'd never wanted to compel her into any such Nietzschean slave-master bond. "She and I talk, Chase"—here he hiccuped, leaving a gap, which we ignored except for his wheeling eye, which seemed to search the room's walls for the missing words—"just talk, nothing more."

Ava also seemed a key to one of Perkus's new motifs, a disquisition in progress on the constructed nature of all consciousness. He worked repeatedly to perfect the thought aloud, seeming to believe he and I had both been persuaded we lived in a virtual reality, and needed to feel better about it. We might as *well* live in a concocted environment, according to his new epiphany, since our awareness was a sort of virtual construction to begin with. No baseline reality existed to worry over. "All memories are replacements, Chase, I read   about this, it's the latest   neurological breakthrough." Why the hermetic skeptic should credit fresh scientific dispatches I didn't know, but never mind. I obliged by asking him to explain. "Each memory is only a photo-copy   of the previous, rather than referring back to some stored 'original.' We trash the original, like some theatrical troupe   that always tears up its script and   bases their performance on a transcript of   the night before, complete with mistakes and improvs, then   destroys that script too, and so on. We have no sugar mountain   to journey backward toward, Chase! Glance   back and the mountain is gone. Better not to glance, and imagine you feel its weight at your back. All we've got   is our working draft, no more final than the   last, just as ready to be discarded. Memory is rehearsal for a   show that never goes on!"

Fair enough, but what did this have to do with the dog? "Each day Ava traces the scent map of the real, beyond which nothing matters to her. She's aware   that the world requires   reassembly each time through it. And think of what   Manhattan is to a *dog*, Chase! If she can endure living in our   daydream, we should be able to tolerate living in someone else's!" Now that Perkus hiccuped openly before me, with evi-dent relief he allowed the gasping intervals to open in his speeches, ellipsis made audible. The asynchronous music of his potholed speech united the Friendreth

Purities with their opposite, those floodgates of paranoiac explanation that periodically opened. "Something
happened, Chase, there was some   rupture in
this city. Since then, time's   been fragmented.
Might have to do with the gray   fog, that or
some other disaster. Whatever the cause, ever since we've
been living in   a place that's a replica of itself,
a fragile simulacrum, full of gaps and   glitches.
A *theme park*, really! Meant to halt time's encroach-
ment. Of course such a thing is destined always to fail,
time has   a way of getting its bills paid. So these
disjunctions   appear, and we have to explain
them away, as tigers or epic sculpture. If   Noteless didn't exist the city would have had to invent him,
Chase!" The more Perkus fleshed this theory the more
the holes in his speech began to seem a kind of necessary
reply to the temporal lacunae he felt the city had fallen
into, as well as to Laird Noteless's bottomless pits and
absent structures.

Perkus seemed to need Manhattan to be both a false-
hood and in ruins (*"This town is wearing tatters!"*) to
make good on his intuitions. But Manhattan wasn't
shattered in the sense that Mick Jagger had indicated in
1978, the way Perkus needed it to be. By recent measures
the city was orderly, flush with money, a little boring,
even. That was, if you trusted the complacent testimony
of the millions who checked TigerWatch in the morning
before donning their April snowshoes and subwaying to
work as usual, then in the evenings filled the bars and restaurants, or stayed home to watch *The Sopranos* or the
Yankees, speed-dialing to stir Chinese-delivery bicyclists

458

to flight. There was Perkus's point, proved: the slumbering millions who never pierced or even nudged the veil of dream. I was one of them, a born sucker, but at least I was here listening to his dire facts. Was he a conspiracy theorist? He spat like I'd said *rock critic*. The only conspiracy was a *conspiracy of distraction*. The conspirers, ourselves. If I didn't grasp this law of complicity I should go back to the beginning and start again. When he said this, I thought of Susan Eldred's office, my first sight of his antithetical eye.

There was another dire fact Perkus wanted me to know without telling me. Something too big to be told. The sky would come crashing down if he told it, so I had to absorb it by implication. In this mysterious matter I was intended to understand Perkus had spared me the worst (I thought he'd spread pretty bad tidings already), and that this secret had to do with women generally, or with Oona Laszlo specifically, or both. Yet he wanted to dance on the precipice of telling it. One day he passingly referred to Oona as "your chaldron," by which he meant nothing good. I found him scratching this itch again the very last day I visited him by myself. That is to say, the day before the day Richard Abneg and I finally dragged him out of the Friendreth Canine Apartments, too late.

■

These days Ava would come rushing to the door as I came in, plainly eager for more company but also appearing to be concerned for Perkus, wishing to scoot me in to where he sat or sometimes lay on the carpet, twitching in glee over some storage-space flotsam like the Warren Zevon LP *Excitable Boy* (he loved a song called "Roland the Headless Thompson Gunner") or, in this case, the latest find, a commercial videotape he'd rescued from a pug's quarters, a Steve Martin comedy called *Dead Men Don't Wear Plaid*.

"Watch—" A hiccup destroyed this word, so he began again. "Watch this with me, Chase, it's brilliant."

"Have you eaten?" He looked disastrous: sallow, skeletal, unshaved, exultant. "I brought sandwiches." I stuck to his preferences, not daring to have some variation rejected, just wanting to see nutrition go in. So pastrami, Diet Coke, pickle spears. There was no coffee brewed. He'd suddenly abandoned coffee, too.

"It's not   sitting well."

"What's not?"

"Food." Unspoken, but heard, was *You idiot!*

The black-and-white *Dead Men Don't Wear Plaid* was a satirical film noir, and a curious amalgam of twelfth-grade tit jokes and an elaborate intertextual trick: Steve Martin's character, a stooge of a private eye, is allowed by the magic of editing to interact with a number of dead performers from ancient movies, Barbara Stanwyck, James Cagney, Humphrey Bogart, and so on. The element, practically an avant-garde gesture, was fascinating and stillborn, destroying any possible mood or rhythm. But incredibly to me, Perkus had located in *Dead Men Don't Wear Plaid* another sacred item. I guess Perkus identified with Martin's detective, for the way he breezed in and out of the archival footage, reanimating his own pantheon of heroes. This was analogous to how

Perkus saw himself moving amid Brando, Groom, Krim, Cassavetes, Mailer, Marplot, Serling, and all the others.

Or so I was thinking, as I sat trying to grasp Perkus's intensity yet again. It was then we came to what it turned out he regarded as the key scene. Steve Martin, whose relations with the femme fatale are absurdly abusive and overwrought, opens the cabinet behind his bathroom mirror and finds a note he's taped there, intended to remind him on a daily basis of something he needs to know: "Guns Don't Kill Detectives, Love Does." Perkus spoke these words aloud as they appeared on the screen, forcing himself past the urge to hiccup at the cost of a wrenching shudder. "Guns! Don't! Kill! Detectives! Love! Does! You see that, Chase?"

"Funny."

"What's   funny about it?" Perkus's voice was sharp. He was suddenly spoiling for trouble, an inter-pretive high noon. Ava got up on all threes and pointed her nose to the door, to meet whatever invader his tone signaled.

I tried, as ever, to meet his standard. "Well, I guess it distills Raymond Chandler's lifework to a bumper sticker . . ." I'd personally always thought the hard-boiled mode wearisome to begin with, so its sending-up felt pretty fish-in-a-barrel.

"Sure, it does   that, you're right. But that's not what   kills me about this scene."

What kills you? I wanted to scream. What kills me is how you smell as if you haven't showered any more recently than your pit bull friend, how your former impeccable suits have degenerated into the same New

461

York Cosmos sweatshirt worn for weeks on end, how your haircut and speech and self-awareness have all gone as crooked as your eye, how your long intellectual voyaging has culminated in a Steve Martin flick. I wasn't going to be swayed into this latest and least of epiphanies, I swore. The closer I looked the more I felt I'd been overlooking the obvious, my eye trained too incrementally on Perkus's details to survey the whole grim trend. He was falling apart, falling down. I couldn't believe I'd let him fall so far. Or that other eyewitnesses, guilty bystanders, hadn't stepped in—I blamed them for what I hadn't seen myself.

"Have you showed this film to Sadie Zapping?" I asked, craftily, I thought.

"Sadie quit coming around," he said. His hand flipped up to flag contempt. "She kept wanting me to try these stupid cures. I swallowed so much water I bloated like a tick. What I love about this scene, Chase, isn't simply that Martin's epigraph cuts so deep into the heart of the matter, but that having arrived at such an essential admonition, he actually *forgets* it and needs to be reminded each day at his shaving mirror!"

I was glad I hadn't suggested any of my own stupid cures. "What about Biller?"

"So, the point is how we forget the most basic fact of ourselves on a daily basis, even while we go around playing our parts, believing ourselves perfectly continuous. Yet a thing can be blotted from the very center of our vision and we won't notice!

Even the   very thing we should most remember! It's like when I tried to write a   book, Chase. Practically   every day I had to   remind myself what it was even *about*, why I'd even started it! What   do you mean, what   about Biller?" Perkus's gaps just kept on getting more frequent, and longer.

"I just wondered if he still comes around."

"Biller's busy   making treasure."

"Oh, sure, I forgot." I'd also forgotten, if he'd actually mentioned it, that Perkus had ever tried to write a book. But no, he hadn't mentioned it. That I would have remembered. It seemed such a simple and humble confession, and I was embarrassed for him for an instant, for burying the lede, slipping the fact into an aside. Then I returned to more root, more animal, worries. No Biller, no Zapping, Laszlo not since the misbegotten night, Abneg never seen in this vicinity, occupied entirely now with his pregnant girlfriend—I, Insteadman, was alone in charge of the faltering organism before me.

"Guns don't   kill detectives. Love   does!" The film had progressed beyond that moment, but Perkus hadn't. He barked the line, seemingly at Ava, as if this were his new song, one he thought as compelling as a Rolling Stones riff, and they should jump up and dance. They didn't jump up and dance. Perkus remained where he sat cross-legged on the floor, too close to the television, I thought, poised with his hand on the remote, his knobby spine showing where his sweatshirt rode to part from his threadbare corduroys. Ava, in a posture of readiness, had split the difference between us and the

door, not wanting to miss a beat when the situation clarified. She cocked her head at Perkus with what seemed tender sympathy, but might only have been a yen for him to break into the ignored sandwiches.

"What does it mean to you, Perkus?" I asked gently. "I never thought of love as your big nemesis."

"No, true enough, I've largely skirted that stuff. *Skirted*—ha! No, Steve Martin more reminds me of *you*, Chase. Oh, shit."

"Did Ava—?" I started this question and stopped, for I'd craned to see that the dog remained poised where she'd been a moment before, the kitchen tile surrounding her clean on all sides, the scent deriving elsewhere.

"Excuse me," said Perkus, swallowing the words. He pulled himself upright using the back of a chair for a ladder. He'd paused the film, an inadvertent screen-capture of Martin's foolish, cross-eyed scowl frosted in a blizzard of static, and now turned his head from my view, to face the heavily draped window, around the edges of which blazing light leaked, the sky smashing its whiteness against the city. A major storm had been predicted to tumble in before nightfall, though I had no way of being certain Perkus, devoid of newspapers or neighborly gossip, knew this vindicating fact. All of us, Steve Martin, Ava, Perkus, myself, had revealed in the same instant our pensive side, a moment of collective interspecies ellipsis that would have solemnized the occasion if it could have been solemnized. It couldn't. Perkus hiccuped silently—I knew well enough by now when he'd hushed one. There was nothing to lose at this point, tensing against the spasm with the muscles of his gut,

464

which had just untensed more than he'd intended. The smell expanded like a parachute, covering the apartment's prevailing dull canine perfume.

"What happened?" I said, though the question was needless. I knew what had happened.

"I   crapped myself," said Perkus.

23

Anne Sprillthmar, a brilliant young South African magazine writer, had been posted in London before being plucked away and hired by Tina Brown during her brief sensational tenure as editor of *The New Yorker*. When Brown had just as quickly moved on, Anne Sprillthmar stuck, endeared herself to the new regime at the famous weekly, and thrived, in her way a perfect Manhattanite, typical of the international elite who lately seemed more the island's right inheritors than its ostensible natives. Sprillthmar was as tall as me and nicely immodest of that fact, standing up without concaving to shelter her breasts as too many tall women do. Bare of a hat, her long copperish hair carried a frosting of snow when she first appeared to shake my hand and say her name, in that faintly exotic, even scandalous accent—bearing its notes of historical shame but presented unshamefully— and when she came near enough I could spot pinpoint snowflakes perching on the tips of her peach-colored lashes. She was even nice-smelling. When we met she'd been shadowing Richard Abneg through his daily paces for four days, fly on the wall as he transacted his duties, the vital errands of the Arnheim administration, and I doubt I'd ever been sorrier to learn that a beautiful and intriguing woman would be difficult to shake from my immediate company. In fact, it wasn't exactly the first time Anne Sprillthmar and I had met. I hadn't recognized her without her tall, long-snouted dog. My elevator girl.

Our recently long-lost friend Richard had found himself cast as bureaucratic firewall between city hall and the spiraling fiasco of the giant escaped tiger's noncapture—of the mayor's failure even to explain the circumstances and origins of the creature's loosing upon Manhattan. So Richard had been shoved to the forefront, to dissemble and deflect in Arnheim's place. This public scapegoat's role had in turn aroused curiosity about the old semi-reconstructed squatters' advocate, and the saga of his long rightward drift into legitimate power. Abneg as sweaty and pragmatic everyman in extremis had immediately struck Anne Sprillthmar as a type worth working up for a profile, in lieu of the access the mysterious mayor would never have granted. When Sprillthmar pitched him to her editors she'd been happily green-lit.

This explained why Richard Abneg wasn't alone when he arrived at the curb of the Friendreth Canine Apartments that next day, in answer to my pleading call. He'd made a commitment to give the journalist access to one of his typical weeks on the go, and grudgingly quit making distinctions between personal and public destinations after she'd insisted she wanted to portray him "in the round." Richard bolted from the taxicab, punching black shoe prints in the dusty covering that had begun to whirl from the sky, leaving the apparently unflappable journalist to pay their fare, and didn't apologize

467

or introduce her when she caught up to him under the Friendreth's portico where I waited. Richard wore the splendid new coat Georgina had purchased for him, and his shoes were fine now, too—he'd always signified his distance from formality by the rattiness of his footwear, but the Hawkman had lately banished all his favorites.

"This had better be good."

I wasn't sure whether I should be furious at Richard for his abdication of Toothland, only that he was so patently aggrieved at my summoning him here that I couldn't bother trying to reverse the charges. Let Richard be the furious one, whether it was to cover feelings of guilt or not. I needed him today.

"We're taking Perkus in for a checkup, only he doesn't know it," I said.

"Your timing is bad," Richard muttered. I didn't know whether he meant the snowstorm, the particular curses of his agenda, the hovering presence of his profiler, or something else, more basic to my being. I didn't doubt he was right in any case. Anne Sprillthmar introduced herself more fully (my name seeming to mean nothing particular to her, a relief), then fell in with us on our way upstairs. Her presence was unassuming, despite her glamour—I figured it was part of her journalist's talents for putting people at ease when they shouldn't be. It wasn't as though she were recording us with anything more than her warmly puzzled, unjudgmental eyes. At Perkus's door I tried to warn them both, incompetently, mentioning squalor, disjunction, hiccups, a well-intentioned but boundless three-legged dog. Richard pushed past me in annoyance. I held the door for Anne Sprillthmar. By the time I followed her inside the journalist was squatting on the kitchen's filthy tile, restraining Ava from tunneling too far down her throat with those patented fang-bared tongue-kisses. "Sweet baby, sweet *baby*, doesn't anybody ever give you love, you *poor* thing?" The accent made Anne Sprillthmar's endearments super-lascivious. "Oh, *yes*, you're a big baby, *aren't* you, darling?" It was on seeing that Anne Sprillthmar was a "dog person" that I recovered an image of her, riding Oona Laszlo's elevator at my side.

Further inside, the encounter I'd willed was taking place, Perkus startled into semi-accountability as only Richard Abneg's implicit reproach could startle him. He'd been huddled on the couch, with Sterling Wilson Hobo's *Immaculate Rust* in scissored remnants all around him, shattered like everything else that met Perkus's interested eye, digested in his own personal mashup. At first I thought to protest—hadn't Perkus said Hobo wasn't his sort of poet?—and then I saw the pages and verses had been reduced past even Hobo's minimalist intentions, the words and even letters dismembered from one another. Perkus had the single syllable *fal* stuck to his cheek. Here was the final destination of all of Perkus's languages: the ransom note. Perkus, kidnapped by his own theories, had then suffered Stockholm syndrome, in which one preferred a jailer to oneself.

Or maybe I was unfair. Maybe hiccups wrecked him. Anyhow, he'd wrecked, chin shadow become an unkempt whitish beard, scruff become inane wisps spilling over his ear tops, disarray become dereliction. Perkus wasn't the only startled person on the scene. Richard Abneg was

469

silenced, too. I saw Perkus through his eyes, miles deep in self-dungeoning since their farewell on Eighty-fourth Street. I recalled they'd been boys together, that unimaginable land of brilliant New York childhood I'd been made to feel ashamed I lacked. I'd given Richard no chance even to understand what the Friendreth Apartments were about—he probably credited the malodorous decor entirely to Perkus. Close enough. Everything stood for itself. Perkus hiccuped violently to rupture the silence and an exclamation mark of drool decorated his chin.

Richard didn't speak to him at first, but turned back to me, the rage and hurry leached from his voice. "You have a doctor waiting?" he asked. I nodded, and he said, "Take Anne back into the kitchen." Anne Sprillthmar, with Ava nuzzling up into her kneading hand, had come in behind me, and now stood shocked. Perkus gawked back at her. "I'll talk to him for a minute," said Richard, as if neither Perkus nor the journalist could hear him. "We should have kept a cab waiting. There won't be many in this goddamn cul-de-sac."

"We'll go downstairs and find a cab and be waiting for you." I was grateful for Richard's command, eager to expand on my usefulness in return for his taking responsibility for what happened next, perhaps even what had happened to begin with.

"Get two and send her back to the Condé Nast building."

The snows were wilder than even ten minutes earlier, though these were still the sort of brittle pinprick flakes I had trouble imagining accumulating much, not because they'd melt—it was too cold for that—but because they'd whirl and drift and be whisked into piles, never adhering to anything, not even one another. If cab-hailing could be called street smarts, Richard's were unerring: Anne Sprillthmar and I had to walk to the corner of First for a taxi. We rode it back while I explained to her that Richard wanted her gone.

"What *is* that place?"

"Only dogs are supposed to live there. If you Google under Friendreth you'll find out all about it."

"I'm guessing this has nothing to do with the tiger."

"No, or at least not in the way you're thinking. Nothing to do with Richard's official responsibilities."

"Who is that dismal person?"

"I'd rather not say."

"Would I know the name?"

"I doubt it." I could excuse *dismal*, which was easily justified. Yet I felt an obligation to be as flinty as Richard, on his and Perkus's behalves, rather than to act as sentimentally undone as I felt, under the twin sway of the disastrous watershed occasion—I was as amazed at myself for waiting so long to put Perkus Tooth into a framework of emergency as I was that I had finally done so, and that it had, seemingly, worked—and my irrelevant and inappropriate responsiveness to Anne Sprillthmar's voice, height, and scent.

She made one last bid for conversation. "Amazing about this weather, don't you think?"

"I guess—yes." I didn't want to think about the snow, though in our cab we were surrounded at all sides by a theater of white chaos. The snow seemed to be thinking about us. That would do for now. Anne Sprillthmar got out and found herself another cab, smiling placidly through a wiped porthole in my window to let me know I'd done no damage to her undamageable serene curiosity about me and other things.

Richard Abneg stuffed Perkus into the cab just a moment later. He'd got him into several layers of charity sports-gear junk to insulate his skeleton from the cold, and a fleabag hat I thought I'd never seen, until I recognized it as the fur tower Biller had once sported, now crushed and matted, as if Ava had been regularly humping it. Ocelot, I remembered. Perkus seemed to be waking from a spell, slowly. "Who was that   woman, Chase?"

"You better ask Richard."

Richard pushed in at Perkus's door, securing Perkus on the hump seat, hands cradling his knobby corduroy knees. A few bits of language, words and letters jaggedly snipped from their contexts, still clung to his pants amid the melting snowflakes. The cabby's lush incense didn't blot a certain doggy, pukey, unshowered smell. I told him where to take us.

"Is that your   new girlfriend, Richard? What happened to the Hawkman?"

Richard might have known better than to try to wait him out.

"You   make   a   beautiful   pair.   Beautiful coats."

"She's not my girlfriend. She's a journalist doing a profile." Before Perkus could pry it from him, Richard added, "For *The New Yorker*."

"No kidding?"

"No kidding."

"Is Avedon going to take your picture?"

"Your guess is as good as mine."

Perkus was disturbingly gleeful through his debris and hiccups. His eyes were thrilled, one with Richard, the other with the surrounding scene. "So you've *done* it, Abneg! How does it feel?"

"How does what feel?"

"How does it feel to *finally ride the hegemonic bulldozer?*"

Richard let this line die in silence. Our cab got lucky shooting downtown, then made slow sticky progress crossing west on Thirty-fourth Street. Perkus, unanswered, ground into his silent management of the jarring hiccups, sometimes seeming to murmur between them to himself, not daring to speak. "I need to walk Ava," he said suddenly.

"Chase will go back and walk Ava," said Richard, smoothly delegating.

"Maybe you should call Sadie Zapping," Perkus mused. He spoke as if conjuring a figure in mist, some fallen Valkyrie or minor archangel.

"I'll do that," I said. I had no idea if this was possible, but I'd be willing to try. I didn't plan on abandoning Perkus anytime too soon. The Friendreth's volunteers, Sadie or another, would certainly look in on the dog before long.

"Perkus is probably wondering what kind of doctor he'll be seeing," said Richard, his voice weary, as he craned his head at the snow-clotted traffic. He'd fallen into a queer oblique habit of addressing us each through the other, perhaps a measure of how badly he'd been rattled by Anne Sprillthmar's questions.

"Strabo Blandiana," I said. "They've met before. He'll be familiar with Perkus's history."

"The Romanian quack," said Richard darkly. "I know who he is."

"He's a Chinese practitioner," I said.

"Chase must think I'm out of *balance*," said Perkus humorously.

"Ironic," said Richard.

"No, it *is* ironic," said Perkus, his voice an ember reigniting in a damp bonfire, cheek muscle frogging beneath his Unabomber beard. "Given all that's off balance around here!" He was revving up another of his hiccologues. "Seriously, I've got to talk with you, Richard. A lot of this, uh, stuff I've been working on is completely lost on Chase."

"Thanks."

"No offense, Chase, but it's like trying to describe Gnuppets *to a Gnuppet*." Perkus's glee in this superb comparison was tempered by the ferocity of the seizure that marked it, an emphysematous gasp for breath adequate to complete the phrase.

"We'll talk after you've seen the doctor." Richard's unrestrained sarcastic inflection of this last word served not only to reinforce what a poor selection he thought I'd made in Strabo Blandiana but to assuage Perkus that the two of them still spoke above my head, and so his promise of future listening was sincere. Perkus, no matter his state, caught this implication and was reassured. His response was to defend Strabo, halfway.

"Blandiana's an interesting character, Richard. Did you know that before we met he actually troubled to read quite a bit of my work?"

"Really." Richard kept it neutral.

"Strabo's a kind of catalyst person, I think. His offices might function as a message center or way station for higher intelligences . . ." From his vague tone I couldn't tell whether Perkus meant the offices had already been used that way or only had that potential. I wasn't sure he knew. (Perhaps it was an allusion to the framed chaldron poster. Or to the chance of Fran Lebowitz running into Frank Langella in the waiting room.) It was maddening that I even wanted to follow his drift into chaotic abstractions. My friend Perkus Tooth had collapsed, then accepted my help. That truth ought reasonably to end my attempt to collate and refold his many crumpled maps of the universe. Yet he was never so very far from where I'd first met him, a door into my life in the city as I knew it now. And I loved him—if that made me his unteachable Gnuppet, so be it.

"*Hark!*" said Perkus. When he spoke the hiccups emerged as silences, but when he was silent they took the form of these Shakespearean exhortations.

■

Arrived in Chelsea, we got him out of the cab, through the darkening street, under a snow-choked sky, and up to Strabo Blandiana's rooms. In arranging this appointment

Strabo and I had spoken on the phone once the afternoon before, once this morning. Strabo had made any number of confidence-inspiring remarks about chronic hiccups, which I needed him to do, for hiccups, I kept telling myself, were the problem here. The healer spoke of my wisdom in coming to him first, explaining that too many of those enduring chronic hiccups found their way to acupuncture only as a last resort. He'd place needles at E-37, E-1, and E-33, and then we'd be able to consider how Perkus had got to this point, characteristically implying he'd make symptoms disappear *in order* to proceed to deeper matters, the world sickness that by its nature infected every soul. I did my best to preview Perkus's low state, the tatterdemalion soon to appear in his suite. Strabo assured me he'd have any other clients tucked away in their own rooms when we came through—any idea that he'd be affronted himself was beneath mention. Strabo's commitment, once he'd taken a client, was absolute. He had no idea how Perkus regarded him. It wasn't clear to me, actually. Perkus might have absorbed more sincere value from his first visit than he'd ever admit.

Strabo even seemed capable of soothing Richard Abneg's suspicions as he eased Perkus off behind a closed door, leaving us to face that dippy receptionist in a waiting room that had been otherwise cleared as promised. Richard and I didn't make any small talk, too conscious of that possible listener, but I believe I wasn't wrong to sense relief in him. I'd produced a kind of obsequious triumph, having moved the hot potato of Perkus from one bracket of authority to another, leaping the gulf of distrust between the two—the best a Gnuppet might hope to do. I don't know how long I was allowed to reside in that bubble of false satisfaction before Strabo reappeared, minus Perkus.

"Will you . . . ?" Strabo gestured us into another room, and closed the door.

Now, as though he'd been holding it at bay earlier, I felt Richard's gaze working over Blandiana's neat crew sweater and huge gold watch, his etched sideburns, the flawless shaving in the dimple of his chin, his poreless nose. I could feel Richard thinking *I may wear the beard, but I know which of us is the faking fakir here*. Strabo didn't blink, but seemed to grant a tiny interval for Richard's contempt to be withered in an atmosphere of total acceptance. Then he spoke. "As you know, I'm in no way hostile to Western treatment. In the case of certain purely medical emergencies I recommend swift intervention of modern techniques, and this is one of those times." Strabo betrayed no panic, though he inspired plenty in me.

"What's wrong?" I said. "Can't you stop the hiccups?"

"I might, but we haven't the time. I recommend that you move Perkus directly to an emergency room. St. Ignatius Rockefeller, on Ninth Avenue at Thirty-sixth would be best."

Richard saw an opening. "His *aura* came up black and you couldn't handle it, huh?"

Strabo turned and spoke to me, with calm purpose. "I believe our friend may have hemorrhaged internally, Chase."

"*Christ*," said Richard, looking at me, too—I was the one to be looked at.

∎

"Forever hailing taxicabs," murmured Perkus, with amusement, after we'd hustled him downstairs and into another backseat, not saying to him what Strabo Blandiana had said, not bothering with any niceties that might slow us. Richard's attitude toward this wayward visit to Blandiana now struck the defining note, as if I was hardly any more competent than Perkus, though Richard would have had no idea Perkus was in any crisis at all if I hadn't called him. Perkus was completely acquiescent in our care, cast adrift, seeming afraid to wander into the snowstorm, the shifting shroud of which blurred his frail form into a kind of wraith even right beside us. Still, he eked out an assessment. "That's the trouble with you, Chase, you think you can be insulated from the pedestrian view, a wholly stage-managed approach to existence. But the stage gets smaller and smaller, soon you're living in a snow globe!" The daylit sky had darkened to a cave of orange at four o'clock, blotted by flakes which had now found their proper size and viscosity, ash from a cold volcano. Manhattan, schooled in the ceaseless winter, had begun folding its tent under the assault, cars vacating the avenues, shops rattling down gates, surrendering the evening. "That's why everyone loves you, Chase. You're the perfect avatar of the city's unreality. Like Manhattan, you're a sentimental monument, stopped in time. I wonder what would happen if

478

we asked this cab to take the   Lincoln Tunnel? What sort of world   is left out there?"

"There never was much of one," said Richard.

"Probably we wouldn't   be allowed to try," said Perkus. Now he censored himself, as though he'd already displeased the imaginary authorities he'd conjured, the Manhattan Border Patrol, and concentrated on managing the paroxysms rippling through him. I considered whether I might be the trapped-in-amber curiosity Perkus made me for. Whatever he said, I felt adaptable enough—I'd put myself into Perkus's crosshairs, for one thing. That might only make me a *masochistic* Gnuppet. By now I could script Perkus's abuse of me without his help.

Richard and I subsisted in the embattled, fearful silence that fell on us through the agony of the cab's crawl up Tenth, then conducted Perkus past St. Ignatius's emergency-intake doors, tracking snow prints along the tile, in through the low-ceilinged, uninspiring waiting room, presided over by a high-mounted television tuned to some disconcertingly jaunty cable-news broadcast. The waiting-room seats were nearly everywhere filled, a gauntlet of gazes we wouldn't want to meet all at once, or, really, at all. Luckily, that feeling was mutual. Illness shies, especially the self-poisoning kind that appeared to dominate the room. Or was I just defensive about how Perkus had come to resemble an old drunkard or junkie? He had company in that here. It was the comparison that risked dragging him down—I wanted him seen as one of us, not one of them. I wanted Richard's coat and shoes to count for a tremendous amount now—God bless the

Hawkman. I knew how this place worked, or thought I knew: we had to distinguish him in their jaded attentions. We had a head start, finding no parents with children. And nobody bleeding, not on the outside, anyway. Best, there was no one between us and the triage nurse, a stolid black woman who might be thirty, or fifty. She worked behind sliding Plexiglas, like Chinese food in Brooklyn. A door to the right led to her small examining room, but she didn't invite us through.

"This man needs a doctor," I said. Perkus swayed between us, mumbling, making a good case he needed *something*, I thought. Richard plucked the smashed ocelot from Perkus's head and stuck it in his hands instead, like a purse. The improvement was modest.

"You talk to me," came a voice of impermeable thickness, resistant to its root, accent shading to some island. "Then I talk to the doctor."

"He's got hiccups," I said. "And maybe internal bleeding."

"Hiccups?"

"Chronic esophageal spasms," specified Richard. "Which is a recognized medical condition, and has been known to cause injury and even death, so summon a fucking doctor."

"Chronic hiccups," repeated the nurse, writing it down.

"They're sympathetic hiccups," I said. "Sympathetic with an *animal*."

At this the nurse only stared. She appeared to be examining Perkus for firsthand evidence, but his present hiccologue, though practically subvocal, was incessant enough that the spasms came only as lulls in his whispering—he hadn't let out a solid gasping *Hark!* or *Hurryup!* since we'd passed through the hospital doors. In terms of symptoms, Perkus fired blanks.

"Write *suspicion of internal hemorrhage*," said Richard.

She ignored him. "Has he been to see a doctor?"

"That's why we're here, to see a doctor!"

"Chronic refers to a diagnosis that shouldn't come to the emergency room," she said blandly. "Some people live with hiccups five or ten years." Working in the emergency room, the triage nurse, I began to understand, was an enemy of the notion of *emergency*. I recalled an acting teacher who'd sworn to do his best to discourage every student who came his way—those that remained were, possibly, actors.

"He *did* see a doctor, who told us to come to your emergency room," I said, speaking each word carefully. "He felt it was an emergency and that there might be . . . internal . . . bleeding." I hadn't wanted to use the term in front of Perkus, but he didn't notice, or didn't care. He'd assumed the role of patient, if anything, too quickly, seeming now to have held this bent and subdued posture for years. Hard to believe that as recently as the night before he'd lectured me on the causes of death in detectives. I should have left him the way I'd found him, still full of brash authority, a captain going down with the ship. Now all his words were for himself, at least in this place. He showed no evidence of bleeding, but all else was internal. Even his uncanny eye seemed to search inward.

"A doctor with this hospital?" asked the triage nurse. I'd interested her, slightly, for the first time.

"No."

"With which hospital, then?"

"Not with a hospital, a Chinese doctor, I mean, he isn't Chinese, but he practices acupuncture."

In her eyes I had now flown to the moon with my flapping arms, which appeared to be a kind of thing she saw too often and didn't care to see again.

"*The kind of doctor who sticks you with needles!*" yelled Richard.

"Was someone attacked?" she asked.

"Eh?"

"Are you describing a crime and should I notify the police?"

"No," said Richard with maximum irritation, yet seeming to recognize an official jargon that required some minimum of respectful reply. "No, there's been no crime."

"Then keep your voice down, this is a place for sick people," she said, adding ominously, "*some of them.*" Then she resumed her inspection of Perkus. I tried to be persuaded something medical was going in her look. "Can he sign his name?"

"Of course," said Richard.

"One of you can come in and help him fill out a form. The other has to wait." She directed this at me. Richard had made a distinct un-friend: in the triage nurse's index the moon flappers were preferable to the shouters.

After the nurse took Perkus's blood pressure and shone a quick light in his pupils (she frowned at the

482

disobedient one), I jotted my way through the intake form. This meant conducting an interview, one Perkus only partly attended from where he sat across from me, burping, blinking, and murmuring: date of birth, medical history (negligible, he'd not been in a hospital since having his appendix out as a teenager), insurance (none), living relatives (a sister—who knew?), responsible parties should the patient be incapable of making care decisions (he hesitated over this until I thought he'd forgotten the question, then startled me by blurting, "You, Chase, you").

Then it was back out into the purgatorial waiting area, where Richard had negotiated or bullied for three seats together in a row. We took our seats like latecomers in some impoverished theater, Perkus with his grotty ocelot loaf in his lap like something he'd killed with his bare hands. The television, I now saw, was tuned not to a news show but to an endless infomercial, the "anchor" at his desk merely a shill offering leading questions to a grinning middle-aged couple hawking DVDs containing secrets to real-estate wealth. Other guests sat on the seats to their right, nodding and grinning as they awaited their chance to chime in and report what millions the couple's system had netted them. *"Shift into High-per-Hour!"* they kept incanting. *"Not High-Power, but High-per-Hour!"* In our dim company the television's presentation was weirdly irresistible, and we all sat drinking it in. I couldn't help wondering how the staff had tuned to this channel, out of so many. The degree of indifference seemed willful, an expression of the low odds you'd ever feel in the care of a thinking mind in this place. Yet just as one's willingness to board a plane depends on believing a plane's cockpit impervious to the condition of chaos that rules an airport, I'd let myself go on thinking Perkus was destined to meet some upstanding captain of medicine just outside this arena of human vacuity and dismay.

Perkus had just now surrendered some layer of will needed to manage his noise, and gave all the proof he hadn't while under inspection of the triage nurse: "*Hawk! How work! Ha wreck! Shirk! Chute!*" Though proof of hiccups wasn't likely to move him to the front of the line. What was the sound of internal bleeding? A less koan-like question: What did these other denizens suffer, to rate being triaged ahead of us? I forced myself to take a closer look. Two different Hispanic husbands cradled rounded wives, and I guessed there might be endangered pregnancies in play. Hard to be sure under the coats and blankets. Otherwise, male or female, our rivals seemed mostly derelicts who'd come in out of the cold. They might as well have been dressed in brown paper sacks.

"Imagine a transcript   of this thing," said Perkus suddenly. It took me a moment to realize he meant the infomercial. "Just word for word,   every gesture mapped   and reproduced. You could stage it   off Broadway, it would be   like Beckett, Chase, the most   astounding avant-garde spectacle, it'd   run *forever*! Then in a few   centuries it might be the   only evidence of our species   locked in some galactic museum   not the original, but a grainy

484

rehearsal   tape of the show   which in reality would likely have closed during previews, but   anyway the universe could know   we lived under *this* regime"—Perkus gestured at the screen overhead—"and yet were able here and there to   laugh, however bitterly."

Perkus recovered some wellspring of associations, riffing with new vigor, though the gaps kept on growing, like a digital brain on shuffle, and breaking down. He was oblivious to the glares of his unfortunate audience, those who bothered to glare—many seemed to take his sprung presence as a typical cost of entry to this pallid dungeon. Richard hunkered down, glaring back, bristling that anyone might object to us. Me, I listened. What were we going to do—ask Perkus to wind down again? These were signs of life. "Richard, here's what   I want you to understand, and never   mind what Chase tells you,   just so long   as you don't go blabbing it all to *The New Yorker*, hee hee—" He regaled Richard with his succinctest description yet of his simulacra theory of Manhattan, including leading roles for the three of us, and possibly Georgina Hawkmanaji (but not Oona), we who were several of the only real souls still inhabiting the island. He was pretty certain the gray fog, the subway-boring mechanical tiger, the chaldron sickness that had come over us, and the "Brando's dead" rumor were each typical of the slippage at the edges of our reality by its handlers, who were for all their contrivances and capital unequal to the task they'd set themselves. If Richard could cause himself to look squarely at one portion of his investment in these fictions, he'd dissolve all the others. Perkus had been a fool, attempting to persuade Chase Insteadman, cracked actor—it was Richard who was positioned to understand, with one foot in both camps by his nature. Only then Perkus reversed again: Why bother? The world *cannot* be disenchanted, this was his new motto. Reside in whatever small *cave of the real* you can gather around yourself and a few friends. Walk the dog religiously, the dog has things to impart. Only watch the weather— when it stopped snowing, disbelieve his theories. Richard's severity gave way to bleak playfulness: he'd believe anything if it didn't require admitting Brando lived. I saw his bantering as a bid to keep Perkus at the level of the propositional, as though not to strand him too deep in any single foray. I was cheered; this was what I'd forgotten to do. I'd taken him too seriously.

Perkus wound down again. He offered a round of disconnected phrases, attempts at deadpan, though they came out forlorn. "So   I don't   have a   headache   anyway!" I smiled to show him I appreciated the irony. Then, "We should have brought   something to   read." He asked if I'd called Sadie Zapping about Ava—I said yes, lying. Perkus appeared satisfied, though we'd never been apart long enough for me to make a call, and his hiccups turned to a spell of spasmodic yawning, as though his quaking body wished to shutter itself for a nap. His breath was rank. Richard, like me, had an eye on the clock. Almost an hour had gone by. Nobody had been called from the room except one of the

Hispanic couples. A few more gray and weather-smitten forms had trudged inside, accompanied by blasts of snowy air.

"Fuck it, I'm finding a doctor," said Richard. He stood and hammered his fist on the Plexiglas—the nurse was out of view. I saw two policemen step up then, from the corridor to the left, behind doors forbiddingly labeled, leading to the ambulance-entry ramp. The cops had been on the ramp smoking cigarettes and grumbling into their stupid radios, complaining of the cold to lucky buddies back in the station house, I suppose. Now Richard gave them a good excuse to get out of the cold. I saw him lean expertly into their company, talking under his breath. I cheered simply for him to stir up some reaction here in this lifeless zone—Perkus's hiccologues were keeping the whole place going, those and the real-estate infomercial. Richard could play some mayor's trump card and get Perkus seen.

"Chase . . ." Perkus was uninterested in Richard and the police, except as an opportunity to have me alone. However much he disdained my grasp of his revelations, apparently he had some use for my confidential ear. His tone turned from declamatory to intimate. "So, I'm in bad   faith with   you over a couple   of things. Do you remember   what I said about rock   critics, Chase?"

"Oh, sure." Why should I ever be amazed at his swerves? But I wasn't sure I wanted him to switch into confessional mode, as if he thought he was running low on chances. As much as I wanted him to be well, I didn't want him to know he was sick.

"I'm   *one of them*, Chase."

"One of what?"

"A rock critic   I mean.   I knew every
one of those poor   bastards at some   point
Shaw   Nelson   Williams   We
broke bread, Chase.   They taught me   what
I know,   how to think I don't know   why
I ever denied it." He rushed these last words into one
breath between the herky-jerks. I wanted to tell him to
ease himself, not try to talk, but that would be as if to
tell him to fold the only tent he'd ever set up on the
windswept desert of existence.

"Each an   explorer   of new worlds a
Columbus or Magellan.   They were   my
brothers."

"Well . . ." I found myself wanting to give him
some absolution. "They probably knew how you really
felt."

"Listen   forget them   I need to   tell   you
something   important about   me and   you
can't ever   tell Richard. Or Oona."

Richard, in the corner with the cops, had his back to
us, gesticulating, looking less persuasive than I'd hoped.
Perkus still had his opening with me.

"I'm   not like   you, Chase.   I've
never had a girlfriend."

"Some men like to keep free and easy. Monogamy's
not the only game in town," I added joshingly. "Looking
at my own poor outcomes, some might say you've done
the more honorable thing."

"I mean   *none at all*."

He groaned it like a frog. Thank God for the inane barking of the infomercial. If only it could have kept me from hearing, too. I didn't need to ask any clarifying question to know how absolutely Perkus meant me to take his words. I suppose I should have known it from his rage of confusion at my attempt to set him up with the Jackson Hole waitress, poor doomed Lindsay. I thought crazily how the tiger might be Perkus's poltergeist, destroying only what he found himself unable to live with: his kingdom of broadsides, the prospect of a lover, the city itself. I wondered if Oona was safe. Now, as though reading my thoughts, he mentioned her.

"Oona was the one. I should have told you."

I sat staring at the infomercial, unwilling or unable to face him. "So you had *one* girlfriend, actually."

"No, I once tried and was rebuffed."

The word bore all the weird delicacy of his innocence. After so long, the size of his loneliness was hard to contemplate. I suppose his kind of radical openness required barricades in some areas—he couldn't have let women pass easily through him and still make room for all those arcane references, all those wild conjectures, all those drugs, all that cosmic radiation flooding his brain. He'd shut the door to sex and in came chaldrons and Ava and hiccups instead. Well, I couldn't argue with the life-architecture of the most remarkable person I knew, only quibble around the edges like an interior decorator, offering wallpaper for his dungeon. "We'll have to do something to get you up and running, then, when we're past this . . . present . . . episode." I worked to keep a gulp or click or sob from my own voice. My words were addressed to a dissolving person-shaped pile of hiccups, not a ready candidate for Upper East Side pickup scene.

Richard plopped into his seat with a tight sigh. At least confessions were done for now—I'd taken my limit. "What did you learn?" I asked him.

"What did I learn? I learned that they have some squeaky-tight protocols around here and I could be arrested if I pushed through the Staff Only doors as I kept swearing I'd do, that's what I fucking learned."

"Did you tell them who you are?"

"Who I am?" Richard chuckled. "My impression is that if you're a cop working below 125th Street these days pretty much anyone you ever lay hands on or even give the hairy eyeball says *Do you know who I am* or *You know I could have your badge in a heartbeat* or *I've got full diplomatic immunity to be carrying this suitcase full of cocaine-dusted Benjamins*, hence they all find such gambits pretty much outright hilarious." Richard seemed energized in the defeat, his typical response. Perhaps he felt confirmed in the deep truth of his rascal identity—he didn't want to be who his credentials said he was. The eternal police-mind, which saw everyone as a lawbreaker, had seen him true. But Perkus was stimulated, too, and raised his pitch again. He was stimulated by one implication in particular.

"Cops   live in   New Jersey, don't   they, Richard?"

"Jersey, sure, or Staten Island or Hicksville or White Plains, whatever."

"They   laugh   because they   know."

"Know what?" said Richard warily, sensing the trap.

"What's   outside   the   limit, maybe fallout-strewn   wasteland   or   Chinese slave dictatorship,   people   in cages   too small   for dogs."

"In that case wouldn't it be more sensible to use *robot policemen*?" said Richard. The couple overhead were explaining how many people misunderstood the *foreclosure* process, the fact that so many homeowners were simply looking for a partnership plan like the one they offered, to ease them free of their mortgages.

"*Sor-   -ry?*" croaked Perkus.

"Robot policemen wouldn't track so much fallout back and forth from Staten Island, don't you think? And they wouldn't require so many bribes, or toroid pastries."

"*—ut—*"

"What I mean to say is no more fucking *plots* now, Perkus, I mean it."

Perkus grimaced and wrapped himself again deep inside his hiccups, but he couldn't out-glower Richard, not in his present state. I was afraid to negotiate between them, so we slid back into the lull that ruled this human backwater. The policemen had returned to their chilly ambulance ramp, where they stood shaded from snowfall, yet stamping their cloddish shoes, in light dimming blue to purple, another day defeated.

"Chase," Perkus whispered after an interval.

"Yes?"

He peered at Richard to be certain his words to me were going ignored. Richard obliged this need. He'd begun tapping angrily at his cell phone, texting something, working the buttons like a teenager attempting to swindle a vending machine.

"There's one   more   thing," said Perkus. "You won't   understand   now but   later   it's about you   know who."

"Oona?"

"Shhhhhhhh." In some way Perkus wished to resume our secret conversation, but only in fragments, or code, increasingly his two specialties.

"Okay," I said.

"It's   a   joke.   Did   you   hear the   one   about   the   Polish   starlet?"

Could the answer be *guns don't kill detectives, love does*? I waited expectantly.

"You   don't   know?"

"No."

"Make   *her*   give you the answer." He pushed this out with difficulty and satisfaction, like a tennis player grunting a difficult shot into an unreturnable position. The game, surely, was between Perkus and Oona. I was the net.

■

"*Mr. Pincus Truth*," called an orderly from the Staff Only doors where he stood, reading from a clipboard. For the seeming eternity we'd waited, we'd nonetheless bypassed some of the brown-paper sackers, still slumped where they'd been when we entered—I guess *hiccups with a side order of hemorrhage* wasn't the lowest rung on the triage ladder after all. Perkus stood, forgetting the ocelot hat, which tumbled to the filthy linoleum, finding its right place, it seemed to me. We stood with him, Richard shoving his cell into a coat pocket. The orderly held the door and we came to him together, Perkus morally supported by us on either side, though he moved under his own power, kept his own balance. He seemed dutifully passive, a model patient trudging into the inevitable unquestioned. I yearned to see a show of scorn for Western medicine, a proscenium for Gnuppetry if ever there was one. Yet he only appeared to want to go through those doors. The waiting and the fluorescent light had humbled and sold him, aroused his anonymous gratitude to have his name called, in any garbled form—Strabo Blandiana could learn a thing or two about breaking down a skeptic. "Can you walk?" the orderly asked.

"Y-   -es."

"Are these your family members?"

"We're friends," said Richard.

"Then you'll need to wait out here," said the orderly.

"How will we know whether he's being admitted or released?" asked Richard.

"Someone will speak with you, if you'll take a seat."

The infomercial had looped for the third time before I understood this wasn't a case of poor channel selection but of synergy. The hospital must have franchised its waiting-room broadcast, these shadows of avarice destined to flicker over the faces of despondency until the end of time, the two having as obtuse a relation as those birds and that tower. Now that we'd returned to our seats without Perkus I considered that others in our company, bad as they looked, might not be here on their own accounts, but be waiting for news of someone worse off, a friend they'd dragged in as we'd dragged Perkus.

"How's Georgina?" I asked Richard, acting as if this were some cocktail party and we, old friends, had at last been left together to catch up.

"Georgina's nipples are the size and color of those baby Italian eggplants," he said. He seemed to be making a dispassionate report, with no desire to shock. "There's a dark brown line running up from her pussy hairs to her navel, which by the way is distended now like a little thumb."

"I wasn't asking for a nude sketch, but thanks. How are her spirits?"

He ignored me. "Do you know what the brown line and the purple nipples are for, Chase? I never knew this. Too bad Perkus isn't here, he'd find this fascinating. If the mother is somehow unconscious and there's no one else to help the newborn baby find her tits in order to get milk, the baby can follow the line and see the nipples and go get itself a drink. Isn't that freaky?"

"I guess." Perhaps the hospital had put him into a medical frame of mind.

"Georgina's body is literally being transformed into a *milk map*. Just to give you a sense of, you know, the kind of world I'm living in at the moment."

"Are you pissed at me about something?"

"Let's not make this about us, okay? Let's just sit here and wait to find out about Perkus."

"Sure."

"You should have called me sooner."

"Thanks, I'm feeling guilty enough as it is."

Richard began checking e-mails or texts on his phone again. I settled in to once more consider the infomercial—I'd been urged by the broadcast to take my wage and imagine two or three zeros behind it. I wondered what my wage was. My account, residuals seeping in, never emptied, that was all I knew. My fortunes depended on something not unlike this broadcast—somewhere sometime always, on the WB11 or its local equivalent, *Martyr & Pesty* ran, filling the hours on some screen, my childhood japery larded with canned laughter, in an infinite loop, perhaps even in a waiting room, to grate on the nerves of the sick and dying.

A young, bespectacled doctor appeared and beckoned to me and Richard. We hurried to him, our frenetic worry the outstanding flavor in this flavorless zone, though no one bothered to be interested. Perkus's muddy ocelot lay on the floor to mark our seats. "You're Mr. Truth's friends?"

"Yes."

"You had some question?"

"Just what's going to happen," I said, as though speaking to a soothsayer who might offer any number of revelations, Mr. Truth himself.

"Oh, I wouldn't worry. Hiccups can be treated by a great variety of agents. Intravenous chlorpromazine is the current consensus. To circumvent hypotension you'd preload the patient with five hundred to a thousand milliliters of saline"—he recited from mental pages—"or you could try haloperidol, or metoclopramide, ten milligrams every eight hours, I think." Here was the next card turned in Hippocratic three-card monte: first the demoralizing ambiance, then the bland inexplicable jargon. The doctor looked ever younger as he scratched a finger nervously around the perimeter of his glasses—perhaps he'd borrowed them just before coming through the doors, in order to better impress us. "What's fascinating is you can come at chronic hiccups from so many angles; anticonvulsants, analgesics, an anesthetic, like ketamine, even a muscle relaxant!" Our medical prodigy grinned like he'd passed an oral exam.

"Right, so how *will* you treat them?" said Richard.

He shrugged. "We'll find out."

"Have you examined him?"

"How could I, when they sent me to talk to you? Besides, you wouldn't want me, I'm a new resident. Dr. Stern will see your friend. He's the attending."

"Who are you—Dr. Silly?"

"That's unnecessary, sir."

"Let us see him."

"Who, Stern?"

"Perkus, Stern, either of them."

"I can't."

The resident ducked out before Richard could sling another insult. I returned to our seats, but Richard began an angry leonine pacing at the doors through which Perkus had vanished. The waiting room took on a swirling time-lost quality, a pocket in the storm that was possibly also a floe stranded from the mainland of ice. The triage nurse was in hard-bargain negotiation with a newcomer, a gray-coated man in galoshes who clutched his stomach, moaning faintly, as snow dripped from hat and shoulders. As Perkus had more or less commanded, my thoughts radiated outward from this room to migrate across the bridges and tunnels of Manhattan. I thought of Oona but also of outer space and other places I'd rather be. In the Stonehenge restroom you know one thing—you've seen Stonehenge. Here you knew less each minute. I remembered Indiana. Every once in a great while I did. I began dreaming of a Polish starlet. I fell asleep, under a blanket of guilt.

I woke to Richard bellowing. "*Show me, mother-fucker!*" He was in the clutch of his two cops, bellowing as near to the face of a tall, white-haired doctor as their sturdy blockade would allow. The doctor, who wore a bloodstained white smock (unconscious of the cliché any actor would refuse), held his hands open, an apparent plea for reason, though his long, deep-lined face, for all its expressive potential, revealed nothing particularly intimate, no fear of Richard, no pity, his eyes showing a gruesome veteran's steel instead. The doctor appeared less Stern than shorn of human sympathies. It was Richard's face that told too much, told me everything before I knew it. His beard seemed to be sticking straight out in fury, as though electrified, his mustache snot-glistening. "*Where are you keeping him?*" Richard seethed and snuffled. "Let me get him the fuck out of here, he was better off with the puncturist than you murderers."

"You're not listening to me," said Stern. His voice rumbled, deep Bronx, a film noir bookie. "You should appreciate the phenomenon of your friend walking in today in the first place. He'd ruptured his internal organry in ten places, was dead days ago in certain regions of himself, how he'd been ambulating in that state I can't imagine. The layman's term for what we found is a *slurry*. You don't want to go in there and see, you'd rather remember your friend the way he was, trust me."

"I don't believe you," said Richard hoarsely. "A hundred times Perkus told me he was the target of a plot—one day he had to be right. I didn't fucking believe him but now I don't believe *you*. He's alive and you're keeping him. Let *go*."

I'd joined them now, reaching my hands out to where Richard wrestled and lunged between the cops, those weary young sentinels of the permissible, who sighed and rolled their eyes between various bland utterances in the vein of *Get hold of yourself, sir* and *Don't force us to put you in cuffs.* I wasn't sure who I was reaching to assist, or assist in what, I wanted simultaneously to second each of Richard's demands and accusations and to save him from having made them—it seemed to me in my confusion that his outburst, a grotesque error, had been punished by Dr. Stern's pronouncements, not the other way around—but I was embroiled only momentarily, when a sweeping foot dropped me onto my ass on tile made slick with the cops' shoe-meltage. My pratfall drew Richard's attention, and the overconfident policemen freed him from their clinch. I suppose they rated his odds as a real fighter according to his wardrobe, so imagined they'd tasted his best.

Richard left this mistake unpunished at first. He reached to pull me to my feet, not so much a kindness, I felt, as that he was embarrassed by me, or wanted me on my feet to at least represent the possibility of backup to his next raid on the doctor and doors. He lifted me by my collar, as I gripped his wrists. "They say they killed him, but it's *shit*, Chase, they're lying." No matter how Richard raised his voice nothing stirred the other zomboid figures populating the room, they only puddled deeper in despond.

"We wouldn't and didn't say anybody killed anybody," said Stern. "People don't come here to be killed, but sometimes, unfortunately, to die."

"I don't understand," I said. "You were going to give him some . . . stimulants . . . to stop his hiccups."

Stern shook his head almost sorrowfully. "They'd needed to be stopped a week earlier, at least. From appearances this patient had been living in a state of reckless negligence for some time, a background condition to the spasms."

"Reckless . . . negligence . . ." I found myself parroting. "That isn't what the other doctor told us." Reeling, I tried to call to mind Perkus's last words, his final hiccologue. Who'd known he was conducting a self-séance before our eyes? I wanted to reassemble the fragments, gather them in memory like the scissored syllables that might now still be traceable on the floor, if we hadn't brushed them all off in the taxicab. I envisioned his splayed carcass, too, his formerly vital organs, as spilling forth with a riot of clipped lines and syllables. The doctors wouldn't know what to do with those, we ought to retrieve them, at least, reason enough to work with Richard to get through those doors. I wept.

"*Where's Dr. Silly?*" said Richard wildly, spittle flying. "Send out Dr. Silly, he isn't part of your game. I want a second opinion!"

"A second opinion isn't called for in death," said Stern.

"*Les Non-Dupes refusé!*" bellowed Richard in his poor French accent as he punched a cop. When fist found nose at close range, Richard and his chosen target howled almost in harmony.

24

It might have been three or four AM before I thought to ask Richard to explain the sense of the French slogan he'd hurled at his moment of fleeting pugilistic triumph and then cried two or three more times until the enraged policemen muffled him with their own shouts and grunts and pinned us both to the floor of the St. Ignatius Rockefeller ER, to bind our wrists and also bind us together with a double butterfly of plastic cuffs, much like the twist ties uselessly enclosed with certain varieties of garbage bags. By this time we'd accepted the fact that we weren't going to be released despite the ritual palliative lies (*"Don't worry, you'll be out in four hours"*) that greeted each of our serial attempts to conduct a serious and reasoning conversation (our attempts, that is, to give them adequate chance to note our distinguishing difference from their milieu, and of the comic inappropriateness of our circumstantial passage through it, therefore to send us forth into the night with hearty apologies and no further ado, etc.) with one or another of our captors and handlers. These included, first, the young and bruised arresting policemen, who could be excused any grudge against us but actually seemed to revert to generic and jovial carelessness in our regard once we'd been added to the van full of other arrestees; next the detectives, milling in the station as we were initially processed, our wallets and wristwatches vouchered, our shoelaces also confiscated, those detectives who appeared so worldly and approachable in their plain clothes and worn faces (yet these were duplicate souls to the younger police-men, only graduated to a more or less adult mien); and last, the weary and marginally humane janitorial types presiding over the actual cells in that station-house base-ment, who after several rounds of complaining stuck their own quarters in the vending machines to provide us with the cheese-and-peanut-butter crackers that became our only nourishment through our whole ordeal, out of some apparent base sense of human dignity or justice— yet perhaps also with the dull yet inexhaustible curiosity of those pushing snacks through the monkey-cage bars at the zoo. Check it out, the white guys in fancy coats, they eat! Having had no dinner or even snack through our afternoon and evening hours in the hospital, we ate unashamedly, licking our fingertips for the monosodium glutamate crumbs.

Richard and I had pleaded to be placed together and been refused, had instead been housed in proximate cells, each designed for one man but holding two—a short bench for the one, the filthy floor for the other— with others who'd been plucked off the snowstormy streets under suspicion of possession of something or another and gathered in our own van full of fresh arrest-ees before we'd been unloaded here. Neither venue, bench or floor, invited sleep, but in Richard's cell and in my own our cell mates seized the bench and curled into an angry self-cuddle. My cell mate, Darnell, had already played a variety of roles in our confused epic: in the van, where we'd all been uncuffed, then threaded together into a daisy chain, he'd whisperingly badgered and threatened me until I accepted a fingerprint-filthy baggie of some loose leaves (presumably pot, though compared to Watt's steroidal buds this resembled lawn clippings) in order to shift it from the elastic at the back of his underwear where he'd had it hidden, to pass down the line for some unclear purpose. I'd finally taken the contraband behind my back, fumbling it from his fingertips to mine, only to have it refused by the next in line. After some squabbling between Darnell and this uncooperator, and a little more failed negotiation between Darnell and myself (Richard turned his head, disgusted at what I'd gotten myself into), the baggie fell to the floor of the van between us, to be discovered there by one of the officers.

Darnell's next hijink occurred after processing while we waited for removal to the basement cells, in the care of the senior detectives. Here, lined up at a wall facing the second-story window, we prisoners contemplated in silence the snow falling to earth with punishing steadiness. We couldn't, however, see over the high window sill to chart its accumulation, which we judged instead by the inches piling improbably atop a streetlight at eye level. Making conversation to no one in particular, Darnell declared that he sold stock by telephone. "No shit?" said one of the detectives. When Darnell lavished a series of investing tips on the earnestly listening cops, he persuaded them. A few even took notes. When he promised he'd make the detectives wealthy if they called their brokers in the morning, one deadpanned, "Fuck that, in the morning I'm firing him, and *you* got the job," and we all laughed, Darnell too. Yet he seemed to feel he'd earned no special treatment from the police. The credit Darnell had earned was with us, his natural peers, for having been entertaining.

He entertained us, too, during the interminable wait for fingerprinting in the windowless basement, before we'd even seen our cells, let alone been disbursed to them. He narrated what he'd been doing when arrested, cut loose due to his "call center" having closed early for the storm, he'd been going from one nightspot to another in the snow, trying to get laid—*looking for some strange*, was how he put it. Then he reassured us, mentioning the worse scrapes he'd been in in his days, the actual prison time he'd shrugged off. We should be happy to know we were in for nothing so bad tonight, we were so obviously just a load of fools harmless to one another and to society. We'd only been arrested to make numbers, to keep the mayor's lifestyle imperatives satisfied. But we weren't going home, we should be certain of that, too. No matter what they told us we'd still be here in the morning, and lucky to be seen by a judge before tomorrow afternoon. Like Darnell's stock tips, this was, alas, persuasive.

Darnell's final guise was as an angry sleep-talker, from his huddle on that bench. When Richard and I found we could sit together at the shared bars of our two cages, our backs to the wall, to talk, we did so, despite the crud on the floor and the disgruntled chorus coming from those on benches or with their heads propped in their hands, those wishing to soak quietly in their defeat. As my conversation with Richard became the only sound and our keepers even damped the lights, as if guiding a planeload of Atlantic crossers into one of those false, foreshortened overnights to London or Paris, Darnell began adding a keening commentary, his limbs twitching with each exclamation. These nightmare fragments seem to issue from his prisoner's id. "*Clock start the minute you walk in the place*," he warned. Then, "Boy don't need a life preserver, boy need an *ass* preserver." Once, he screamed, "*Attica! Attica!*"

Richard and I spoke of Perkus Tooth without mentioning his name. Richard's rage was gone, worn or arrested out of him. He told me a few things I'd been unable to imagine, about Perkus in high school and the single year of NYU he'd managed, and about the birth of Perkus the broadsider, the invisible overnight fame he'd created for himself when the city had still been open to Beat or punk self-invention, that city Perkus had always chided me for failing to know: Frank O'Hara and Joe Brainard, Mailer and Broyard and Krim, Jane Jacobs, Lenny Bruce, Warhol and Lou Reed, all of it, including Patti Smith and Richard Hell and Jim Carroll, poets declaring themselves rock stars before they even had songs, Jean-Michel Basquiat writing SAMO, Philippe Petit crossing that impossible distance of sky between the towers, now unseen for so many months behind the gray fog. Richard left Perkus's name unspoken but he named a lot of others, threw in a few of his own heroes, too, and if he didn't mention Perkus's the reason might be that it would have seemed too complete a processional, the sound of a door being quietly but firmly shut forever.

"*Les Non-Dupes?*" Richard repeated when I asked, then laughed to himself. "A joke. One day he told me it was the basis of our friendship: we weren't dupes. The Two Non-Dupes of Horace Mann, he called us. Really he'd only flatter me to set up another teardown session, I'm guessing you know what I mean. He used to mock me for airing out my high-school French, so I insisted we call our gang *Les Deux Non-Dupes*. We'd shout *Les Non-Dupes refusé!* at boring assemblies, stupid bullshit like that. Or write it on our homework."

Richard spoke of himself as much as of Perkus. In return I reminisced, too, of my life before I came to New York City, such as it was. I talked about Bloomington, about becoming an actor in junior high, my emancipation. (I only didn't mention Janice Trumbull, for I found myself confused about her whenever I tried.) The two of us memorialized Perkus by talking of ourselves, talking simply, as we'd never done before. Murmuring through the bars of those two cells, we were careless about which ears might listen, for we each made certain to say nothing to betray him. Perkus was dead and we protected him the only way we still could, by not offering his secrets in this ashtray of human freedom, littered as it was with stubbed-out ends.

■

It was close to four when a weary detective came downstairs and began whispering to the pair of keepers that had been stationed here below. I caught a tone of sarcastic delight in their exchange. Then, without raising the lights, the keepers came to our two cells and curled a summoning finger at us where we sat.

"You really got some pull to go with your camel-hair coats," said one of the cops, impressed despite his chafing tone. "I'd have sworn you was just another pair of bozos."

"What's going on?" asked Richard.

"Somebody got a judge out of bed," said the cop. "So now, you tell me, who are you guys?"

"I'm not sure," said Richard. "Let me see who got the judge out of bed and I'll get back to you on that."

In the booking area we discovered Arnheim's short aide, the blonde I'd seen maneuvering the mayor at his party. She carried such an air of machinelike destructive efficiency that they should have set her to digging the Second Avenue subway tunnel and saved themselves a lot of heartache. She wore a comically practical parka, snow glistening in the furry unibrow of its hood, and creamy leather boots engulfing her tucked slacks to her knees. When she saw us coming, shuffling moronically, toes curled to keep our feet inside our laceless shoes, she shoved a BlackBerry into her purse, rolled her eyes at Richard, and stuck out her hand to me. "I'm Claire Carter," she said, and before I could speak, added, "Believe me, I know who you are."

"Sorry to have woken you. I appreciate your getting us out of here."

"My driver's waiting," she said. "I'd give you both a lift uptown, but I've been informed you've got about half an hour's worth of paperwork before they can decommission your shoelaces, so you're on your own. I spoke to your pregnant common-law wife, Richard, she knows you're not dead."

"Claire, have I told you lately to go fuck yourself?"

"You're welcome." The smile she brandished was no less convincing than any I'd seen her produce.

A sleepy half hour later Richard and I stepped out, in shoes with laces, onto the white-smothered pavement. The snowfall had eased to a trickle, having satisfied itself to barrage the city beneath a foot or so. The moon was gone, dawn not close, the pillowscape of buried cars and newspaper boxes and trash cans lit only by street-lamp and the red warning blinkers of the scarce passing plows, which seemed as much to be tunneling for their own survival as breaking a useful path for anything that might follow. Nothing tried. The notion of a cab was too forlorn to speak the word aloud. Perkus Tooth was dead and we didn't deserve a cab and none was given. We trudged, plowing with our feet in our laced soaked salt-ruined shoes six long blocks to the subway, the Lexington line. I wouldn't have known how to find it, but Richard did. That underworld was steamy and ferocious and constant and a spectral empty car of the 4 train drew us up to Eighty-sixth Street.

We set out walking together through the snow again, downtown to where we'd part, he going toward Georgina Hawkmanaji's, on Park Avenue, myself east toward home. Or at least I let him take that impression. We didn't speak. I meant to keep walking all the way to York and Sixty-fifth, to the Friendreth. I'd keep my promise to walk Ava, that hiccup assassin. Now that we were safely out of hospitals and jail cells and subterranean trains I could admire the night's supreme reduced stillness, the storm now just dotting the i's and crossing the t's of its masterpiece. It might be my task to abide with this night until exhaustion killed me as hiccups had killed Perkus. Until I saw the vacated rooms I might believe he had somehow transported himself there, just to drop the needle on "Shattered" or "Roland the Headless Thompson Gunner" one more time. I didn't need Richard to know. I felt he was called home (for Richard now had a home, however improbably) as a baby is called to crawl the darkened line pointing through his mother's navel. Richard Abneg had a head start on me, I now understood—he'd begun saying farewell to Perkus Tooth sometime just after high school. I'd only had a few months, or a few hours. I wasn't sure when I'd begun, but it wasn't enough.

At the corner of Eighty-fourth we came upon the giant escaped tiger, moving silently along the side street to cross Lexington there, heading east, away from Central Park. We froze when its long streetlamp-foreshadow darkened the intersection, so stood rooted like statuary in our deep footprints as the creature padded to the center of Lexington's lanes, under the dangling yellow traffic lights which shaded the great burgeoning white-and-yellow fur of its ears and ruff now green, now red, the procession of timed stoplights running for miles beyond through the calming storm. The tiger was tall, a second-story tiger, though not as enormous as its legend. Still, it could have craned its neck and nibbled the heavy-swinging traffic light which hummed in the whispering silence that surrounded us. I found myself thinking the tiger should be measured in *hands*, like a horse, perhaps because I found myself wishing I could rush to it and grip its striped, smooth-ridged fur with both hands and also bury my face there, then climb into its fur and be borne away elsewhere, out of Perkus's city, out of my own. This was a death urge, and I did nothing. The tiger had no remotely mechanical aspect to it, nor appeared in any sense to have emerged from underground or be about to return to fugitive excavations, seemed instead to be wholly of flesh and fur, leather-black nostrils steaming above a grizzly muzzle baring just the slightest fang tips and fringed with beaded ice, its own refrozen breath or drool. There seemed no reason to rub Richard's nose in this fact, which he'd certainly be capable of observing himself. The tiger's passage across the empty avenue was languorous, hypnotic, serene.

We weren't hidden, and when the tiger leveraged that mighty head from one side to another, looking both ways before crossing, we were caught in the psychedelically deep-flat headlamps of its pale gaze for an instant and then released. The tiger either didn't see us or didn't care. We were beneath or beyond its concerns, wherever it was going, whatever it might be pursuing or, less likely, eluding. Fearless and splendid, the tiger seemed quite outside the scope of TigerWatch or of the tracking throngs that massed to rubberneck at its destroyings. Possibly there were two tigers, the famous and chaotic one that lit the tabloid frenzy, and this more dignified one, who showed itself to us alone. It was after all moving along Eighty-fourth Street, toward the block where

Brandy's Piano Bar and Perkus's old apartment lay condemned. Perhaps this was the tiger that put things back together instead of destroying them. Its touch seemed light enough, unlike mine or Richard's tonight. In that spirit it regarded us or didn't, shone its light on us and then shut it off again, and was gone, leaving only claw prints and, with its tail, an inadvertent serpentine signature lashed into a parked Mayflower van's snowy windshield.

25

I pushed the buzzer for O. LASZLO, just my second time in her building and I'd found the courage to actually buzz. While I waited I ran my eyes over the other names, and found a couple that meant something to me, A. SPRILLTHMAR and T. SLEDGE. Sledge lived on Oona's floor, not a major surprise. Despite Perkus's admonition to me, I'd never played a detective, hadn't struck anyone, I suppose, in the brief duration of my post-childhood career, as deep or sad or crafty enough to be persuasive in that sort of role. I wondered if that would be different now. I buzzed Oona a second time and when I'd satisfied myself that no reply was coming I buzzed T. SLEDGE. The sandy little man hadn't seemed the type to be wandering out the morning after a major snowstorm, and I was again unsurprised to hear his query to me on the intercom. I said my name and he let me inside the building. (A. SPRILLTHMAR I kept in my back pocket for the time being.)

Out of the elevator I looked to Oona's door, wondering if she was somehow huddled silently inside, pretending not to be home for my benefit, but the door told me nothing—it wasn't as if there were milk bottles set outside it. Then I examined myself in the mirror in the corridor there, as I suppose no detective would have. The muscles of my calves pinged from my night of trudging through unshoveled snow. I'd steered the grateful and untiring Ava north again, from the Friendreth, to my apartment, and introduced her to my own bed before collapsing there for a few dream-fuddled hours of sleep in morning glare. Ava had draped herself across my legs, and if she'd wondered about Perkus or this change in her circumstances she did nothing to show it. When she woke she pogoed on her forelimb to give my rooms close-sniffing inspection, then circled into my softest chair. I'd left her there, with only a bowl of water and a few slices of Muenster cheese, to go by myself on this new expedition. But first, prisoner of vanity, I'd showered, shaved, slicked my hair. Now, too vain not to use this mirror to judge the result, I couldn't locate the disenchanted and fearsome character I wanted to believe the night had made me.

It was my curse to look unruined in my ruins. If the bereaved had no language for speaking to the unbereaved, my own bereavement had no language for making itself known on the outside of me. You'd cast this face as the astronaut's ineffectual fiancé to the end. My solipsistic fugue might or might not be justified by the discoveries presently dawning on me (or perhaps force-fed, by Perkus, and finally, reluctantly, swallowed by myself). Anyway, I was interrupted by T. Sledge (Thomas? Theodore?), formerly known to me as Blurred Person, the pale sidekick presence lolling around Oona's apartment waiting for delivery sandwiches the only time I'd been here before. He'd opened his door just a crack at the sound of the elevator's ding, and now stood watching me with one eye. Now I understood he was more than Oona's best friend. He was the model for "Sledge," the gardener, the other American trapped aboard the space station with Janice Trumbull.

Sledge's door was triply locked from the inside, including an iron bar extending to a slotted plate on the floor, to form a reinforcing buttress a battering ram couldn't have overcome. Inside, I saw he had every reason to want to be sure a visitor was alone, not flanked by some team of DEA agents. The light inside was all artificial and warm, the smell sweetly fungal, like a rain-forest floor. Bulbs hummed and seeping watering systems chortled, bringing throbbing life to the hundreds of sprouting marijuana plants visible in long open tanks covering every spot of floor in the maze of rooms. The humid false summer here was as oblivious to the snowstorm outside the building's walls as it would have been to a dry desert heat or the void of space. When I stepped inside I felt I was as near to entering an orbital station (one orbital station in particular) as I'd ever be. There didn't look to be a bed or even a couch for sleeping. I suppose Sledge spent his nights in some small extra room in Oona's spacious apartment. Possibly they'd nicknamed it the Attic.

Sledge and I stood in the only bare zone, around his kitchen table, a sort of processing station that included a digital scale for weighing buds and two Tupperware bins full of Lucite boxes, one loaded with empties, the other with those already bulging with zesty-looking wreaths and braids of dope. Between our feet rolled several empty Starbucks to-go cups and crumpled white delicatessen bags. I wouldn't have been shocked to have a leaf-cutter bee alight on my knuckle, but none did.

"I'm sorry about your friend Perkus." As before, Sledge seemed to be half asleep, a nodding dormouse. His words squeaked, as if they slipped past unguarded sentries on tiptoe. I wondered if it was possible to die of yawning, as one died of hiccups.

"How did you know?"

"Apparently somebody notified the *Times*. Their fact-checker called Oona this morning about some details in the obituary."

I wasn't interested in having Oona's reaction to the news, at least not in Sledge's paraphrase, so I changed the subject. I plucked up one of the full Lucite boxes. Though unlabeled, it had a familiar weight and ambiance. "Do you do business with someone called Foster Watt?"

Sledge pursed his lips in mild gray surprise. "Among others . . ." He spoke almost introspectively, as though I'd forced him to realize he did business with anyone at all.

"Why doesn't Oona buy directly from you?"

"Oh, gosh, I'd never ask her to pay."

I suppose Oona would have been glad to have Perkus cheat her on the back end and pocket the difference, as I'd always suspected he did. It was Oona's way of throwing Perkus a periodic donation without causing him to lose face. I wondered if she even smoked as much as she purchased, or whether she simply ferried it back to Sledge to recycle into his supply, a trick to give her pity gesture double value.

"Oona isn't here, is she?"

"No, I'm sorry."

"Not hidden in her apartment?"

"Do you want to have a look? I have the key." Sledge's air was slyly apathetic, as if he might be curious himself to see if she was there, and felt no more loyal to her than to me at the moment. "I was just going in to see if she had some orange juice, anyway. Would you like a glass of orange juice?"

"No, thank you. Do you know when she'll be back?"

"Oh, she left a message. She told me to tell you to meet her at the museum at four o'clock."

It was just after two. I'd have time to return to my apartment and walk Ava. First, though I believed I understood my instructions, I needed to be sure. "The museum?"

"The Metropolitan," said Sledge. He scratched his invisible left eyebrow with the tip of his thumb, gently. His whole body seemed a kind of eraser. I imagined if he rubbed himself too hard he'd crumble away. Perhaps I found myself prickly confronted with one of life's obvious Gnuppets, being confirmed as one myself. "She said you'd know where."

"Yes, thank you. I do."

"Chase?"

"Yes?"

"Be kind to her if you can."

26

By the time I crossed Park and Madison, retracing the tiger's park-ward pilgrimage of the night before, the city had accustomed itself, struggled to a half-life, snow dredged right and left, most parked cars only sculpture. The four o'clock sun was already in submission to the high wintry haze over the Hudson, the light feeble, and when I found myself at the foot of the mountainous museum, the park behind made a dark screen only relieved by a pale-blue snowy band, bright filling in an ominous sandwich of night. The Metropolitan, though mostly uninhabited, was open for business as usual, collecting its imperial "suggested donation" and handing out its little tin badges of entry, the whole engine not so much resolute as indomitable or blithe. The great building housing the art museum was an island city itself, or a virtual universe or space module, operating according to its own necessities, perhaps with its own mayor, and it wasn't hard to picture it plunging onward unchanged though the surrounding city might be in ruins, as Perkus Tooth had imagined New Jersey or Staten Island already to be. Treasures lived in these vaults never seen except by curatorial guildsmen; a given human form drifting beneath these monumental ceilings was of no consequence to the larger story of the building as it pushed through time.

I knew my way through the echoing maze to the Asian galleries, and within them, to the Chinese Garden Court, though I couldn't say whether I'd passed this way a handful of times or hundreds, whether last week or not in years. (What I couldn't remember could fill a book, one written by a ghostwriter.) The court had a smell, one I'd just now previewed in Sledge's pot factory, of controlled indoor growth. The museum's internal weather, its vast thermostatic lungs, carried this scent along the neighboring corridors, and if I'd been lost I might have followed it to the place where Oona waited, in the shadow of the teak bower and slate-shingle roof, looking down onto the tiny curved bridge and the arranged rock garden, all the marvelous stuff that had been shipped here and re-created with such immaculate fakery. I wasn't lost. My footsteps were full of intent, of personal purpose. What made a better model of free will than a walker in the city? I could have gone anywhere, even hailed a taxicab and asked to be taken across one of the bridges, or through the Lincoln Tunnel, to call Perkus's bluff.

But I was tired of models, even ones as cute and complete as the Chinese Garden Court. I didn't want to *model* free will, I wanted to embody it. What I'd learned was that I didn't. Even if every worst suspicion Perkus had urged on me was untrue (they couldn't all be), I'd been forced to understand I was an actor in a script. As according to my long training, in my only avocation. And I was a less-out-of-work actor than I'd believed. Those obnoxious young producers I'd lunched with *had* enlisted me in the role of my lifetime, after all. I was wrong to think their script had never arrived. I'd obviously memorized my part so well that I could lose myself inside it, forget it was a script, live it as my own life. I was the ultimate Method actor, better than Brando—or as bad, I suppose, as any performer on *Jerry Springer* who, having agreed to pretend to be defiantly astounded by some cartoon version of their life, then feels the emotions surge in him for real when the red light blinks on and the studio audience begins hooting. My script's updates arrived periodically in *The New York Times* in the form of Janice's letters, and all of Manhattan was my studio audience.

I wanted to think I was here to enact free will at last, as I came to where Oona stood at the railing, overlooking the lily pads and bamboo in the court's shallow waters. So far, so good: my footsteps had carried me all this way into the museum, the blocking quite perfect, but when it came time to speak I found my lines were missing. Then I recalled I'd been supplied with my line the night before, in the hospital waiting room.

"Perkus told me a riddle, but he wouldn't give me the answer," I said.

"Shoot," said Oona. She raised her hands to make a little mime show of it, surrendering to my nonexistent weapon.

"Did you hear the one about the Polish starlet?"

"Oh, sure," said Oona, not meeting my eye. "*She fucked the writer.*"

"Ah."

"Everyone knows that one."

"Maybe in your circle," I said defensively. It would be as near as I'd come to saying to her that I couldn't try to live anymore inside her boundary, her *circle*, or glancing against it, as I mostly had been—that with Perkus's release from his hiccups, and having read and reread the last weakening report from Janice Trumbull, those words Oona could only risk letting me hear through her forlorn devices, I now found myself also released, into a different life, however unknown. Post-Oona, post-Janice, now that I knew the two were one and the same.

"Chase, please don't leave me."

"I wasn't ever really with you," I said, unable to hold the bitterness from my voice. "I'm engaged to be married, you know that as well as anyone."

"Forgive me, Chase. I wanted to make you love me both ways."

"Both ways?"

"Janice . . . and Oona." She barely got it out. Her voice was frail, not in the old brittle manner of cracks showing in a façade, but molten, her throat full of tears. And how sad that she put herself second. I think I'd never heard her say her name aloud before, *Oona*, and it sounded to me now like a fading pulse, a formless thing half swallowed in doubt, the double O's like a pair of dice that had miraculously come up twice zero. If you wanted to love two ways you had to be prepared to lose two ways, I suppose.

If at the very last moment I'd become my own director, I couldn't think of an instruction for this scene, other than *cut*. Then I found a stray Perkus witticism I could use. "Two fakes don't make a real, Oona."

"No, I guess not."

"Or three," I corrected. "I think we're three fakes, thanks to you. In fact, Janice might be the realest of the three of us."

Oona fell silent. I'd attained that much, if it was anything to be proud of. I was ready to leave her there, in her precious Chinese Garden Court, yet I couldn't quite move. We stood in silence, then Oona freed the long-hidden glasses from her purse and showed her true face—I suppose she did it simply because she wanted to see mine, and I'd always been a bit blurry. (The story of my life.) We couldn't bear the look between us for long, however, and bowed our gazes to the pond instead. A black goldfish meandered there, in and out of rocks directly beneath our feet, and when it wriggled through Oona's reflection and mine, rippling the tender screen that bore our doubles, Oona turned her head slightly and one hinged corner of the heavy black glasses frames seemed to squirt free for an instant, wholly separate from the glasses or from Oona's outline, a thing born, tadpole or guppy, and wanting its own life.

27

This was another kind of waiting room. I had no appointment and so it should not be so strange that I was left there to wait a while. Yet I was left to wait a long time. It began to seem to me that my appointment here was with the room itself, that I'd been installed here in order that I understand what the room had to tell me, and that I was expected to need a while to absorb it completely. At the mayor's party I'd been cushioned by the occasion, the crowd's mania, from this room's full severity, the pressure of that thunderhead of plaster ornament, the gravity of the furnishings, the majesty and provenance radiating from the French chairs, arrayed like bewigged justices. I found it almost impossible to stay seated in one.

The room was not precisely as I'd remembered it. I now saw that inlaid-rosewood panels, so impressive in themselves, were only covers, the room an enormous magician's cabinet, beautifully joined, made to slide aside in order to reveal a gallery and library, all the fetishes and collected works that had needed to be protected from the grubby hands and eyes of the guests at the champagne reception. I was idiotically proud to recognize the oils as examples of the Hudson River school, verdant mysterious panoramas of the Palisades, of ice floes bottlenecking at West Point. The books were bound or rebound in leather succulent as amber. I tried to read their fine gilt titles and found my eyes stinging. I might have pulled one down to examine it but my fingers felt numb and weak, nearly immaterial, as though the density of a hardbound volume would pass through my hands. This may have been the effect of a day where I'd steered Ava through snow three times, grappling with the weave of her leash in my childishly soft palms.

I was also embarrassed. I no more wished to be caught fondling the books as be seen creeping upstairs to ogle Arnheim's hologram. I didn't want the setting to unravel the meager poise that had brought me here to make my stand. Yet by the time Claire Carter appeared, it had almost done that. She'd left me long enough for me to feel she'd rescued me by appearing, that if I'd been there longer the age and force of the place would have wholly disintegrated the small pretense of me. Nearly dark out when I'd approached the town house, the windows were black now, as if I'd risked the vanishing of all nurturing illusion by entering this chamber, this sole place certain of its purposes. I apprehended here the indifference of the ancient and unchangeable city, the incidental nature of its use for me. Claire Carter didn't say "Any further questions?", but she might as well have. The room was lit by one standing glass lamp, and it didn't seem to light me at all, but Claire Carter in her peach-sherbet pantsuit glowed like the green shores so luminous with under-painting, glowed like the amber spines of the Collected Works, glowed, yes, like a chaldron, a thing glimpsed only to deny you.

"Thank you for seeing me," I said.

"You're always thanking me, Mr. Insteadman," said Claire Carter. "But that isn't what you came for."

Her brittleness gave me some courage. "No offense, but I hoped to talk to Mayor Arnheim."

"Here's how this goes. You get five minutes with me, and the meter's running on that, so skip the formalities. The mayor will join us at some point. You should tell me anything you need him to know."

"Is he listening now?"

"How can we help you, Mr. Insteadman?"

Again I was voiceless. No wonder the Polish starlet fucked the writer. I wanted to spellbind and scald Claire Carter with a hiccup-punctuated tour de force of accusation. Yet after all I knew nothing, had no evidence, only dubious questions wilting on my tongue. "Is the tiger . . . being used to destroy . . . the city's enemies?" I asked her.

"The tiger is a distraction," said Claire Carter firmly, as if placing it in a bureaucratic category beyond further consideration. I recalled Perkus's commandment, *no conspiracies but of distraction*. I didn't suppose Claire Carter was about to use that other word. If I used it myself I was a fool.

"Does Richard Abneg know the truth?"

"The truth about what?"

"About distractions like the tiger . . . and me." I surprised myself.

"Richard's like you," she said. "He forgets a lot of what he knows, forgets everything except what he needs to carry on, and do his job."

"What about you?"

"What *about* me?"

"Do you forget?"

"I'm the same as anyone else," said Claire Carter. "Don't mystify things."

"Do you know Oona Laszlo?"

"We've met." The weary tone suggested my questions had drifted into irrelevance, that she'd begun wondering why she'd bothered to grant me even these five minutes.

"My friend died," I blurted out, not wishing to fail in my only secure complaint. Yet I didn't wish to give Perkus's name aloud here, feeling as superstitious as I'd been in the police-station basement, though I believed him beyond Claire Carter's or the mayor's harm now, either dead or gone underground ... I'd begun telling myself that if Marlon Brando could be alive, the same was possible for Perkus. The medical world could form an anti-conspiracy, a form of underground railroad originating in hospital emergency rooms, to hide the *Non-Dupes* from their enemies. I remembered a phrase Strabo Blandiana had mentioned, Médecins Sans Frontières, which might be a cover name for this secret society.

"Richard mentioned it," she said.

"My friend told me ... a lot of things. He believed Manhattan had become a fake. A simulation of itself. For some purpose ... he couldn't guess, but he died trying."

"What on earth makes you think it could possibly be only one purpose?"

"I'm sorry?"

"Pay attention, Mr. Insteadman. I'm astounded at your naïveté. How could a place like Manhattan exist for just one purpose, instead of a million?"

I had no answer.

"Do you *personally* believe Manhattan is fake?" asked Claire Carter.

How could I reply? Perkus's theories proved themselves ludicrous while demolishing any castles of consolation to which I might hope to retreat. They unmade those as they unmade themselves. Our sphere of the real (call it Manhattan) was riddled with simulations, yet was the world at hand. Or the simulation was riddled through with the real. The neat pink seam of Ava's surgery scar, which I'd traced with my finger this very morning while giving in to her cuddling demands in my bed; the brown stripe—the "milk map"—across Georgina's pregnant belly which, though I hadn't witnessed it myself, had plainly reordered Richard Abneg's helpless mind; the exact flavor of Oona's kisses (or Ava's, for that matter), the sugar dust on a Savoir Faire almond croissant (I have my weaknesses); these details could no more have been designed and arranged than Laird Noteless could have thought to include discarded baby carriages and crushed crack vials in his sketches for *Urban Fjord*. The world was ersatz and actual, forged and faked, by ourselves and unseen others. Daring to attempt to absolutely sort *fake* from *real* was a folly that would call down tigers or hiccups to cure us of our recklessness. The effort was doomed, for it too much pointed past the intimate boundaries of our necessary fictions, the West Side Highway of the self, to shattering encounters with the wider real: bears on floes, the indifference and silence of the climate or of outer space. So retreat. Live in a Manhattan of your devising, a bricolage of the right bagel and the right whitefish, even if from rival shops. Walk the dog, dance with her to *Some Girls*. Why did Perkus have to be killed for his glance outside the frame? But maybe he hadn't been killed, had only died. And again, maybe absconded. I was sick with ignorance, and my own complicity.

I'd been like Steve Martin in *Dead Men Don't Wear Plaid*, playing scenes opposite phantasms, figures unreal and deceased. Yet Perkus had made me peculiarly brave. The Polish starlet was also the detective who couldn't kill or be killed by guns, but might brandish love. It struck me that Oona had done me a favor, too, enmeshing me in such a lame script. How many ever know they're in one? "Being until recently one of the local fakes," I told Claire Carter, "I take the matter seriously. Forgive me if it strikes you as tendentious."

"Let me make a suggestion," she said. "*Follow the money.*"

"Sorry?" The glib cliché shattered my reverie, returned me to the tangible fact of the mayor's operative, her dress-for-success pugnacity, her horrific *completeness*, how she made in her whole earthly self Perkus Tooth's true opposite, and how vile she was to me, real or fake. She might begin clubbing me, as a pelt prospector clubs a baby seal, with further phrases such as *do what you love, the money will follow* and *show me the money*, and I might die here yelping on the mayor's superb

Oriental. I couldn't brandish love in this encounter, had to choose my battles, flee.

"Take a look at who signs your checks. If it isn't a city agency, and it isn't, then you've brought your complaints to the wrong door."

I wondered, for the first time, if my residuals weren't all residuals. "I get . . . direct deposit."

"We're in the coping business around here," said Claire Carter, ignoring me. "Like any administration, we *inherited* the problems we're trying to solve." Her tone was almost sulky. Perhaps my accusations had reached her, in whatever slight place she could be reached. Or maybe the phrases were a secret signal, for now the mayor arrived. He wore a brocade robe over silk pajamas, and inspected me like a disgruntled father in a black-and-white comedy, or Sherlock Holmes resigning himself to lecturing Watson on the obvious. He should have been carrying a candelabra. But these weren't Hugh Hefner or Rossmoor Danzig pajamas, tailored to jollify ugliness, these were no laughing matter, the pajamas of power wakened from its deserved repose. I had to make myself worthy of interrupting these pajamas. I felt I might have wandered into another joke besides the riddle about the Polish starlet now, that like a penitent who'd ascended a snowy Tibetan mountain to speak with the hermit guru, I'd be permitted a single question before being returned to my exile. *Why is it snowing? Is Marlon Brando alive or dead? On what support does the weight of the world rest?* I couldn't choose, and so exhibited my traditional mask of placid stupidity. Yet before the swarming pressure of the unreal rose up and swallowed us three where we stood, Arnheim's impassive features deflated in an approximation of human sorrow, and he beckoned with his short arms to encircle me, and like a giant infant I was for a moment comforted against his shoulder, which was surprisingly knobby under my cheek, as though it had knuckles.

"I'm deeply sorry for your loss," he said. "Our city mourns with you."

"Thank you, sir." I tried to conceive that Perkus would be granted this tribute after all, and whether I should accept it for him. On the other hand, it might be an attempt to persuade me not to look into the circumstances of his "death."

"She won't be forgotten."

"She?"

"The Chinese will pay some price for this, don't doubt it."

Arnheim meant Janice Trumbull. The ghost-astronaut had been declared dead at last, I gathered, though I'd have to buy the *Times* the following day to learn that rather than linger any more in fetid cancer and agriculture, the space captives had serenely directed their station into the path of the mines, to be cleansed in vacuum fire. Did the mayor believe I still believed that stupid tale? Did he? Perhaps Claire Carter was simply being truthful when she told me I'd come to the wrong door.

I had nothing at all to say to him, or anyone, about Janice Trumbull. But in the comedy we now played, in which the billionaire Arnheim, veins so notoriously icy, now steadied me by the elbows and gazed into my eyes with avuncular wartime bonhomie as if I were some far-posted confidential agent coming in briefly to receive encouragement from the home office, I could let "her" stand for Perkus Tooth. This suited me. Perkus could be everywhere and nowhere, as I'd often felt him to be. I hungered to dismay Arnheim, to let him wonder if the operative in his embrace had gone over to the other side, even if I had no idea whether another side existed. "I learned certain secrets from *her*, before she died," I told him. "Secrets about the city. The tiger, for instance."

Arnheim stepped back from me, placing his hands in his robe's deep pockets as if he were suddenly ashamed of them. He didn't have to bend his elbows to do so. "I'm glad you mention it."

"I didn't want there to be any confusion."

"There's a Sufi aphorism that's apropos to this situation—have I ever mentioned it to you?"

I stared in confusion. Arnheim spoke as though we enjoyed some long association.

"*The secret protects itself.*"

"That's the Sufi aphorism?"

"Go with it, my friend. You can do no wrong. The secret protects itself."

I found this notion, that *I could do no wrong*, demoralizing in the extreme. If I believed it I might have to hurl myself into one of Noteless's chasms, perhaps the *Memorial to Daylight*, during the opening ceremonies. Though I suppose my most flamboyant suicide could be incorporated readily enough into a tale of the astronaut-fiancé's bereavement. Better to drift into the gray fog and be forgotten. I noticed I'd now officially *contemplated suicide*, an act no one warns you is involuntary, unfolding as it does in contemplation. All it had taken was the crushing force of this parlor's decor, and a mayor who might himself be a memorial to daylight, as though he'd drunk it all for himself and left nothing on the table. Who required even hiccups to destroy me? In my despair I tried one more code word on Jules Arnheim, a gesture in commemoration of the now-dissolved Fellowship of the Chaldron. "*Les Non-Dupes refusé!*" I said, producing the slogan with all the useless courage of Nathan Hale on the gallows.

The mayor had a ready response, one which seemed to gratify him, not at the layer of his bogus joviality but in the deeper stirrings of his killer's soul, on view at last. "*Les Non-Dupes errent,*" he said, gazing unblinking and unavuncular into my eyes. My own high-school French, flickering in memory, supplied the interpretation. Like knights-errant, we non-dupes were not only lost but mistaken. We wandered in error. To be unduped was not to live. There was no way out, only a million ways back in.

"What do I do now?" I asked him, helpless not to turn to the authority before me, the father we dream of in joy and fear.

"Go back to a city that needs you."

"You mean, Manhattan?"

"No one disputes your place here. You own your apartment outright, don't you? I understand it has a fine view."

If I stayed a moment longer Arnheim might describe those birds and that tower, my heart's last sacred quadrant of sky. I fled into the night and snow before I could hear it.

28

This is the story of Bloomington that I told Richard
Abneg, the night of Perkus's death and the night of our
arrest, while we sat with our heads leaned close against
the bars of our cells, in the quiet that descended in the
dark there. Richard had finished speaking of his teenage life, and Perkus's. He'd asked how I'd come to the
city, how a person becomes a star in a television show
filmed live on a soundstage on West Forty-seventh Street
while still the age of a high-school junior, leaving parents
and friends and a world behind in distant unimaginable
Indiana. I tried and faltered over making him a portrait
of my parents, my old and helpless and perfectly kind
parents so confused by their youngest son, and the story
of my legal emancipation from them by the talent agent
who discovered me, in order that I could travel and
be tutored and work for the benefit of myself (and the
agent) before I'd attained a legal working age. It was all
a bit much and likely too boring to tell.

So I instead drew a loose portrait of myself, how
strange and also strangely happy I was, waiting for something to happen, knowing it would. How I grew into
my big rangy handsome body that attracted so much
notice from my school's coaches, and how it attracted so
much notice from girls and women after it had finished

disappointing the coaches. I wasn't interested in or gifted at sports at all, which to others might have seemed the only thing to do with the problem of me. I probably should have been homosexual but wasn't—then I could have been a mascot of the girls, or a dodgy runaway, of whom everyone could say they'd seen it coming. Instead I was good and big and straight and something of a chameleon. I wanted and tried to be funny, and sometimes was, but my curious formality, diction borrowed from P. G. Wodehouse and Cary Grant instead of from my peers, was funnier without trying. I was like a thing born for something else. Tolerated and teased in school, but dreamily destined, and unafraid. Destined to be adored. Destined for sex. I waited for someone to put me to right use, and when I was fourteen the talent agent did that, an old story, like someone discovering Kim Novak in a cornfield. So I set it up by painting this picture of myself and then I told Richard a particular story of a moment from just before my emancipation and my first journey to Manhattan.

Bloomington kids, the good and bad ones, the professors' children and the ten-generations-in-the-same-house kids, the athletes and the losers and those who would get away and even those who we all knew were secretly homosexual, we all of us did the same thing in the summer months, together and apart, in groups that overlapped and broke apart as much as our cliques in junior high during the school months: that was to swim in the abandoned granite quarries scattered in the fields and forests outside of the town. The kids who wanted to be ruffians would swim in the most dangerous and most forbidden, those farthest into the woods and with the deepest cuts, where the water was black with legends of drownings. The losers puttered in a wretched shallow quarry where a kitten couldn't drown. And the popular kids swam in a clean high-walled pit known as Turtles. I was, after all, a part of the popular crowd—I was the not-gay unathletic daft handsome mystery among them. Turtles, named for creatures often sighted there, lay hidden in overgrown fields whose owner trimmed thistles from the worn path and made us welcome as long as we carried out our Strohs empties, was also outfitted with a raft, a bobbing wooden platform anchored by some method to the center of the water, and ladderless, so one had to clutch with both arms as it tilted and then haul a leg over one side, or be helped by someone standing above. One tumbled crevice led to easy entrance to the water, and this was where we gathered to swim, though sometimes a show-off, a diver on our high-school team, would plunge in from elsewhere on the rim—the water was clear and deep enough to make it safe. All who swam eventually congregated out on the raft, which might have been ten or fifteen yards from the crevice's entry point. All but me.

It began as a matter of fear, then a prideful obstinacy. I began as a poor swimmer, though I got better. (Slipping my body through water seemed to me more like sex than athletics; I had an instinct for it, but like masturbation it felt private, and I hid my improvements.) The more I was ruthlessly mocked for not joining the laughing throng that teetered atop that raft (and frequently cleared itself in a paroxysm of shoving), the more I distinguished myself in the calm of my own mind for not caring to join it. The raft was where everything eventful was transacted, all the famous gropes and shames and confidences, somehow hidden in plain sight, secreted within the mob, or just at that moment when everyone else was in the water to miss them. So I'd exiled myself from society, shunning that artificial island. It made me who I was, the act of not going there. I attached a certain feeling of irreversibility to the choice, as if those who'd gone that mere distance of strokes to clamber aboard had in a sense never returned, or not completely. Perhaps after I overcame my swimmer's fear I was still afraid of the disappointment that awaited me if I joined them there. Somehow I was patient enough to have another island in mind for me.

The part I didn't tell Richard was this: the summer before I began high school—my last year in Bloomington, it would turn out—and had begun to draw the attention of the high-school girls, even the graduated seniors with their college destinies turning them into forms drifting out of reach before our eyes, the most extraordinary and fierce and unforgettable of those girls was one named Janice Trumbull. She was leaving Bloomington forever three or four weeks after the day she acknowledged me, though later I'd know that she'd been aware of me a while before.

At the time I thought it was by not swimming to the raft that I'd gotten Janice Trumbull's attention. Turtles was well behind her by then. She'd been goaded to swim there that day by two of her friends for whom it was an ironic act of instant nostalgia. Their future was more

535

real than their present and they shone with it, most particularly Janice Trumbull, who had won a scholarship to MIT and none of us had any idea what that meant, not the sun-blazed afternoon they came through the crevice and began swimming among us with their insane bodies, these girls who were more like floating hallowed names than real persons in the life of the high school I was supposed to attend.

They weren't going to board the raft, they certainly weren't going to do that. Janice's two friends swam out and around it, performed mocking leg splits and whirlies to an awed contingent, and Janice came back to where I paddled at the sheer granite wall, sole member of my refusal society. She asked me my name and I told her, and then she said in so many words that I was in a quiet hell here in Bloomington and I should know to get out. She told me I looked as if I knew but she couldn't live with herself if she didn't say so. I didn't explain what I couldn't have, my dreams and certainties, of which this encounter with her made a perfect harbinger. Was struck dumb by even my own dumb standards. Janice Trumbull then told me where to meet her that night. It was a few months into my freshman autumn that I'd learn, through the younger-sister grapevine, how Janice had told her friends she'd have me before she left for college, and that they'd brought her to Turtles that day partly or even largely to call her bluff, which was no bluff. For the last weeks of that summer she taught me how to swim to the raft of a woman's body and what to do there. Then she went to Massachusetts and eventually into space, to die. I never met her after that summer, though I did watch her triumphant launch to join the Russian crew, on television. In fact, I'm almost certain—as certain as I can be of anything—that Janice Trumbull was killed, with all her compatriots, within a few hours of the distribution of the Chinese mines into their orbit path, rather than living on for so many months, and doing space walks, tending gardens, writing letters.

The day after meeting with Claire Carter I'd done as she suggested, and traced the origin of the surplus flooding my checking account. The signatory was the treasurer of the Manhattan Reification Society, that shadowy philanthropic trust appointed to enact the city's little Gnuppet shows. I suppose the callow producers who'd long ago enlisted me to play the part of myself as astronaut-fiancé were on their payroll, too, and Oona Laszlo, the writer. When it had been decided to give the remote and perished astronaut a lease on life—to take the cruel and stunted tale of the space station's collision with the Chinese mines and distend it into an enthralling melodrama of foot cancer and orbital decay—they elected also to humanize Janice Trumbull by awarding her a mopey earthbound boyfriend. (It took a lot of melodrama to keep the War Free edition from seeming a tad thin, I guess.)

So how did they come to pick me? I suppose the footnote of our crossed paths as teenagers, mentioned here and there in magazine profiles, must have bobbed to the surface in Oona's research, once she took the job. The ghostwriter had surely found it irresistible—as though a pair of Gnuppets had conspired in the distant depths of their Midwestern past to make their Gnuppeteer's fiction that much more lively and persuasive. (It wasn't that I'd ever mentioned that Janice Trumbull and I were teenage lovers, but Oona had guessed this, or decided to make it up.) If I was faithful to the dead astronaut it made a fine sentimental motif; if I betrayed her, fine too, sentimental in the other direction. I could do no wrong.

29

Perkus Tooth's sister was a twin sister, that was the major surprise. It was Sadie Zapping who'd put together the memorial gathering at the Friendreth, in Ava's former apartment. I suppose in some way I thought of Sadie Zapping as Perkus's twin, his female half, now that Oona Laszlo had been disqualified, turning out to be something so much more baited and treacherous than the sibling she first resembled. But no, Perkus had a real twin sister, June Tooth, named for the month of their birth and the month of the gathering at which we met.

June Tooth lived in West Haven, Connecticut; managed what was left of their deceased folks' silver and pewter works, Tooth Knife and Fork; was divorced and with a kid "on the spectrum" who was wonderful and brilliant but nonetheless sucked up all of her time and attention, ran her ragged with his endless devotion to railway maps and timetables, like some nutty train scholar at twelve years old, and who'd demanded she take a digital photograph at each station stop on her Amtrak journey here today. She'd had to switch off her cell phone so he wouldn't call her every five minutes to check that she had. As stoical and earthbound and modest as Perkus was anything else, both of her eyes meeting ours in tandem, June nonetheless evoked Perkus in her voice and form, some little swerving energy she couldn't rein in though she didn't acknowledge, a part of her, like him, an arrow aimed into the infinite obsessive, but in her, unlike him, curtailed. She'd been there all along, tucked into the middle distance of the tristate area, cutting Perkus regular checks from the sturdy little forge works that was their shared legacy (a riddle: How many benefactors did it take to keep one Perkus on the Upper East Side?), proof enough if Perkus had wanted it that his Manhattan's-a-Black-Iron-Prison theory wasn't concretely true, that *some* kind of life went on being lived across the bridges and tunnels connecting us to the mainland and the other islands—or at least not true enough to exclude the persistence both of the Connecticut suburbs and of a small but sustaining North American market for hand-forged pewter fittings and furnishings.

I wondered, but didn't ask, whether they made anything resembling a chaldron. In truth, I found June Tooth too painful, too much his spitting image, to do more than be introduced and express the passingest of condolences, so the majority of her story I gathered eavesdropping as she explained herself to others in rattling Toothian monologues, making herself known and visible to the astonished others for whom Perkus had always rendered her unknown and invisible, unnamed. Besides her, the party consisted of myself and Biller and Sadie Zapping and Richard Abneg and Georgina Hawkmanaji, now ruddy-cheeked and protruding and huge with the kid forming inside her, plus a couple of scrappy old comrades whose names I'd caught in Perkus rants but never expected to greet in the flesh, Seidenberg,

Breithaupt, Roe, men failing in their upkeep, whose idea of funeral garb was black sneakers and practically braidable nose hairs, men keeping the contract with squalor that Richard Abneg had only denoted when I'd met him and now under Georgina's guidance had voided completely. I didn't talk to these men, either, I found I wasn't interested and couldn't have gotten a word in edgewise if I had been. Besides Richard and Georgina I talked mostly to Biller and Sadie Zapping. I should add that the party consisted also of a number of dogs—I'd brought Ava to see her old place one last time, while Sadie culled a few genial creatures who had apparently also been guests here. Perhaps some were the former owners of *Some Girls* and *Dead Men Don't Wear Plaid*. If so they couldn't tell me.

Sadie was garrulous and funny and did the talking for both of us. She told me what I didn't know about Perkus's Friendreth afternoons—she was a kind of obverse witness to what I knew, presiding as she had over his new daily rituals, dog shit and cribbage and hot chocolate, adamantly impatient as she was with his theories, which had waited for my visits to explode into life. With sudden frankness she told me of their disenchanting rift, a squabble over her attempted hiccup cures, then confessed that she'd believed them headed beyond cribbage. "I felt something was developing between us. Did he ever mention it?" I told her he was shy about such things, and didn't reciprocate her frankness with the facts about just *how* shy I meant. I pictured Sadie Zapping attempting a pass at Perkus over mugs of Swiss Miss—would it have even been legible to him? Had Sadie Zapping been, to use Perkus's word, "rebuffed"? Well, I didn't need to know.

After the others left, I stayed with Sadie Zapping and Biller, gathering the paper plates and plastic cups in a garbage bag, scraping Mallomar crumbs to the floor for Ava to snuffle. It was then that Biller told me what he'd learned from Perkus about Claire Carter's brother. Linus, the hoard of chaldrons Linus had bestowed on Claire, and the far castle where they lay under supposedly impregnable defenses. Though Biller had never been, as Oona once accused, a "virtual thief," he had lately spent some time in avatar form casing the joint, and believed he'd located an imperfection in the redoubt's security. *We could take them*, he told me simply.

That was two months ago. We've only had two snows in August so far. The newspapers are calling it summer, and mostly I find people are content to do the same. There's only so much you can listen to yourself complain about snow. Ava is mine now, in the sense that she lives with me, eats on my floor, and sleeps in my bed, and that I walk her three times a day (you might as well say that I'm *hers*). Sometimes I think I hear her hiccup once or twice, and it sends my heart racing. In those moments I always think of the advice to *keep your enemies close*. Yet I don't think it is right to be paranoid about dogs. Perkus was murdered as he'd always expected to be, not by Ava or hiccups but by complicity, by having one of his theories, his worst suspicions, come wandering in and befriend him. So the real enemy is one I could never do other than keep close.

I've been seeing a bit of Anne Sprillthmar. I try not to be ashamed of my habits, or my fate, which always seems to come in the form of another woman, each to follow the last more quickly than I ever learn to expect. We do all have our ways of moving through the world, our regular situations. Ava gets along splendidly with Anne's Afghan hound, a fixed male named Century. The two frequently tussle to exhaustion over woolen socks knotted into a chewy rope, then climb onto my bed and wend themselves into a fond, seven-limbed canine pretzel. This is not so different from how Anne Sprillthmar and I like to spend time, when the bed is available. She and I and the dogs stick to my place. I avoid Anne's building for the risk of running into others who live there, though I suppose it is eventually inevitable. I suppose, too, that Oona Laszlo will regard it as an act of minor vengeance, that I should take up with a woman in her very own building, but I know myself well enough to say I don't have a vengeful bone in my body. One recent afternoon while Anne and I were fucking I found myself unable to keep from laughing hysterically, to an extent that put a crimp in the proceedings. I tried to explain to her what had popped into my head, that my friend Perkus Tooth might have called what I was doing *riding the hegemonic bulldozer*, but Anne didn't seem to get the joke, or maybe just didn't find it funny. That she didn't know Perkus is, most days, a relief.

Richard Abneg, when he heard about me and Anne Sprillthmar, was properly infuriated. I'd guess that despite the new life that has enclosed him, Richard's competitive ire told him Anne was rightfully *his*, least compensation he could expect for the indignity of his profile being killed by Anne's editors at *The New Yorker*, who finally didn't concur that Richard was so signal a figure in the present life of the city. (I didn't explain that I'd noticed her first, figuring it would only irritate a sore point.) As for the escaped giant tiger, it hasn't been captured or killed, nor bent to the purpose of digging subway tunnels, and goes on wrecking only things it seems to me the city can spare. Rumors abound of late-night standoffs with worshipful mobs, but mainstream coverage has fallen off, more enamored lately with the coyotes that have been terrorizing joggers at the Central Park Reservoir. I do find it hard to believe the wrecking-tiger is the same one Richard and I met in the fresh-fallen snow, but I've never tested this two-tiger theory on him, and have no plans to. Anne Sprillthmar mentioned that a friend at the *Times* claimed they were market-testing a Tiger Free edition. I don't know whether she was joking or not.

I spend a lot of my time on the computer now (I bought myself a new one). Apart from frequent visits to Marlon Brando's Wikipedia page, where controversy over the truth or rumor of his death remains fresh and interesting, I'm mostly immersed in Yet Another World. There, under Biller's leadership, my newborn avatar has joined a commando unit, made of dozens of others, volunteers or mercenaries hidden behind their contrived personae, which has been readying itself to storm Claire Carter's redoubt and seize her cache of chaldrons. I've spent not a little of my own money (Reification Society stipends, that is, as well as genuine *Martyr & Pesty* residuals) compensating the weapon and armor-makers' guilds for what outfitting our force requires, to ensure success in the coming battle. Our existence is a tightly held secret at the moment, but Biller promises me that if we succeed no one in Yet Another World will fail to hail our name: *Les Non-Dupes*. What exactly we'll do with the extravagance of chaldrons once they've been liberated remains to be seen. Biller speaks of opening a virtual museum, placing the treasure into a public trust, where all and any may commune with the impossible objects, but I suspect this would only be to inspire marauders more powerful than ourselves. As well, it may be a mistake to assume that our confederation will hold at the seams once the chaldrons are in our hands. There's no honor among thieves.

Speaking of Biller, I've acquired another paperback copy of Ralph Warden Meeker's *Obstinate Dust*. Though it's hardly easy going, I'm doing my best to push through to the finish line, in Perkus's memory. I read it on the subway, another new imperative in my life—I've renounced taxicabs. Once in a while on the underground trains I look up and see another rider with a copy of Meeker's bulky masterpiece in their hands, and we share a sly collegial smile, like fellow members of some terrorist cell.

Two days ago I left Ava at home and went to visit Richard and Georgina on Park Avenue, in Georgina's penthouse, less than a week home from the hospital. If I thought the brown stripe had unraveled Richard Abneg's cynical poise, that was a mere preview of coming attractions. Richard hovered over his new family with tiny plates of prepared foods, tomatoes heaped on cottage cheese and laced with balsamic vinegar, a small, dubious feat of cooking of which he was unduly proud, explaining to me how many calories Georgina needed to sustain her breast-feeding. In his enthusiasm he tipped the plate and dripped balsamic down the infant's neck, but Georgina only ever basks in his brutish attentions, and the three seemed bound in some human energy field impossible to deny, as if glimpsed in the core of a flame. The boy looked in my direction but seemed to see right through me, an effect both parents assured me was in every sense typical, in no sense a judgment upon my status as Cheese Unperson. His name is Ayhar, meaning Ruler of the Moon. Ayhar's brow is blotched with evidence of his birth, a ruddy archipelago the doctors say will fade. He has the Hawkman's eyes.

I let Ava lead me where she wants to go, finding traces on the snow-scraped pavement where she or some acquaintance (though many are only scent-acquaintances, inhabitants of a virtual world inside Ava's snout) has made some statement that needs to be footnoted or overwritten. It was only a week or so ago when it occurred to me how Ava's paces, her bold and patient pissings, must have been immensely comforting to Perkus, and in a sense familiar. Ava's a kind of broadsider herself, famous within a circle of correspondents, invisible to those who don't care. She's flying under the radar, not a bad trick.

Yesterday Ava and I went out walking, and she tugged me to an unfamiliar block, Ninety-fourth Street, beyond First Avenue, almost to York. There we discovered a street corner where a flock of gray-jacketed, white-bellied birds were scattered like jimmies over a mound of snow, a mound some custodian must have heaped up in the process of clearing the gated courtyard where it lay—a church courtyard, when I looked up to see. The birds pecked at seed strewn over the icy heap, until Ava, uncharacteristically, and despite the heavy black iron that divided them, made a leash-snapping charge and scattered the birds to the sky. It was as if she wanted them in the air. Only after they found the altitude they liked, that which made them feel safe or free or whatever it was birds found in their places in the sky, and began wheeling, passing between buildings and repeatedly in and out of view, did I judge the shape of the church's spire and knew that these were my birds, that we stood at the foot of my tower.

We watched a while and then headed home, and when we had ridden up in the elevator and gone inside and I'd freed Ava from the leash I went to my window for the first time in two months to see if they were still aloft, to catch a bit of the aerial pandemonium ballet it now seemed to me I'd been heedlessly neglecting. The birds were there, still satisfyingly continuous in their asymmetries and divergences, as if I'd been abiding with them through all these weeks and days. But I noticed something else as well. The Dorffl Tower had shifted a little to the right, shaving another margin from my window's view. I don't know how this can be possible, but then again there are so many things that escape me. It's still a view I can live with. I only hope it doesn't get any smaller.

Note

With gratitude I return the tiger to Charles Finney, *The Unholy City*; "In the midst of these variations the theme was always ingeniously and excitingly retrieved," to Saul Bellow, *Humboldt's Gift*; "The Beatles family goes back to Jack Kerouac, etc.," to George W. S. Trow, *My Pilgrim's Progress: Media Studies* 1950–1998; "But in truth, moderns live in a world-order in which the primitive, etc.," to Kenneth Smith, *The Crypto-Revolution of Our Age XX. Power Versus Reality (Comics Journal* no. 185); "Perhaps such secrets . . . in which the person perished," to James Baldwin, *Another Country; The New York Times* as "the commissar of the real," to Seymour Krim, *What's This Cat's Story?*; "I want it on record, right here and now . . . Captain's birthday cake," to Jane Poynter, *The Human Experiment: Two Years and Twenty Minutes Inside Biosphere* 2; everything else to everywhere else forever and ever amen.